A Secret to Remember

A NOVEL BY

WENDY J. LEVENFELD

To Suzanne – my beloved
Coffeemaker –
Love our chats
Hope you enjoy my "Secret"
Wendy

ISBN-9798709790629

For Drew...as always and forever

Author's Note

In 1973 I began my professional life with a teaching position at Dawson Skill Center located on the South Side of Chicago. I have used that location as a backdrop for this novel. The characters and events as written within these pages are fictional, developed solely for entertainment and to advance the story line.

This is a work of fiction and should be read as such.

Contents

Prologue

1974

The school was a sterile, windowless, cinderblock box dropped senselessly in the center of the Robert Taylor Homes on Chicago's Southside. Tucked under the El tracks, I often thought that distinguishing between the subtle differences, the noisy nuances of the squealing, rust-scrapping sound of the various trains above was the true extent of many of my students' learning. Bars and chains on doors, keeping out, binding within; walls verging on collapse from railway vibration and anger; pressures squeezing; murders considered commonplace at the bar across the street; raw emotion everywhere pushing the quest for knowledge deeper, deeper within to where the struggle to let it surface was just far too great.

Babies had babies. Babies carried weapons. After having been abandoned by the mere occurrence of their birth - no by life itself - these babies were murdered. These babies murdered. They scratched through each day simply to survive their seemingly impossible quest to reach the next layer of life, the next day.

Struggling, they were always struggling, fingers raw from the effort, hearts hardened, their humanity burned beyond recognition by the firebombs of their reality. With gang wars bloodying their streets, their hands, they would come to this place. Oh, and what a place this was. Under the auspices of the Chicago City Colleges, this was a skill center. Labeled a skill center not a school. The goal was to impart life skills, something to help its students with their lives. But what did any of us really know of *their* lives, these supposed to be students?

This was where I worked. This was the environment into which I was thrust immediately upon graduation from college.

Ah yes, college. My life. My experiences. My childhood. What a contrast to the lives, the experiences, the childhoods of my students. Contrast? What a gross understatement. Surely there's a better word than merely a contrast. My suburban childhood memories were of ice-skating winters and beach filled summers, school and summer camp, and then came fraternity parties that eventually gave way to campus protests and smoking dope.

Alien existence seems a much more apt description of the difference between my upbringing, my entire world, and that of my students. Alien. Yes, that's it. Much better.

For we had the luxury of dreams...oh, such dreams we had. We worried not about whether we would be alive tomorrow. We wasted not one moment in fear that perhaps another sunset or dawn would never be seen. We were expanding our minds with each inhaled toke in the hope of changing the world. We were going to make a difference, really make a difference. We were going to save the world. We were not going to fall into the same routines as our totally *out of it parents*. What did I know of a place like Dawson Skill Center, or of the people it served?

I grew up in the upper middle-class lifestyle of an Ozzie and Harriet household. Then, for four years I resided in that proverbial intellectual bubble of sheltered academia. What did I know of this life, of their life?

So, I began my career, the onset of my adult life, at Dawson Skill Center. There seemed not a teaching job was to be had back in that time but, unexpectedly, a position opened up mid school year at the Center. While unfortunate for the critically ill teacher I was replacing, his misfortune proved to be a blessing for me.

Initially perceived as a blessing, soon the bubble within which I had resided for so long definitely burst the day I walked through those doors. Life as I had known it, was comfortable within, would never be the same again. Everything changed the day I walked into Dawson.

This was an adult education facility where men and women who had dropped out of high school came to be instructed both academically and vocationally. The hope being that they would obtain enough knowledge and skill to pass their GED exam and acquire enough practical workshop ability to make them employable.

I had my first real job at last. The once summer-employed, part-time cashier at Muntz Cartridge City, a retail outlet for eight track tapes, had a real career now, a real job. Dawson Skill Center. Life was at hand. Dirty, dangerous, reality-filled life surrounded me now. I was a teacher.

Willie

His skin, polished to a red highlighted glisten, is what first struck me as he entered the room. He looked to be at least six feet two inches of pure muscle. Arms of mass swung boldly, intentionally exposed by his having rolled up the sleeves of his tee shirt. My first thought was that this guy was a hunk. His fists were balled powerfully and hung at his sides and his eyes sparkling playfully at me. Was all of this a joke to him?

"Hey, look at da curves." A short, wiry, thirty-something looking man, whose skin was the color of burnt bacon and whom I was to learn later was named Henry Barton; commented loudly while he elbowed the ribs (two quick jabs) of *the hunk* as they came further into the classroom.

"Did ya fuck yer ol' man last night, curves?" Henry continued with a smirk as he fully entered the room.

Henry's head suddenly hit the wall. He was easily being held, suspended a few inches off the ground, by the large hands of *the hunk* around his throat. He was apparently my self-appointed defender. A moment passed as all eyes were on the unfolding scene. A surge of pressure, beginning at the exposed shoulder of my defender, rippled down his arm and culminated in a tighter grip around the other man's throat as Henry finished his question, oozing sarcasm, when...THWACK! Again, his head hit the wall. The sound resonated throughout the classroom.

"Polagize," my black knight growled. Then under his breath, whispering through clenched teeth, "Asshole."

Henry, shocked, speechless, finally found his voice after a quick shove produced a rib-cracking moan.

"Sorry," he managed.

The focus was now squarely upon my response. I saw the anticipation on all of their faces. I would be setting the tone for my entire relationship with the class. My first teaching job and the first words uttered to me by a student, *Did ya fuck yer ol' man last night?*

Oh my God. How to handle this? I wasn't prepared. I had such a nice little speech rehearsed. This was not what I had planned.

I glowered at Mr. Fowl Mouth while searching desperately for the right thing to say. Having grown up with two older brothers, I had perfected a pretty nasty glower. But what to say? How to handle this? Once again, he came to my rescue.

"Siddown! Stop starin' like a bunch a idgits," he commanded.

His voice was as powerful as his countenance. And they all obeyed. The moment had passed. I had yet to say a word, utter a sound.

I watched eighteen men and women take their seats. Many were older than I. Eighteen different reasons why they had not finished high school. Reasons that made them eligible to be instructed by me in english, social studies, math and science in the hope of passing their GED exam. They split their school day between my academic classes and vocational training in the machine shop. I had a shot every day to break through. I wanted desperately to ignite some kind of spark or perhaps re-ignite an ember long since lain dormant, to create a burning desire on their part for knowledge. God, I was so very young and naïve but equally determined to succeed.

I kept coming back to him as I scanned the faces watching me expectantly. I kept coming back to his look, his posture as he sat front row, center seat; tall, erect, so disciplined.

I leaned on the edge of the desk looking them over for one moment more, hoping they didn't notice the deep breath I took in order to push the words out past the fear blocking their path.

"I am Lauren Gates. I'm here to help you to achieve your high school equivalency diploma."

When I couldn't take their staring at me for one moment longer, I turned and walked behind the desk. A deep breath later, I began to write my name on the blackboard. There was total silence in the room until the chalk squealed. Oh God! I turned, anticipating the remarks to come, ready to face my punishment for being so totally inept.

Silence. DEAD SILENCE was all that followed. Not a sound was made. Not a snide comment nor sarcastic remark was uttered. I scanned the faces, uneasy with this totally unexpected lack of response. What was going on? Then, I focused my attention on him and the mystery was solved.

There he sat, glaring about the room as if daring a comment. His eyes shot from face to face, silently threatening. His expression was deadly serious. A bit shaken but certainly not thrown, I found my voice.

"Now that you know who I am and why I'm here, I want to learn the same about you. Please tell me your names and why you have decided to come back to school for your GED. Who would like to start?"

There was a lot of squirming, a few snickers but not a single volunteer. Before the lack of response became unbearably uncomfortable, once again, he saved me.

Sitting tall, proud he said, "I's Willie Taylor. I wants a good job so's I can get me a white Eldorado wiff silver buckles on da trunk." He smiled.

Oh, how he smiled. A toothy, wide, warm, totally engaging smile spread across his face.

It mattered not what he had said. I was awed by the pure power of that smile, like he knew exactly what he wanted and exactly how to get it. I had never seen a smile quite like his before.

I found myself smiling back at him, instantly at ease. No, it was more than just at ease. I was happy to be there. I was happy to have the opportunity to impact his life. Was it what he had said? No. Such a ludicrous ambition yet his voice thickly spread through the sentence having it make total sense. Or was it the eyes, those eyes so sincerely playful? Was he kidding, making fun of me? No. I didn't think so...but was he?

"Thank you, Mr. Taylor for beginning."

Before I could go any further he continued.

"Jess call me Willie." And there was that smile again.

"O.K. Willie." I redirected my attention somewhat begrudgingly to the rest of the class. "So, who's next? Why are you here?"

Not surprisingly, no volunteers.

"How about you?" I pointed to a middle-aged woman seated next to Willie.

A heavy, flat voice echoed dully off of the walls as she responded in a tone laced with defiance.

"I'm Ann Vance. I got three kids ta feed and I get more in my welfare check if I show up here." Smugness spread across her face as my expression must have exposed my disbelief.

Some muted verbal and nodding-head agreement with gloating on the side and poorly concealed laughter billowed across the room, spreading slowly like some giant cloud of smug engulfing my students, one by one, in what looked like a snide conspiracy of purpose. Was this possible? I scanned the faces. As I searched the expressions, I realized that it must be so. Not one of them reacted to my gaze with anything other than an agreeing nod, confirming murmur, or smirking sneer. Everyone except Him.

I continued undeterred and heard sixteen more names. PreDennis, James, Annie, Bernadine... Different names but sixteen variations on the same theme. To get more money in their monthly government checks seemed their sole motivation for showing up. The more classes they attended, the more money they received.

Certainly not the first lesson I expected taught in my classroom and certainly not the student I had anticipated to be the first to learn something. Yet, learn it I did and as unexpected as it was; I was determined not to let this revelation of motivation sidetrack my enthusiasm.

O.K. then. So be it. Whatever the motivation for the system putting them into my care for several hours each day; I was going to alter their lives. I was going to make the difference that all of my friends and I talked of in our classes at school when boasting of what our lives would be like.

So what if they thought that they were here for the money. Whatever their reason for showing up to this classroom; I had my own reason for being here. I would be standing here in front of them every day of the week and I was going to make a difference in their lives. They might have come for the money, but they were going to leave with an education. I would give them something more valuable than merely the immediate pleasure of a few more dollars in their pockets. I was going to give them a future.

Thinking back on that moment, I can't believe just how very naïve I was not only to their plight but to their world.

I must have gotten through my description of the class, my expectations of them, requirements, goals. But all I recalled later was how he looked at me; followed my every move, laughed at my attempts at humor, squelched any disruptions by others.

Who was this man? Why was he so damned appealing?

And then, all at once, my first day was over. I had gotten through it, shakily at first but I was basically unscathed. As they all left, he remained.

"Hope I din't seem too pushy. I think I comes off too pushy sometimes."

While apparently searching for the right words, his tone remained confident. He was such a paradox. Every time he opened his mouth the words which he spoke never seemed to convey the true meaning behind the vocabulary choices he made. It was the way he said things and his incredibly powerful presence; I had never met anyone so very self-assured. I had to really think to focus on what he had said, I was so caught up in his delivery. He mistook my silence.

"Sorry. You was a shock. Dat's all," he apologized defensively. "I gets kinda *pushy* when someone shocks me."

"A shock? Me? How so?" I was intrigued.

"I weren't 'specting...you...ta be da teacher...someone like... ya know?"

"You mean a white woman, here, in an all-black school?"

"Not jess color. You's so young...'n pretty."

Was it a sincerely-stated compliment? With no further thought I replied, "You certainly don't seem the type to be thrown by a mere woman."

UHHHHG. I was sorry the moment it came out of my mouth. The way it came out. Was I flirting? How was I coming off in front of him? I had to keep this professional.

I walked to the small closet at the back of the classroom and retrieved my coat. As I turned back toward him, in what I thought to be a very professional sounding tone, I stated,

"Well, Mr. Taylor, it really is time for me to go. I will see you in the morning."

He seemed genuinely sorry.

"Do ya think we ken talk sometimes or somethin'?"

Before I could answer, he was helping me on with my coat and his hand innocently brushed my cheek.

Oh, there *was* something. I was not imagining it. We stood a good few seconds just stupidly staring into each other's eyes. Hadn't I seen this scene a thousand times in a thousand different "B" movies? But still, there was definitely something going on here and I knew that he knew it.

"I'm sure we'll be doing a lot of talking as the term proceeds," I stated as coolly as I could manage.

"Ya know dat's not what I means." He spoke sincerely with nary a hint of snide nor sleaze.

I was thoroughly taken in. I had to get out. This was ridiculous. I didn't even know this man. He was everything I did not want to be involved with. Was I getting involved? Was I making a total fool of myself in front of this stranger? And one of my students no less? Was I reading more into all of this than what was really happening?

I stood looking up into his beautiful face.

"What do you mean?" I whispered. It was hard to get the air I needed.

"I means I wants ta talk...ya know?"

There was shy anticipation in his voice now. He was a big, very big, adorable kid, unsure of what my reaction would be but hoping for acceptance.

"I'd like that," I answered evenly, honestly.

What I didn't say was at that moment I wanted more. I wanted to feel his strength all around me, holding me tight, not letting anything or anyone ever hurt me again. I knew that no one could guaranty that I would never be hurt again but my heart just hadn't been steeled to that conclusion yet. My instincts told me that if anyone could protect me, he would be able to do it. Just the look of him, the feel of having him close; I knew that he could do that for me.

"I best walk ya ta yer car. It's get'in dark," he offered.

I agreed gratefully.

President Carter had just recently made a fervent plea to the nation requesting a concerted *energy conservation effort* and the school administrator was doing his part by not turning on the lights in the parking lot. It was winter in Chicago and fully dark by the time school ended at 5:00 P.M.

As the foot thick, solid metal door clanged shut behind us; I noticed dense clouds blocking what little light there might have been

14

from ascending stars and moon. No wind. High- pitched screeching from the El above, spiriting their rush-hour commuters on rumbling tracks, painfully pierced the cold, then still silence as we left the building.

Large structure barren plots of earth surrounded the school. Huge piles of so much more than mere garbage lay all about us abandoned, rooted from neglect. There was the faint reek of rot masked somewhat by the smell of cold.

In the distance looking north, lights were flickering on. At first, they formed ad hoc clusters of twinkles which then turned into symmetrical patterns as more were illuminated in the otherwise darkened sky. I knew each twinkle to be representative of the upper class of Chicago coming home to their opulent high-rise lifestyles after a day of mastering the universe. The Chicago elite shined their blazing light in the blackening winter sky with the flip of a switch heralding not only their return to their homes but in some cases more importantly their wealth and power for all to see.

Funny how when planning and then building the Robert Taylor Homes, the powers that be thought that a high-rise design would in some way create the same feeling of empowerment and self-confidence that the occupants of the high-rises of the rich experienced in their ivory towers. They were sure that the result would be that the Taylor residents would then take pride in not only their homes but in themselves. Now, years later, all that the experiment in high-rise public housing accomplished was the creation of vertical slum living.

Off the lake a sudden, blustery gust unexpectantly pushed me back. As I began to stumble he reflexively wrapped me in a protective hug, anchoring me, holding me steady against the blast of cold air. It was so natural, felt so very right. All I could do was smile. I didn't know if he saw it or not, nor did I care. I had never felt so safe before. And God knew that I needed to feel safe.

Not a word was spoken.

We walked through the parking lot, his massive form shielding me from the legendary Chicago wind which had picked up, threatening to push me off course. As we reached my car the wind once again died down. His arm remained securely holding me. There was nothing to say. He watched as I unlocked the door. He helped me in. I smiled my thank you as he closed the door with a gallant nod. In his long, heavy, black coat he vanished completely, instantly, as he turned and walked away. And then he was gone.

WHOA! I sat staring after him but could not make out his form. Where did he go? Was all of that for real? What the hell happened?

Who was He?

I took a deep breath and started the engine. Out from the world of Willie Taylor and Ann Vance I drove. With each minute, every mile logged, the garbage and chains and deafening rumbles from the El above became easier to ignore, to forget. But I could not forget him. He was just there. The miles diminished not one moment of the memory of him. I heard the timbre of his voice. I felt the power of his presence. I missed the contentment I felt in his all-too-short embrace. What had happened? What had really happened?

And that night. What a night I spent sleeplessly, caught in tangles of sheets battling with an uncooperative pillow. I doubted my recollections, questioned my interpretations. Late into my battle with sleeplessness, tossing and turning in total confusion, apprehension, self-condemnation; finally, finally blessed sleep overtook the turmoil. But, all too soon, I found myself in those wonderful moments, just before full wide-awake consciousness overtakes, when all things seem possible and the simplest solutions to the most menacing problems miraculously appear.

How stupid of me. Rewinding and replaying the actual words exchanged, reliving the walk to the car. Surely, he was just being polite, interested in his new teacher, getting a feel for the rules of my classroom game. There was nothing more to it.

How stupid I was being. I had to rein it in. The reality was that I had gotten caught up in some kind of fantasy. One that had nothing to do with the actual events. It all seemed so clear. I had better just snap out of it.

I felt so much better. I regained control. I had identified the problem and could now effectuate the solution. What a relief. Why can't these insights ever appear *before* one wastes a good night's sleep?

I glanced at the clock. Too early to get up, yet too late to go back to sleep. In my sleep –deprived mind's eye, I saw his face. I saw those powerful arms and hands, actually glowing mahogany, slamming Henry Baton against the wall in my defense...explosive, fierce, then touching my cheek gently. It was all so very exciting. It all kept rerunning in my mind allowing me to relive it like a scene from a favorite movie which when viewed over and over again fostered the contentment of knowing what was to happen next. I was not only anticipating what kept happening in my own personal rerun, but actually longing to see it yet one more time. God, why did I keep tripping on my memories of him along the way to my solution?

I tried to think only of the day ahead. But his words, that smile, our time together the day before seemed to seep into every moment. I tried harder to prepare for my day but all I could think of was whether he would prefer my hair down long and loose or tied back with a ribbon. Should I wear a dress - I had decent legs - or would a pant suit be better?

This had to stop! Where was my self-control?

I had never been so instantly, totally wrapped up with a man before. My experience with men had, to this point, been pretty traditional. In reality, my experiences with men and life in general had actually been quite boring, the thought of which just added to the excitement of what was happening now.

As I stood in front of the mirror, I let the straps of my nightgown fall, releasing the silky fabric into a puddle around my feet.

Great body woman. You know a good body is a woman's best asset! My ex-husband used to tell me.

Well, my best asset hadn't changed at all in the year since our divorce. In fact, it was still pretty much the same as it was when we first started dating in my sophomore year of high school. We were the proverbial high school sweethearts. Going steady throughout our high school years led to my being pinned, engaged and then married while still in college. We had followed the pattern that our society set, to the letter.

He was my first exposure to the male being in a role other than family member or friend, and my first exposure to sex. I knew that I had a lot to learn and I was convinced that he was the only person I wanted to teach me.

The sexual aspect of our relationship did not start out well at all and, as is so often the case, it only got worse. I was so very young and needy. I was shy about telling him what felt good and what didn't for fear that he'd find someone more accommodating and less trouble. So, when he demanded satisfaction, I saw my role as providing it. It seemed more than reasonable at the time. I would give into his desires and he would continue to love me. I wasn't too concerned in the beginning. I was sure that I'd get the hang of it and begin to enjoy all of the sex stuff later. And in the meantime, I had Glen Jacobson all to myself.

Glen

I awoke to the smell of fresh lilacs. Today's were whites and purples. The most glorious lilacs in the neighborhood bordered my mother's garden. One day, teeny little buds covered the branches, too small to even hide the stalky underpinnings of the bush. Then, in season, the day finally arrived when the blossoming grew so abundant, full and lush; all that could be seen was vibrant bursts of color. Deep purple, pale purple, white and cream colored, each year they heralded the blooming of the rest of my mother's garden. And the fragrance...I had a new vase full in my room every day, scenting my world with the aroma of spring.

I felt oddly akin to the garden this year, for I too was blossoming after what had seemed a long winter's preparation. I too had a sense of awakening, finally, finally reaching maturity. My life was beginning at last. I had waited oh so very long. I was seventeen. I was in love.

Growing up in the North Shore suburbs of Chicago was a childhood upon which dreams are based. Old solid oaks and massive shade-producing elms lined the streets filled with well-kept houses. A huge toboggan hill and an ice-skating rink adjoined a lovely golf course; the large picture windows in the back of our house overlooked the second fairway.

We were what most would consider an athletic family. The proximity of the course made golf a family affair. My mom was a good golfer. My dad was a really good golfer and my two older brothers were excellent golfers. If you do the math, that adds up to four people, and if you know anything about golf you know that it is played in foursomes. So, by the time I was of age to play, our family foursome was already filled. But, before you think that I was neglected or felt left out, let me tell you that I wouldn't have competed with my older brothers on that turf in a million years. Rather, growing up, I picked my arenas of sibling competition very carefully with a vigilant eye to contests I actually had a chance of winning.

My life with two older brothers always seemed a challenge. My eldest brother reigned supreme, threatening to beat up the younger if he sided with me in any dispute. They were both quite industrious at times, even as youngsters. They once tied me to a tree when I was around six years old and sold looks up my skirt to their friends for a quarter a peek.

My best friend in my adolescent years was our pure white, ninety-five-pound German Shepard, Levi, named for the lead singer of The Four Tops. It was to him that I confided my deepest feelings. It was with him that I shared all of my fears of never finding the one boy who was right for me. And it was he who, every weekend, licked away my lonely tears as we watched *Saturday Night at the Movies* on T.V. together.

That was, until Glen.

Glen. How on earth can I describe what he was, what he meant to me? He was everything, had everything the movies I watched instilled in me to desire. He was the romantic, chivalrous hero of so many of the British novels I was reading in literature classes. I thought of him in clichéd terms for as a young, inexperienced girl that's all I knew. If asked at the time, I would have said *Glen came into my life like a burst of lifesaving air, filling me up. He was an essential part of my existence. How had I lived? How had I breathed? How had I made it through even one day before him?*

Yep, that's probably what I would have said, and meant every word of it!

We had been dating for two years, since I was fifteen. We had progressively spent more and more time together during those years.

And now, this was a summer filled with Glen...wonderfully, joyfully filled with Glen. On days I wasn't working, he would pick me up in the morning and we would take long, beautiful drives up and down the Lake Michigan shore. We varied our routes, sometimes opting for roads less traveled. Glen would maneuver twisting streets through heavily wooded terrain while at other times he would stick to the very popular sightseeing route, hugging the shoreline.

We talked for hours about everything and nothing. He was charming. He was handsome. He was so smart. He was rich and by some miracle, perhaps an intervention by the divine, he said that he loved me.

20

One such day, we were driving, engulfed in the opulence of the estates bordering Sheridan Road. This was my favorite route. Huge mansions of a time past had what looked like mile-long driveways and were bordered by trees bent, hanging low by the weight of their age on their massive limbs. At some points, as we wove our way along, the shade from the trees guarding the estates from view was so dense; we almost needed headlights to maneuver the twists and turns of the road.

It was at one such point, in the Ravines, a particularly hilly, twisty, wooded area of the drive south from beautiful Lake Forest, that Glen informed me that we were going to his house. It took several more minutes of glorious scenery to get there.

I had no idea that one of the fabulous properties that I had been gawking at on our drives actually belonged to his family.

We turned into a circular driveway lined with weeping willow trees curtsying a greeting. As a breeze caught their skirts, they seemed to bow slightly, waving us on. One after the other, as the wind moved through their midst, their long arms motioned as if ushering us on up to the front veranda.

"Oh, Glen," I managed to whisper before the sight of the antebellum mansion caused me to totally lose my train of thought.

I was unable to speak. I thought we lived in a pretty nice house, but this was a plantation for heaven's sake, right out of *Gone with the Wind*.

This was where he lived? Amazed, I could do nothing more than shake my head in disbelief. The estate was complete with swimming pool, riparian rights and a staff, housed in quarters above the garage, to take care of it. I half expected to be greeted at the door by a mint-julep bearing Mammy!

I wasn't that far off. As we entered the house, we were greeted by Annette whom Glen introduced to me as their Housekeeper. She was clothed in uniform; black dress, sensible black shoes with a white apron no less. Without another word or a smile, Glen told her to summon the staff so he could introduce me. I had to stifle a giggle. He was so - I don't know - authoritative. I wondered if I should pinch myself to make sure all of this wasn't a dream.

"The staff has been advised by Mother and Dad that when they are out of town, which is quite often, I am in charge of the household," he proudly informed me.

The Jacobson's estate had five full-time employees: Paul the chauffeur, Jake the groundskeeper/handyman, Mary the maid, Juliet the cook and Annette the housekeeper overseeing the others. Each nodded a greeting as Glen introduced me. He was so in control and he displayed that control with obvious enjoyment. How I marveled at his poise in power.

God, was I impressed. He actually *handled a household* in his parent's absence. Was I the luckiest girl in the world or what? He just knew so much about everything.

You were young once. I don't have to tell you what teenaged dating is like, what the progressive sexual ritual consists of. Glen and I were no different. We went through it all: the incredibly memorable first kiss, the fighting over the first feel, my tugging at that persistent hand trying to make its way into my pants.

We had gotten to that hot and heavy place enough times for a routine to have been established. I knew exactly what to expect and what was expected of me almost second to second.

For the previous two years we had progressed to the point where, being seventeen and totally inexperienced, I thought there was only one thing left for us to do. I was going to have to give in and let Glen *go all the way.*

It was an August afternoon, hot and steamy, when we had progressed on our sexual journey to the point where, naked bodies entwined, Glen emphatically announced that the time had come; and so would he...inside of me! Even as the predictable words of refusal were escaping my lips, I knew that my virginity was short lived.

Heavy drapes blotted out most of the sun but allowed, none the less, a deep, rich, muted glow to be cast into Glen's parent's bedroom where we lay. Three walls of floor-to-ceiling windows comprised the boundaries of this lovely room that was filled with live plants and a king-sized bed. That was all. Adjoining the bedroom was a large sitting room, a spacious separate dressing room and the cavernous bathroom. I had never until this summer of Glen seen a true Master Bedroom Suite. In this big old house, this suite encompassed two of the original bedrooms and an adjoining sleeping porch beautifully redesigned into the most spectacular bedroom I could ever have imagine.

It was ninety-five degrees outside and at least one hundred and ten in that bed! After months of his attempts to disrobe me, my clothes were now piled on top of his on the floor beside the bed and he was viciously alternating between fingers pushing and probing, and stiffened penis poking into my thigh. I know he thought that I was enjoying it, assuming that I was into it every bit as much as he was. I was too afraid to tell him I wasn't.

I was distracted by the same troubling questions that had been haunting me throughout our relationship since our first kiss. What was wrong with me? I should like it, shouldn't I? Was there something really wrong with me? In truth, I liked so very little of it. The rubbing and the kissing were nice and God how I longed for the gentle touches and caresses, but I was never able to build up to anything. I didn't know how and I just couldn't ask. He was so in control of everything. I just couldn't admit to my shortcomings. He deserved more, better than me.

So being the loyal, obedient girlfriend, scared to death of losing him, I faked it. I moaned and panted and clung on and bit my lip. Hell, I was good at this. I discovered that I possessed some truly accomplished acting ability. I was so good, sometimes I almost convinced myself!

As the afternoon sun waned and my impending deflowering approached, he reached to the floor and deftly produced a little silver foil packet from his pants pocket. One gasp later the condom was securely in place and his seemingly huge penis was ripping through my innards.

I truly remember very little of the actual sensations. But I vividly remember one thing: I hated every second of it. There was blood everywhere. It was all over Glen's thighs and dripping in large "plops" off of the tip of the condom precariously hanging from his now-limp penis. My belly was smudged crimson.

I was aghast at all of the blood. I had no idea I would bleed like that. God's wrath was upon me and my fate was sealed. Bleeding to death in a mega-million-dollar estate seemed my just due!

"My God, look at the sheets!" He shrieked. "We've got to do something! My folks might come home any moment. Hurry, Lauren, get dressed and help me strip the bed. We've got to get these sheets changed."

He began fumbling with his clothes, pulling at the sheets, scurrying about the room with not a single thought or word of inquiry as to my condition. Good God in heaven, I was bleeding to death and he wanted to do laundry!

While he finished stripping the bed, I made my way, naked, across the dressing room. As I sank near ankle deep in the plush, pale peach carpeting, I prayed that the piece of Kleenex I was holding between my legs would prevent the proof of Glen's victory from staining more than just my memory of the event.

White marble with peach and gray veining walled the entire space of the master bathroom. A huge tub of the same marble was on my left and two massive vanities were on my right as I entered. Straight ahead was a door leading to the shower stall. A small room housing the commode and bidet jutted left. The glass wall paneling one side of the tub afforded the soaker a view of a greenhouse filled with various varieties of orchards which, I was later to learn, Glen sarcastically called *Jake's children.* A sincere, *oh my* escaped my lips as I looked about me. This was really more than I had bargained for. Could it really be that I had Glen and he had all of this?

I stood for a moment staring at my reflection in the mirror. My hair (raven in color as Glen called it) was sort of wildly appealing with wisps hanging kind of sexily disheveled. My face seemed different too, more mature than a mere hour ago. But nothing had really changed. I was still just plain old me. What in the world could someone like Glen see in plain, drab me? I stood for a moment seeking an answer in the mirror. Nothing. Nada. No change.

How many countless hours had I spent in front of my makeup table in my bedroom at home doing just as now, staring into the mirror, searching, wondering when, if ever, I would *swan.* When, was it going to be my turn to have a beautiful me reflecting back?

I sighed in disappointment. Well, at least IT had finally happened. Not exactly in the way I had hoped for, but Glen would have no reason now to doubt my love for him.

As I washed the proof of his love from my body, I regained the sense of urgency that the situation required. I was relieved to find a Kotex pad in one of the vanities. Now armed with the proper protection, I quickly dressed and led Glen on a mad dash down the stairs with bloodied linen in hand, looking for the laundry room. Annette stopped me in my tracks.

"Miss Lauren, what have you there?"

I couldn't speak, couldn't move. I was mortified. Glen came up behind me.

"Take these dirty sheets to the laundry room and have Mary remake my folk's bed...NOW!"

Glen grabbed the sheets from my arms and shoved them into Annette's chest. She stood, unflinching, as he pulled me back and on up the stairs.

"I'll be waiting in their room," he commanded.

I couldn't speak through my embarrassment. As I turned a backward glance, I could see Annette's steady gaze. What was it that I saw in those knowing brown eyes? Not judgment. No...sympathy. It was sympathy that struck me.

With no time to spare, Glen supervised the remaking of his parent's bed. As we started down the massive, ornately tooled, heavy wooden staircase; the front door swung open below us. Arthur Jacobson guided his wife Cynthia into the expansive foyer.

Glen instantly put his arm around my shoulder as we continued our descent from the second floor. My God, the embarrassment! What would they think, coming home and finding us coming down the stairs? And the worst part was they'd be right. How could I have let this happen?

When I decided that I had examined the marble entrance hall floor long enough, I lifted my gaze and was immediately struck by Cynthia's sea green eyes set firmly on me. I felt them gush over my whole body, soaking every inch of me in shame and humiliation.

She stood taller than I and radiated a dominance that instantly heralded her superiority. I was awestruck. I was totally unable to move.

Her complexion was smooth and heavily made-up but done in such a way as to look healthy and natural. Her hair was richly tinted red and hung shoulder length in perfect harmony with her total look. She wore navy blue and white from neck scarf to sandals, crisp and proper in every detail, each accessory perfectly selected. On this incredibly hot and humid day she was the epitome of cool. She equaled the magnificence of the estate, and more.

Arthur, at six feet tall, had the build of a man half his age. Broad, squared shoulders served to support an elegantly tailored suit. His white shirt contrasted with his deep, reddish tan bringing the actor George Hamilton to mind. His striking coloring highlighted his large angular features giving him a manly handsomeness which Glen had inherited. Arthur and Cynthia, oh, they were quite a pair. Arthur spoke first as he extended a large, soft hand and a warm smile in my direction.

"Who is this little doll?"

With an expression of pure disinterest, Cynthia walked over to the foyer table and began busying herself with the mail.

"This is Lauren Gates. You know, I've told you about her," Glen answered very curtly.

I was momentarily surprised at Glen's tone. So, was he playing the *best defense is a good offence* thing here? I never would have used that tone with my dad. I didn't know what to expect Mr. Jacobson's response to be.

I certainly didn't expect what followed. Totally ignoring Glen's combative tone, he looked at me and smiled broadly.

"Well, Lauren Gates, I hope that we will be seeing more of you." His voice was soft and kind.

Then, he walked past us and on down the long hallway leading to his study. He had a warm gentleness about him that almost succeeded in putting me at ease.

"So, did you have fun today?" Cynthia asked Glen, obviously not the least bit interested as she continued, absorbed with the mail.

Glen beamed. I sulked (and bled).

"Yeah, had a great day. We went to the beach," he answered over his shoulder as he led me out the front door and out of earshot.

"For God's sake, Lauren, you look like death warmed over!" He hissed, tightening his arm around me as he continued.

"C'mon, baby, you've just had the greatest experience known to man. Can't you look a little more excited? Wasn't it great? Wasn't it something?" His tone had softened.

I looked up at him. Really looking at him for the first time since *the greatest experience known to man* I was struck by his expression. He had never looked more elated. There had been so much craziness, with the bloody sheets and his parents coming home, I hadn't had a chance to really look at him until that moment.

His face was a little flushed, intensifying his deep tan. His eyes, so green, sparkled emerald. And that smile. Oh, how I adored that cocky smile of his.

Then it hit me. I had done this. I had given him this joy. I had never seen this kind of elation wash over him before. Just thinking about our tryst was the catalyst. I had done this for him. God, how I loved making him so happy. This had to be what real love was all about. And in that moment of clarity, I knew that this was certainly enough for me.

He was looking at me expectantly. Or was he actually seeing right through me? Either way, I knew that I had better muster up some enthusiasm about the afternoon's events... for his sake.

"Yeah, it was really great!" I smiled my best smile.

I received no response from him. Thinking back now, I realize it hadn't really mattered what I said or how I really felt about what had happened. He was into his own reveling, not even hearing me. So what if my insides were aching, my head spinning and I was afraid I was bleeding to death. Glen was in love with me and at the time, that was enough.

Reflection

These memories bombarded me from the mirror. I had been so
very young. We had been so young. That's what everyone told us.
We were too young to be so seriously involved. But we wouldn't
listen. We spent every possible moment together. With the absolute
surety of youth, we knew exactly what it was that we felt. True,
everlasting devotion; an unparalleled love. We knew what we had. It
was everyone else who just didn't understand. They couldn't
understand what we felt for each other. No one had ever felt what
we felt for each other. That's what Glen told me and as he lovingly
whispered the words into my ear, I knew them to be true.

At nineteen, I knew all that I needed to know. He was handsome.
He was so generous. He even wrote me sonnets. I couldn't figure
out why, but he truly loved me. What more could I ask for? What
more could there possibly be? I needed so desperately to be loved.
I don't know why I was so desperate, from where such insecurity
came. I had a great childhood with loving parents, a seemingly
storybook life. But, for some reason, it simply was not enough. I
was not enough.

I guess like most teenagers I was having trouble handling it
all...this thing called life. I think I was searching for a guaranty that
the security of my childhood would flow, uninterrupted, into my adult
life, and Glen was that guaranty. Or so I thought.

Aw Hell, do I really know why? Does it really matter? The bottom
line is, I needed to belong to someone and, my God, he was so much
more than a mere someone.

So, without asking the really important questions, we married. It
took three years for me to discover that everyone had been right.
We were too young. We had a lot more growing up to do and boy,
did we grow up differently in those three years of marriage.

Now at twenty-three, I had never had a chance to experience boys
or men for that matter. From the time I was old enough to date I
was with the boy I would marry. Since the divorce, I had shied away
from anything, but the occasional blind date insisted upon by a well-
intentioned friend or relative.

There certainly was never anyone like Willie. The sheer power he exuded. His body, his voice, just the memory of the few hours we had spent together sent my thoughts racing. I saw such sincerity – no, so much more than that. Could it have been passion I saw, felt in that moment we stood staring into each other's eyes?

If just the memory of a moment could produce such a response from me, what in the world was I going to do when I actually saw him again?

I glanced at my body in the mirror; took a critical look. What would it be like to have those huge hands touching me? What would it feel like to...this had to stop!

Oh God, where was my self-control? I kept asking myself that question as I dressed for the day to come. Where, indeed, was my self-control? Did I have any at all? Had I ever had any and just suddenly lost it?

Such a gray, winter day; such heavy thoughts. Even the drive south on Lake Shore Drive with the splendor of Lake Michigan outside the car window couldn't seem to brighten my mood. Most winter mornings the sun rising behind the Adler Planetarium, reflecting the platinum sheen of the water in the early morning hours would energize me. It would fill me with a spirited resolve to soften the day, kneading it, like unbaked dough, into a wonderfully aromatic delight that, once baked by the experiences awaiting me as the day progressed, would provide a feast fit for the senses, good enough for the gods. But what exactly would be awaiting me this morning? If I were one to believe in omens, the fact that the drive hadn't lifted my spirits did not bode well.

By the time I pulled into the parking lot I had resolved to just wait and see what happened...like I had any other choice! I wasn't really sure what had actually transpired between the two of us. I was going to just start fresh, a clean slate. The sun had risen on a new day. Well, at least it was trying to poke through the clouds.

Walking from the parking lot to the school, I couldn't free my mind from the incredible feelings I was experiencing. The closer I got to the building the more the adrenalin flowed. My pulse was quickening with each step. As hard as I was trying to remain calm, every nerve twitched, the blood within my veins throbbed, the very essence of my being seemed to be pulsating with excitement. Hard as I tried to contain them, the feelings I had experienced the day before kept surfacing. Oh, how wonderful it was to be reminded. I had forgotten just how thrilling life could be. In a moment of weakness, I reveled in the glorious feeling of true excitement. What a great feeling.

There are times in life when we are so bogged down, for whatever reason, with the mundane, the meaningless day-to-day, that we forget, we actually forget the feeling. You know what I'm talking about. I know you do. We don't even realize it until something happens, some wonderful thing happens and all at once our senses are brought back to life again. It's as if God is playing some awful practical joke; the older we get the fewer and farther between those wonderful moments occur.

When we're young they seem to be happening rapid fire...BANG, BANG, BANG, explosive excitement erupting almost non-stop. Then we grow up. Life's realities muffle the sound, buffer the impact until all of a sudden, without even realizing it; we are caught off guard when it does occur.

BANG! Here it was, one such *thing.* The something had happened and I was suddenly aware and so grateful to be alive again.

But were these feelings based on reality, or just some fantasy I had concocted in my own mind? Was I that desperate for some excitement in my life that I had exaggerated or, even worse, simply imagined the situation?

I looked around me, shivering from not only the harshness of Chicago's winter but from this barren, depressing environment as well. Suddenly any thought of Willie or what actually happened or didn't happen left my mind completely.

I saw not a single soul. At seven thirty in the morning, I found myself in a modern-day ghost town...early morning in the middle of an inner-city housing development. Gusts of wind carried the paper and trash sagebrush swirling, twirling it mixed with the spraying snow in an urban dust storm whipping through the alleys, collecting on the exposed, grated catwalks of the buildings' exteriors.

As the wind picked up speed, bright red fabric caught my eye billowing out of a window several floors up from the street. What a contrast to this otherwise gray, deserted, deathlike environment.

31

How strange indeed. Who would have a window open on such a frigid morning? I then noticed that many - actually very many - of the rows upon rows of windows stacked to the sky were open. Most were just ajar but some were really opened.

I later learned that the Chicago Housing Authority had trouble regulating the temperature in these projects, so rather than risk the wrath of the watchdog groups by providing inadequate heat, they erred on the side of excess. The tenant's only recourse in solving the excessive heat problem was to open the windows, even when temperatures plunged to below zero outside.

On an historical note, it took many more years for the city to acknowledge that these high-rise experiments in public housing had turned into nothing more than high-rise slums providing a somewhat safe haven for gang members and thugs and an urban hell hole for the other residents who simply wanted a place to live that they could afford. Years later when developers and city planners alike realized that the property, just blocks away from the lake and the Loop, was ripe for urban gentrification and development; the city began demolishing the buildings one-by-one.

But in 1974 those buildings were bustling with hundreds, if not thousands of people that very well might become my students in the future and many that already were.

The blood red flag of poverty, flapping in the gray, early morning gloom had caught and held my attention. What a God-forsaken place this was. Who could live in a place like this? Could I really work in a place like this?

The heavy metal door of the Center slammed shut behind me as a mighty blast of cold air came off the lake. At least it was warm in the building. I shook the snow from my coat as I began to once again focus on what to do about Willie Taylor. How was I going to handle the effect he had on me now that I was here? I was preoccupied with the very distressing fact that I didn't have a clue as I walked into the administrative office to get some copies made for my class.

"Don't you waltz in here thinkin' I'm gonna jess drop everythin' ta do yer shit!"

Mellie Thomas was the school's secretary and possessed the power of the Xerox machine. Without her, no one made copies. She wore the code key thing around her neck and word was, only after your quota of groveling and kowtowing was fulfilled would she go forth and duplicate for you. I was actually grateful for the sarcasm. It gave me a chance to focus on someone, something other than Willie. I could definitely use a diversion.

"Well, good morning to you too, Mellie." I smiled, sincerely hoping she was just crusty and not genuinely mean.

She grabbed a file from atop the copier. In one swift movement she turned in front of me and spat in my face.

"Fuck you, Sugar!" She viciously snapped, wiping her mouth dramatically with her free hand.
Then she was gone.

I stood there like a dumbstruck idiot. The warm spittle making its way down my cheek brought me around as I searched my purse for a piece of Kleenex with which to mop my face. My anger built with each swipe of the tissue. I was virtually consumed with fury by the time Nancy Martinez, the only other non-black face in the entire school, found me standing there moments later.

"Lauren? You O.K.?"

"Fine. Just fine." I was afraid to say more as I walked out of the room.

And I had welcomed a diversion? What the hell was going on here? I was furious. No, I was Irate! Who dared to actually spit in someone's face? What had I done that was so terrible? What had I said so hateful to make her respond that way? Nothing. I had done nothing. Then, why? Why such anger; such vehemence?

I had never before had the pure intensity of feelings that I experienced in the two days of being in this place. Such a surge of emotion, so strong, so disarming. Yesterday, it was Willie. He had completely overwhelmed me, and now Mellie had managed to insight a rage in me I never knew I had the capacity to experience. They had both evoked such passion from me. I had never experienced the power of it before. A power that instantly buried my background, my methodical reaction process, my very nature seemed to be overtaken. I had never before felt such anger, so immediate, intense than that which I felt for Mellie Thomas when she had the audacity to spit in my face. I had never before felt the desire - so immediate, intense - like that which I felt for Willie Taylor as he held me wrapped in his gaze.

What was happening to me? The me I was so sure I knew was suddenly, inexplicably unrecognizable. My very nature was in question here. I had the real sense that it was imperative for my personal wellbeing that I maintain some semblance of what I was still sure was the real me. My logical, sensible mind sought answers. There had to be some logic to all of this. There was always some logic. Yet here, things were so very different. Even logic seemed different here. The logic I was used to always demanded a reaction to any given act that was, if not predictable, at least understandable. Yet there was nothing anywhere close to resembling predictable about Mellie's reaction to my simple request for help. And there certainly wasn't anything predictable about my reaction to Willie Taylor's touch.

As I walked the halls toward my classroom, I was filled with such confusion.
What was this place?

It had to be this place. I couldn't believe the things that had happened to me in just two days. No one would believe them, at least no one that I knew anyway. This place, really, what was this place?

I began to examine the realities of what had happened. It was as if each time I entered this building I embarked on a totally foreign experience. An environment populated by people who spoke the same language yet said things, did things, made me feel things...I wasn't sure I could adjust to so much raw emotion. I had to learn to adjust, and fast. I could no longer rely on my obviously limited frame of reference to handle this...place.

Could a place have that kind of power? I feared I was as close to a logical explanation as I was going to get, and it was totally unsatisfying. But, out of necessity, I grabbed on to it.

This place was so unlike anywhere I had ever been before. People had the power to open others up here, piercing through in only a moment, the deepest emotions pouring out. Everything seemed to happen so quickly here. Was it me? Was I losing my mind? I was really having trouble accepting such an illogical logical answer!

I had to focus on something. Get my bearings somehow. I reduced my thoughts to the very basic problem at hand, how the hell was I going to get my copies made?

I was pondering that dilemma as I walked toward my classroom.

I was aware of him before I actually saw him. Was it his scent? What was that strong, very appealing smell? I realized that I had smelled it before, before I was taken in by it, by him yesterday. It was vaguely familiar. I struggled to remember. *Sandalwood* I thought to myself as he joined in step next to me. Sandalwood incense is what came to mind.

Incense-filled rooms, reminiscent of a time in my life not so very different from this one in one respect. I was as totally unprepared then as I found myself to be now. A situation. I was caught up in a situation for which my experience, my truly limited experience, could provide no help.

Des Moines

Returning from our honeymoon, Glen and I embarked on a totally new life: Marriage. I was married to a wonderful guy who loved me. How did I ever get so lucky? He wrote me passionate love letters and I was showered with constant surprises. Was I the luckiest girl on this planet or what?

He had one more year of college; I was beginning my second. We moved into a little house not far from campus. It was a block away from the Des Moines River, the filled with sludge, always brown Des Moines River...very earthy! But I loved it as only a 19-year-old newlywed brimming with enthusiasm for the future could.

While our house was a newly constructed, two bedroom, bath and a half adorable bungalow, it was in a just-beginning-to-be-renovated area which was big on vacant lots spewing gravel dust with any slight gust of wind and shy of much charm. Who cared if the walls were paper thin and the windows cheaply sealed? Even trying to keep the soot that permeated the air from accumulating on the furniture and window ledges was a joy.

Playing house, going to class, concocting meals every night from my various cookbooks; to my mind, this was a young newlywed's dream come true.

Oh how the enthusiasm of youth can make one ignore, even relish, the trials of existence which after years of experience and the mere act of living come to be revealed as nothing more than sodden dreams rather than the pure fantastical. Don't you agree? When one looks back, thinks back, many harsh realities become so damn obvious, so transparent; one has to wonder how in the world we had misjudged the obvious?

I was, to myself now, so mystifyingly oblivious to the fact that my college experience was different in every way from that of the typical coed, so completely wrapped up in a dream world of Glen's creating was I. Living off campus we were *commuter students*: arriving on campus for classes, leaving immediately after. To me, I was missing nothing. To the contrary, I was Glen's wife.

One crisp, sunny October Saturday, Glen and I took a walk down 34th Street, Drake University's fraternity row. It was homecoming weekend and the frat and sorority houses had really gone all out. Hundreds of people were working on floats, exhibits, or simply milling about laughing, joking and just enjoying the perfect fall day.

The laughter from one small group produced a billow of chilled breath, which rose from their mouths above them as an unmistakable symbol of the pleasure of the cool outdoors. Their sounds were happy and warming even though their noses and cheeks were reddening.

Footballs were being tossed. Pin-mates from out of town were being kissed. And we were so much in love.

Such traditions observed on most every campus across the country were not the only staples of college life at that time. Drake University, like every other university in the late 60's and early 70's, was caught up in a set of new traditions emerging as being equally as important to its student body.

Smokin' dope had become a big portion of campus life...and of our lives. We were no different from most every other Drake University student at the turn of the decade. It seemed everyone smoked...all the time.

We got stoned to go to class. We got stoned to relax after class. We got stoned to more thoroughly enjoy the movies. We got stoned to go to concerts; we got stoned at concerts. We basically got stoned to get stoned. It had reached the point where I had forgotten what being straight felt like.

At first it just sort of happened. It was what everyone was doing. It seemed O.K. Then Glen decided to take it a step further. See, in addition to buying for our own personal use, Glen had established quite a thriving little business supplying a few regular customers with their smoke as well. And as our marriage progressed, so did Glen's ambition. It began with his rationalization that if he sold some weed, the profits would pay for our personal consumption. But it didn't stop there. I began to see changes in Glen, subtle and then eventually not-so-subtle changes. Glimpses of a man I didn't even know emerged as his business grew.

It is so easy, in hindsight, to be perplexed at our inability to recognize the signs of problems to come. I was so blinded by the image of the marriage we would have, the life we would share, the future we would build together; I just didn't get it. Of course, I can see now that the reality in which we lived was very different from the one I had unwittingly constructed in my mind.

"You know baby, with the amount of dope smoked on this campus; we could make a small fortune."

Glen had taken up pad and pen one night to figure.

"Why would you want to do that, take that kind of risk? We don't need the money. We have our great little house. Our tuition is paid for. My dad sends us spending money. Your dad sends us spending money. Everything is perfect. Why risk it?"

What the hell? It seemed like such an obviously bad idea to me. But maybe I was missing something. Maybe there was some kind of plus side that I just wasn't aware of. I really wanted any kind of explanation that would make some sense.

Looking at Glen sitting before me, I saw his usual loving gaze morph into an expression that I was beginning to see more and more of lately. The one that made me feel like his little uneducated child. No, it was even more than that. It made me feel like someone he had to explain everything to, someone he enjoyed knowing that he had to take care of because I was so naive. How cute that I would have to ask such a question.

I would grow to hate that expression.

"Shit, baby, it's the knowing you're doing it. God, how to explain it to you...it's inside. It's something in here." He tapped his chest. "It's the planning it. Seeing it through. Doing something better, something others can't do. Don't you feel the excitement of investing two hundred and making a thousand?"

No, I couldn't feel it, but he obviously did. His face was lit by the excitement. I walked over and sat beside him.

"It's just the trouble you could be in if you get caught. It scares me."

He held me tightly.

"Don't worry, baby. Nothing's going to happen. I won't let it."

He gently kissed me, kissed my whole body until I could think of nothing else except how much he loved me.

As had become the norm, I rose from our lovemaking unsatisfied but totally contented with the closeness we shared. Surely there was more to true, everlasting love than great sex. The mere physical was certainly less important than what we shared.

I began to think that no woman actually attained that much-advertised, over-estimated orgasm. It was a huge, silent conspiracy of women afraid to admit that they didn't climax. Their love for their men, like mine, prompted the greatest faking of feeling possible with each attempt. Oh, I enjoyed the touching and the warmth, the kisses and embraces. Indeed, I yearned for the closeness and tenderness. But it never seemed to build into anything. And Glen seemed so sure of his sexual mastery; I just couldn't tell him I simply wasn't getting off. It wasn't his fault. Really, I just couldn't tell him.

The young have such dreams. I had such dreams. No more than just dreams, expectations. I just knew that if I found someone to love and if that someone truly loved me in return, the minor things, you know, those little and not-so-little irksome things that plague any type of partnership could and would change. I would be able to explain or cajole or simply reason them away and the blissful, yes blissful, life that was possible would become reality. I knew, really knew, that bliss with Glen would be my life. Oh, to have that surety of youth, that hopefulness, that...oh, I don't know, euphoria that can only overtake the young. While obviously unaware of it, I truly was that naive waif Glen seemed to adore.

Had I not had more important things to worry about, I'm sure that our inadequate sex life would have played a more important role than it did that first year of marriage. But I did have more important concerns, made even worse after receiving a phone call one evening from Glen's supplier.

He told Glen about a girl named Alice who made a big score of some *primo hash* that Glen just had to buy.

"I mean REALLY primo, Glenny boy. You gotta get your hands on some of this stuff." He spoke so excitedly, that sitting next to Glen I could hear him through the receiver.

So, after dinner Glen and I drove to Alice's house.

A Buddha-shaped girl with long, stringy blonde hair answered the door.

"I'm Alice. You Glen?"

And I'm Tarzan, where's Jane? God, I hated this. Glen nodded as we stepped into her home.

"This is my wife, Lauren." He responded to the look of apprehension my following him in through the door had produced on Alice's face.

The room we entered was intimate and very tastefully decorated. There were lovely oriental rugs and unusual brass candlesticks creatively placed on tables and fireplace mantle to softly light the room. There was a fine mist of smoke wafting above a square, very low to the ground, table in the center of the room. A subtle scent of sandalwood incense filled the air; nothing overpowering as so often the case with incense. This was more like a slight flavoring of the air, a lightly seasoned sensation, just pleasantly there.

"This is just lovely." My tone must have exposed my surprise.

"Some drug dealers have taste," she answered harshly.

I decided even an apology wouldn't help so I attempted none.

Glen and I sat on a wicker couch covered with a multitude of pillows forming a collage of softly toned Indian prints. Café au lait backgrounds with rusts and cool blues patterned the heavily fabriced room. While somewhat sparsely furnished, the effect was truly handsome.

Rather comically, Alice attempted to sit cross-legged atop one of the large pillows on the floor facing us but her protruding belly restricted the completion of the position. The result was a very awkward looking contortion. Her back was perfectly straight as if in defiance of her uncooperative limbs. She lifted a stone pipe carved in the shape of a penis, filled its testicle bowl with hash and offered it to Glen to sample. He drew deeply sucking on the tip as she held the match to the bowl.

I had to stifle a laugh. How ridiculous did that look, Glen sucking on a stone penis? She spoke softly and radiated a genteel composure.

"I think you'll like this stuff," she almost whispered, lifting one eyebrow coyly. "It's Afghanistan and really quite good. In fact, I think it's the best stuff I've ever been able to score and I've been doing this for more years than I want to remember."

Glen picked up a small chunk of the hash from the table and examined the color. It was very black. He rolled it around the palm of his hand to evaluate the texture. It wasn't reduced to crumbs as he rolled. A broad smile erupted. I had learned that he preferred this moister consistency rather than the crumbly quality he sometimes bought.

"It's Primo O.K. Let's have another taste."

Alice returned his smile as he once again took the carved stone shaft from her hand. Just as before, he inserted the tip into his mouth and drew deeply as he held a match to the bowl. He instantly produced a closed mouth grin, which I knew meant that we had just scored.

I was getting more uncomfortable by the minute. Watching Glen sucking on a penis, smiling with glee gave me the willies!

They agreed on a price as Glen pulled a wad of bills out of his pocket.

"This hit is my treat." He refilled the pipe and passed it to Alice as the front door suddenly crashed open.

Fright squeezed the breath from me. A tall, dark, figure of a man loomed large before us, backlit by the flickering porch light. His size became even more exaggerated by the massive shadow cast by the candlelight as he walked into the room.

Dominick Del Torio had just entered our lives.

I didn't know if he was going to bust us or kill us. I just knew that it was going to be something terrible. He stood six foot four with a few strands of greased, black hair flopping down over a broad forehead to precisely tweezed but obviously thickly bushed eyebrows. Black was definitely his signature color! Hair, eyes, even his demeanor screamed dark, ominous.

His full Italian featured face showed the remains of many teenage knife fights. And every fix of heroin with which he had soothed his cravings for escape was reflected in his kohl- ringed, chill- producing eyes.

I sat perfectly still hoping he wouldn't see me if I didn't move. I took shallow, soundless breaths praying that they were inaudible.

Alice put the pipe down on the table and rose with a degree of difficulty.   With a toothy grin of welcome, she walked over to where he stood. They spoke too softly for us to hear what was being said. Glen picked up the pipe and approached them.

"Care to join us for a smoke?" Glen handed the monster the penis, ever the generous dealer.

The huge black fiend looked at Glen, then at the pipe and finally at me. His eyes came alive momentarily in the candlelight. I could feel goose bumps exploding as he methodically examined every inch of me. As his gaze slowly traveled from my sandaled feet up to my eyes, which I am sure had to look like gaping, wide-open orbs; I felt trapped by the impending doom I instinctively knew this creature brought with him. Scared and flustered, I sought the security of Glen's eyes as a shiver overtook me. The now flat, black, eerie dead looking eyes of the intruder followed mine to Glen.

"She yours?" He asked Glen, cocking his head in my direction.
Glen smiled at me, a genuine loving smile.

"She's mine." He answered not taking his eyes off of me.

Dom smiled broadly, taking the pipe from Glen's outstretched hand. The old wooden floor moaned from the weight of his large frame as he walked over to me. He loomed above me, dark and scary, just standing there looking down at me. Then, he dragged noisily on the pipe and handed it to me. I just knew if I didn't take it, he would kill me.

With a shaking hand I reached up and took it. I hesitated to bring it to my lips, but he nodded his head, prompting me to draw in lightly.

I thought I was going to retch as my lips touched the tip of the cool stone penis pipe; it was all wet. I handed it back to him unable to utter a sound. He just stood there looking down at me. It took every bit of self-control I had to muster, not to wipe my mouth with the back of my hand in disgust.

Once again he cocked his head to one side and just looked at me. In my mind I shouted, *GET THE HELL AWAY FROM ME!* I just wanted him to leave me alone. But I was powerless to speak. I don't know how long he stood there, stood there just staring at me.

Finally, he pulled his gaze away from me with what appeared to be reluctance, turned and walked back over to Glen handing the pipe back to him.

"Lucky man," he stated flatly over his shoulder as he covered the distance back to the door in two long, easy strides, flung the door open and left.

Glen turned to Alice, excitement on his face, fascination in his voice.

"What the hell was that?"

"That was Dom," she answered softly.

Dom

As the evening progressed, Alice entertained us by relating Dom's story.

"The man has had incredible experiences with dope. He began with codeine cough medicine hidden in his fourth-grade locker at school. Coming from a strictly religious household, with a very domineering, nosy mother, he knew he couldn't keep it undetected at home. Shit, by age twelve he could tell the quality of LSD, mescaline, MDA and most any other hallucinogen with one small lick better than a chemist working on the analysis all day!"

She boasted as if he were her child that had become a famous neurosurgeon. I was having trouble sharing the admiration that she obviously had for Dom's background.

"Sounds to me like he could be the poster child for the *using any drug leads to using more serious drugs* proponents," I stated sarcastically, truly proud of what I thought was a very clever retort.

Both Glen and Alice glared at me. I guess I was wrong.

Glen chose to ignore my comment.

"Go on Alice. Tell me more about him," Glen urged.

"Well, his attitude back then was really very simple. His life was such a drag, why not artificially help with the day-to day. By age twenty he was addicted to heroin...but he licked that habit long ago. Actually, he has kicked it all including the attitude. See, he learned the hard way that the very best thing to use dope for is to make money. And once you have the money, you don't need the escape anymore. You can just enjoy the profits. I mean, what is there to escape from if you have everything you want? Right? Making money. You know; the profit and some good smoking dope on the side, that's what he's into now. That's really where it's at if you're smart."

She turned, nodding to Glen.

"But I don't have to tell you that do I?"

I don't know how, but she knew that Glen looked to capitalize on the college drug scene in just such a way. He seemed to be so obvious to everyone else. Was I that dense? Is love truly blind? Why hadn't I seen it sooner? Maybe I could have done something about it if I had truly understood. Was it too late? Of course not. I could still make Glen see what he was doing. God, it was so destructive. I had to make him see. But how?

"Dom's the best partner I've ever had," she continued, sitting back down on the floor and taking the pipe.

"How can I get in touch with him?" Glen asked after sitting for a moment in quiet thought.

"He'll be here tomorrow night, same time."

Oh, no. No no no! I had to go home. I had to get out. I had to get Glen out of that house. What was going on now? I had to talk to Glen away from this woman. Had she cast some sort of spell on him? Had the hash been laced with something that caused him to totally lose his common sense? How could he want to be with that...thing again?

"You know, it's getting pretty late. I've got an early class tomorrow." I hoped my imploring gaze would prompt Glen to get me out of there quickly.

His eyes met mine soft with understanding and love.

"I better get you home then." He turned to Alice. "Thanks for the stuff." He lifted the paper bag in a salute.

"Come on, baby." He took my arm as we approached the door. "We'll see you tomorrow night," he stated matter of factly.

"Peace." She nodded approval and with her right hand raised in the vee of the peace symbol she closed the door behind us.

I remained quiet until we were safely inside our car. The fear began escaping my body in spasms.

"Please Glen, let this one go. He's awful. You can't really want to get involved with him?"

I spoke softly, so afraid of what he would answer.

"Come on, baby, this is the fun stuff." He turned in his seat and stroked my arms. "Lauren, come on, lighten up," he pleaded.

"Didn't you see the way he stared at me? Glen, he really scared me. God, he's awful!" A streaking shiver shook me at the memory of his darkness staring down at me.

Glen examined me with concern.

"Wow, baby, you really are scared." And he began rubbing my arms as he continued. "He was just a shock, busting in like that.

That's all. It was strictly the drama of the situation that shook you."
He laughed. "What a show. What a get-up. Did you see the leather
bracelet with the silver spikes? And what about all of those homemade tats? What a total trip, huh?"

He was looking to me for some sort of affirmation, confirmation
that Dom was indeed a *total trip.* I could only think that the details
Glen found so exciting about Dom's appearance, I hadn't even
noticed. I was never able to get past the initial grip of terror.

"I find nothing appealing about being horrified," I answered.

"It was all show, baby. He's just really into the image thing...Big
Bad Boy. Come on baby...you have to admit, he does it pretty well."
And, once again my husband got that damned look on his face.

"Aw, don't be scared. I know what I'm doing, baby. You don't
even have to think about it. You know I'll take care of everything.
Don't I take good care of you? Would I let anything or anyone hurt
you?" With his sincere eyes imploring he continued. "Don't be
scared, babe. I'm right here, always right here. No one will ever
hurt you. I won't let that happen," he stated with total surety.

He leaned over and kissed my cheek. He was right and I knew he
would do anything to keep me from harm's way. I instinctively knew
I had better just snap out of it.

I had never been equipped to argue with him. No matter what I
said, he would always manage to make things end up his way.

What was wrong with me? Why didn't I just say *we're not going
back there?* But I knew the answer. I was afraid; afraid of losing
him, afraid that if I said such a thing; he would find someone else
who would go along with him. A deep, rationalizing, all too familiar
sigh escaped my lips. Was it so bad? He loved me; of that I was
certain. He took care of me; truly gave me any material thing I
wanted. And, he was right. Things always did seem to work out just
the way he said they would. Was it so bad to give him his way in
return for all of the security I was receiving?

I slumped in my seat the entire drive home feigning sleep. My
forced peaceful expression hid the conflict deeply brewing, the full
extent of which was unbeknownst to me.

Glen kept his rendezvous the next night. I went along, too afraid
to stay home alone. As anticipated, Sal was at Carol's house when

we arrived.

"Hey, man, I'm glad you're here. I wanted to talk to you." Glen began the conversation as we seated ourselves on one of the couches.

"So I heard." Sal smiled at Carol, but his tone was anything but encouraging.

"I think we have a lot in common." Glen proceeded anyway.

I sat somewhat stunned as Dom reacted instantly to Glen's statement. He began to shake. It took a moment but then his silent shaking erupted into raucous laughter, the most genuine, hearty laughter I had ever heard. It seemed to originate in the depths of his being and generated spasms of pure joy as it overtook his body. In the time it took for me to inhale deeply from the shock of anyone finding this situation funny, Alice was laughing right along with him. And much to my unwitting amazement, I too found the urge too great to stifle and began laughing myself.
So viscerally sincere Dom's laughter, it proved very contagious. Within moments, both Carol and I were heartily laughing right along with him.

Glen sat somberly observing the scene. He seemed to be waiting for something. He waited some more as the tears rolled down our faces. I had to clutch myself to contain my lungs, fearing they would explode from the enormous gasps of breath I was forced to inhale in order to fuel the laughter. Looking back on it, I realize that my uproarious laughter was a release of my pent-up fear.

Finally, Dom spoke. His laughter stopping as quickly as it had started. His expression turned deadly serious.

"We got nothing in common." He sneered. A truly menacing creature sat glaring at my husband as I helplessly watched. My laughter immediately ceased as the realization that I could not defend him from the attack that I was sure would follow. I silently prayed it wouldn't get physical. While being in excellent shape, Glen would be no match for the obviously streetwise alley fighter that sat before us. I tensed at the battle brewing not knowing what form it would take.

Undeterred, Glen proceeded as if not even hearing the overt threat.

"I heard you've had some pretty heavy experiences with dope." There was ill-concealed envy oozing from every word.

Dom picked up on it right away.

"I've had a few hard knocks, but I managed to come out on top. Know what I mean?" With pursed lips releasing a conceited sigh, Dom sat back smugly.

"Man, I sure would like to hear about 'em," Glen almost begged. It was obvious to me that he was feeding the huge ego. What I couldn't figure out was why.

"Ya know, when you've worked for the Mob, you can't say too much, ya know?" He cracked the word Mob for effect, then watched for Glen's reaction.

"No shit? Far out, man," came Glen's wide-eyed reaction.

Oh, this was not Glen. What was he up to? As I looked closely at my husband's expression, I realized that he was playing Dom...he wanted something. I looked at Alice. And all at once I sensed from her gaze that Dom was playing Glen as well. I kept shifting my attention from Glen to Dom in an effort to gain some understanding of what was really happening here. What was this? I felt like I was observing some kind of warped tennis match. Did they each think that they were exposing a weakness in the other, just waiting to smash the game-winning slam? The artificial banter lasted a few more moments.

All of a sudden, Dom broke into that contagious laugh once again and Glen began to roar uncontrollably. Alice and I both sat back rather dumbfounded as they slapped each other on the back and shook hands.

"Let's talk business," Dom spoke first.

"I thought you'd never ask," Glen replied.

I was totally lost. Maybe it was the primo affecting my brain. I had definitely missed something, something important and I knew, in that moment, whatever it was had bonded Dom and Glen together.

What was all of this? I sat stunned and terrified as I watched them together, smiling and talking animatedly. The two of them were now acting like old chums grinning ridiculously at each other. There was only one thing of which I was sure at that moment; I didn't like it, any of it. Nope, I did not like it at all.

And my fears became harsh reality as Dom became an everyday visitor to our house. While I did the laundry, the two of them would go to the gym. Or the three of us would go cruising around, visiting people and getting high. Glen and I still went to class every day, but Dom knew our schedules and seemed to simply appear whenever we had free time.

Their relationship soon grew from a friendship into an extremely profitable business partnership. Dom would arrange the score. Glen would fund the buy and they would both sell to their distinct clientele. Between the two of them, with their totally different spheres of contacts, they had all of the bases covered. It was an ideal partnership.

Can there be room in one's life for more than one ideal partnership? Why wasn't Glen able to recognize that I was becoming a nervous wreck? I don't think that my fears were unfounded, for it wasn't long before my husband was supplying the entire city of Des Moines with their smoking dope, and my newlywed lifestyle had changed dramatically. No longer was deciding which recipe to prepare for dinner my greatest concern.

By the end of the first semester of school their reputation had spread and strange faces were constantly tromping in and out of my house, picking up stuff and dropping off money. It was unreal...surreal. I was terrified by the constant stream of strangers. And, as the traffic increased so too my nervousness. I dreaded the knocks at the door. I hated the bricks of grass being split up on my kitchen table and the stashes of hash being sampled in my living room. I resented Dom for being the force that created this havoc in my life.

But I loved my husband and I had to admit, he was absolutely thriving. The more he sold, the happier he was and the more I feared his getting busted.

It's funny how I never thought in terms of my involvement. Talk about naïve! I just assumed that when it happened, Glen would be arrested, and I would be left alone to suffer without him. My fear was solely focused on what would happen to Glen. God, how I dreaded the thought of Glen being convicted and sentenced to jail time. He would die. This was a guy, so vital, energetic, so used to doing as he pleased. How could he possibly survive incarceration? And what in the world would I do without him?

I lay awake at night crying in anticipation of the trouble Glen was bringing upon himself. I walked around each day with a piece of lead lodged in my belly, just hanging in my stomach, weighing me down; a constant reminder of how I felt about our present situation.

"I heard you up again last night. You sick, baby?" Glen asked.

He seemed so genuinely concerned. Was this my chance? Perhaps I could finally get him to stop before something terrible happened.

"Glen, haven't you had enough yet? Can't you stop this dealing now before you get in real trouble?" I actually shocked myself with the degree of concern I was able to convey through my whispered plea.

"Stop worrying, baby," He soothed. "Relax and enjoy it. You know I'll take care of everything."

"I can't stop!" No longer whispering, my words now spewed forth, frenzied, crazy.

"You're going to get caught and put away. I'm so scared. I can't stop. I can't!"

I ran into his arms as he cradled me tenderly. Why had my words failed me so miserably? My plea sounded so lame and so crazy, even to my own ears.

"I love you, Lauren. I get that you're worried. I know you love me and think that you know what's best for me. And I appreciate your concern." He held me at arm's length looking intensely into my eyes. His voice was soft, and oh so tender with love.

"Honestly, I do appreciate it. But you don't have to be worried. I know what I'm doing. Trust me, baby. Have I ever let anything hurt you? Would I let anything hurt you?"

"It's not me I'm worried about..."

"Let me handle this," he gently interrupted me. "You just put all of this out of that gorgeous head of yours. Can you do that for me? Just enjoy the benefits? Can you try to do that for me?"

So many times over the next several months we had variations of this same conversation and each time they ended in the same way. He would wrap me tightly in a loving, secure embrace. I felt so warm and protected there. And this time, like so many of the others, all I could do was struggle to get closer, needing to be closer to him. I needed to feel his love.

I wanted desperately to share his desire, to feel the power of fulfillment he often spoke of. I lifted my face to him, started to kiss him. And then with a forceful surge of strength, he interrupted my gentle kissing of his forehead, his cheek and all at once I was pinned on my back. So urgent his passion, he ripped at my clothes, buttons flying, seams giving way and yet he spoke softly, lovingly as he pushed inside of me.

"Don't worry, baby. I'll take care of you," he whispered. "God, your body feels so damned good..." His whispers turned into a hiss in my ear.

I couldn't speak for his thrust had caught me without breath. Never before had I truly felt violated. How had our love turned into this? He came as I closed my eyes tightly...and my thoughts kept repeating, repeating, "I love you Glen. I do love you."

Nothing changed as the school year progressed. I desperately yearned for it to end so we could move back to Chicago. Glen's father had offered him a job after graduation. He would finally be out of this crazy, dangerous business and he could put his abundance of talent to legitimate work. If I had learned nothing else, I knew for a fact that Glen had the stuff of which success is made.

Once in Chicago, we would have a real life and maybe, just maybe I could find the right time to talk to him about my feelings...my desires. I grew increasingly excited as our last semester in Des Moines drew to an end. All of the negatives of this first year of marriage would be relegated to the past, a past I was very anxious to forget.

Standing at the sink washing fruit, my view from the kitchen window delighted me. Spring was upon us without my even noticing it. Whether memories from the first sight of my mother's garden coming to life each year, or now seeing just the few tulips that I had planted in the backyard poking their delicate red heads out for a glimpse of the world; I loved that first cognizant thought that spring is finally here. There was pure joy in my step as I carried the bowl of fruit into the living room and caught the tail end of a conversation Glen was having with Dom.

"...so, it's a perfect set-up, a last BIG score to send you and Lauren back to Chicago with a bundle of bread. I got this friend in Iowa City who's expecting a huge shipment of acid."

Glen leaned forward to listen more intently. I sat down hard on the couch, petrified, with the bowl of fruit in my lap. I was unable to set it on the coffee table.

We had never had anything to do with LSD before.

"All's we gotta do is drive there, pick it up, cap it, and deliver it...I already have it sold, the whole bunch, one buyer! It's golden, Glenny boy."

Dom sat back, puffed up with pride, picked a pear out of the bowl still resting in my lap and took a huge bite out of it. He chewed behind a closed mouth grin.

"Is it good stuff?" Glen asked, ignoring the theatrics.

"The best. Timmy Leary's Sunshine," was Dom's wide-smiled response.

I had no idea what that meant, but it got a huge returning smile from Glen who obviously did know exactly what Dom meant.

"Tell your friend we're in," Glen beamed.

They were so involved in the celebration of their good fortune, after all how many people get a chance to voluntarily screw up their lives royally, to notice that I sat stunned, silent, contemplating our total demise.

When Dom left, I confronted Glen.

"How could you commit to being involved with anything like that? My God, isn't it bad enough that every doper in Des Moines buys his smoke from you? Do you have to supply their chemicals too? It's not using the stuff that has you addicted, it's selling it!"

Whoa...even I was shocked by my outburst. But it was short-lived. I found I couldn't continue. Emotion choked my words. Glen was utterly stunned. Never before had I used that tone of voice, had the anger I felt been exposed so nakedly.

"Baby, baby, baby, I had no idea you'd be so upset."

His surprised expression confirmed his words. He put his arms around me in an effort to comfort me. But for the first time I didn't yield to his embrace. I pushed him away as through muffled sobs I managed to continue.

"I've been telling you for months how I feel about all of this. I can't stand it any longer. I just can't take it."

He reached for me again. This time I gave in. He rocked me gently, in sync with my sobs.

"I didn't realize, baby." That was all he said until I had cried it out. Then he began again.

"Baby, this is the last, I swear. I had no idea you felt so strongly about it. This is the last deal and we'll be back in Chicago. I'll be working for Dad. This is it. The very last, I promise."

There was absolute resolve in his voice. He was so God damned sure of himself. I wanted to scream, *you're so anxious to please me. You say you'll do anything for me, yet you're still going through with the deal! What difference has it made that now you realize just how strongly I feel about it?*

But I didn't. I couldn't. I was all too aware that I wasn't equipped to argue with someone who was that self-confident. But for the first time in our relationship, I really wanted to.

The Last Big Score

Iowa is so crisp and pretty, shimmering multiple shades of green in the sunlight of spring. And the drive from Des Moines to Iowa City engulfed our car in the deep rich beauty of newly planted fields with their perfectly symmetrical rows extending, extending on and on. Linear vision, peripheral vision, it all looked the same for as far as the eye could see. The sporadic tuft of trees, standing as an oasis amidst the flat expanses spreading in all directions, the only variance.

Thousand-acre farms, such huge fields surrounded us, shadowed by the occasional grouping of giant silos standing as if on guard over the crop. Massive protectors, they towered high above any structure, every field, steadfastly assuring the safety of anything within the shadows they cast. Some of them shone glistening silver in the intensity of the unobstructed afternoon sun as if clothed in sterling armor. Others sparkled in cobalt blue mail.

I once had a neighbor many years later that was a genuine Wisconsin farmer's daughter, peaches and cream complexion, long blonde hair and all, who told me that the type of silo one had on their farm was a status symbol and that the *blues* were the Rolls Royce of silos. We were definitely passing through the wealthy part of Iowa farm country.

Most of these massive, sturdy cylinders stood beside huge pole barns in view of the occasional tidy white farmhouse dotting the green expanse. There were no people to be seen, just the quiet planted stillness. Not a child scampered, nor dog romped, not even a scarecrow lent a lifelike form to the landscape.

A weather-beaten, faded, barely legible advertisement popped up before us on one of the barn sides evidencing a time past when the harvest hadn't yielded profitably and income needed to be supplemented by those lucky enough to have visibility from the interstate.

It smelled country and clean as we sat three across the front seat. It was a warm spring day. Wide-open windows freed the mild breeze outside to expand, exploding as it whipped around the interior of the car gaining in velocity, hair tangling, wild. We were wild. We were young. We were stoned. We were free.

The radio blasted our favorite tunes. We passed a pipe full of hash as the corn fields, packed tightly with soon to be full bulging stalks, standing straight up, erect, just poking up into the slowly oranging sunset, whooshed past us.

Up in front of us a tip of something glowing white rose from the horizon. The sun was almost set behind us; the orange-ness had grown redder and the glow ahead of us was growing larger. And, the radio played on. I, somewhat dazedly, realized that the ever growing glow was actually the moon lying right there on the road in front of us. Whoa, far out! And as if he had read my thoughts realizing it himself, Dom went into a lengthy, totally stoned, completely serious explanation of how the moon was rising and would definitely be off of the road by the time we got there. Glen and I glanced at each other and cracked up laughing.

The wind picked up and clouds began to roll in. Within moments I was shocked by the starless black sky that seemed to instantly engulf us. It had happened so quickly. With hardly a tree and only flat terrain abounding, there was nothing to obstruct the force or magnitude of the winds so, once blowing, they had free reign, changing the conditions as if on whim.

Finally, we neared the city and began our search for a bar called the Deadwood. Dom's contact was supposed to live in one of the apartments above. That was where our meeting was to take place. Where the deal was to go down.

Dom was the first to spot the bar. "There it is, on the right, up ahead there."

Having no previous way of knowing the actual reason for naming the bar, The Deadwood, one look at the structure and I was immediately struck by the appropriateness of that name. Decaying slats of wood marked the entrance. So many layers of paint had worn off the structure that fine lines of varying color covered the boards, marking each painting, repainting and peeling. If one can tell the age of a tree by counting its rings in a cross section, one could certainly see that this structure was very old just by the quantity of layers of paint exposed. I was fascinated in an out of body experience, flyin' high kind of way. From the safety of the car's confines, I had the luxury to be merely an observer of this funky place.

For the entire drive I had conveniently forgotten why we were making this trip and what we intended to do once we arrived. But now, as we approached this decrepit structure, the reality of the situation crept into my consciousness. By the time we found the stairway on the side of the building leading to the apartments above, my fear had firmly squatted, claiming rights to inhabit my being totally.

The stairwell was solid darkness, blackness filling the space harboring a narrow, splintering set of uneven risers. Holy shit! Was this the staircase? Indeed, it seemed to be at least what was left of one. O.K. Enough. I was ready to head for home, but I found myself uncomfortably caught in a squeeze between Glen, leading the way up, guiding us through the obstacle course of broken steps and missing railing, and Dom's knees bumping into my bottom if I didn't move along quickly enough.

I didn't know if I was relieved or even more petrified when we reached the top of the stairs. So dark the cramped space of the landing was, that the air actually felt to have increased in density. A thick soupy atmosphere seemed to be seeping into the area, pushing any hope of a fresh breath of plain old air out of the realm of possibility.

While the night had turned cool, I was perspiring. The dew of fear had settled on the landscape of my body, irrigating the steadily growing terror I felt blossoming.

"What now?" The apprehension in my voice must have been blatantly obvious.

"Don't worry, baby. Now we just find Eric, make the score and split. Dom, which way, man?"

"Turn left and feel your way along the right side of the hall until you come to the last door."

I was suddenly aware of what was meant by the expression *skin crawling with perspiration.* My fear had taken on a life of its own, traversing every inch of my body. It was damp and drafty, dark and dirty and I wanted to run like hell out of there, but before I could finish my train of thought, someone grabbed my arm. I jumped with fright.

"Sorry, baby," Glen whispered. "Listen...music. This must be it. Maybe we had better knock, huh?"

"Nah, he knows we're coming. Just walk in. It's never locked," Dom whispered back.

"What do you mean, never locked? With that much stuff he doesn't even lock the door?"

"There's no reason 'cause he ain't got the stuff here."

"Then why the FUCK are we here?"

I could hear the disappointed anger in Glen's voice. The tension was getting to us all. Dom's voice was also wrapped in the strain.

"When Eric sees us he'll send someone to get it. Don't worry, Glenny boy. We get a few free hits of whatever he has around while we wait. The stuff gets delivered, we pay, and we split. That's the way he works it. It's his game so we play by his rules. Okay?"

No! It is not O.K. My thoughts were screaming at me in my head.

I held my breath hoping the silence was an indication that Glen didn't like it any more than I did and we could leave. But his answer destroyed any hope of that very quickly.

"Yeah, go on in."

Dom opened the door into a room dimly lit by a few candles. The only things immediately visible were a stereo and a hot plate balancing on the unusual carpeting of wall-to-wall mattresses. The room was wallpapered with tinfoil. I was momentarily fascinated by the bizarre decorating.

Glen turned to me with an excited grin on his face and I couldn't help but return it as I looked around us.

"What is this?" I giggled under my breath.

Glen shrugged and jerked his head to one side drawing my attention to something across the room I hadn't yet noticed.

Sitting propped up by pillows in a corner was a sickly thin, boy-like man staring out of the only window into the black sky. His eyes were barely visible at first from my angle and the lack of light but in the next moment he turned slightly and without a sound or apparent provocation, I saw them open wide, blankly stare and then squint back to their original gaze. I can't explain the mesmerizing sensation this subtle sequence of events had on me. I felt lost, so very out of my element and yet somehow intrigued.

As we all stood there watching him staring, just staring silently; I took stock of the situation. How had it come to this? Here I found myself totally encased in this eerie setting, standing on mattresses with faint candlelight ricocheting off tin-foiled walls and Peter Townsend blasting from the stereo about a magic bus, waiting for a bizarre, manlike creature to say something.

Dom broke the silence at last. "Eric, hey Man, it's me, Dom. This is Glen and Lauren, the friends of mine I told you about."

In what seemed to take several minutes, Eric slowly, almost painfully, as if the effort was just far too much for his frail body to handle, turned his head and motioned for us to be seated. There wasn't a hint of recognition in his face. In fact, I began to doubt if he was reacting to Dom's statement at all or if his tremendously labored movement had been some kind of stoned reflex to the cosmic shift in the air of the apartment due to our disturbing the serene tranquility of the sheltered environment for which he so obviously strove!

Dom tried once again.

"Eric, it's me, Dom." He paused. "Whatcha been up to?"

"Traveling, as usual," barely audible was his whispered response.

Dom turned to us.

"Ya see, Eric here never leaves this room. He cooks his brown rice on the hot plate, listens to The Who day and night and drops acid. His theory being that you don't never need to physically move to see the world or to have a fulfilled life. Drop some Sunshine and anything you want to see is right before your eyes. He just sits in front of that window and watches morning turn to evening and days blend into weeks all over the world...and beyond."

Holy Shit! O.K., I had seen and heard enough. I grabbed Glen's arm for support but as I looked into his face, I could see that he was totally absorbed in this whole, unbelievable thing.

As my eyes grew accustomed to the strange things the candlelight did to the tinfoil, I focused on Eric. He appeared such a frail little thing with almost bluish-white skin set off vividly by dull, coal black hair cascading in ripples below his shoulders. While displaying no luster, its texture seemed abundantly healthy in stark contrast to his otherwise sickly countenance.

Again, he labored with the effort to turn his head slightly. This time he looked directly at me. So intense was his stare, I had to look away. I buried my nails into Glen's arm. What the hell was this character and what in the world had we let Dominick Del Torio get us into?

The door behind us slammed shut and I jerked around exposing my naked fear in front of those penetrating eyes.

"Don't be frightened," came Eric's soothing, gentle response. "That was just Janet leaving to get your package."

What was happening to me? I certainly wasn't that stoned. Any semblance of the mellow effects of the hash we had smoked in the car had long since been banished from my system, never to be heard from again by the almost debilitating fear brought on by this horrifying situation. Yet my perception did seem almost surreal, my reactions seemed distorted. Something was definitely wrong with me. I wasn't even aware that there had been another person in the room with us until this Janet person had slammed the door behind her. I had always thought of myself as being pretty observant. What was this all about?

"Here, Dom, fill the pipe. Let's help miss Pretty here relax."

Oh God, it was getting worse. He spoke with sincerity, with no condescension intended. He was attempting compliments, trying to be nice.

I looked to Glen then to Dom. Both sat pleasantly smiling. I was having trouble understanding why I was the only one of the three of us that seemed to be uncomfortable with this situation. In retrospect, I guess that really wasn't anything new.

While Dom filled the pipe, there was no small talk attempted. No niceties exchanged. Not a word was spoken by anyone. I became aware of repressing the urge to squirm. I could not just sit there. I remember thinking that maybe a little conversation would lessen my fear. Dom had made that totally ridiculous statement about Eric never leaving the room. I found that incomprehensible.

"Is it true you never leave this room?" I found myself shouting the question to be heard over the music.

Eric just stared at me as if my words were as incomprehensible to him as the fact of their meaning was to me.

"I mean, don't you find it lonesome, boring, never coming in contact with people? Never doing anything?"

Dom shifted his bulk uncomfortably, shooting me a glare that sent me sinking deeper into Glen's comforting embrace. What had I done? I just asked a question. How was I to know that I had broken some kind of rule when no one told me the rules to begin with?

As Eric smiled with the answer to my question, Dom relaxed, nodding agreement and smiling forgiveness at me.

"But I am doing things. Wonderful things. Just the same as you do." The tenor of his voice was lilting almost melodic. "I just utilize different energies to achieve them. You walk or drive to reach a destination, while I go to all of the same places by using my mind. The exciting day-to-day experiences that you enjoy, I too enjoy. My imagination writes the scripts and the action takes place in my head."

He spoke with a gentle quality no louder than the wisp of a breeze fluttering past my ear. Involuntarily, I secured a few strands of hair back behind that ear. Until that very moment I hadn't noticed that my hair had fallen into my face as I leaned forward to hear him.

His voice had now become hypnotic.

"My reactions are the same as yours too," he continued. "When I'm somewhere exciting my pulse speeds up just like yours. When I am just at the beach soaking up the rays, I too relax...I just don't get the tan!"

Oh God, he was attempting humor. I was not amused.

"And as for my not seeing people..." his voice now took on a humming quality. "The ones that I want to see don't stay away too long. Friends like Dom come by for a pick-up. There are always people coming and going. So you see, my life is quite well rounded."

This time we all turned as Janet entered the room, my mouth being the only one agape resulting from Eric's monologue. Janet handed Eric a paper bag and retreated to the shadows of the far corner. As my eyes followed her, she nearly disappeared completely into the unlit crevasse. Aha! So that was why I hadn't spotted her earlier. Mystery solved. Well, at least that made me feel a little bit better.

Meanwhile, Eric lifted a corner of the one pink flowered mattress from amid all of the other blue and white stripped ones and took out what looked to be a pound of hash from the floor beneath it. He opened the bag Janet had given him and dropped in the hash. I was getting pretty good at assessing quantities of dope.

"Dom, here's a pound of that primo you liked so much. I made another good score...figured 800 was a good price for a full pound...don't think you can afford to pass it up."

"Sounds good to me," came Dom's instant reply. "Can we have a taste?"

"Of course," Eric slowly turned his eyes toward the far corner of the room.

"Janet, fill the pipe for us, won't you?"

He didn't even move. We all watched in silence as Janet reappeared to do his bidding.

This was getting ridiculous. I kept forgetting this Janet girl even existed. I couldn't take my eyes off of Eric. And I thought that Dom was strange! But I had to focus. I couldn't let myself become any more absorbed in this bizarre Twilight Zone episode. There were practical matters needing attention. Where would Dom get the extra $800.00?

As if he had heard my thoughts, Dom spoke.

"Eric, I don't have the extra cash on me, man. Can I owe it to ya till Glen and I get this acid sold?"

There was an uncomfortable moment of silence. Dom continued his plea.

"Won't you trust me for it, man? I'd sure hate to let a righteous score like this one slip past me just 'cause I don't have the 800 on me and you find another buyer before I can get it to you."

Eric turned from the window to face us directly for the first time since we arrived. He stared squarely into Dom's eyes. His whole demeanor had changed.

"I don't put myself in the position of having to trust anyone for money." Both his demeanor and tone had taken on a no-nonsense quality as he continued. "Look here."

With that he pulled back the solitary flowered mattress to reveal the entire space below it filled with perfectly blocked chunks of hash.

"You know how it works, Dom. Bring the money and you'll get the hash. As you can see, there is plenty here. You don't have to worry about my selling it all to someone else."

It looked like a giant Hershey Bar of primo under that mattress, a twin bed sized hash candy bar. Well, he had done it; my mind was now officially blown!

Dom stared, momentarily examining the neatly divided chocolate bar treat and then produced a rather pathetic pout. I hoped no one noticed me slightly shaking my head as I watched Dom at his dramatic best. I still marveled at his pension for *just a little theatre thrown in* as he himself described his antics.

"Shit, if I know you, man, and your clientele, by tomorrow it'll all be gone. You know I'm as good as my word. We got all of that acid sold already. We have one buyer for the whole lot. We sell it all tonight. It's a slam-dunk. As soon as the deal's done ... Tomorrow, you'll get your money for the Primo tomorrow, you have my word."

We all held our breath. One of the candles sputtered, scattering shards of light about the room. Eric exhaled noisily.

"Take it. Take it, Man. Mail me a certified check," came Eric's begrudging reply.

A huge toothy grin heralded Dom's instant change of mood.

"Thanks a lot, Eric. Really, I won't forget this."

"Do me a favor and forget it fast. All I need is for the word to spread that I've gone soft on requiring cash on the spot...now get out of here. I've got somewhere to go. Catch ya later."

Immediately following that distinctly brash dismissal, he resumed his previous position of staring blankly out of the window.

What a Trip!

As we reversed our earlier journey, Glen selected a mellow mix of music, I think in an attempt to soothe my frayed nerves. A comfortable silence had overtaken the car. The trip home seemed to take significantly less time than the trip there. And, then all too soon the spell of serenity was broken. There was something very unsettling about reaching the city limits of Des Moines. The stillness of the farmland in which we were engulfed had apparently helped to foster that sense of security within me. Somehow, I managed to rationalize that as long as we were out in the country, within the confines of the car, everything would be all right. I realized that the quietude into which we had lapsed reinforced that feeling of security for the entire drive home.

I can't venture to say what occupied their thoughts, but I was wrapped in melancholy, languishing in the knowledge that we were safe and this bizarre lifestyle we had slid into was almost over. Not wanting to jinx the last leg of this journey, I tried not to dwell on, not even to think about the prospect of leaving this whole seedy scene behind us and starting anew after Glen's graduation.

Flashes from streetlamps illuminated the ivy-covered college buildings as we sped by the campus. Up and down the glacier-created, roller coaster hills of the city, we drove on towards the final destination of this oh so bizarre night.

I have always felt very defensive about Des Moines. It is a very beautify city; unlike the hick farm town thought of by most who have never been there. With its charming Ivy League style campus, its beautifully diverse terrain and its citizenry insisting on high culture and art, Des Moines is truly one of the great secrets of this country. A very respectable art museum tucked into a lavish, expansive park and a pre-Broadway stop for many theatrical productions (coupled with the vitality of a college town) make it a true gem.

I had often thought that if I should choose to live in a small city, Des Moines would be it. But as we neared our destination, all I wanted to do was leave it and leave it in a hurry. I wanted, no needed, to get out and actually begin a real life instead of living one moment longer in this smoke induced, fairytale existence we had created. God, how I wanted a real life.

We continued driving in silence as Glen headed for Second Avenue. The plan was to use the house of one of Dom's buddies to cap the acid then to proceed with it to the drop off spot. Thus, we were making our way to *Fox's House.*

Guys had names like that then: Fox, Stinger, Turk were all among our acquaintances. And all of them had very good reasons for their monikers. At least, at some point in time the reasons were thought to be good. But no matter the reason, a cool name was a cool name. I never did find out what Fox's real name was but his tag was obvious. With his brilliant red hair and slight, lanky body, everyone called him Fox.

I had only met him once. An unfortunate circumstance caused our relationship to never fully develop into a friendship. One-night Fox was quite drunk and couldn't hold his bladder. His relief came when, in his diminished mental state, he mistook a dark front yard for a deserted field.

There he stood fertilizing a lady's front lawn at three in the morning when her dog began to bark. Light erupted from several windows and a gasp was heard three houses down when the front door flew open and the night clothed elderly woman got a look at what Fox was holding. Apparently unimpressed, she phoned the police and before Fox was able to totally comprehend just what had happened; he was arrested for indecent exposure and some other offence which simply meant pissing on the lady's lawn.

Once at the police station, the stash of grass that he always kept in a baggie rolled in his sock landed him in jail...minimum sentencing had recently gone into effect in Iowa...so he was in for a three year stint. In his absence, his house on Second Avenue was temporarily in Dom's care. Actually, instead of defining it as a house, I think the more apt description would be a run-down, three-room shack which continually flooded in the spring when the Des Moines River over-flowed its banks. A damp stench permeated throughout as we entered.

"After all, it is spring." Dom needlessly pointed out as he unlocked the front door and we were attacked by the odor.

"Holy Shit!" Glen's wide-eyed reaction to Fox's décor mirrored my own. "What's with all the flags?" He asked.

Dom smiled.

"The little guy has this far out need to relive the past, man. Yeah, some trip, huh?" Dom swept his arm around emphatically. "He has a fuckin' forty-eight-star flag fetish. Oh, sorry Lauren."

In his own way there was a certain warped gallantry about the normally beastly Dom that surfaced on occasion. Using the "f" word in front of me always produced the same apology with the same dumb-assed, got caught with his hand in the cookie jar, grin.

And Glen's return grin could not have been larger. Dom continued as Glen shook his head in fascination.

"See, Fox is convinced that the U.S. had no serious problems before Alaska and Hawaii joined the Nation, so he collects these old flags and fantasizes on how great things would be if we still had only forty-eight states. Simple as that," he concluded with a shrug as if he had merely stated the obvious.

The forty-eight-star flags were literally everywhere in the house. They were his drapes. They were his bedspread. They were his closet doors, wall hangings, even his bathroom ceiling had a flag, suspended in the corners of the room by four thumbtacks.

"How did he get them all?" I asked as I wandered the three small rooms, utterly amazed at the sight.

"He bought new flags and went around to people's houses on flag flying occasions and swapped the new ones for the old ones. The people were thrilled to get the updated version and he was delighted to add yet another and another to his collection...What a guy, huh?"

I didn't ask where he had gotten the money for all of the new flags. For the majority of kids on campus with whom we came in contact, money was really never an issue. They were like Glen and me. Our folks sent money and we got *educated.*

By the time we got around to the serious business that had brought us to this flag-bedecked place it was very late. We set up shop around the kitchen table. I removed the bag of stuff from my purse. Immediately, Glen and Dom grabbed for it, both securing a handhold on the paper bag. Neither let go as they glared at each other.

After a few seconds of the minor tug-of-war (God forbid they should tear the bag) all of the tension building during our long day's ordeal seeped out into the muggy dampness and spread across the room in a giant wave. The three of us began laughing. We laughed till we roared. Dom intentionally slipped off of his chair making Glen and me scream for him to stop.

Pressure relieved, we got to work grinding the orange tabs into powder and filling the empty capsules which Dom had withdrawn from the bottom of the bag.

"Where'd those come from?" Glen asked upon seeing them.

"Eric includes them with all of the tabs he sells. He's a full-service drug dealer!" Dom's grin spread across his face but vanished just as quickly as he became deadly serious.

"Listen, you guys; you've never capped acid before. I guess I better tell ya, after a hundred or so caps you'll begin to feel it."

"What do you mean, feel it?" I was confused.

Dom's black eyes actually sparkled as he turned to me excitedly.

"All's you need is a little of this stuff to seep into the pores of your hands...you're good for an eight-hour trip!"

"You're kidding. How can that be? You have to ingest acid for it to affect you."

I vigorously nodded my head in agreement with Glen's statement.

"Okay, alright, but remember, I warned ya." Dom couldn't contain his grinning.

How ridiculous. Who was he kidding? We were new at this for sure, but we weren't stupid. Come on, seep through your pores?

After about ten minutes of capping there was no doubt about it in my mind. I was in the midst of an LSD experience.

At first, I was intrigued when bizarre things began to happen to my hands. They were huge...no they were teeny-tiny. Then they weren't attached to me at all! They were just capping the acid on their own.

I began to laugh. It was all so funny. When I realized that I had no idea why I was laughing, I sobered immediately. O.K. then, that was better. How ridiculous; I was in total control. I simply had to concentrate. Concentrate. I mean I really had to try to concentrate to keep working.

I kept being distracted from my job by little things like my fingernails jumping from their rightful positions at the ends of my fingers. Onto the table they leapt and then, scooting off of the edge of the table, they scurried across the floor. And the caps themselves were like melting in my hands. As hard as I tried to get the powder into them, it just kept flowing, flowing, oozing orange, smoking lava out of the caps and spilling over my hands, hot on my hands, scalding my hands.

But that couldn't be. The more I shook my head trying to clear it the more befuddled I became. I knew one thing for sure. I wanted desperately to get this over with. We had to get this over with so Glen and I could be finished with this dangerous, crazy stuff for good. God, I hated this stuff, all of this mixed-up, melting hands, disappearing fingernail, lava burning me, stuff. And the drugs in my house and the strangers coming and going and Glen's sheer pleasure when I was scared to death...Death. Oh no. Don't think about death. I wasn't dying. Concentrate. Concentrate. But on what? My fingernails were disappearing! I wanted this trip to be over. I had had enough. I wanted it to end. I wanted this lifestyle to end.

Then, all at once, the flags started to come at me. Tall red and white stripes with blue star-studded hats made their way across the floor, dancing toward me. They leapt from the walls and ceiling, dancing, dancing, dancing to music that came from the kitchen sink. Plunk, plunk, splash drip, the beat clanged on.

I got it. I finally figured it out. I was in a Disney animated movie with colors bursting, shapes, sounds blending in unbelievable patterns. That was it. I was in my own version of *Fantasia*. Now, wasn't that just great. God, I think I am the only person in the whole world who hated that movie and here I was stuck in my own crazed version of it!

Then the flags were coming again. No. They were just getting bigger. No. They were folding themselves up on the floor. Wait a minute. That seemed so funny to me, I was folding myself up on the floor instead of them, laughing uncontrollably. Then I was crying. I was crying out of fear. I couldn't stop. The tears kept coming and coming. I was going to die. I was definitely going to die.

I ran to the bathroom and stared at my reflection in the mirror...BIG MISTAKE. HUGE MISTAKE. My face began mushing and squishing, oozing out of its form. I screamed and screamed, the shriek ricocheting, careening round the small room. As I turned to follow the sound of my own demise, the noise, like a great, silvery, gleaming, threatening, lightning-like flash; I was suddenly engulfed by red and white stripes...no, not stripes, flames.

The more I screamed the faster the noise was gobbled up by flames. I was being swallowed whole by the flames. I felt their hold on me tightening, the heat scorching my skin, the smoke suffocating me. They were all around me, holding me tight like a straitjacket binding my arms. I couldn't move. I couldn't breathe. I was caught. I was going to die. I was suffocating. I was burning.

But no, there were no flames at all. There was no straitjacket. Glen. He was there, all around me, cradling me, pulling me to the floor away from the horrible sight. And he was whispering in my ear, then shouting that it would be fine. Everything would be fine, I just had to hang in there, just flow with it, turn it around, use the energies to enjoy it instead of fighting it. But instead of me flowing with it I was sure that it would be my insides, my very essence that would be doing the flowing...right out of me.

Then, I once again realized that it was Glen. He was right there with me. He was holding me so tightly, keeping my innards within my body. He would not let my essence escape. He had that power to hold me together.

Somehow, all at once, it was O.K. Huddled on the floor together he kept talking to me. In my delirium he was making no sense, but his voice was such a comfort nonetheless, so familiar, so soothing. Even if I understood not one word of what he was saying, I could trust him. I needed to trust him. And I did. Yes, he had that power. Thank you God for sending him to me. He had that power. I was safe.

There we sat, Glen holding me, binding my very being within the fragile boundaries of my body until finally I settled into an incredible, controllable high.

I didn't know how long my terror-filled feature film had lasted. I was just greatly relieved that it was over.

Dom never spoke of what had happened to me in that house of horrors. Never a sneer nor smug, I told you so, glace was cast my way. With all of his disturbing oddities, I had grown to realize that there was a strange "gentlemanliness" about him; his own unique brand of gallantry. Never a door would be held open for a girl or coat assisted with; yet he would go to the grave before he would have embarrassed me about what had happened in that flag-bedecked shack of terror.

Somehow the acid got capped. All 1,230 hits of it were ready to be delivered as promised. With the acid and the new pound of hash in the glove compartment of the car, we assumed our position of three across the front seat to complete the day's lunacy. As we drove, I allowed myself brief moments of joy at the prospect of it all being over but quickly banished the thoughts from my mind, fearful of putting a hex on the remainder of the endeavor.

How Glen even drove the car is beyond me. All I saw were streaks, lights, bolts of shimmering opal just above street level and stars shooting through the sky in time with the music throbbing on the radio. The whole car pulsated. I was so rapt in the show that I was able to forget all of the fear, all of the worry. I had turned the corner, progressed on my trip to the point where I could settle into just bopping along for the ride. I was tuning in and out of Glen and Dom's conversation.

"See the next stop light, Glenny boy? Go straight on through till the next corner."

So, being the perfectionist that he was, Glen did just that. He drove straight through the red light. And a very conscientious policeman followed him.

I was totally oblivious to what was going on until a red flash interrupted my sky gazing. There was some kind of red beacon reflecting in the rear-view mirror. What a nice red light! Where was that coming from? I turned to look out of the back window.

Dom's words were the slap that brought everything into crystal clarity.

"Jesus Christ. Holy SHIT! Now you've done it. That's the Man. He's got us now. You'd better pull over."

"Why the FUCK did you tell me to go through the red light?"

"Me? You're driving. I meant for you to go straight through AFTER it turned green, you Schmuck!" He sighed in exasperation, then continued.

"It don't matter now. Pull over. Get out. Go back there and take your ticket. Say thank you and we'll still have time to complete the exchange."

At that point there was no doubt in my mind that Dom and I were two totally different types of people. Maybe not even of the same species. A vision of me in jail with a fifty-year sentence to serve was what was on my mind and he worried about being on time to complete the deal. What a guy. He was just what we needed to get us through this. I had to believe it. He could handle this. After all, he was the pro. He was weaned on desperate situations. I waited for my instructions as Glen calmly got out and walked back to the squad car. When none came, I turned to look directly into Dom's now very serious eyes. I stared speechlessly at him without a clue as to what to say, willing him to reassure me that indeed he had some plan to get us through this.

I needed to wait no longer.

"We've been through a lot these past few months. I really love you guys," Dom said turning to face me with genuine affection in his eyes. "Keep your eyes glued to that mirror and tell me if the Man gets out and starts to walk in this direction."

I nodded my understanding of my role but confusion about exactly what would happen if the cop approached must have been evident on my face.

"Don't worry about a thing. I'll down the stuff before he gets here. You and Glen will be in the clear."

With that, he opened the glove compartment.

I sat dumbfounded. What? That was the plan? Dom was willing to kill himself to protect us? Looking back now it seems absolutely ludicrous. There is no way he could have swallowed all of those capsules before the cop was upon us, even if indeed he had wanted to; but at the time all I could think of was how had I ever been frightened by this big lug who had just placed himself at the top of my martyr scale?

I sat; eyes fixed on the mirror. Dom sat forward with the contents of the glove compartment now in his lap. I could see Glen as he sat motionless in the squad car. He faintly smiled and nodded his head as the cop wrote the ticket and spoke to him. My heart leapt into my throat as the cop opened his door and got out.

"Dom! He's out of the car!" I wailed.

The tin foil was ripped open exposing what looked to be a million orange capsules. He was really going to try to do it! I caught Dom's arm before he could shove the first handful into his mouth.

"Wait. It's O.K. Glen's smiling. They're shaking hands."

The tension drained from Dom's body proportionately to the color draining from his face as he slumped back into his seat. He released the handful of capsules back into the foil. I watched the policeman get back into his car and pull away from the curb, out into the street and out of our lives.

By the time Glen returned to the car I was sobbing so deeply, not a sound came out, just rippling spasms moved my body at regular intervals.

"How the hell'd you do that?" The volume of Dom's words exposed the previously well-hidden fear.

"I don't know. Instinct, I guess." Glen fell into his seat slamming his head back in exhaustion.

"Come on, Glenny boy, don't quit on me now. You just pulled off the greatest scam I ever seen. But we got to get to Waterworks Park. Come on, kid, we got more work to do. We got a ton a money waiting for us."

The rest of the escapade is really just a blur. We drove to the park in a numbed silence. Dom got out just in time to meet his contact and make the exchange. I asked no questions wanted no information about any of the details of the deal. I didn't want to speak nor did I want to hear anything at all. I just wanted it over and done with.

When Glen and I were finally home, safely alone, I snuggled in close under his arm as we lay in bed.

"What a day," I whispered, afraid to even talk about it out loud. "I can't believe this whole day."

"Shit, what a high!" Glen was almost shouting.

"Glen! A high? You sound...I don't know...almost thrilled."

I didn't have to see his face to know that it contained a broad smile. Apprehension overwhelmed me. He had enjoyed it.

"Oh, Glen, you promised that this would be the last. You promised..."

I couldn't contain the tears as I rose to an elbow and saw the excitement radiating from him. He stared at me for a moment, cocked his head as if assessing what I had said, the sincerity with which I had spoken and then he pulled me close.

"I swear, baby, this is it. You're right. That was just too close. But you got to admit, it was something. Wasn't that really something?"

I started to laugh with relief.

"It was something alright. But now it's over. I can't believe that it's finally all over. No more dealing. No more worrying. We'll be back in Chicago and we can start again, really fresh from the beginning..."

He interrupted me with a gentle kiss. It stopped me short, making me smile.

"Oh, I do love you, Glen. It's going to be alright now that this nonsense is all over, isn't it?"

"It hasn't been nonsense, baby. It's been adventure, business, BIG business! Don't you feel it? God, I feel so damned alive."

"But Glen..."

"Don't spoil it, Lauren. Come on. We made thousands of dollars tonight and Dom hasn't even sold the hash yet. Don't you understand how that makes me feel? Don't you feel it?"

"No, I don't. Feel what? Being so scared you can't talk? Never sleeping through one night without jerking wide-awake in a cold sweat? Help me here Glen. What is it I'm supposed to be feeling? Is it the money? Is it the risk? What makes it so damned important to you?"

He sat up. Now he was the one leaning on an elbow looking down at me for a long moment. Then he spoke softly.

"Power. I guess it's a kind of power. I need the power of it."

Even in the darkness his green eyes blazed with the truth he spoke. "I need to know that I put a deal together and have the profit to prove how good I really am. And with the profit, you have the power to do it again and again for more profit, for more power, again and again, bigger and bigger each time. Can't you understand that?"

I wanted to understand. I really did. I wanted it to mean as much to me as it did to him. Somewhere inside I knew that if I couldn't understand, didn't really feel it, there was no future for us.

He kissed me hard on the lips, then down my neck.

"I've got the power to make it big baby," he whispered snidely.

He nipped at my left breast, then my right. He did it so forcefully, it hurt, but I couldn't spoil it for him. It would be as it was so many times before. I felt I owed him his pleasure.

The next morning, as I was putting his clean socks away, I noticed some orange capsules in a baggie hidden rather poorly in his top drawer. There were at least two hundred hits of acid in the bag. Holding the bag up, I turned as he entered the room.

"Where'd these come from? Didn't Dom sell the whole score to Nick last night?"

He approached, hair still dripping from the shower. He grabbed the bag and casually tossed it back into the drawer.

"Oh, these were just some extras. Nick got the full amount promised."

"Why didn't Dom take these home with him?" I was furious. "Why do you always have to be the one taking all the risks?"

I was just settling into my new-found sense of security at the prospect of being finished with the whole drug dealing shit and here was yet one more, one last *deal* that Dom was thrusting upon us. Why couldn't he just leave us alone, take his damned Sunshine and leave us alone? Were we never going to be able to be free from his influence?

With that look on his face, Glen came to me and kissed my forehead.

"Listen, baby, don't mention this to Dom. I have my own buyer for these. What he doesn't know won't hurt him."

He finished drying himself off as he returned to the bathroom.

Reality

God, if only it could have turned out differently. We had started out so innocently. My concept of love so simple: make your husband happy and he'd make you happy. I thought we'd be young and in love forever. How stupid could I have been? How naïve I was back then. While only a few years in actual time, it was so very long ago. Had I learned nothing in the years that had passed since then? In the here and now at Dawson, was I still that naïve little girl without a clue?

"Mornin," Willie interrupted my thoughts, joining in step beside me. "Hey, I was thinkin' lass night. What'll I call ya?" He asked in all seriousness.

"What? I'm sorry. What did you say?"

"Good mornin!" He grinned broadly. "Ya sure looked miles away."

"I was...yet not quite as far as I had thought."

"Huh?"

"Oh, nothing." I shrugged. "Really nothing."

I was very aware of just how closely he was walking beside me. Oh God, it was starting again.

"So, what should I call ya...Teach?"

"Lauren'll be fine. So many of you are older than I am, I'd feel pretty silly insisting on Miss Gates."

"Miss Gates?...hmmm...Lauren?...I still likes Teach best." He smiled.

"That's fine," I said absently.

I had nothing else to say. Not a thought was in my head that I could possibly articulate. I had to sort out a way to deal with all of this.

"Somethin' wrong?"

"I have to figure out how to get some copies made."

He began to laugh so gaily, I had to smile to myself.

"So ya met Mellie, huh? Aw, don't worry. It's nothin' ya said or did or even you as a person. You's white. She's a true-for-shit bigot. We got's lotsa em. Whites don't got no monopoly on bein' stupid. Here, give em ta me. I'll get yer copies made."

He took the papers from my hand before I could get a word out, turned and instantly vanished around the corner.

"Now I know we're not in Kansas, Toto," I muttered to myself.

Before I had finished writing the agenda for the day on the blackboard, he had returned to my classroom with a stack of copies. He handed them to me accompanied by that enthralling smile.

"Thank you, Mr. Taylor." I don't know if it was relief at getting the copies made or simply that engaging, expectant smile on his face; I found myself smiling in return.

"Ya know, Teach, anytimes ya needs copies in da future, save yer self da hassle, jess let me handle it for ya."

"I do appreciate your help and for the time being I will take you up on your offer, but eventually I will have to figure out a way to work with Mellie Thomas." I smiled gratefully.

"It's no trouble t'all, really. I likes ta help ya." He returned my smile.

Maybe I had overreacted. For sure this place was different from any I had experienced before, but I could adjust. With Willie on the bench just waiting for the call to enter the game to pinch hit, I felt comfortable in the knowledge that I could put off dealing with Mellie Thomas till later. Then, once I had established an effective game plan, Mellie and I would play ball.

The Situation

The door was kicked shut behind him. A large figure of a man was silhouetted in the shadows cast by the moonlight seeping through the slit joining the two halves of the closed drapes. He seemed familiar. I couldn't quite make him out in the muted darkness. He was big, shoulders broad, tall, and oh so confident; just the way he occupied his space, this room. He was so self-assured. It must be his room. This must be his place. Who was this man? Why was I here? Everything, all memory was so fuzzy. I looked down. I was naked. Nope not a stitch of clothing covered one square inch of my body as I stood motionless. That was odd. Why did I feel no shame, no shyness even though I knew he could see me? He stood there, intent on just watching me. As I looked around, I saw familiar things. But no, how could they be familiar?

The wood paneling, deep and richly polished, that big English bed guarded by solid head and foot boards and the very masculine colored fabric on windows and furniture, brown and gray and black swirling in a muted hurricane of pattern...I knew this place. Where was I? Who was this Man?

As he approached, his movement was so familiar. Long, cocky strides as if he owned the world, brought him close to me. I moved. I didn't want to see him clearly, to know. I turned away as a powerful arm reached out toward me.

"Don't. I don't want to know," I whispered, yet longed to know it all.

He spoke not a word but enfolded me, caught me, held me, brought me into his warmth. I closed my eyes as we seemed to glide, him guiding our path. I kept my eyes closed knowing that I had nothing to fear, comfortable in the charge that he was taking of me.

I knew who he was, had always longed for his touch; he so very different from Glen in every way. It was unnecessary to open my eyes for he was so familiar yet so totally unknown to me in this way. Knowing it could never be, I had secretly always wondered what making love would be like with him instead of Glen.

As we neared the bed, I felt the questions fade, the apprehension give way to desire. I had to find out. I would at last experience Glen's younger brother, Matt. As I gave into my decision, I opened my eyes...OH MY GOD!

Shocked into wide-awake alertness, I was up out of bed before my eyes were actually focused. What a dream! It was Willie, not Matt, Willie! Oh God. I smiled at the remembrance of the anticipation. Shit, what a dream.

As I drove to work, I marveled at the human mind. What a dream. What a surprise. What the hell was happening to me?

My life had never before included such surprises but now they seemed never ending. Was it me? Was it some mysterious energy constantly teetering precariously on the brink of combustion at Dawson? Could it really be a place? Was it Willie? Could it really be a person? Or was it the entire situation...all of the above and much more?

The situation. I had to concentrate on the situation. I had a job to do, a job that was not easily come by. Enough time spent on all the rest of the nonsense going on; I couldn't allow myself to be bogged down in self-analysis. Besides, I was never very good at it anyway.

The situation. That was the issue here.

My education had prepared me to teach high school English and this was indeed a high school equivalency program. But I was soon painfully aware that unlike the well-defined educational levels of your average high school class, I was, in fact, teaching multiple subjects to students of vastly diverse abilities and skills. In effect, I was a throwback to the frontier, one-room schoolhouse teacher having to deal with whatever difficulties the varying levels of competency presented in my classroom. Vastly different from your typical high school, for sure, but my experiences in the teaching profession had never included anything very typical. From the very beginning, back to my student teaching position, I just always seemed to situate myself in unusual circumstances and environments. Just a talent, I guess!

Student teaching...the memories started flooding back.

Oakstream

Once Glen and I returned to Chicago, I continued my education locally. I became aware of a change in my attitude almost immediately. Instead of merely passing the time in school, I began to anticipate the pleasure I would derive from actually teaching. Each day seemed to bring more excitement as the idea of a career edged closer and closer to becoming a reality. I became enthusiastic about my future. I looked forward to each day in class with purpose and determination. Unfortunately, the more excited I became about my future as an educator, the more threatened Glen became.

My motivation for entering college was mostly to be with Glen. My ambition was pretty much based solely on being his wife. My English classes in high school came so easily to me, it seemed only natural for me to have my college major be English education. After all, I had to major in something so logic dictated it be something in which I excelled. But surprisingly, as my formal English education progressed so did my motivation. I was going to be a teacher someday, and a good one.

I wanted desperately for Glen to be proud of my abilities and excited about my successes. But instead of supporting my desire, he belittled it. The more finite my plans for fulfillment outside of his domain, the more demanding and stubborn he became.

He wanted me at home, in his house, running into his arms upon his return each evening saying, *Oh Glen, I've been so miserable but now that you're here everything is wonderful.* And he made no bones about it. Subtlety was never his strong suit.

For the first time in our relationship we really argued. This absolutely shocked him. He had no frame of reference with which to deal with my wanting something different for myself than that which he wanted for me. Constantly, with little provocation, he would put forth his rationale for why I should do exactly as he wanted.

"Why don't you just quit school, Lauren? You don't have to work. We don't need the money."

His arguments always seemed the same. I sat next to him on the couch hoping to finally make him understand.

"It's not about money, Glen. I love school. I really want to teach. I think I can be good at it. You have your work that you enjoy. Can't I have mine?"

That look spread over his face.

"Why, baby?"

Frustrated and tired of trying to explain, anticipating what was going to come next, I leaned back into the corner of the couch only half listening to his routine oration on the subject. Mind wandering, I looked about me at the beautiful house in the suburbs we owned. Glen had bought the house without my even seeing it. It was located in North Stream, one of the many new *in* communities spreading west from the old moneyed North Shore of Chicago. The community was built on the site of former corn fields, sold off by the children of farmers unwilling to dirty their hands with the soil which had supported their families for generations. They couldn't resist the profits from selling the prime farmland to developers who then proceeded to transform the masses of land into multi-acre lots to be built upon. This was where the hip Young Turks of the Chicago financial scene had created neighborhoods of opulence. LaSalle street lawyers, investment bankers, traders from the various exchanges, the young movers and shakers of commerce in the city had created modern day manor-esque estates boasting rambling homes on acreage expertly designed by landscape architects to blend the hundred-year-old trees with spectacular, newly-planted flora incorporating the mandatory swimming pool and tennis court into the designs.

In some cases, the children of old money decided to forsake new construction and opted instead to reside in the *old family home*, replacing the mahogany libraries and artwork in oils of the masters they grew up seeing in their parent's mansions with sleek glass and chrome great rooms and numbered copies of soup cans.

Not to be outdone, Glen had purchased a three-year-old, five thousand square foot home that had been built by a young couple, the children of one of Cynthia's acquaintances. They had decided to retire, dividing their time between their home in Aspen and a newly purchased Co-op on East Lake Shore Drive in Chicago. After seven years at the Merc, the husband had amassed enough to make his wife's dream of a life of travel a reality. And Glen had agreed to their asking price with the condition that they be out of the house by our anniversary so he could give it to me as a gift. While not thrilled at being so rushed, they could not pass up the offer. So that is how I became the proud owner of a home which, in years prior, I could have only dreamt of actually living in. Glen had also given me a checkbook and told me to furnish it. I never even knew what the balance was in the account. When asked, Glen would just answer, *buy whatever you want and don't worry about it.*

On my next birthday, there sat a lemon-yellow Jaguar XKE in the Driveway. Even though it was February and the temperature was in the low teens, the top was down exposing black, glove-leather seats complimented by the burled wood dash. A huge red ribbon running from rear bumper to front grille completed my birthday package.

I was twenty years old.

Soon thereafter there came another addition to our household. Glen surprised me with a spirited kitten which he had named Profit. Glen thought the dual meaning of her name to be very clever. I didn't object. To the contrary, I was thrilled to be the recipient of unconditional love for a change as I mindlessly stroked the silky fur and she revved up to a methodic, almost hypnotic purring.

It hadn't taken long for Glen's enthusiasm, ambition and business acumen, that I was so painfully aware of taking root in Des Moines, to fully blossom in Chicago.

Arthur Jacobson's company Leasco, which began as an equipment leasing concern, had grown through the years into a diversified, multinational conglomerate with more than a dozen companies under its umbrella. The Leasco corporate offices were housed in one of the old, prestigious 1920's era buildings across from the Chicago River on the corner of LaSalle Street and Wacker Drive. The structure had some 30 odd stories and Leasco occupied an entire floor of the rather ornate Deco tower.

With windows looking down LaSalle Street over the river to the North and an unobstructed view of Lake Michigan to the East, Arthur's corner office, comprised of over 2,000 elegantly appointed square feet, was often featured in various design and style magazines.

Glen also had an office with a view. While not a corner, he did face north, his vista spreading over the river and encompassing a wonderful cityscape. And once he hit LaSalle Street, from that office, Glen devoted his very being to learning his father's business from every aspect. He was determined to learn what everyone in the huge corporation did and be able to do it better. No boss's son stigma for him. He was going to earn the position handed to him.

As for me, the silly, naïve little girl that Glen had married began to grow up quickly as I realized that the high expectations of that blissful, happy life I was so sure we would share in Chicago might never come to fruition. To the contrary, all that we used to share seemed to be gone and the distance between us only seemed to increase.

I sat one evening looking around me at what was truly a palatial abode thinking about how adamant in our resolve to wed Glen and I had been when our parents told us that we were too young to get married. How sure we were that no one knew the kind of love we shared. How could they? There had never been a love like ours before. I began to wonder if my surety was indeed based purely on Glen's or had I really felt that way back then?

"Lauren, are you listening to me?"

I was startled from my thoughts.

"What? Did you say something?"

Glen bristled. "What has come over you? Why don't you listen to me anymore?"

"I listen, Glen. I hear every word you say. What I don't do is agree."

"See? That's just what I mean. Listen to yourself. I'm worried about you, baby. I think you are under too much pressure with the move and furnishing this big house and then you throw the crazy demands of school into the mix...I think you need a little bit less in your life. Quit school. You don't need it."

He rose from his chair, dropped the newspaper to the floor and came over to the couch to sit next to me. He put his arm around me and nuzzled my neck, kissing my ear.

"If you're serious about teaching kids, we could get started on a few of our own. I think we should have a baby," he whispered.

A baby! Now? I didn't even know if I wanted children at all. I wasn't finished with school. I just had to finish school. Why was he doing this, bringing this up now? Had he no clue as to how much getting my degree and teaching had come to mean to me? What? Why?

I calmed myself knowing that I would not give in on this one. I was staying in school. I was not going to have a baby, not yet anyway. I was going to teach.

I could feel his anticipation. I silently willed my anger to morph into steadfast resolve. I decided that another approach rather than all-out battle would be more effective.

I looked pleadingly into his eyes.

"Oh, Glen, I only have one more year...and finishing means so much to me. Wouldn't it be silly for me to quit now that I'm so close?" I kissed softly all around his lips. "It would be pretty dumb to quit now, wouldn't it?" I was the one purring now.

I felt the tension relax. The competition was almost over, yet he gave complete victory one last try before giving into compromise.

"But you don't need to finish school..."

"I know you're right about that, but it's something I want. Haven't you always told me that I could have anything I want, that you would make sure that I had it all?"

"It just seems so silly..."

"Then please let me have this one silly thing."

He looked squarely into my eyes.

"If this is what you really want. You know I could never refuse you anything."

And that is exactly what I was counting on.

So, he had given in, but he wasn't about to make it easy. At every opportunity it seemed he had a snide remark or sarcastic comment about me staying in school. It became an almost daily ritual.

By the time I secured an interview for a student teaching position that was reported to be an amazing opportunity, I had totally given up on trying to make him understand. I had to reluctantly acknowledge that I would have to content myself with simply a truce.

The morning of my interview, I was a frantic combination of excitement and nerves. I dressed with purposeful care, attending to every detail. It was very important to land a good student teaching assignment because jobs were extremely scarce and if I could distinguish myself as a student teacher it might pave the way for a full time position if one opened up in that school for the following year. These thoughts played over and over in my mind as I put on what I thought to be a schoolteacher dress (white collar and cuffs) and combed my hair in what I considered a schoolteacher do: long, soft, feminine curls held back off of my face with a barrette.

Glen was sitting in the kitchen drinking juice and reading the paper when I walked in.

"Well, how do I look?"

He glanced up, smiled and put the paper down.

"Look at you. You definitely look good enough to eat...come here," he growled.

He grabbed me so roughly I thought he would rip my dress.

"Glen, don't. I'll be late."

"Who cares?"

His grip grew tighter as he really started to hurt me.

"I care! Please, Glen, you're hurting my arm. You'll ruin my dress."

I couldn't struggle loose.

"This means a lot to me," I began to plead.

He angrily shoved me aside.

"Get out then. Go to your fucking interview if it means more to you than I do."

The anticipation was all over his face as I straightened myself up. But I couldn't reassure him that he was being silly. I couldn't say that of course he meant more to me than any interview possibly could. I just couldn't say it.

Oh God. Did this job mean more to me than Glen? Was it truly a revelation or just a result of an extreme case of nerves? I shook off these thoughts.

Not another word was spoken as I readied myself and left. Glen sat there dazed.

I had no time to waste thinking about it now. That would all have to wait till later. For the moment getting this student teaching position would have to take priority. Yes, that was my priority now. I had to concentrate intently on the task at hand, getting this job. I could afford no distraction. But it was difficult not to think about Glen and the disturbing attitude about our relationship I was developing.

I proceeded to bite my neatly manicured nails down to the quick during my drive to Oakstream North High School. I sat for a moment in the parking lot surveying my surroundings and collecting my thoughts. What a moment this was. I was on my own; no one to help me, no one to handle it for me. I had once thought that my life would begin when I married Glen. I now knew that one's own life begins when you make it your own...on your own.

That was one hell of a realization and looking out of the car window, this was one hell of a school.

An immense glass and brick, one story structure wrapped itself around three different, beautifully landscaped courtyards. The wealthy suburban taxpayers demanded that attention be paid to every detail of the twenty acre campus on which their children would spend the majority of their day.

The courtyards were manicured to an almost eerie perfection. As I maneuvered my way through the halls, I realized there was no way for the students to get into the courtyards. They were not allowed out there at all, only to look at their beauty through walls of glass, never to enjoy being a part of it.

I asked a blue jean clad teenager for directions to the English department. When I was in high school, not only couldn't we wear jeans, but the English department was a small room stuffed with the desks of all of the English teachers. Now, only a few short years later, I noticed that all of the kids were in jeans, as I was led to the English Resource Center. It consisted of small offices and seminar rooms surrounding a large library-like work area designated for use only in the subject of English.

In the far corner sat Eddie Morton behind a glass partition separating his office from the work area. This was with whom I would be interviewing. I would be working in his classroom if I got the job.

I knew instantly that I would like him. He was a small man with youthful features. There was just the hint of a beard on his heavily pock-marked face that exposed, for all of the world to see, what must have been a painful, acne-filled adolescence. But there was such joy and kindness in his eyes as he greeted me. That was what held my attention.

Greetings, pleasantries and my resume out of the way; we spent another hour talking. I did my best to come off intelligent, enthusiastic, capable and most of all agreeable.

"Lauren, you have the opportunity here to be involved in something very different and exciting. It's a unique position and needs a unique teacher to fill it. This is a special, Government-funded, Title I Project...we're supplied with virtually unlimited funds to meet our mission."

WHOA!

"That really is unique. The inner city schools I have visited as potential job sites have trouble even getting enough books to go around. And 80% of the students suffer from eyestrain due to inadequate lighting in the classrooms. This sounds like a teacher's dream. Please, Mr. Morton, tell me more."

"Please, call me Eddie." He shyly dipped his head as he spoke the request.

"O.K., Eddie, if I may get to the guts of the matter...what exactly is the job and what's the program's mission?"

He seemed pleased by my straightforwardness.

"We have thirty-six students divided into two classes. They meet for an hour and a half straight each day. You would be one of four: two regular teachers, two student teachers working together. The students receive credit in both English and Social Studies."

"Why these particular students? Are they gifted?"

He laughed.

"Not only gifted students deserve special treatment."

You know the expression that there are no stupid questions? Well, while he wasn't making fun of my question, I still felt truly stupid. He must have sensed my discomfort.

"These students are your classic under-achievers. They all have at least average I.Q.s but they just can't seem to adjust to the traditional classroom environment. Without this program they would be hitting the street the day of their sixteenth birthday. It's our job to provide an open, stimulating school experience which will, ideally, inspire them to learn and keep them in school."

I had a glorious time talking about the program and the kids. And when our hour was up and the conversation had concluded I was aware of wanting this job more than I had ever wanted anything in my entire life. I loved Eddie. I loved the school. I wanted this job.

He made no commitment, merely directed me to go to Oakstream South School for the second part of the interview. I was to meet with a Dr. Archer who was the staff person in charge of the student teachers for the Oakstream School system.

As I wound my way through the suburban streets on my way to "South" as Eddie called it, I became aware of the huge grin splitting my face when the muscles began to ache slightly. Shit, I really did want this job.

Not quite as impressive in style, "South" definitely had "North" beat when it came to size. It was an immense, intimidating structure which took me more than a half an hour to maneuver winding halls before finding Dr. Archer's office.

There, sitting behind a solid desk was an equally solid, quite handsome woman of about fifty with short-cropped red hair, appropriately dressed in tweed. Her complexion was freckled and quite outdoorsy. It was obvious at first glance that this was a former P.E. teacher.

After about fifteen minutes of routine questions, I rose to leave as the phone rang. She answered it and before I reached the door, she motioned for me to sit back down. Quite a few yeses and ahuhs passed and as she finally hung up she smiled.

"That was Eddie Morton. Welcome to the Oakstream team." She extended a masculine hand and shook mine enthusiastically.

I drove home. I really don't know how I got there. As I tossed my keys in the dish on the entrance hall table, the clash of the metal on china startled me into awareness. I got the job. I GOT THE JOB!

I picked Profit up and began dancing a highly stylize waltz throughout the house. We glided through the living room and executed a simply awful dip in the dining room. I decided to try it again as we tangoed into the kitchen. There the dip came off much better.

Quite aghast at the disturbance of her mid-day nap, the cat sped down the hallway, seeking asylum from her lunatic "mother" as soon as I put her down to answer the phone.

"Hello?" I sang into the receiver.

"Where have you been? I've been trying to reach you for hours."

I was totally unaware of Glen's angry tone, too thrilled with myself to notice it.

"Oh, Glen, I have such wonderful news. I got the job. I'll be doing my student teaching at Oakstream. They interviewed over twenty people and they picked me. Can you believe it? They actually picked me. I got the job!" My enthusiastic delight exploded.

"Lauren, calm down for Christ's sake. The phone company installs sound boosters in the phone lines every few miles just so people like you don't have to scream to be heard.

The intensity of his sarcasm more than matched my previous enthusiasm. His angry annoyance needed no phone line boosters to be heard loud and clear.

I lost my breath as tears filled my eyes. The ability to speak was gone. It was actually a struggle to breathe as he continued.

"Christ, it sure took long enough. I've been calling you since ten."

At last I knew that I could speak, but what to say?

"Lauren, are you there? What took so damn long?"

I barely recognized the voice as a monotone response escaped my lips.

"I had to drive to Oakstream South for a second interview. It took extra time."

"Shit, they've got a lot of nerve making you drive all over town like that. They should have had everyone right there for you."

"Glen, they weren't there for my convenience. They could have chosen any number of other people...it's a great opportunity, a great job."

"Well personally, I wish they would have chosen someone else. Now you'll probably want to take the damn job...Oh baby, that's a call I have to take. I've been expecting to hear from L.A. for over an hour. I'll be home about six-thirty. Love ya, baby."

The receiver went dead in my hand. And at that moment I wished I were...I truly wished I were dead.

As the day proceeded, the dread of the nasty encounter, that would surely come, increased. I knew that Glen would do anything in his power to stop me from accepting the position. My working was not in his plan for my life. I knew if I wanted to teach I would have to come up with something to insure that he would let me take this job.

When Glen arrived home he was greeted with soft music playing. The wine he preferred was opened and I was in the kitchen arranging the finishing touches on his favorite dinner. I had spent the majority of the afternoon preparing this feast. I took extra time pounding the veal cutlets until paper-thin taking great care not to go so far as to tear the delicate flesh.

My homemade marinara and freshly grated parmesan and mozzarella cheeses were combined into my own veal parmesan that Glen adored.

I actually discovered in Des Moines that I loved to cook. Not only did I find it to be a truly gratifying creative outlet but also I relished wondrously losing myself in the active details of the process. Ah, to lose myself. And what a perfect day it had been to just get lost!

"What's all this?" There was genuine admiration in Glen's voice as he entered the kitchen.

"Well, I thought it's been kind of unpleasant around here lately and maybe we could do something to change that tonight. You know, have a really special dinner..."

While I had certainly not intended the statement to be accusatorial, Glen instantly became defensive.

"It's not my fault that you have been so preoccupied with this teaching shit!" His anger started to rise.

Even though not totally unexpected, his angry attitude stung nonetheless. I was determined not to cry but I could not stop the tears from welling.

"I just wanted to do something special for you and you're already yelling."

His expression changed instantly. He got *that* look on his face and within a moment he was all around me.

"Baby, I'm sorry I yelled at you. Don't start crying, please. It's been rough these past months. I know that. I've been really frustrated with work and I miss not being with you all day like we were in Des Moines. But it'll get better. Trust me. It will get better."

As he kissed my neck the guilt began to grow. Why couldn't what I had said been true? There was a time when my desire just to be happy with him would have been the motivation for such a feast. How had our relationship changed so drastically? Or was it only me who had changed?

"Sweetheart, stop," I pleaded. "If we're going to enjoy this meal, I have to finish getting it ready. We have all evening."

He squeezed me tightly and whispered.

"Fuck dinner."

"No, Glen, really. Stop." I pleaded once more.

I tried to wrestle myself out of his embrace. He began grabbing at my clothes. Looking into his eyes and at that moment I realized that he was totally unaware of what I was saying.

"Glen, please, no..." I moaned.

I was helpless as he shed the clothes from my body.

"You are so beautiful. How did you know that this is just what I need? Oh, baby, you always know what I need," he whispered, lost in his own desire.

And all I could think of was maybe this was for the best as he lowered me to the kitchen floor. I closed my eyes tightly. The floor was cold, hard against my back. I felt his weight heavy on top of me. The Italian stone tiled floor was so uncomfortable under his rhythmic pressure. But I was actually glad for the discomfort. I deserved it.

I was suddenly aware of his heavy breathing, then the pressure of his lips all over my face, roughly kissing me, hurting me.

"God, baby that was so good."

And again the powerful kisses and massive hug extinguishing breath, hurting my ribs. Then, in the next moment, he was standing over me staring down at my nakedness.

"You know, you're even prettier now than when I married you. Great body, woman!" He proclaimed proudly.

He tossed a dishtowel down to me, smugly assessing his possession. I wanted to cover myself. I felt exposed and embarrassed. God, how I wanted to just be left alone. But there he stood.

Finally, without another word, he walked out of the kitchen. My relief was quickly overtaken by my realization that I hadn't discussed my job yet. I just couldn't let this opportunity pass. I followed him into the den fully aware of my motivation for not dressing first, totally cognizant that somewhere along the way I had evolved into a manipulator.

Student Teaching

I took the job. As the days passed, I grew to realize that never before had I felt so alive, so inwardly content as when I was in that classroom. I had the freedom to experiment with different teaching methods and the funds to support unusual, interesting projects.

As Eddie had explained, this unique class was taught by four teachers. Each of us brought our unique talents to willingly share with the others. Eddie had chosen the other student teacher well. His name was Brad and he was bright, energetic and extremely capable. At first I was a bit intimidated, thinking that I would surely let the others down. But I soon came to realize I too had much to offer.

I was allowed to implement a system by which the class decided what they would like to study. We broke up into four small groups, each teacher taking five students at a time who researched the agreed upon topic for the week. The group would then present their findings to the entire class. The kids loved it because they were allowed to study any topic in which two or more of them shared an interest. They really felt like they had some control over how they spent their time in school. I was thrilled because I was fulfilling my obligation to get them excited about learning and even more importantly; I was getting them to read.

I became acutely aware that these experiences were equally as meaningful for me as they were for my students. For the first time in my life, I really had something to offer on my own. I slowly became aware of a growing sense of worthiness, a self-worth that I hadn't realized I had been lacking. And it felt good; really good. My students seemed to be learning. I was learning. And the kids came up with great topics.

O.K. then. Yeah, this was going well!

My group did segments on living off the land, superstition, drug abuse and many more unconventional topics for high school study. It was working. I could teach. I felt I was really making a difference with these kids. Never before had I experienced such pure pleasure. Whether pride or conceit, I didn't care. Whatever it was, it was a totally new emotion and I liked it. I needed it. In the classroom I was in charge of my life. And with each passing day my confidence grew. I was able to recognize that I had value and that I could contribute. This represented a polar opposite environment from that which existed within the confines of my own home.

Rather than improving, the situation in our house just seemed to be getting worse. Glen showed no interest at all in what I was doing. When he did acknowledge my *other life* as he called it, it was with scorn. He had given in but he wasn't going to make it easy for me.

One break period Eddie approached me with a peculiar smile on his face. I had left our classroom en route to a well-deserved cup of coffee as he neared.

"Dr. Ford wants to see you in fifteen minutes."

"What did I do? Am I in trouble?"

He shrugged his shoulders.

"I don't know, kid. There was a note in my box to have you in his office at 1:15. That's all it said."

"Have you picked up any rumors or anything?" My apprehension was building.

"Not a peep," was his terse response.

We walked the corridors in silence, my thoughts zipping through everything I had done while at Oakstream. Sure, I had made some mistakes, but I could think of nothing so dramatic as to warrant a middle of the day meeting with the Superintendent of the school system. I was one of those kids that NEVER got sent to the principal's office!

I blinked wildly, trying to focus on the classrooms we passed, as my chest tightened and I silently tensed.

All at once a terrifying thought occurred to me. Had Glen done something? Oh God, as soon as the thought came into my head I couldn't shake it. Did he have something to do with this?

As my professional pleasures grew, those of my personal life diminished. We argued constantly. We had gotten to a point where he preferred that I not even *trouble myself* with any of his day-to-day activities...thinking that I could never understand the complexity of his professional life. At the same time, my triumphs and misgivings were simply unimportant to him.

We just didn't talk about our days. But the one point that he did make over and over was that he was not pleased with my pursuing a career. He wanted...no, needed to be the sole source of my happiness and fulfillment.

Could he have, would he have, taken matters into his own hands and somehow gotten me in trouble or manipulated my dismissal in some way?

My God, what was I thinking? I was letting my imagination run rampant. How could I even think that Glen would do such a thing? Certainly, we had our problems but he wouldn't...

I struggled to dismiss the thought that he had anything to do with this meeting. It was absurd. The meeting didn't have to be for something bad. Dr. Ford might just want to see me, have a chat. After all we hadn't met yet. I didn't even know what he looked like. In a large school system like Oakstream, the Superintendent was strictly a political position with very little hands-on management. Maybe he just wanted to get a look at me.

Oh God, who was I kidding?

After what seemed to be hours of walking the halls but was, in reality, only a few minutes; we finally arrived. Dr. Ford's secretary politely and professionally asked us to take a seat, stating that Dr. Ford would be with us shortly. A chill began at the base of my spine and traveled up, freezing each disc until it melted into a throb as it entered the back of my skull. God, I had an awful headache all of a sudden!

Soon, we were ushered into a lovely office, orderly arranged within walnut paneling. Sitting at a meticulous desk was a meticulous little man, well-tailored right up to his short, blonde, feathered haircut. He rose as I entered.

"Ah, there you are. Please, sit down, Lauren."

My mind raced wildly. A lisp. A feminine hand dangling from a loose wrist motioning for me to be seated. Was he gay? I lost control of my thoughts as they jumped from one unjust reaction to another before this poor man had a chance to utter another word.

Oh, how I wished I knew more about homosexuals. To my knowledge, I had never even met one. Did they hate women? This oh so elegant man seating himself before me had tremendous power. It was well within his purview to black list me; oh yes, he could actually do that. An unofficial, intra-school buddy system was rumored to exist. Often in my college classes this subject would come up among my fellow students. There was no question in my mind that he could indeed see that I was never offered a job in a decent school.

Why didn't I know he was gay? Why didn't I know more about homosexuality? What a totally inept human being I was and how truly arrogant I had been. How could I have thought that I would be a good teacher when my own knowledge of the world was so very limited? He had heard about me somehow. Sitting there watching me, he could now see right through me to my total incompetence.

I took a deep breath, silently praying it went unnoticed. How stupid of me. I had to get a grip. I didn't know anything about this man, except that he preferred men to women as sexual partners...and did I really know that? One more glance at him poised across the desk from me assured me that at least that much I did know.

My hands were clammy as I folded them in my lap hoping he didn't notice them shaking. What if I couldn't get a job when the time came because this man knew the truth about my complete ineptitude? At least I knew at that moment that Glen had nothing to do with this. He was too homophobic to have any dealings, whatsoever, with this man.

I was faintly aware of Dr. Ford pleasantly dismissing Eddie from the room. Left alone; it was time.

He looked directly at me. I returned with a straightforward glare. Go ahead. Do your worst!

"So, you're the pretty new student teacher the whole school is buzzing about."

Was it spoken as a compliment? Having braced myself for an attack, I wasn't sure of his intent. I sat quietly confused as he continued.

"I have received quite a few phone calls from the parents of your students and each has mentioned how impressed they are by the progress you've been making with the class. I felt it was time I got to know you since there will be an opening in our English Department for the next school term."

He sat back gently, obviously pleased with himself...and me. His words finally sank in. Thousands of teachers unemployed across the country and out of nowhere, unsolicited, he was actually talking about a job for me? I knew that he was waiting for a response, but what to say?

"It's always nice to hear that others think you are doing a good job, but I really can't take the credit for how well the class is doing. Eddie and the others are really great teachers, and the kids are a trip and a half. I'm learning more than they are!"

Damn that sounded so prissy, kiss-ass. What was I saying? He had to think I was a total dolt!

He gave me an obligatory smile. I was mortified. Here he had actually given me a great compliment and all I could come up with in response was a garble of gag-producing, self-deprecating hooey.

When I was young my mother told me that most people just don't know how to handle a compliment. They verbally stumble about trying to be cute or funny or intelligent or, as in my case, humble when all that is really ever needed is a simple, sincere "thank you." Why had I forgotten that lesson at this oh so important moment?

Dr. Ford seemed unaware of my internal turmoil as he continued.

"Of course it's important that you learn from this student teaching experience, but from my perspective it is more important for us to recognize the potential of a good teacher and not allow her to slip through the proverbial Oakstream fingers."

Humored by his own attempt at brevity, he exposed a brilliant, to the point of unnaturally, white smile as he leaned forward with hands clasped atop his desk. His neatly manicured fingernails, buffed not polished, contrasted dramatically with my previously gnawed down versions. I immediately hid mine in my lap.

"Lauren, quite frankly I have been advised that you have that potential we are looking for."

His smile now warmed me. He had me. I was suddenly totally

relaxed and smiled back.

"Thank you."

My ego trip lasted for a good fifteen minutes during which time we discussed my work. He seemed impressed by my evaluation of the Individualized Learning Program that Oakstream utilized and when I politely suggested that the contracts used to commit a student to his weekly activities could use some specific revisions, he actually took notes!

We ended our conversation with my detailing the progress in the small group individualized topic experiment.

"It's working wonderfully well. We each take five students so the individual attention we're able to provide is more than five times that of a conventional classroom. And by letting the kids choose their own subjects their cooperation level soars. Plus, it's an incredibly fun challenge for me. Finding appropriate materials and resources can become difficult at times. With topics such as witchcraft-that's what we're researching this week-it can be quite a challenge. Believe me, this segment was not easy!"

I had to laugh at his expression of surprise, but I pushed on with my explanation.

"I was able to find a rather large cult in this area." He actually gasped at this revelation.

"Believe me; I was as astonished as you are. But, I did find out about a couple of guys that have a program on the subject and I was able to arrange to have them speak to the class tomorrow. They will be lecturing on the Black Mass. I've been assured that they are intelligent and very professional speakers. They supposedly put on quite a presentation. It should be both educational and entertaining. I thought it perfect for last thing on the Friday afternoon agenda. The kids are really looking forward to it." He looked at me in astonishment. Is that good or bad, the question flooded my thoughts. But I continued. "Perhaps you would like to sit in on the class?"

"Thank you for the invitation. But I'll have to make it another time. My schedule tomorrow is booked solid." He sounded utterly relieved by that fact as he continued. "It does sound like a good challenge for you. I'm confident that you will meet it head on and do a fine job."

He rose offering me a hand signaling that our meeting had ended.

What an outstanding day! I wanted to celebrate. I wasn't going to let anything spoil this day. I'd make a wonderful dinner and even if Glen was in a bad mood...I was going to make sure that he wasn't!

As I scurried about the kitchen attending to last minute details for our dinner, I heard the front door slam. As I approached him, Glen flung his suit coat in a wad at the entry hall table.

"Jesus Christ! I can't believe it," he growled.

Even though he wasn't yelling, his anger came blasting through. Having grown accustomed to his usually loud, animated anger, this quiet venom was truly scary. With apprehension I went to him.

"God damned bastard," he continued in softly spoken rage. "I just can't believe that my Dad could do this."

"What has he done this time?" I asked timidly.

"The fucking business has just gotten too big for him to handle. He's making bad decisions...oh what's the use."

Through the years as Glen was growing up he had built an image of his father as some sort of Corporate God. There was no way any mere mortal could have lived up to the idol Glen had created. Had he not gone to work for Arthur perhaps the image could have remained intact, but seeing him daily, working with him and realizing that the man, like any other, had his flaws and weaknesses had done something to Glen. As the weeks passed, Arthur's management style and even his abilities seemed to become a constant aggravation to Glen.

I picked up the wad of his jacket from the table and followed him up to the bedroom trying to straighten the jacket out as we climbed the stairs. I watched in silence as he angrily snapped his tie from his neck and threw his cufflinks at the dresser.

"Sweetheart, I hate to see you so upset."

"I'm alright. Everything is fine. There is nothing for you to worry about." He turned a vacant smile at me.

He had said these same words so many times lately they had become a reflex rather than a conscious statement. They began to sound more like *it's none of your business.*

"Will you tell me what happened? Please?"

"It doesn't matter. Really.   There's nothing for you to worry about. I shouldn't have brought all of this home, not here, not in our house."

But this time I refused to give up. If I could get him to let me into his life again, maybe, just maybe, he would want to be a part of mine.

"I would really like to know. I'd like to help," I implored.

He looked up at me as he sat down heavily on the bed. But he wasn't looking at me at all. He was seeing something that brought a contorted, red-faced rage spewing forth. He began very softly, enunciating each syllable with precision.

"He expanded the company's Board of Directors."

I didn't understand the severity of this action, but I knew enough not to question it. Glen rose slowly and walked to the armoire. He flung open one of the doors with such force I was certain it would fly from its hinges.

"He expanded the Board of Directors but was so fucking afraid of what the stock holders would say, he didn't put me on it."

He turned, walked several steps and stood leaning with his palms flat on the dresser looking at his own reflection in the mirror, his face contorted with fury.

"I will never be free of the boss's son stigma, he bellowed as a clenched fist raised and then smashed down on the dresser. "Shit, what's the use?"

His rage was so intense I could hear his teeth grinding as he stood up straight trying to gather control.

"I know that business better than anyone, anyone including the old man. I've got plans. But how the fuck am I going to get anything done if I'm not in a position with any power?"

Even though his back was turned, he was speaking to me. God, he was finally, really talking to me as an equal.

"This is a bad one, Lauren, you mark my words. This mistake will come back and bite him in the ass!"

I walked up and put my arms around him. I nuzzled my cheek below his shoulder blade and smelled his familiar, pleasing scent. I felt so inadequate. What could I say? What could I do to help him?

"I'm so sorry, sweetheart." I whispered.

He turned and held me. Ripples of tension passed through his body as he began to cry soundlessly. He had never let me see him cry before. I don't even know if he ever had cried before. It instantly endeared him to me. I felt the anger and disappointment right along with him. And it felt good. It felt so very good to have him this close to me again. He had finally opened up to me. He was finally sharing himself with me.

I didn't want to move. I hardly drew breath, afraid of losing this wonderful feeling. Glen needed me, needed me for more than what had become his usual sexual seizures.

In that moment I came to an amazing realization. I had begun to doubt that I had ever really known this man I married at all. I was afraid he had never been anything other than the controlling, hurtful man with whom I was now living. I had begun to believe that I had been unable to see him for what he really was due to my own insecurities, my own tremendous need.

But now, here was this man, my husband, in my arms, vulnerable and needy. He actually allowed me to see that he needed me. I was sure that I had finally broken through to the boy with whom I had fallen in love. That sensitive boy who had written me sonnets and professed to only wanting to make me happy was still there. The pressures and problems of manhood had just made it too difficult for him to show himself. Glen had been hiding behind the bravado for far too long. But now here he was again. I began to weep at finally having him back.

It felt wonderful and what a relief. Lately, I had begun to think that perhaps he was right. I was to blame for all of our problems. I was the one selfishly blinded by the money and the power he possessed, but most of all I was afraid that I had been blinded by my own need to be loved and to be taken care of. I had begun to feel incredibly stupid for being so needy as to be totally oblivious to the true nature of the man I married. As all of these thoughts rushed through my mind, grateful relief followed. He *had* been different then. Hadn't he? I wasn't as pathetic as I had feared I was back then. And now he was back. Here, this man in my arms was the proof.

We stood in the embrace for several moments more ...several wonderful moments.

I felt his anger wane. Then his mood began to brighten. He finally pulled away from my arms, actually looking gratefully into my eyes. Yes! This was how it should be between us.

He finished undressing without another word. As he changed his clothes, he even began to whistle. I sighed at the very look of him. He was back. The man I married was back. I could see it in his entire demeanor. That's when I remembered my good news. I knew that now he was finally ready to listen and share.

"Glen, how about some really good news? You'll never guess what happened to me at school today."

He grabbed a tee shirt from the armoire and pulled it over his head as he left the room totally ignoring me.

"Glen?" Oh no!

"Not now, baby."

He began to mumble the rest as he left the room.

"I really don't care what happens at that place..." He was lost in his own world once again. He resumed his whistling.

I listened to the shrill sound becoming faint as the distance between us grew. Sitting down hard on the bed, I tried to blink away the tears. His statement wasn't said with malice or with the intent to hurt me. All of the optimism, the joy, the relief of the past several minutes was wiped out in one brief sentence. I was finally, painfully, totally aware that he had spoken the absolute truth. He simply couldn't care less. I had, indeed, been that pathetic, idiotic, child blinded by insecurity. Oh God, no wonder he treated me that way.

I lay wide awake late into the night making up all kinds of excuses for our failing marriage. I finally fell asleep reliving the experience of my afternoon at school. Nothing could spoil that for me. I would learn to enjoy my small triumphs alone until Glen could or would share them with me. I was aware of the enormous satisfaction I had gained from knowing that a man as important as Dr. Ford knew that I was a fine teacher. I could and would be contented with that...for now.

Dream On

I heard the alarm go off, felt Glen get out of bed, but decided to indulge in a few more moments of sleep.

It was a warm August day. The sun was hot. I was hot. The breeze picked up but it was anything but refreshing. It caused the sand to swirl and I felt a multitude of gritty particles stick to my oiled body.

"Oh, yuk Glen, look at this. I'm covered with sand."

He reached over from his beach chair and tried to brush the sand from my arm.

"Stop! That hurts. I feel like you're filing my skin off." I feigned anger, and he knew it.

We met half way and kissed long and hard.

"God, baby, I love you."

"I love you too, sweetheart."

He leaned back contentedly.

"How's this for one hell of a honeymoon spot, huh?" He asked.

"As the natives would say 'Je t'adore,' I answered playfully.

"I hope that means you love me, 'cause I sure as hell love you, woman." And I could see the truth of his statement in the blazing green eyes looking adoringly into mine. "How do you like Cannes? This is great, isn't it?"

"I love it. It's everything I've dreamed of and then some."

My response pleased him. He was so generous and caring and protective of me. I loved pleasing him, and now that we were finally married, I would have the opportunity to please him, as he pleased me, for the rest of my life.

He leaned over and kissed my neck tenderly. He spoke softly but emphatically, causing wisps of air to flutter past my ear with each word, tickling me, sending chills up my spine.

"Let's go back to the room, baby. We haven't officially initiated France yet." He was grinning wickedly.

He helped me out of my chair and we walked arm-in-arm through the formal gardens bordering the beach. The wind had once again picked up but this time instead of sand, I was bombarded with the deep, syrupy-sweet fragrance of fresh flowers. The colors were more intense than I had ever seen before. Everything was more intense here; or was it just that I was so very much in love?

I found myself wrapped in a sensual experience unlike any I had ever known. I was luxuriating in it. Smells, sounds, colors all combined, stimulating my being. The people looked happier here, the trees more lush, the air wonderfully fresh. I grabbed Glen's arm.

"God, I'm glad to be here."

"Me too," he answered kissing the top of my head.

As we arrived at the door to the Bridal Suite, he lifted me effortlessly, in one swift movement, up into his arms. I squealed and squirmed knowing with certainty that he would not drop me. His arms felt so strong wrapped around me, his embrace secure. He would never let me go. I never wanted him to let me go.

"What kind of marriage would this be if we didn't start it off properly?" he teased.

I wrapped my arms around his neck in surrender and buried my face under his chin. A wonderful combination of the sea and sand and manly scents filled me with anticipation as he carried me into the sundrenched living room. Straight ahead the calm, clear sea filled the floor-to-ceiling windows, so blue and motionless; it looked to be frozen. I smiled at the magnum of champagne along with two stunning crystal flutes into which our names had been etched delicately, sparkling atop the dining room table. These had been waiting for us upon our arrival in Cannes earlier in the day, compliments of Cynthia and Arthur Jacobson.

Glen carried me directly to the bathroom, put me down gently and began filling the tub.

"Let's get this sand off of us."

The tub filled. The mirrors steamed up. And we undressed, each occupying our own space, quite removed from each other. The anticipation was building. Though far from being the first time, this would be THE first time for me, I just knew it.

The room was floor-to-ceiling tiled in black; sleek, shiny black. The wall opposite the tub had the top half mirrored, with a black marble-topped vanity extending the entire length of the room under it.

I stood naked watching Glen as he gauged the heat of the tub with a swish of his hand. He adjusted the tap. His golden body looked outstanding with a black marble-tiled backdrop. I could feel myself losing control of my thoughts as my desire for his touch grew.

He extended a hand to me and guided me toward the tub. He helped me lower myself into the soothing, wet heat. When I was settled, he reached across me for the soap and ever so slightly touched my breast. An involuntary shiver sparked through me as if jumpstarting my expectations once again, heightening my senses for what was to follow.

He lathered a washcloth and ever so gently slid it over my body. Then he picked up the hand held shower spray, adjusted the flow to a fine mist and began spraying my shoulders.

As he moved the nozzle down my body, he turned the controls to increase the pressure of the spray. Across my chest, around each of my breasts, he continued to build the water pressure. As he moved the spray down my belly and finally between my legs, I thought I would surely explode from the sensations that the rhythmically pulsating water produced.

"Lauren, wake up!" I felt strong hands shaking me awake. "Come on, baby, you'll blame me for not getting you up on time."

I then felt hard kisses leaving a moist path down my neck. I shivered as the morning air hit the dampness, painfully aware I had been awakened from a wonderful dream of what might have been.

"Come on Sleepy, get up. I have to leave. I have an early breakfast meeting and I need my goodbye kiss before I can start my day!"

"Okay, okay, I'm up. You don't have to..."

He kissed me squarely on the lips.

"You sure you're up? You're the one so crazed about this job of yours. You don't want to be late."

"I'm up. I said I'm up." I replied sourly.

I didn't want to start another day angry, but I seemed to have little control over it. Everything he said, everything he did, even when he was being thoughtful, like this morning, making sure I wasn't late, was predicated on something he wanted for himself. His morning kiss was his impetus this morning. It just made me so mad.

He left the room. As I lay there, I heard the door slam and then the noise of the garage door opening and closing a few moments later. He was gone. I sank back into the contentment of bed with relief. I could dress and ready myself for the day in peace.

My God, what had happened to us? Why couldn't our honeymoon night have been like that of my dream? And now, even after over two years of marriage, I just couldn't seem to get our relationship on track. But it wasn't only my failure. No. I had had quite an epiphany that previous night. I wasn't the only one to blame. After all, what could I do alone?

I shook the question away, buried it deeper and deeper the more progress I made into my morning. After dressing and driving to Oakstream I was ready to think only about my day ahead.

The Black Mass

By the time I reached the school all I could think about was how anxious I was to continue deserving Dr. Ford's praise from the day before. Then the two guest speakers arrived, and I had something else to think about. Good God, what had I done?

They were monstrously proportioned, caped and dressed entirely in black. Their facial features were totally obscured by scads of black hair billowing from below black hats. One carried a small black bag resembling a doctor's case with one slight distinction, his had a large skull and cross bone decal plastered across the front. They literally swept into the room with capes flowing out behind them uttering nary a sound, effortlessly capturing the undivided attention of the kids.

The class sat in gawking silence, jaws dropping wide open, eyes even wider. As I looked around I couldn't help but smile also having been taken in by their initially shocking appearance. This was great! But then I began to worry about their presentation. How would these two creatures handle this class? But I had to give it to them. What a first impression!

The kids began looking around at each other, smiles erupting on their faces. They were eating up the drama of it all. Since the class consisted of students with behavior problems and their main objection was the sterility of school as a whole; having two guest speakers arrive looking like Count Dracula and sidekick Renfield was a fantastic change of scenery for them.

To my surprise and relief, the lecture/show was excellent. These two characters really had a well-prepared presentation on the history of the Black Mass and on the various cults practicing it today. It was the perfect combination of history, folklore and Goth. They were organized and kept the kids wide-eyed and wildly excited for the entire hour and a half.

They had brought various props with them that were used in creating the proper setting for performing a mass. From the black bag they produced all kinds of ghoulish paraphernalia that elicited approving howls from the kids.

We burned incense and passed around the literature they brought.

But the piece-de-resistance was when one of them withdrew from the bag a black, bejeweled dagger enshrined in a magnificently beaded sheath.

The room went silent.

"We use this holy dagger to perform our sacrifices," one of our large, spooky guests whispered.

"The usual procedure is to climax a mass by sacrificing a lamb or goat," the other one added.

The group was speechless. Then slowly a few whispered wows and far outs could be heard. At the end of the presentation the kids couldn't wait to tell their friends about their experience as they exploded from the room.

After what proved to be a surprisingly exciting presentation, since it was Friday, I had the mundane task of writing up my weekly evaluation of the group. Meanwhile, our two guests were gathering all of their goodies back into the bag. Two of my students, Joe and Mike, had remained to watch them clear away their stuff.

Joe's evaluation would be a difficult one for me. He kept totally to himself in a corner of the room making only the occasional, usually hostile, contribution to the class. I had read his file and was not surprised to find that he had exhibited violent tendencies toward other students as early as the second grade. While he had never overtly taken on any of the students in this class, he did demand and always received deference. In truth, he even frightened me a bit.

As I wrote, I cued in on Joe's conversation.

"Wow, look at that dagger. It's really something. Look at the jeweled handle..."

He had turned toward the larger of the two men.

"You say this is used for sacrifices, huh?"

Thank God my instincts told me something was happening here and I had better pay attention, because as I looked up, Joe had taken the dagger from its sheath and in a swift move, a moment later, was slashing it toward Mike as he began to scream, "Let's sacrifice Mike!"

His face was wild with passion, eyes wide with excitement, he closed the gap between himself and Mike in one agile lunge.

Mike instinctively turned away, trying desperately to avoid the stab, as I jumped up and reached for Joe's arm. I was too late. The knife slashed Mike's shoulder.

I can tell you that all of those stories about incredible power being achieved from adrenalin flow in stressful situations are true and I am living proof of it. Joe had at least forty pounds on me yet I was able to push him away from Mike, stopping him from slashing out again at the stunned and now injured teenager.

Joe now stood motionless with his arms bent at the elbows as if he were about to run and would need to be pumping them for speed. In his right hand the knife still remained grasped in his fist pointing downward. There was a small drip of blood making its way down the blade and then, almost delicately, slipped off of the tip onto the flood. I approached him slowly but soon realized that he had no idea that I or anyone else was even in the room. I easily managed to get the knife out of the hand of the now totally incoherent Joe.

The two men stood there in utter shock. One turned to the other and whispered in disbelief,

"Shit, we only sacrifice animals. This kid wants to off his buddy!"

Meanwhile, as Mike's shoulder began bubbling blood, Joe stumbled to a corner of the room sliding down the intersecting walls into a crouching fetal position. He remained there staring, coldly staring unemotionally, just staring at Mike.

"Faaaauck. Look at the blood. God damn, look at the blood," Joe practically whimpered with satisfaction, breaking his silence.

I ran to the door screaming for help. Eddie entered the room with a horrified look, gauging the situation. He stood in shock.

"I'll take Mike to the nurse if you can handle things here." I was still shouting.

I had to grab Eddie's arm tightly to focus his attention on what I was saying. I handed him the bloody knife.

"Did you hear what I said?

He nodded his assent to my plan as he looked at the crimson-smeared weapon in his hand.

I was never so glad to leave a room in my life. My mind was blank as I guided the surprisingly calm Mike through the hallways, now teeming with curious kids, to the nurse's office.

With several students craning to get a better look through the glass door to the office, the nurse in a most professional manner assessed the bleeding shoulder. After cleaning the wound, it became obvious, even to me, that stitches were required.

"Shall I call the paramedics?" I asked, hoping of be of some use.

"Not necessary, I'll drive him to the hospital myself."

I was greatly relieved. It wasn't so bad. He didn't even need an ambulance. Oh God, who was I kidding? Wasn't so bad? A child in my care was stabbed...by another child in my care. Could it get any worse?

Here's a tip: one should never, under any circumstances, ask that question because you just know what the answer will be.

"Oh, and I'll call his parents." The nurse's very organized mind was working overtime to make sure every detail was attended to. But one look at my obviously ashen face and her all businesslike expression softened.

"I think you have other things to worry about just now." She patted my shoulder in obvious sympathy which I was too numb to acknowledge.

Finally, I nodded unable to find any words at all. What was there to say? What was there to do? I was lost unable to think.

Focus Lauren. Pull yourself together. My mind kept saying to me.

And as I watched them hurry down the hall, the nurse's attention seeming more devoted to shooing away curious students than with Mike's condition; I just stood there.

I finally managed to softly say, "I'm so sorry" as they turned the corner.

So, they were off to the hospital, leaving me utterly paralyzed. I knew I had to do something other than stand there staring down the hallway, but I just could not muster the energy to move. There I stood. Some students walked by looking as if they wanted to say something, ask something but instead they continued on past me staring and still I could not budge. Oh, Lauren, what to do now?

I stood motionless for what seemed to be hours. I was vaguely aware of the hallways clearing. School was out for the weekend. None of the kids wanted to stay one moment longer than necessary.

I had assumed that all of them knew what had happened. Apparently, I was wrong, for had they known surely they would have been curious. Surely they would have discovered what a true failure I was, how I had totally fucked up! They would never trust me again. Their parents would never trust them to my care again.

And time passed. I was now alone in the deserted hallway. I saw that the sky was darkening over the courtyard in front of me. I had braced myself against the wall. When had I done that? How long had I stood here? I had to get a grip. I knew I had to go back to my classroom but how could I? How would I ever be able to go back into that classroom again? So, there I stood. *Come on Lauren, get it together*, I told myself. *You're stronger than this.*

I was actually surprised when my legs started moving as if all on their own. I nervously walked back to my classroom. I took a deep, calming breath as I hesitantly opened the door. Eddie began shouting instructions to me before I could even enter.

"Jeez, Lauren, where have you been? I've been waiting for you. Ford wants to see you, NOW. You better get right over there." I turned and left without a word.

I walked the halls to his office in a daze. This time I knew exactly why he wanted to see me and there was no need to even hope that our chat would be as pleasant as the one we had just yesterday.

Once again the door opened on the man sitting behind the desk. But today there was no softness, no gentle expression on his face. Instead a man twisted with fury sat before me. I knew instantly that even my preparation for the worst before yesterday's meeting was not going to be enough for what was to come today.

"You idiot! How could you have allowed a knife in your classroom?" He bellowed before I had even fully entered the room.

"But, Dr. Ford..."

He wasn't listening. He was rapt in such fury, my words went unheard. Then he interrupted me before I could even try to explain or defend myself.

"I am not going to take the fall for this. Oh, no young lady, you'll be the one sued. I'll see to that and believe me, when I am finished, you'll never be allowed to step one foot in a reputable school district, let alone teach in a decent school. I am not going to the wall for your stupidity."

He was spewing his venom as he began to slowly rise, as if being hoisted up by a massive crane from his chair in measured increments: crank, crank, crank. I was utterly bewildered. The horror of the event was just now taking hold in my mind.

"I had no control over what those men brought with them. I didn't know a knife was part of their presentation material," I stated defensively.

Then I started to get angry.

"No one could have done more than I did under the circumstances. Christ, if it weren't for me, Joe would have killed Mike. Those two big, tough men just stood there gaping. If that had been my reaction you would have had a murder on your hands!"

To this day, I don't know how I continued.

"And I have read Joe's file. He has no right being in a regular school in the first place. This kid has been violent for twelve years. It's documented. He needs special attention. You know it and I know it, so cut the crap! If there was a mistake made it was not by me. And I'll be damned if I'm going to sit here and take verbal abuse from you after what I have just been through."

He immediately became defensive.

"Well, in my twenty-five years in education, I have never had such an overt act of violence performed in my school..."

I began screaming now. I was the one interrupting him this time.

"I have only been teaching a few weeks and I was there watching it, so think how I feel about what happened!"

With that, my emotional release was drawing to an end. Sensing it, Dr. Ford simmered down too, at least enough to make a feeble attempt at comforting me.

"Now, let's not let a bad situation deteriorate into an even worse one."

The poor man had really had quite a day, first the stabbing and now this ranting female with which to contend. I'm sure he was greatly relieved to usher me out the door.

He managed a very unconvincing, sympathetic arm around my shoulder.

"We'll see what happens. I'll get back to you on Monday."

I left his office and headed back to my classroom out of habit more than anything else. I didn't know where else to go and couldn't seem to collect my thoughts.

Could I have done anything to have prevented it? I kept going over the events in my mind. When I first saw the knife should I have stopped the program right then? I hadn't been prepared for anything like this. How would one prepare for a stabbing in one's classroom? Yet, I had reacted quickly. I truly believed that I had saved Mike's life.

The memory of that deadly, maniacal look in Joe's eyes pulled me up short. I stopped in the hallway. With legs quivering I anchored myself against the wall once again until I felt strong enough to continue on my way.

As I entered the room, I don't know why but I was surprised not to see Joe still there huddled in the corner. Instead Mike was enthusiastically telling his tale to Eddie. The nurse couldn't reach his parents, so she had brought him back to school. His wound had taken 18 stitches and was now encased in gauze. His madras shirt was stained deep burgundy down the entire right side and had a large gaping tear as if the stain were not evidence enough of the attack. At the end of his saga, Eddie accompanied us to the parking lot.

"You both need to get some rest...it's been one hell of a day." He turned a sympathetic look in my direction.

"Everything will be fine, kid. Try not to worry," he whispered unconvincingly, then kissed my cheek.

"You'll see. It will all work out," he continued much more confidently.

He opened my car door for me and I got in. I motioned to Mike.

"Come on. Get in. I'll give you a lift home."

It was against the rules for a teacher to drive a student home, but I figured I couldn't possibly get into any more trouble than I was in already. What a day!

So, I drove Mike home. He lived *on the island* in the only, very small, section of the school district that could be considered blue collar. The island was totally surrounded by upper-and way upper-middleclass homes. The bit of irony that it was a kid from this side of town that got stabbed by one of the offspring of one of the more prominent members of the community instead of the stereotypical other way around, did not escape me.

Mike's parents were still at work. The nurse had finally reached them both by phone but each had indicated that as long as their son was O.K. they didn't want to take the time off work to rush home. I had a king-sized picture of my parents reacting that way. If I had been stabbed, they both would have dropped everything and gotten to my side even if they had to run all the way. But Mike seemed fine with being alone, so I guiltily made my apologies for what had happened for about the millionth time, waved lamely as he closed the car door and headed for home.

It was a relief to close the front door behind me. I knew Glen would be late, so I was assured of some safe solitude. I needed some time, with no interruptions, to put it all into perspective. Was there an acceptable perspective into which I could put it? Was there any sense to be made of the horrifying events?

In the brief time span of 24 hours I had gone from young educational wunderkind to totally irresponsible idiot. Shit, what a day!

Profit was rubbing a loving greeting against my leg, purring her pleasure at seeing me. I gathered her up into a tight hug. Burying my face in her fur, I began to cry. No racking sobs or wailing keening, just a soft, tragic, mournful recognition of the stark reality that my dreams had been shattered and would never be whole again. But all at once I realized that it was not just for my dreams of being a teacher that I mourned.

I expected little consolation from Glen. I received even less. The weekend amounted to one of the worst of my entire life. I was sick with nerves and to top it off, Glen's reaction to the sequence of events as I related them served only to make matters worse.

"Now, Lauren, I'm sure it wasn't that bad. The kid didn't die or anything. Besides, what's the big deal? You're not going to teach anyway." He shrugged it off.

And then I was aware of his shifting in his chair. After a moment I could feel his anger rising.

"And who the HELL does that bastard Ford think he is? I won't have him talking to my wife that way. You should just quit, baby. Monday you walk into his office and quit. You don't need this bullshit! Christ, you're doing the work of two teachers and not getting one lousy dime for it. He's got a hell of a lot of nerve. That's what you should do; you should quit."

I was oblivious to what Glen thought or said. I knew that my whole future was at stake here.

I waited for the two days to end. I stewed and paced, wishing the time to pass quickly and when Monday morning finally, finally dawned; it was the last thing I wanted. My thoughts kept fluctuating between uncontrollable fright and almost irrational defense of my actions.

Though uninvited, I went directly to Dr. Ford's office upon my arrival at Oakstream. I couldn't wait to be summoned. I wanted it fast and straight and I would deal with whatever was going to happen. By the time I was admitted, I was ready. Bring it on, Dr. Ford. I was not about to be taken down without a fight.

Oh God, please let me be able to handle this, I silently prayed.

"Lauren. Come in. Here, come in and sit down." He was quickly up from his desk ushering me to a chair.

"Would you like a cup of coffee?" He was calm and casually smiling.

"No, nnnno thank you," I stuttered through my shock.

I had been prepared to do battle. I awaited his fury.

He took his time returning to his desk chair. He spoke simply.

"Lauren, my dear, you have been blessed."

What the hell was this? Blessed? Did he actually say I had been blessed? I had witnessed a stabbing. This man had threatened me with losing my career and a lawsuit to boot. My husband was a total bastard about the whole thing. I had spent the entire weekend in utter hell and he casually sits there telling me that I am blessed? I would hate see what being cursed was like! He continued.

"It seems that in as much as Joe's father is a very wealthy and influential member of the community and this type of incident could only cause damage and pain to all concerned, Mike's parents have decided to let the whole matter drop."

He smiled broadly, leaning back in his chair quite contentedly.

"The whole unfortunate incident simply never happened." He concluded.

Never happened? What? I was momentarily confused, stunned by this totally unexpected turn of events. I had been anxiety-torn for two days, truly sick over this. What the hell was going on? It took only a moment for the reality of the situation to sink in. Oh, this was bad. One hears of cover-ups and corruption but to actually have it thrown into your face.... and here was this man assuming that I would just go along with the arrangements that were made. But it wasn't quite that simple for me to just brush it aside, no matter how the powers that be decided to handle it. I wasn't about to make it easy for the smiling bastard facing me.

"I don't quite understand, Dr. Ford." I almost purred with feigned bewilderment. "What do Joe's father and his standing in the community have to do with having the *matter* dropped?" I blinked up at him wide-eyed; flashing him my most sincerely bewildered expression. It was essential to my well-being, at this point, to make someone else uncomfortable...and I succeeded. He shifted about in his large leather chair.

"Try to follow this," he began with an unmistakably condescending tone. "Joe's father came to an acceptable agreement with Mike's parents and was then able to arrange to have none of this mess in any official files. Everything is just as it was before Friday's little mishap. Do you understand now?"

Of course I understand, you little bastard. It was now quite clear how Joe had been able to remain in public school all of these years with his record of violence. God only knows what other *little mishaps* weren't on the record. No one wanted to embarrass his father. But I waited to answer him, choosing to let Dr. Ford shift uncomfortably in his chair for a moment longer. He looked so miserable, waiting for this unpredictable, possibly unstable female to respond. And I had been afraid of him?

"Yes, Dr. Ford, it is crystal clear. I presume that I will be unable to convince anyone in authority of the need for Joe to get some serious attention?"

"I believe you to be quite right about that."

"But, surely it is obvious that at the very least, this boy needs extensive psychiatric treatment."

"That decision will have to be left up to his parents."

"And they have done such a great job in the past of getting him the help that he needs?"

"Lauren, this is not our concern..."

"Not our concern..."

"Like it or not, think of them as you will, but I would caution you about telling anyone about what actually happened," he rather forcefully interrupted me.

"Anyone wanting to verify your story will find no records anywhere to support your assertions of the events...nothing anywhere will indicate that anything unusual occurred in your classroom last Friday afternoon."

I was astounded

"I don't know how you can condone this, but you have obviously been *convinced* yourself by Joe's father as well so I guess I have no choice but to let it be. But know this; there is no way in hell I will ever concede that it never happened!"

I simply could not remain seated looking at his self-satisfied grin. I had to move. I had to get out of there. I just wanted to get away from the gloating little bastard.

"Well, if there is nothing else to discuss, I'd like to get back to my classroom."

"Yes of course," he answered quickly, seemingly relieved that I wasn't asking for any *convincing* from Joe's father and that our talk was over.

"And if you should have any problems in the future, please feel that you can come to me directly." His tone having changed completely, he was now back to being the gracious benefactor.

"There is one thing you can help me with."

His lips thinned into a hint of a grimace as I took him up on his offer sooner than he had expected.

"I will not teach with Joe in my group. Will you arrange for him to be transferred immediately?"

He smiled in relief.

"Consider it done. Oh, and about that teaching position for next year; we should have a contract ready for you to sign tomorrow afternoon. Can you stop by after two to sign it?"

I guess he thought that I was now worthy to be a member in good standing of the elite Oakstream team. He had waited to make completely sure that I would make no waves and this was my reward, his added insurance policy. Or so he thought.

"You can shove your contract up your ass," I stated sweetly with the most genuine smile I could muster as I got up to leave.

The appalled expression on his face was almost worth all of the trauma. I ever so gently closed the door behind me as I left. God, how I love a dramatic exit!

My conversation with Dr. Ford had me more upset than the incident itself. One hears about payoffs and crooked officials, but you never expect to witness them firsthand, especially with an incident with the serious, even potentially deadly, ramifications of this one.

"Can you believe that money can actually convince all of those people to ignore such a dangerous problem?"

I was so upset, I didn't even care that Glen sat reading his newspaper apparently giving me very little of his attention, if any at all. I had to talk, if only to myself. I had to actually *hear* the words spoken. What had happened had to be reinforced. It all happened so quickly, the stabbing, the convenient resolution. It all really happened. If I couldn't convince myself of the harsh reality of all that occurred, I feared madness would overtake me. And so I continued.

"I mean Joe is going to kill someone one of these days and then the news media will tap into all of the experts who will speculate on how something like this happens. And millions of people like you and me will be sitting in our living rooms shaking our collective heads in bewilderment mumbling, *what a terrible thing, and from such a good family too*, while all the time I'm going to know damn well that it was that good family's fault for not attending to their sick child's problem. Someday Joe is going to do something to someone who won't be bought off!"

Glen finally lowered his paper and stared directly at me.

"What did you say? Who was bought off?"

"Haven't you heard any of what I've been saying?" I asked in desperation.

"Joe's father paid off the world, for Christ's sake, to keep his kid out of trouble with the authorities."

Glen leaned forward. I now had his full attention.

"So, how much did you settle for?" With the paper now in his lap, his eyes blazed into mine demanding an answer.

I shook my head slowly. I couldn't control a slight, tentative smile on my lips urgently needing, imploring Glen's laughter at his own joke. But the smile faded as he just sat there somberly. And then he most sincerely asked again.

"Well? How much did you get out if this?"

I wasn't smiling anymore as he continued.

"Don't tell me that everyone got a piece of this but you!" Now, he was angry. "Who all got paid?"

My tears of shock and disappointment began to build as he continued.

"How many of them, Lauren?" He stalked over to me, grabbed my shoulders and began to shake me. "Who?" His fury released my words.

"Mike's parents, Dr. Ford, the nurse...I don't know who else," I spat out my answer.

"Shit, Lauren, none of them went through what you did. That brat would have died if it weren't for you and the other one would be behind bars. You should have gotten the yeoman's share!"

I had no answer for him. I began to cry so hard I had trouble breathing and those God-awful gasps for air kept shaking my body. I was mortified at Glen's reaction, appalled by his attitude. The angrier I grew the harder I cried and the more ghastly the noises I produced.

Glen was glaring at me at arms length for what seemed quite a long time. Finally, his expression began to soften changing from one of fury to "that" look, that God-Damned, patronizing, condescending look.

"Now, baby, stop that horrid noise."

He drew me into his arms cradling me and began to rub my back gently.

"Come on now. Ease up, baby. It's all right. Come on."

I felt my sobs begin to lessen. Still unable to speak, I just listened as he continued.

"That's better. No need to feel so badly."

I was waiting for some sign that I had misinterpreted his meaning. Yet I knew that it would never come. And then he spoke the absolute confirmation.

"I'm sorry I upset you so." He spoke softly now, gently.

"Come on, baby, that's right. Breathe, baby, just breathe."

As my breathing calmed, he held me at arm's length, rubbing me gently from elbow to shoulder.

"There, that's getting better. Oh, baby, you're just not experienced enough to handle this kind of situation. I shouldn't have jumped on you like that. I don't know what I was thinking." His voice was laced with concern.

"I love you so much. You're my sweet, naïve baby girl. It's all my fault for upsetting you. Shit, I am so sorry. I'm the stupid one. You would never think of getting your fair share from a situation like this. It's just all too messy for you. You shouldn't even be exposed to this kind of stuff. The bastards never should have exposed you to all of this," he continued, now gently rubbing my back.

"This is what you have me for, baby, to protect you. This is why you need me."

He gently rocked me back and forth as my crying continued to subside. I was trying to process what he was saying when I felt my body stiffen on its own accord as his rubbing of my back began to take on meaning. I tensed. Then he began to kiss me. I felt his hands sneaking down my sides then up the front of my blouse.

"Baby, you are the softest thing on this earth. God, I love the way you feel. Come on, that's better, ease up."

I was aware of being touched yet I felt nothing. He gently laid me down on my back and was on top of me, lightly kissing my neck, my shoulders. I watched him carefully unbutton the front of my blouse and kiss down my neck and chest. He continued to whisper between the kisses.

"That is what I love the most about you, baby. You are so vulnerable. I love taking care of you. I will always take care of you."

He was gently stroking my cheek now while laying his head on my chest. I couldn't recall the last time he had made such an effort to be gentle and slow. I still felt nothing. And I said nothing as he undressed himself and then me.

His body was young and tight with sleek, lean muscles. When he knelt beside the couch and gathered me up, I felt totally secure in his arms. He lifted me without the slightest effort. In one fluid motion I was up off of the couch and on my way up the stairs to the bedroom.

I looked directly into adoring green eyes as he stood over me for a moment in silence. I finally found some words.

"Glen, I want you to know something about what happened today."

"It doesn't matter, baby," he whispered.

And, before I had a chance to tell him that I wasn't naïve; that I had very consciously handled the situation the way that I felt was right, his lips were smothering my words. It was no use. It was just no use.

He continued his uncharacteristically methodical kissing. I lay staring off at nothing, unable to feel, unable to respond. How many times had I hoped for him to take some time with our lovemaking as he battered in and out of me? How often had I pleaded for him to go slowly only to be reminded that if I weren't so damned sexy, maybe he could control himself longer? And now, here he was laboring over my body with care and love and tenderness and it was all too late.

I closed my eyes tightly, concentrating, concentrating on his lips upon my body. I tried desperately to flow with his gentle rhythm, to be carried away someplace new. But there was too much reality blocking the way. I had heard too much too clearly. I tried to turn my memory off. I tried to fill my mind with thoughts of loving tenderness, but I was unable to feel it. I was all at once aware that there was nothing left to feel except the heaviness of Glen's body on top of me.

Then I concentrated on his heartbeat. There was a time in the beginning when we lay together; the coursing of his blood had felt as if it was a part of my own body. I had loved him so much, needed to be attached to him as if there was only one source of life's blood flowing between the two of us, binding us together. But no longer. Silly, foolish girl that I was.

I felt the pace of his beating heart lessen, as did the depth of his breathing. He lay perfectly still. Then he raised his hand once again and began to gently stroke my cheek.

"I love you, Lauren. I really do love you."

"I love you too, Glen." I was the one answering reflexively now.

Reality

That seemed like a lifetime away from here, now, at Dawson Skill Center. Yet it was the blackballing by Dr. Ford that left me with no other options than teaching in the inner city if I wanted to teach in the Chicago area.

I had to learn from my past. I was making the rules for my own life now. I had begun to build on my knowledge that I was a good teacher. I would adjust to this situation better than I had managed at Oakstream. I had to somehow make this work.

I could do that. I would do that. After all, this class wasn't *that* bad.

The reading levels varied from second grade to twelfth, math skills likewise and science acumen was non-existent. Those were the negatives. What I did have going for me was ME. I was such an oddity, they arrived curious to see who I was and what I would do.

My reaction to Henry Barton's foul-mouthed greeting that first day, while totally unplanned and completely unintentional, apparently made a good impression, for they came to my classroom thereafter with a degree of respect. Even the students just showing up to be logged in for attendance points, while not contributing or even exhibiting any interest at all, still did not inhibit or interfere in any way with the rest of the class's growing enthusiasm. I felt confident that I could help them and have some fun doing it.

And I had Willie. His dominant presence, so willing to learn, totally open to the experience, affirmed to the rest of the class, especially the other macho men, that it was O.K. to let me teach them something. But he did even more. He encouraged them all, with my blessing, to use me, my knowledge, to help them achieve their own personal goals.

Yes, I had Willie. But he was still such an enigma.

Who was this man? What was he really doing here? As of yet, I had not gotten the answers to those questions, but no matter. I was really teaching, and I liked it.

I had begun by concentrating on basic English grammar.

"Ann, please tell the class which of the words in this sentence are nouns."

I pointed to the sentence, "I enter the classroom" which I had written on the board.

"Sheeeeeit!" she hissed.

The class broke into laughter. I smiled.

"You mean *merde*. If you must swear, I'll teach you to do it with a bit of elan," I quipped good-naturedly.

"Whud you mean?" Ann asked.

"Whud she say?" PreDennis poked Willie.

Willie shrugged looking around as the whole class started murmuring. I had somehow gained the attention of the entire class.

"I said merde. It means 'shit' in French."

Everyone was smiling then laughter began to course through the room.

"You knows French?" One of them shouted.

"Yes. I took it in school. I think I can still remember the important words like merde!"

They all laughed again. I looked around amazed at having their total attention. Nary a one was distracted or whispering with another or even fidgeting. Maybe I had something here.

"J'entre dans la salle de class." I spoke very slowly.

A respectful din erupted.

"You hear dat?"

"Whud she say?"

I noticed Willie's intense gaze. He looked very impressed. Looking around the classroom, they all looked so impressed. I was utterly embarrassed. How could they be so impressed by something which to my mind was totally unimpressive? I had taken French in school beginning in the sixth grade. There was nothing unique or particularly significant about the fact that I could now speak a few phrases. But I saw the looks on their faces and I knew that I had an opportunity here. Perhaps I could use this undeserved admiration to reach them in a different way.

"I stated again slowly, 'J'entre dans la salle de class." I then repeated it once again.

I wrote it directly under the same sentence in English that was on the board as I spoke it again.

"Anyone want to guess what it means?"

No one looked around. No one snickered or laughed. They were all staring intently at the words on the board.

One timid hand shot into the air, the pure joy of discovery all over PreDennis' face.

"I enter the classroom!" He shouted excitedly before I could call on him.

"Yea, dat's it. Jess like da one in English." The voice came from the back of the classroom. It was a voice I had not heard since that first day when everyone had to introduce themselves. I had to smile.

"Look at dat. Some a da words is almost alike," another student erupted with a spontaneous observation.

There was general amazement circulating through the room. The excited energy was building.

I spoke the sentence again. No one moved. I had them. They were listening.

"O.K. now, listen once more. Remember a noun is a person, place or thing. See if by the way the words sound in the sentence, the emphasis put on the words, you can pick out the nouns in this sentence."

I repeated it slowly. No one raised a hand. I knew I had to do something before I lost them. This was too good an opportunity to miss.

"O.K. that might have been a bit hard for the first try. What's the definition of a noun again? Anyone?"

"Person, place or thing..." The answer was shouted out.

"That's right; a person place or thing." Heads were nodding in agreement.

"Now in English; 'I enter the classroom.' What are the nouns?"

"I n classroom," Willie's unmistakable voice sang out confidently.

"Good. Now in French. Listen once more and see if you can pick out one of the nouns. 'J'entre dans la salle de class.'"

I repeated it several times before someone in the back shouted out.

"I think, Class!" Robert volunteered.

I couldn't believe he actually spoke without the threat of death!

"Yea, dat." Someone else shouted and everyone seemed in agreement.

"Well, you all think almost right."

He beamed.

"Classroom is one word in English, 'salle de class' in French"

"So dat was kinda a trick question you tossed us, huh?" Robert reprimanded.

I smiled.

"I guess it was. But you caught it and not only did you volunteer an answer but you volunteered a correct one at that."

"Yea." He beamed as PreDennis got out of his seat to give Robert a high five.

"So, English: 'I enter the classroom.' French: 'J'entre dans la salle de class.' Repeat the French with me: 'J'entre dans la salle de class.' They all repeated.

"Excellent! You have all just spoken French."

The entire class was literally basking in their accomplishment.

"Now, Mr. Barton, why don't you try this one?"

I wrote another sentence on the board as I spoke it slowly.

"Je dit bonjour au professor." What word is the subject in this sentence?"

He looked around embarrassed. He still was uncomfortable in my presence after the way he had greeted me that first day and Willie's instant retaliation.

"Come come, Henry," I said playfully.

"I picked this sentence especially for you," I teased.

"Je dit bon jour au professor." I repeated it for him once again.

"Remember, the subject is the noun that does the action. Give it a try, Henry. What's the subject?"

It was obvious that Henry was not going to join in the fun. He was beginning to look truly miserable. And, as happened so often when I needed help, just when I was beginning to feel uncomfortable about joking at Henry's expense, Willie stepped in.

"Whut's it means, Teach? Why's it 'specially fer Henry?" Willie asked.

Pausing for effect I stated flatly.

"It means, 'I say hello to the teacher'."

The class roared at poor Henry's expense. My guilt was eased when Willie did manage to coax a small smile from Henry after some playful rib-poking.

I hated to see the day end. I wasn't sure what I had really accomplished, but it sure felt good. They were curious and attentive and I realized that I just might have a chance to get through to them. I could teach them English grammar by teaching them French.

"You really is differnt."
As had become his habit, Willie stayed after class to talk with me.
"How so?" He took my coat from the closet and brought it to me.
"I donno...you jess got a differnt way a seein' thins, sayin' thins; gettin' me ta see thins...I don't know zactly...like French. I means French, here at Dawson? French?"
"I'm just doing my job, Willie. I have to use any way I can think of to get through to you guys. So, if French works, then I use French. It's my job."
"Dat's jess what I means. An you'll do it too. No one usually gives a damn. Dey jess shovel out da same ol' shit an if we don't git it, too fuckin' bad fer us. But you's differnt. Ya don't jess say ya wants ta help. Ya really will help. I knows ya will."
"How can you be so sure when I'm not?"
"How kin ya doubts it? Ya can do anythin'."
I started to laugh. I was immediately sorry when I saw the expression on his face. He thought I was laughing at him and this was not a man people laughed at.
"Willie, I was laughing because it wasn't so long ago, when I was married, that I wasn't even sure I could make it on my own, let alone help others to do so."
"Married?"
"Yes for a short time. I was very young."
"Ya gots kids?"
"No. He wanted them but...I don't know, something made me stay in school and finish my education first. I guess my instincts served me well. I had to establish control over my own life before I could be responsible for another's."
"Woowee! Was ya born sensible?"
This time we laughed together.

"No, actually. For a time there sensibility wasn't even in my vocabulary."

He looked at me quizzically.

"It's a long story," I quipped almost dismissively with a wave of my hand.

"I gots time," he stated sincerely.

I looked at my watch. I really had no plans and it was nice just talking. There was something about him that made me want to tell him all about me. And he seemed so hungry to know. What harm could it do?

"Where should I start?" I was actually talking to myself more than to him.

"Beginnin' always works best fer me." He flashed that totally endearing smile at me.

"O.K, the beginning then. I guess it truly started one August day when I was fifteen.

My parents belonged to a country club and I spent a good deal of time that summer at the pool hoping the rays would bake me brown enough to last well into the winter. I had all the typical teenaged self-esteem problems. I thought I had really terrible skin. At times I felt like my face looked like a pepperoni pizza. I thought I was way too chubby and my hair, ugh, I could never get it to look as cool as Cher's! My solution was to get a great tan, thinking then I'd have some semblance of appeal to the guys when school started up again."

"Ya gots ta be kiddin. Country club? An I jess knows ya wasn't fat. Ya musta been somethin' ta see even den."

"Now, whose story is this?" I feigned irritation.

But I was smiling at the compliment.

"I really did feel that way. I was very insecure."

Willie gave me a 'who are you trying to kid' look so I just continued with my story.

"Well, anyway, I saw this beautiful boy strutting around the deck of the pool. I had never seen him there before. Believe me, I would have noticed. I remember thinking that his blonde hair seemed to flow into one continuous golden haze with his tanned body as I squinted in the sun's glare.

He dove smoothly into the water. Back and forth he swam with rhythmic strokes while the sun reflected off of the golden beads of water studding his back. I was mesmerized. I had never before seen anything so beautiful. He was long and lean. It was as if his body wasn't moving at all...only smooth, reaching arms and fluttering feet pushed him across the pool.

And then, there he was in his deep green trunks dripping puddles of water at his feet as he came out of the pool toweling his hair dry. I wondered how I could get his attention. Without even thinking, when he dove back into the pool a few minutes later, I dove in after him. But my timing was a bit off and his foot cracked into my jaw as I hit the water.

I knew I wasn't hurt, but I swam up to him anyway and said, 'Hey, didn't you feel that? Is my mouth bleeding?' He turned the darkest green eyes I had ever seen on me and sarcastically said, 'What do you want me to do about it, kid, kiss it and make it better?'"

"Man, Willie, my anger flared instantly at his blatant arrogance. You should have seen the smug look on his face. Who the hell did he think he was? What an ego!"

"Wad ya do?"

"I responded with all of the venom I could muster and a glare I had perfected on my brothers.

'Yea, big shot, kiss it and make it better in front of all of these people!'

And almost before I had time to finish the sentence, he grabbed my shoulders and planted a Hollywood style, huge kiss right on my lips in front of God and everybody!"

"Ho Teach, I dint see dat comin'?"

"Neither did I. I was so startled I said something really stupid like, 'you don't waste any time, do you?' And he said, 'If you know what you want, you should go for it.' And then he smiled so broadly it surrounded me."

"Sounds like a man I could like!" Willie said.

"That's exactly what I thought too so I introduced myself. And he did likewise:

'I'm Glen Jacobson,' he stated simply, confidently. 'I would offer you my hand but under the circumstances, I think this is more appropriate.'

And he wrapped me in a massive hug and kissed me...I don't even know how many times he kissed me there in the water, with the heat of the sun on my shoulders and the whole world watching."

I was smiling at the memory.

"Man, he had his self some style!"

"Yes, he did," I agreed softly.

"Well, what happened?"

"I fell in love."

"Dat was alls it took? I din't know'd you'd be dat easy," he teased.

"You have to realize I had never had anything like that happen to me before. He was older and gorgeous by anyone's standards. And I was hopelessly smitten not only by his looks but by his confidence. He knew what he wanted and he simply took it."

"I guess dat's whud it takes..." Willie was mocking me.

Oh God, why had I told him all of this? What the hell was I thinking? Was I thinking at all? What a mistake. How stupid. Yet, he made me feel like I could tell him anything.

I looked at my watch again. Now it was getting late.

"I really do have to go. It's a long drive home and I still have some work to do to prepare for tomorrow's class. It looks like I'm going to be boning up on my French! I'll have to revise my lesson plans."

"Oh, ya cain't stop now. Sounds like ya's gettin' ta da good stuff. I got's ta know whud happened next."

"We married then we divorced...end of story." I was the one doing the mocking now.

He smiled. "O.K. O.K. I'll let cha go, fer now, but ya gotta promise dat we'll talk again."

"Only if you'll promise to do some of the talking next time instead of letting me ramble on and on."

His arm draped across my shoulder as he helped me on with my coat. We were so close; I smelled what was becoming his familiar scent, sandalwood. I liked it. I was sure he was going to kiss me, grab me by the shoulders and kiss me. But he just stood there looking into my eyes. We stood there as that incredibly sensual moment passed. I felt cheated. What was he waiting for? Perhaps he expected me to make the first move. He was a man that women probably threw themselves at all of the time. I saw how they surrounded him in the hallway. Didn't he know I couldn't be like that...I just couldn't? Why didn't he understand that? He seemed to instinctively know so much about me, how could he not know that? But he didn't kiss me. I'm not sure if I would have let him if he had tried. God, who am I kidding?

Confusion erupted anew. What was I doing here? What in the world made me think I could actually make a difference in the lives of my students? I mean really?

WHO WAS THIS MAN?

We walked silently out into the eerily darkening evening. I wanted to find bright starlight or a huge beautiful moon to match the glow I felt must be emanating from me. I felt good. But the deep grayness of dusk darkening to night in a cloudy sky was all I found there.

What a place this was. Such wonderful highs, instant gratification when I felt I had somehow gotten through to my students. But what alarming lows. It was dizzying. I kept swinging from one extreme to the other. I had to gain control, stabilize my equilibrium before I totally lost my balance and fell flat on my face. Could Willie be the anchor I needed? Did I really need an anchor? I had to start making it on my own. Could I successfully break that very old habit of always having to rely on a man?

"See ya tamorrow, Teach."

"Weren't you going to call me Lauren?"

"I means no disrespect. I jess think 'Teach' feels right." He was visibly shaken at the thought that he had offended me.

"If ya don't likes it, I'll call ya Lauren." He so wanted to make it right.

"It's O.K., Willie. Teach is just fine. Actually, I would respond to whatever you called me."

God, I regretted it before I was even finished saying it. I was doing that a lot lately. I was so damned frustrated. All of our conversations since that first day ended with the same feeling of tremendous frustration. I could see how he looked at me. I could sense his desire, as I knew he sensed mine. How much longer was this going to go on? Why didn't he just get it over with already? It was the 70's for Christ's sake and we were two adults. Yes, he was my student but he was almost ten years older then I. This was not your typical student/teacher relationship. Nothing at Dawson could be classified as typical, for that matter. And it was something we both wanted, two consenting adults, so why not? We could then put it past us and get on with our lives.

But what would happen once the barriers of propriety were dropped? I sensed he felt the same way I did. Scared. There was more to this than just animal attraction. Neither of us wanted to risk all that we were beginning to share with a stupid false move. No matter how different we were, our background, our cultures, in this we felt as one.

Our daily good-byes were always the same. The cold Chicago winter the setting for a brief smile, a simple *see ya tomorrow* and he was gone, disappearing into the darkness. Where did he go? Where did he come from? How did he end up in this place? Who was this man?

French!

The noises were not those of a school. I think that is what struck me first upon entering Dawson. The whirring of electric tools, the clanging of metal hitting metal, the grinding of gears were the echoes within these halls of learning. Although a new structure, the building itself was designed and constructed with self-preservation as the only concern. There was nothing breakable, damageable or the least bit unnecessary to be found within its walls.

Bare-boned construction was the term to describe where I now found myself spending the majority of my waking hours. Nary a window through which to daydream was to be found. Nor was there a carpet or even a piece of fabric of any kind anywhere to take the metallic tinge off of the constant noise of the shop.

Like the revving of a car, the noise seemed to fuel the internal engines of the skill center's population, building, ever building toward the moment when, popping into gear, an explosion of speeding energy erupts. I could see the pent-up energy in their eyes. Even their walk exuded ready-to-burst, emotion. There was not a casual, even gait to be seen in the entire building. Instead, arms swung from rotating shoulders with heads bouncing in opposite directions from hips swinging and swaying. Every muscle seemed to be called upon to exaggerate the simple act of walking.

Constant grating noise, sterile industrial landscape, hip-hop bravado required, not what one would consider fertile ground in which to be planting the seeds of knowledge.

My classroom, like all of the rest in the building, was floor tiled a muddy brown. The walls were painted a greenish-gray. My desk was gray metal with a stark architectural design that screamed pure function and was bolted to the floor. My chair was of the molded metal variety with no seat cushion and was also gray. Gray metal desks, styled like the functional wooden type of decades past with one bulging arm extending like a flat seatbelt holding the student in, were the only other furnishings in the room. But unlike their ancestors, these had none of the warmth of wood nor did they offer the friendly possibility of leaving a secret message or even just one's initials etched for eternity, or just for the next student to conspiratorially partake of.

There were no bulletin or display boards. No extra paraphernalia of any kind allowed, or so I was told upon my employment. Nothing was allowed that could be stolen...or *don't bother complaining when it was!*

The school had no funds to provide anything but strictly educational necessities. This was a learning environment totally void of any of the educational stimuli that I had simply taken for granted in all of my experiences as both student and teacher.

Still, as the weeks went by, I approached my task enthusiastically. I could ignore the negatives. I had made a start, a good start and so very quickly! I cautioned patience during my soul-searching, knowing that an undertaking such as this would take time to be deemed truly successful.

I felt good. I sensed true growth potential here. For what I considered to be a relatively small capital investment of time and energy, I was convinced would generate major returns for my students. And Glen thought that I had not a clue about successful business concepts!

I was going to succeed. But most importantly I was beginning to feel that some of my students sensed their own success as well. For many of them, this was the first time in their lives that they had experienced such feelings. And they liked it.

As the weeks passed, I became aware of more and more students showing up in my classroom for the last half hour of the day. This was the time I set aside for French. During this time we played with the language in the context of what we were studying during our English Grammar lessons.

For some of my students this was the only time I saw them. Others were not on my class list at all. They were simply curious. Word had spread quickly around the school. I was astounded. I actually had students from other classes crashing my class. I hated to send them away, but I had no choice. I knew that I couldn't be responsible for them skipping their other classes.

So I wasn't surprised when my door opened during one of my French classes. Mellie Thomas entering my classroom did surprise me.

"Mr. Jackson wants ta see you NOW!" She yelled from the back of the class then she turned to the students. "Class dismissed!" She hissed.

No *excuse me for interrupting* or *may I speak with you in the hall a moment?* No, not Mellie. She turned on her heels, glared at me then stormed out of the room.

I had to smile. She was a joke.

"Well, I guess that's all for today." I said as lightly as I could. My students responded warmly.

"What's her problem?" PreDennis expressed the apparent sentiments of the class.

"Not to worry, guys. What you need to think about is reviewing the material for that quiz we're having tomorrow."

There were the expected frowns and moans. Even though adults, students of any age were all kids at heart with the same reactions to homework.

"I'll see you all tomorrow," I smiled.

As I pulled my things together, I couldn't help wondering what in the world Jackson wanted to see me about. I surely didn't want to make being summoned to the principal's office a habit. It was as if Willie read my thoughts.

"Whud ya think he wants?"

"Don't know."

"Do ya wants me ta go wicha?"

I smiled.

"Willie, that's sweet, but don't you think it would look a bit odd if I brought one of my students with me?"

"I'd jess be dere if ya needed me."

"I doubt that I need a bodyguard to talk to the administrator of the school. But thanks."

We stood for a moment. It was all so damned innocent.

"I'll wait here ta walk ya ta yer car when you's done."

I nodded in appreciation as I left the room.

Now What?

Leonard Jackson was the Administrator of Dawson Skill Center. He was short, squat, very dark skinned and sported one of those silly little moustaches that was a cross between the one atop the lip of Cab Calloway and the one worn by Adolph Hitler. He was not an educator; he was a bureaucrat. He was not the man who hired me. My employment had been approved by the board of the Chicago City Colleges. Dawson was under their auspices. The program at Dawson was considered one of the City College's experiments in adult education.

I had only a brief encounter with Leonard Jackson on my first day on the job. And a perfunctory nod constituted his response to my introduction. What did he want now?

"Sit down, Gates," he ordered without the slightest attempt at courtesy. "I've been gettin' complaints 'bout you."

"From whom?" I was shocked into the chair facing his desk.

"Whom doesn't matter." He mockingly stressed the ooom with derision.

"I hear you let 'em smoke. And just look at your clothes. You prance 'round here like some goddamned hippie. And where do you get off teachin' French when most of 'em can't even manage English?"

His growing anger caused mine to begin to flair as well. What was this place? Why did everyone that worked here seem to hate first and find out the facts later?

"I don't know where you're getting this information." I began trying to hide my defensive anger.

"First of all, I do not let them smoke and there is nothing inappropriate about my clothes AND I am not teaching French, I'm teaching English grammar..."

"You're teachin' French," he interrupted before I could explain.

"Don't you go takin' me for no fool, girl. You think I don't know what goes on here, everything that goes on here? I've heard it from several people."

"Look, these students dropped out of school because it wasn't important to them. For whatever reason, something other than school had a greater appeal. Now they're back, if only to get a bigger check each month. We've got another chance to reach them. They're interested, curious about French. It's different. It's simply a new way to look at an old subject that they only remember as being boring and useless. But using something new and kinda sexy, French, they're learning English grammar in spite of themselves. What difference does it make what tools I use as long as they're learning? Isn't that what I'm paid to do?"

A mask of pure hatred covered his face. Oh no. Not him too.

"You look here you white-assed cunt, I don't wantcha here. None of us wants you here. I fought the board hirin' you. Hundreds a black teachers outta work, good teachers who understand the way thin's really are, how thin's get done. And they stick your pasty looking face in here for me to deal with. What do you know 'bout a place like this or these people? You drive here from that other world each morning and rush right back to it as soon as you can get your skinny ass outta here at night. French...shit, the machine shop's where their future is, if they have any future at all, not the fuckin' Louvre. But I'm stuck with you...for now. I don't like it and believe me, I'll make it so's you don't like it neither! We don't need no do-gooder comin' here slummin. You're gonna end up hurt...or worse."

All of my shocked amazement at his foul-mouthed, utterly insulting barrage morphed into anger as his last words sunk in.

"Are you threatening me?" I couldn't believe what I was hearing.

"Predictin', that's all. You're not the first."

There was such hatred in his voice he left me unable to respond.

"NO FUCKIN' FRENCH! While you're here, just put in your time and go. You got it?"

Maybe he was right. It was very apparent I did not understand; not him, not this place.

I felt the tension flow down my legs as I rose from the chair. I left the room without another word. I felt wobbly; dazed from the glancing verbal blows I had endured. Halfway down the hall I was aware that I had tightened my face into a half-smile mask of my own, instinctively trying not to let him see just how very effective his scare tactics really were. It took great effort to relax the gritted teeth behind the mask and to ease my facial muscles back to their normal state.

What was this place?

"Sweet Jesus, what happen' ta you?" Willie greeted me at my classroom door. He hesitated then gently laid a hand on my shoulder.

"I'm not quite sure." I whispered.

"Sid down. Ya look terrible."

The moment that passed in silence did not help. I just couldn't quite focus on what had just happened. Sentence fragments kept flying through my brain and I rewound the conversation and played it over and over again. Willie sat patiently, just waiting, as if he knew there was no way I could be rushed into an explanation.

"He doesn't want me here. He said no one wants me here. They all resent that I got the job instead of a black teacher. He won't let me continue using French to teach English." I turned to face him.

"Oh, God, Willie, I am in big trouble here. I think he threatened me. No, I know he threatened me. He said I'd end up hurt...or worse if I stayed."

Willie sat quietly listening, his face totally expressionless.

"I think I'm in over my head here."

A multitude of confused thoughts were building. What had I done wrong? Mellie Thomas, Leonard Jackson, who were these people? What were they?

"What is this place?" I looked pleadingly into his eyes hoping to see something there that would make some sense to me.

"I'm so confused. I'm just trying to do my job," I could only pitifully whisper.

"You's really shook. C'mon, calm down. I's here. No one's gonna hurtcha." He put his arm around my shoulder.

"You gotta know I won't let no one hurtcha." He put both arms around me in a protective hug.

It was so easy to forget the fear and confusion while in his arms. Easy to let him fold me into soft, secure, wonderfully comfortable warmth. No one could hurt me. He made me believe it while in his embrace.

Not again! Not another man that wanted to protect me! This

wasn't gonna work...or was it? If it wasn't right to let him comfort me why was it so damned easy to accept?

Once he sensed that I was O.K. a vicious, hate-filled voice interrupted my thoughts.

"I'll kill da bastard fer doin' dis ta you."

It was a stranger holding me.

"Willie, you're scaring me. You sound so serious."

I pulled away and stared into his eyes. I saw them change from steely resolve to the soft endearing gaze I had come to rely on when he looked at me.

"Da last thin I wants is ta make ya more scared. I jess wanna do somethin'. Make him see dat it's not O.K. ta treatcha dat way. You's special. He cain't be treatin' ya dat way."

"It's O.K. Really, I'm fine now. It just took me by surprise. Man, he totally blind-sided me. Everything in this place is so foreign to me. I guess he was right about that. I do feel like I have dropped onto another planet each time I come through the doors. But it's O.K. I'm going to handle it."

I had to pause. I steeled myself, willed myself not to start crying. I had to stop reacting to every uncomfortable situation with tears. That Lauren was the past. I had earned the right to a new Lauren. I had the right, now I just had to embrace her. Man, that was a good pep talk to self, yet I still struggled to get the words out without tears.

"It's just I love this class, you know, I really do, and I think that I have something valuable to offer but I can't do that if he's going to tie my hands."

I paused again for composure.

"But it's not just him. It's all of the staff here. At lunch I sit alone, every day, not by my choice. And, I'm totally ignored when I try to strike a conversation in the halls with anyone except my students. At first I thought it was because I was new. I figured it would take a little time. God, how stupid could I be? Time will only make it worse. Just like he said. They are all just waiting to make it uncomfortable enough for me here that I'll finally just quit. They all hate me so intensely. Mellie actually spat in my face...she SPAT IN MY FACE, for Christ's sake! And Jackson just did the same thing with words."

One angry tear escaped the corner of my eye and made its way down my cheek. Willie gently wiped it away with his thumb.

"You seem to be the only person here who doesn't hate me," I whispered pitifully more to myself than to him.

Before I could say more he had engulfed me in a loving hug. We just stood there as my tears of rage and confusion began to flow.

Damn! I felt so stupid. First, at being so naïve to my situation and then, even more so, by letting him see me so unhinged. Who was he to me, after all? How in the world had I allowed myself to totally lose it in front of him? Was it because he was with me that I allowed myself to expose my vulnerably, so nakedly displayed in front of him? I knew he would provide unquestioning support. How did I know that? What made me so sure of his feelings, his reactions?

And he did not disappoint.

As I regained control, I knew that I had to say something to bring things back to 'simple conversation' once again.

"Maybe I'm just destined to never get along with any authority figure. Jackson is just the latest in a long list of people that I wish I had had someone like Mellie Thomas on my side to handle for me. Where are the Mellie's of this world when you really need them?" I made a pretty feeble attempt at humor.

"Like who else 'sides Jackson?"

"Well, I sure could have used someone to spit in my ex-mother-in-law's eye." I started to laugh.

"Yep, I would have loved to have seen someone do that."

"She was bad news, huh?"

"That, my dear Willie, is the understatement of the year."

"Whud she do?"

I walked toward the desk and began fusing with some papers on it.

"I really don't think you're interested in my ex-mother-in-law."

"I is...really. She musta had some kinda major impact on ya fer ya ta bring her up first thin like dat."

I laughed, nodding my head in agreement.

"'Major impact, definitely sums it up."

"Well, whud she like? Whud she do?"

"I don't know." I took a moment to reflect on all that had occurred between Cynthia and me.

"It's not that easy, in ten words or less, to describe. It was more her entire being."

I was truly at a loss to put Cynthia Jacobson into words. But I became aware of the tremendous relief I felt to be thinking about something other than my current problem, even if it was one of my past problems that was creating the distraction. But it wasn't the past that had caused the relief. It was Willie. He had managed to completely divert my attention from the fear and confusion. It was all Willie.

"Let me give you an example. And mind you this is just one of a multitude of equally obnoxious incidences that I can call to mind about the woman."

"Sounds great." He settled into his seat as I leaned against my desk facing him.

"Great or not here, goes."

"It was the day before the wedding. Glen - that was my husband to be - his dad, Arthur, his mom, Cynthia and I were running a ton of last minute errands. Glen had bought his tux at an exorbitantly priced shop on Oak Street. We all went in to pick it up.

This trés chic salesman greeted us with, 'Ah, bonjour, bonjour, Madame, Mademoiselle, et Messieurs.' He led us deep into the store. With an oh-so-suave gesture, he directed me and Glen's parents to sit and wait while Glen went to try on the suit. I sank deep into one of the huge leather chairs he pointed out to us."

"No wonder ya knows French so good. I don't go nowheres I needs ta know it!"

He was teasing me but I really didn't mind.

"Alright, come on, I know you see my point. I was overwhelmed by all of it. They were rich. I mean RICH. And this store just made it all suddenly sink in. You had to see this place. There were fashion magazines casually strewn about on a large glass and chrome coffee table and several very highly-styled *browsers* whispered to each other while they gingerly fingered the expensive fabrics. I was impressed."

I realized that I had become very wrapped up in my recollections. I thought that I must have been boring Willie to death. But then I took a good look at him. I was surprised to see just how truly engaged he seemed to be. Why in the world would he be so interested?

"Ya tells a great story." It was as if he had read my mind and was answering my question. I didn't know if he was teasing me or not.

"Yea right..."

"No really. Ya describes thin's, like how stuff looked n what ya was feelin, not jess whud happened. I likes dat. Like I was really dere. Kinda like why books or movies is good. You's a nachal born storyteller, girl!"

It was one of the nicest compliments I had ever received.

"Maybe this wasn't such a good idea." I had suddenly become uncomfortable. What was I doing telling him all of this?

"No, no, go on, please. I's interested...really," he stated firmly.

"Really?"

"Really."

And I was treated to one of his mega-watt smiles. How in the world could I ever say no to that smile?

"O.K. then."

Willie actually looked relieved.

"Anyway, I could hardly believe this store. Everything was so elegant. It was quiet, almost reverent. I felt if I were to pick up one of the magazines and look through it, just turning the pages would make too much noise; disturb the piety of the setting. Then Glen stepped out of the dressing room in his tux.

Whoa, did he look great. His eyes never left mine, the excitement they held was infectious, there was nothing in the world I wanted more than to marry this man. Then as if out of nowhere...

'That's awful!' Cynthia screamed.

'Twelve hundred dollars for a suit and the shoulders are lop-sided. He's getting married tomorrow. Arthur, just look how this suit fits!'

She shook with anger, face red in distress. The salesman came running. All of a sudden there was turmoil throughout the store.

Other shoppers were stopped in their tracks by her bellowing. The tailor rushed over to us while the store manager began trying to convince the other shoppers that nothing was wrong but having both eyes and ears it seemed a useless task. Cynthia's face was contorted in an irate scowl and the vehemence of her words echoed off of the walls. Everyone that could, seemed to make a bee line for the door. Cynthia had created such havoc; I scarcely recognized the store from just one moment before.

Then the tailor took his tape from around his neck and measured both arms from shoulder to wrist. He pulled at the jacket's sleeves, first one then the other, critically examining how much linen from Glen's shirt sleeve showed.

I remembered hearing my mother tell my brother, as he dressed for a prom, that a proper gentleman always had bit of the linen from your shirt sleeve showing from beneath your coat sleeve."

"No shit? I never heard dat. Course I never wore no tux neither!"

"You never went to prom?"

Willie just smiled waiting for what I had said to sink in. DUH! How stupid could I be? He had dropped out of school before the 8th grade. Genius. That was why he was in my class! Had I been able to slink out of the room without explanation I would have done so instantly. What an idiot.

"I'm so sorry Willie." Was all I could lamely offer.

"Forget it," he smiled and without skipping a beat asked; "So, what happened next?"

"Well, the tailor, after determining that the sleeves were indeed the right length said softly to Cynthia. 'But Madame, the fit is exquisite. Look, it measures perfectly.'

Meanwhile, Cynthia had taken her gold cigarette case from her purse and began waving it in the man's face.

'Don't you tell me it's perfect. Those shoulders are lop-sided.' And then she cracked Glen in the small of the back with the gold case as she began once again to shout.

'Stand up straight, darling. Show this idiot how far off those sleeves are.' She stood back with a satisfied smirk challenging the tailor to contradict her."

"Man, she sounds like a real..." Willie shook his head as if deciding silently not to continue.

"BITCH! Go ahead and say it. But wait Willie, it gets even better. 'Arthur, do something.' She demanded.

'Do you want your son to walk down the aisle looking like this?'

Then she angrily pulled a cigarette out of the case and inserted it into her grimaced lips. And as if nothing had just transpired, Arthur gallantly produced a lighter and lit it for her.

'Sweetheart, calm down. The suit looks fine,' Arthur soothed.

Cynthia inhaled deeply as if in deep concentration and then her face morphed into a contorted mask.

I'm telling you Willie, I had never seen anything like it. All I could do was stare in fascination.

Slowly she began spitting out the words as the smoke oozed from her mouth and nose.

'I should have known.' She moaned. 'You're siding with them against me.'

She stood rigid, poised with arm cocked, jerking the cigarette in and out of her mouth a la Bette Davis. I could barely make out her features for all of the smoke swirling about in front of her face.

'Sweetheart, no one's siding against you. You're just nervous. It's understandable. Your first born, your baby is getting married. You want everything perfect. But look at him. He looks great.' Arthur spoke soothingly again.

A blast of smoke struck his face. His demeanor changed instantly and, as if bracing himself for what he knew was to come, took a deep breath and stood there facing her in silence.

'He looks great? It's perfect? It Shits!' She shouted through clenched teeth.

'I am so humiliated at your total lack of loyalty...and in front of all of these people, and Lauren!' Now her voice was quivering."

"She really pulled a scene like dat?" Willie seemed suspicious.

"Could I make something like that up? No, she created quite a stir."

"An ol' Arthur? How'd he react?"

"Arthur started fawning all over her, rubbing her back and finally got her settled into one of the chairs promising to handle it. Then he went and helped Glen out of the suit coat and threw it at the tailor who had been standing there in total disbelief as the scene unfolded before him.

Being smacked in the face with a wad of fabric brought him back to the reality of the situation and he scurried back into the workroom as Arthur commanded,

'Make the alterations. We'll wait.' Then Arthur went and sat next to the now gloating Cynthia and patted her hand.

'Better, dear?' He whispered.

Leaning her head on his shoulder she purred, 'Yes, darling.'

All of the crazy shouting and suit-coat throwing had now been replaced by an eerie silence. I sat dumbfounded. I looked over at Glen to reinforce my sanity. Seeing my glance, he came and sat next to me. Quietly I whispered,

'Oh God, I'm so embarrassed...' but he interrupted me.

'Embarrassed? Why? Screw 'em! We're paying for the suit; it should be perfect!'

'That's not the point.' I told him.

'She didn't have to make such a scene. There are other ways to handle...' But he interrupted me again.

'She's getting it fixed isn't she?'

Before I could make my case so Glen would understand what I was trying to say, the tailor was back with the jacket and motioned to Glen to try it on again."

Willie had begun to shake his head.

"What are you thinking?" I asked.

"I jess don't see how ya stayed mixed up wiff folks like dem. How'd ya marry dat guy?"

Looking back on it now, I had to agree with him. But at the time...

"I was young and insecure, and I kept making excuses for them out of...fear, I guess. Fear of my own naiveté. Fear that Glen would see the truth about who I really was and not want me. He'd see that I didn't really know any of the things that I thought he would want in a wife and I figured the Jacobson's surely must know everything to have all that they had and live the way that they lived. What else can I say, I was nineteen."

"So, did he have da tux fer da weddin'?"

"You bet. He tried it on again and although it looked exactly the same to me, Cynthia was satisfied that the tailor had made significant changes and it was now perfect.

Everyone was smiling. I couldn't take my eyes off of Cynthia. As their driver drove the car up to the curb, she winked at me and linked her arm through Arthur's and propelled him out of the store and into the backseat. As we pulled away into traffic, she snuggled close to him, looked directly at me and chuckled, then said,

'If you want something done right you have to know how to handle the help.'"

Willie sat back in his seat smiling.

"I think you's right. A tussle tween her an Mellie could be da bout a da century!"

Before our laughter had fully subsided he asked, "So what's yo mom like? How'd she handle Cynthia?"

"Let's just say my mother had her own way of dealing with Glen's mom."

I had to smile at the recollection of the two of them together. I must have appeared rather smug for Willie reacted immediately.

"Oh, no girl. Ya can't hold back now! Not flashin' dat look. Let's hear it." He insisted with a don't mess with me look on his face.

"Alright, let me think where to start."

"There was that evening just after Glen and I announced our engagement. I had been invited to dinner at the estate. We were just finishing when Cynthia issued a command: 'Annette dear, I'll have my Courvoisier and coffee in my sitting room, with Lauren. Arthur, you and the boys occupy yourselves elsewhere.'

She rose from her mammoth Queen Ann, wing-backed chair elegantly upholstered in silk, which served, with its mate, as the host and hostess chairs within the ornately paneled dining room. She proceeded to noiselessly glide across the Oriental rug and into the two-story, domed-ceiling entrance hall, pausing briefly to beckon me to hasten my departure and follow her.

I quickly brought the Italian lace napkin from my lap to my lips and whispered, 'Excuse me.' Glen's father smiled and nodded as I rose, following Cynthia's avenue of departure."

"My God Willie, I was so scared. For the brief journey up the stairs to Cynthia's sitting room, I was filled with apprehension and sure I would do something stupid. So stupid, like tripping and falling down the stairs, that she would forbid Glen to marry such a fool. And then to compound my fears I began to wonder why she wanted to see me alone? I wished Glen had insisted on joining us."

"Man, she really had ya freaked."

"You can't even imagine."

"But I began to feel a bit better when we entered the room and she so very kindly said,

'Sit down, Lauren, Dear' directing me with a delicate flourish of a hand onto the couch. She then sat down in a chair facing me."

I had to hesitate in my story telling as the memory of what was going on in my mind at that moment came flooding back. I was not about to tell Willie that I was worried that Cynthia had found out that this was not the first time I had been in her sitting room. I was scared that she had found out about the many times we had walked through that room on our way to their bedroom when they were away. I was panicked that she somehow knew that I had lost my virginity in her bedroom and that Glen was using that bed for his own satisfaction regularly, explaining to me that it was more exciting in his parent's bed. I was convinced that she would blame me for the awful invasion of her privacy. And wouldn't she be totally justified? I didn't want to see disgust in those penetrating green eyes, Glen's green eyes, as she looked upon this little slut seated before her. I was petrified of being the target of her wrath.

Before Willie acknowledged the pause, I began again.

"Annette entered with a silver coffee service and the most beautiful brandy decanter I had ever seen."

"I ain't never seen no brandy decanter. Hell, any one you'd show'd me would be da mos' beautiful one I'd ever seen!" He teased.

"Stop making fun of me. Do you want to hear this or not?"

"I wanna hear it, brandy decanter n all."

"O.K. then. I'm just trying to describe her style. She never just simply did anything nor did she do anything simply. And I was so impressed with it all. I had to make a conscious effort not to gasp at the grandeur."

"Annette had left us alone. I watched with fascination every move that Cynthia made. As she poured, she spoke and I listened somewhat mesmerized. I suddenly became aware of being pleased with the opportunity of having the magnificence of Cynthia all to myself. To think, she actually wanted to have a talk with me.

We spoke of the dinner and she commented on what a great help Annette was in running the household. As I glanced around the room, so many beautiful pieces surrounded me.

'I just love your Lalique bird bookends there on the desk. Oh and that Baccarat vase is truly wonderful.' I gushed.

'You know fine crystal?' I felt a tinge of pride that she seemed impressed.

'It is one of my passions. I know a little about it...I'd like to collect someday. Oh, but I can't imagine ever having a collection like yours.'

'Oh, but you shall.'

She rose and retrieved a beautifully detailed small Lalique crystal elephant from the coffee table and handed it to me.

'And you'll begin with this little piece.' She smiled and patted my knee.

I couldn't speak. I sat stupidly, silent staring at the delicate creature in my palm, thinking that this must surely be a dream.

'You have fine taste, Lauren. You did after all choose my son.' She smiled. 'Of course you will have a wonderful collection of crystal if that's what you want. My Glen will see to it.   There is nothing we won't do to make you happy.' Her smile seemed to increase in sincerity."

"Wow!" Willie didn't have to say another word.
"Exactly what I was thinking!"

"And as the brandy decanter began to empty and the ashtray to fill, we laughed together, grew very comfortable and then she said, 'Lauren, Darling, there is one more thing I would like to discuss before I let that lucky boy of mine have you all to himself for the rest of the evening.'

Her expression had suddenly grown a bit askew. Then, somewhat off-balanced, she pushed her face much too close to mine as she seated herself next to me on the couch. With relief, I watched her settle back into a position reasonably removed from me. Now, that's better. Lauren, I just want you to know how thrilled I am to be getting such a lovely girl for a daughter. You know that Arthur and I always wanted a daughter but we have had to content ourselves with our two boys. Now, Glen is giving us a daughter!'

I was touched by her words but confused by her actions. There was a slight slur in her speech all of a sudden.

'Thank you, Mrs. Jacobson...' was all I could manage.

'Please, please, call me Mom. You must think of me as Mom now that you are engaged to my boy.' She interrupted a bit too loudly. Then she leaned tipsily and kissed my cheek.

She had become awfully high awfully fast. A bit of fear began to overtake me. What was this surprising quick change in her demeanor? I was unsure just what to do. Before I had too much of a chance to think about it, she was speaking again.

Lauren!' She shouted as if discovering buried treasure. 'It just occurred to me. My God, why didn't we think of it sooner? You'll have your wedding here...here in my beautiful house. Why, it was just meant to be. This house was just built for entertaining.'

I was startled by the intensity with which she spoke, and the volume. I had to think for a moment. Ever since I was a little girl I had always dreamed of being married in the sanctuary of our temple. I had never considered myself very religious, but it was just something that I knew I wanted. Before I could speak, she had her arm around my shoulder and continued with contagious enthusiasm.

'Just picture it. The reception on my blue stone terrace, surrounded by the rose garden; why I...we can make this wedding the social event of the season!'

The idea of the ceremony at temple and the reception in the Jacobson's garden filled my mind. God, it seemed absolutely grand. All of this elegance was at my disposal. The more I thought about it the better the idea seemed; a fairy tale wedding and me the princess. I turned my attention gratefully to Cynthia.

'It sounds spectacular! Are you sure you don't mind?'

Her expression changed instantly. She sat up, posture perfect and straightened the fabric of her skirt that had wrinkled in her lap.

'I wouldn't have it any other way, my dear.' She stated flatly. And, without another word about the wedding, she dismissed me to join Glen downstairs.

'Guess where we're having the wedding?' I gushed as I raced down the stairs. Glen stood smiling at my excitement.
'On the blue stone terrace,' he answered.
My shocked reaction caused Glen to break into laughter.
'How did you know?' I asked.
'I know my mother.' He pecked my cheek as I made my descent to the bottom step. 'You'll learn.'

I didn't know what he meant nor did I care. My wedding was going to be the social event of the season.
When I glanced up, there was Cynthia standing soberly at the top of the stairs silently observing my enthusiasm."

"Oh Teach, she really did a number on you, honey."
"I know. My naiveté back then actually makes me cringe now. I was just so caught up in the possibilities. I was envisioning the most beautiful wedding imaginable. The reception in Cynthia's garden...I mean you should have seen it. It was truly magnificent."
"Problem was, she an dat son a hers went along wiff it!"
"Yes they did. And at that point in time I was thrilled about that too." I saw a bit of confusion cross Willie's face. "Look, try to imagine a very sheltered young woman, girl actually, being thrown into such a world. I was smitten. I was overwhelmed...in a good way. Everything was happening fast and it was, I don't know, unbelievably spectacular. Can you kinda see what I was feeling?"
"Yea. I kin see hows ya gots yoself sucked in. So whad Glen have ta say 'bout it all?"

"Well, as Glen drove me home that night, he pulled the car off of the road and turned to me. There was such adoration in his eyes as we sat for a moment saying nothing. I snuggled close. He picked up the small crystal elephant I held in my lap, looked at it and then into my eyes. Without a word he kissed me deeply, passionately.

Baby', He said. 'This is just a sampling of what's to come. You'll have it all, baby. I'll see to it. You'll be dressed in the finest, housed in the best on the block and never want for anything. I promise. You're my private jewel and I'll take care of you so you'll never lose your sparkle.'"

"Man, what lines dat guy had! He really talk like dat?"

"Yep. And did I ever fall for it. I thought he was incredible. I couldn't believe that he wanted me. How could one girl ever get to be so lucky?

When I got home, even though it was late, I wanted to tell my parents of my decision. As I climbed the stairs I tried to anticipate their reaction. I knocked softly on their closed bedroom door. My mother called quietly to me, 'Come on in Sweetie.' As I opened the door, she beckoned me to her side of the bed. My father lay sleeping beside her. She clasped my hands in hers and I sat down.

'Well, how'd it go? Good dinner?' She whispered.

My description of the evening began to explode. She quieted my enthusiasm with a finger to her pursed lips. Finally, I got to the point of my chat with Cynthia.

'Mom, what would you think of the idea of having the reception at the Jacobson's house...out in the garden?' I asked not knowing why there was hesitation, almost apprehension, in my voice.

'Why? Are you thinking about it?' She asked searching my face in the darkness.

'It's just that she offered and it's so beautiful in the garden...I don't know. It seemed like a good idea.'

She cupped my face in her hands. They felt very warm. 'Is that what you want?'

I couldn't contain my smile. 'Oh yes, won't it be great?'

'If that's what you truly want.' She kissed my forehead. 'Get some sleep now. We'll talk more in the morning.'

I had just stepped out of their room and into the hallway when I heard my father's voice.

'Isn't this getting a bit out of hand? Glen has totally dominated her life and now his mother is calling the shots for the wedding.' I heard and felt his anger. Why was he so angry? Cynthia was allowing me to use her beautiful estate. I waited for my mother to explain it to him. I knew that at least she understood.

'Richard, calm down. She's in love with a very wealthy boy.

Lauren's young and so impressed with all that's ahead of her now, all that he can provide for her. She's entering a new world and she's excited about it...'

'Have we done so badly by her? He interrupted. 'She's had everything she's ever needed and most of what she's wanted. I make a hell of a good living.'

I heard my mother begin to soothe him.

'I know that and Lauren knows it too. But Rolls Royce's and mansions are what she's marrying into. Can't we try to let her enjoy it all? She's a smart girl and we raised her well. This fascination will wear off. Meanwhile, what is so terrible about letting Cynthia pamper her a little bit...if it's what Lauren wants?'

'I have always given her the best...'

"As I walked down the hall to my bedroom, I kept hearing my mother's words: 'This fascination will wear off.' I didn't like the sound of it one bit. Getting into bed, I snuggled with my dog, Levi. I was going to have my reception in the Jacobson's garden and be grand and elegant just like Cynthia. I would make Glen proud that he was marrying me."

I looked at Willie expecting to see that he had grown bored with my saga but all I saw was anticipation on his face. I said nothing waiting for him to comment.

"Well, wad happened? Ya don't tink dat I's gonna let ya stop dere?"

I had to smile.

"Really? You really want to hear more?"

"I wants ta hear it all," he stated resolutely.

I spent a moment more scouring his face for some indication that he was teasing me; I mean really, how could he be interested in all of this? But I found none so I continued.

"Well, the phone was ringing the next morning when I woke up. It was Cynthia. She suggested that we meet to finalize the wedding plans. I thought it to be an excellent idea. We agreed to meet for lunch to work out the details."

"I entered the appointed restaurant at the appointed time but neither my mother nor Cynthia had arrived yet. I went outside to enjoy the beautiful weather and wait for them. It was a glorious day, Willie. You know one of those days when everything looked perfect. Even the smell of the flowers and newly cut grass was perfect. There was a slight breeze carrying the scents swirling gently around me as I walked out of the restaurant. I inhaled deeply the sweet aroma of...contentment." Willie had a puzzled look."

"Yes, it was contentment. As the breeze played with the hem of my skirt, I contemplated the true meaning of the word contentment. I had often heard people talking about being content but I had never actually felt what it was like to experience it, until that moment."

Willie puzzlement turn into a smile.

"Don't get dose kinda days 'round here. We don't wants da smells a da projects swirling 'round us!"

Seeing my embarrassed expression, he continued.

"Jess kiddin. Really, I love's da way ya talk. Loves ta hear bout how ya felt n whatcha said. Don't stop...please." He sincerely implored.

"Are you sure I'm not boring you?"

"Let's hear some more, Teach. I's ready fer more."

"O.K. You asked for it."

"I remember thinking that everything was working out perfectly. Glen was all that I had ever dreamed of in a husband and Cynthia had welcomed me into their family by graciously offering me the opportunity of having the reception at their estate." I paused in my tale-telling just long enough for Willie to interject:

"Time fer da bubble ta bust, right? Dis has all gotta be leadin' ta a huge KABAAM!"

"Ah, my dear Willie, the wisdom you do possess!" I was then treated to one of his dazzling smiles derailing my thoughts momentarily.

"So anyway, I recognized my mother instantly in the back seat of the cab as it turned the corner and pulled up in front of the restaurant. She swung the door open and I helped her out. Her movements were graceful and her eyes shone with excitement. She appeared, as always, petite and beautiful. Her coloring is the exact opposite of mine, fair-eyed and blonde-haired. Her grooming is meticulous and while she is always appropriately dressed, she's never hard or cold. Her demeanor is proper yet oh-so-comfortable and she has the ability to blend all of that with a wonderful sense of humor. I not only love and admire her; I like her.

I had learned so much through her gentle instruction but there was so much more that I felt I needed to know to be the wife that Glen deserved."

"Getting out of the cab, she looked quite crisp that day in her smartly tailored, beige, tone-on-tone blouse and skirt.

'Hi Sweetie, you were early,' she said in greeting.

'Not too early, Glen just dropped me off a minute ago. I haven't been waiting long,' I replied as she kissed my cheek and I hers.

'Did you check inside to see if Cynthia's here?' She asked.

'She's not here yet and since it is so beautiful out here, I decided to take in the fresh air while I waited.'

She nodded agreement. We stood in silence a moment and then began to talk.

'What did you and Glen do all morning?'

'He picked me up about ten, right after you left, and we went back to his place to get another car...so I could follow him. He had to take his car into the shop to be fixed. Something different for a change!' I cocked my head with a shrug looking contrite.

'You'd think an expensive sports car would work once in a while. That little car is more trouble than it's worth.' She spoke my thoughts exactly.

'I guess, but Glen really loves it. And he says it suits me too.'

She smiled at me a bit insincerely.

"You know Willie, I think the money part of it really bothered her. Although we never had words about it, she believed, as my dad did, that one should earn what they receive. I knew they saw Glen as a demanding, spoiled boy with overly indulgent parents."

"Dey had a point." Willie mumbled.

"I wasn't stupid." I replied somewhat defensively.

"I could see how they might think that. And with the advantage of hindsight, of course they were right. But what they couldn't see and what I guess you are having a hard time understanding is how wonderful his love made me feel. Oh, I can't explain it," I was searching desperately for some way to make him understand.

"All else was eclipsed by it. There was just Glen...until all at once the Silver Shadow limousine pulled up in front of us and the Jacobson's chauffeur helped Cynthia from its confines."

"The shapely, tanned legs, contrasted by gray, lizard shoes appeared first. Then, with one swift emphatic surge, her brightly printed, Pucci clad body stood erect in front of us. The smile was fixed on the mouth, but all else was hidden in shadow by mammoth tortoise-shelled sunglasses.

'Lauren, darling!' She extended both hands, one to me, one to my mother. 'It's so good to see you both.'

She then swept past us carrying us into the restaurant in her wake. Over her shoulder she yelled instructions to the chauffeur.

'Paul, I'll be one hour, and then we must pick-up Mr. Jacobson for his hair cut appointment.'

Without missing a step, she continued her convergence on the restaurant. I caught my mother's eye. She shrugged and smiled coyly. I did the same in response. That was my soon to be mother-in-law!

We were seated immediately. Cynthia positioned herself between us. Before anyone could speak, she caught the attention of the waitress.

'Miss? Oh, honey!' She grabbed the woman's arm. 'I'll have a Bloody Mary with two limes. Nora, what will you have?' She turned asking my mother.

'Oh, Cynthia, I don't care for a drink, thank you. But you go right ahead,' my mother responded.

'Lauren, my dear, a drink for you?' Cynthia turned her full attention on me while still holding onto the waitress.

'I'll have coffee please.'

As the waitress escaped Cynthia's grasp my mother spoke.

'I certainly think that this meeting was a good idea. There are so many details to be settled quickly,' my mother began as she casually looked over the menu.

'Yes, I quite agree. I thought it imperative that Lauren and I meet as soon as possible, but frankly, I didn't expect to see you here, Nora.'

My mother's expression darkened but only momentarily as she casually put down the menu. I inwardly winced at the insult. Why would she say such a thing? She continued as if she had said nothing wrong.

'Of course, I am delighted you came.'

My mother sat silently, taking it all in. I watched her as she watched Cynthia. Oblivious to all else, Cynthia sipped her Bloody Mary and rambled on about caterers and stocking the bar. As she continued to talk, she produced her gold cigarette case. Without missing a beat, she pulled out a cigarette and after a moment of examination, lit it. The inhalation was the only interruption of her diatribe.

'Of course I consulted with Glen and he yields to whatever we decide here,' She spoke as she exhaled creating a swirl of smoke to rise in front of her eyes.

I grabbed the opportunity to speak as she paused for a moment to drink. I was hoping to create some kind of bridge between them. After Cynthia's thoughtless greeting, I hoped my enthusiasm would unite them in the common mission of making this one hell of a wedding."

"Ya really thought dat was possible?" Willie asked almost disbelievingly.

"Yes. At that time, I really did." My response was greeted by a quick head shake and a smile.

"O.K. girl. If ya says so. Less hear da rest."

"Are you sure?"

"Positive! Common; I's itchin ta hear how'd ya made out?"

"Well, as I said, I wanted to defuse the tension that was building between them so I just jumped right into how I envisioned the wedding.

'A sundown ceremony in the sanctuary of the temple would be wonderful, wouldn't it?' I turned to my mother. 'It's so beautiful in that room at sundown.' She nodded approval as I continued, turning to Cynthia.

'And I accept your generous offer to have the reception in your garden.'

Before continuing, I noticed that Cynthia's smile had instantly drained of any pleasure. She turned abruptly, shouting to the waitress across the dining room.

'I asked for two limes!'

The waitress scampered over apologetically.

Yes you did, ma'am. I'll get you another right away.'

"Uh oh, dis don't sound good."

"You have no idea, Mr. Taylor."

"All I could do was look around in total embarrassment. My mother's expression remained constant, never taking her eyes off of Cynthia. I felt the sudden pressure of Cynthia's hand clasping my arm. She stared deeply into my eyes.

'Lauren, dear, I thought it was settled. The wedding will be in my home.'

I smiled at the obvious miscommunication.

'The reception will be in the garden like we discussed, but not the ceremony...'

'But, darling' she interrupted, shifting her weight in her chair and tightening her jaw. 'Just think how lovely it would be to have the ceremony in my library instead of at the temple.' Her gaze now so intense, I was the one shifting my weight as she continued her emphatic plea.

'Oh, Lauren, think about this. Just any of the members can have their wedding in the sanctuary. So very common; it's almost a commercial venue, for Christ's sake! But my library...and the reception to follow in the rose garden and on the blue stone terrace...why, it's perfect. A one-of-a-kind, once in a lifetime event. Surely you can appreciate the difference?'

She commanded me to think so I thought a minute. She certainly could be convincing. But no, my mind was made up.

'Thank you again for the offer. It would be beautiful, I'm sure, but I have my heart set on having the ceremony in the sanctuary. I've pictured my wedding there my whole life.'

Two orbs of stone-hard jade stared at me. Her grip on my arm tightened slightly.

'But it would be PERFECT, just what you want. My house was absolutely designed as if to have your wedding there. I have no daughters. Let me do this for you and Glen.'

"Wow...what pressure." Willie interjected.

"You're not kidding. And was I feeling it too! It was torture under her intense gaze while she waited for my response. I was struggling to figure out how I could get through to her? I was sure once she realized what it meant to me she would understand and want for me what I wanted for myself. But, as I continued to explain, I think I was beginning to realize that it wasn't going to be easy."

"'I'm sure it would be wonderful, but I have always looked forward to being married at temple...always.' Even I was aware of an almost desperate pleading in my voice.

She released my arm and leaned back in her chair. She calmly stirred the ice in her glass with her index finger.

'You know, dear, Glen has always loved the library. It's his absolute favorite room in the house. I think it would mean the world to him to be married there.' Her words were encased in velvet.

God, what could I do? After all, it was Glen's wedding too. But I knew he couldn't care less where it took place. I looked to my mother for help and she did not disappoint. Her words were soft and quite calm.

'Cynthia, I'm sure that Glen will want what Lauren wants in this case. She has always dreamed of being married in the sanctuary...'

Cynthia interrupted, 'but surely, Nora you must...'

It was then my mom's turn to interrupt, 'I shouldn't have to remind you of how generous Glen is when it comes to Lauren. Do you really think that he would deprive her of a life-long dream, and one so easily realized? Shall we consult with him on this? I'm sure the maître d' would let us use the phone.'

All I could think at that moment was, bravo, mom! But my sigh of relief was premature. Cynthia locked her glare on my mother, a contorted, angular smile crossing her face.

'It's just that I assumed that the entire wedding was going to be at my house. Nora, surly you can see how much more significant this event will be at my estate rather than at a mere *hall for rent*. This childhood dream of hers means nothing when considering what a pictorial spread in the Tribune, complete with color shots of the storybook setting, can do for their social status.' She stopped for a beat and then continued. 'Why, wouldn't you have absolutely killed to start your married life with such a Society Splash?'

My mother said nothing. She sat steadily looking into Cynthia's eyes. I found myself silently rooting for my mom, totally forgetting that I was involved in the conflict. I didn't want Cynthia's feelings to be hurt, but on the other hand, it was, after all, my wedding.

Cynthia was infuriated by my mother's silence.

'Nora, think what you're giving up here. We are talking about my house...my house!'

Her volume grew in direct correlation to her frustration with my mother's silence. By the end of Cynthia's speech every eye in the restaurant was fixed on my mother, waiting for her response.

My mother waited one more moment for effect.

'Yes, it is your house, but it is Lauren's wedding,' she said quietly, steadily. Her words, though voiced softly, had a bite to them.

They sat silently facing each other. My mother's expression hadn't changed since we first sat down. The muscles in Cynthia's jaw started pulsating. I braced myself for another explosion. But finally, a casual smile replaced the tautness.

'Aren't we being silly? Of course it's Lauren's wedding.' She patted my arm. 'If you want the sanctuary...then that's what you shall have.'

But the tension of the moment never truly passed as we settled into casual conversation. My mother's gaze never left Cynthia's face. I was aware of a victory of sorts but couldn't quite comprehend the scope. I was just so relieved that the fighting was over."

"In the cab going home my mother turned to me with concern.

'Lauren, you must watch out for her. She's tricky...and oh so good at playing the game. She will try to outmaneuver you at every turn.'

'I'll be fine. I'm marrying Glen, not his mom.'

'If you're smart you'll listen to me. She'll be trouble if you let her. Remember one thing sweetie: all the money in the world doesn't give her the right to run your life for you. I know you're impressed with the rose but don't be blind to the thorns.'

"At the time, I thought she was being incredibly melodramatic but I should have paid more attention to her clichéd advice."

"Why should ya been differnt from any other kid? We all shoulda paid more 'tention ta our folk's advice. Dat jess goes wiff bein' young. So, whud 'bout yer ol' man; whuds he like? It sounds like he done all right by ya...Aw, I kin see dat smile happenin' dere...you's a daddy's girl!"

"I guess I was, but I never realized it until the day of the wedding."

"That morning the door to my room opened slowly and my mother poked her head in. She smiled, acknowledging that I was awake.

'Good morning, I guess the phone woke you. It hasn't stopped ringing all morning.'

'Now that you mention it, it does seem like it's been ringing a lot. What's going on?'

'Everyone's calling to talk to you. Shall I say you're still sleeping?'

'No, I'll talk. What's the big deal?'

'Well, with the rain and all, they're all worried that you'll be upset. You know planning a garden reception...'

'RAIN? What rain?' I pulled back the curtains.

'Oh God, its pouring! What are we going to do? It can't be raining.'

I envisioned all of my beautiful flowers and lovely plans seeping drenched and muddy down storm drains...mingled with my tears. She came to my bed and took me in her arms.

'You can't let a little rain get to you Sweetie. Crying never solved anything especially when it comes to the weather. Come on now, you don't want to have big puffy red eyes for your wedding, do you?' She cradled me comfortingly.

'I guess not.'

I gave into her logic. After all, we had rented a huge yellow and white-striped tent, complete with dance floor and crystal chandeliers for just such a contingency. But I had so hoped we wouldn't need it and that the guests could wander the gorgeous gardens.

We sat there for a moment in silence, she cradled me in her familiar warmth. I heard the rumbling of the rain and wind outside whipping against the house. She began to speak softly after taking a deep breath.

'There must be a million things that a mother should tell her daughter on her wedding day. Why can't I think of any?'

"Oh jeez, don't tell me she's gonna start wiff da birds 'n bees stuff! She couldn'ta thought ya needed dat talk!" He interrupted, wildly amused. "Or did ya?"

"No, Willie, I did not and she did not," I stated firmly which stopped his fun making.

"She wanted to tell me that marriage is hard work. She worried about my being so young. She hoped that I would be willing to work at it...she knew that I was in love with being in love as much as I was in love with Glen. She was just trying to bring some reality to bear."

"So'd ya listen?"

"Oh, I listened. But what I heard was not what she had intended to say. I interpreted her words as meaning I was the one that had to work to make Glen happy. I truly never considered that he should be willing to work just as hard. And I knew that I could and would do just that. I would do whatever it took. I would never let him regret that he had married me. It certainly didn't sink in that I should also work at making myself happy. Like my mother and her mother before her, I was convinced that if I could keep my husband happy that's all I would need to be happy too. I could do that, no sweat. It was going to be great, that I would have my happily ever after."

"Anyway, as the amount of rain that fell increased, so did the phone calls.

'Lauren, darling, I'm calling to tell you that rain on your wedding day is a good omen. So don't worry, dear, the wedding and the marriage will be a great success!'

As I hung up the phone, I turned to face my dad.

'Can you believe Aunt Dee? Rain, a good omen? I don't know if I can stand anymore of this good cheer.'

'How 'bout a hot dog? Just you and me and no phone.' He smiled conspiratorially.

'You're kidding, right? Today? Today is my wedding, daddy. I can't go out for a hot dog!'

'Why the hell not? It's your day. Who's to stop you?'

"We both looked over at my mother. She had her *you've got to be kidding* look on her face. But before she could say a word my dad linked his arm in mine and propelled me towards the garage door.

As we reached it he turned to my mom. 'So, how much time do I have with the bride before all hell breaks loose and I run for cover?'

My mother looked at her gold-banded wrist.

'Have her back here at three...sharp. That should give us plenty of time to get to temple and dress for the ceremony. Three, Richard, not three fifteen or three thirty. Three o'clock!'

Oh Daddy

"So, incredibly, on my wedding day, the two of us were off to Big Herm's, the kosher hot dog king of Chicago's northern suburbs.

'Daddy, you're a genius. How do you do it?' I put my arm through his and squeezed excitedly. 'Haven't you learned yet; dads know everything?'"

"We laughed yet all I could think was what a very lucky girl I was. I had wonderful parents and I would soon be married to the love of my life."

As if coming out of a trance of remembrance, she noticed a strange look on Wiilie's face and asked, "What is it? Is something wrong?"

"Naw, jess thinkin how differnt our life is. Dis almost like hearin you read a fairy tale. Does people actchaly live like that?"

She stared at him for a moment unsure of his meaning. Was he upset? Should she stop? If it was upsetting him...Before she could ask, he continued.

"Please tell me more."

He had spoken with such yearning that she was suddenly confused. Why was it so hard for her to figure this man out? After a moment, seeing the look on his face, she decided that his plea was sincere, so she continued.

"It was crowded as we quietly entered the hot dog joint. We were both very quiet. It was as if we knew that after today, all would change. Very few talks had passed between us. Very few *I love yous* had actually ever been spoken. But there was a bond there. It was deeply felt and at that time silently acknowledged as a loving look passed between us."

"We walked into the tiny hot dog shack on Dempster Street in Skokie. Lots of people were stopping in for Saturday lunch. My dad announced with flourish, 'This is my daughter Lauren and tonight she's getting married.'"

"To Big Herm he yelled, 'Two with everything, Herm.'

Smiles and good wishes were thrown in my direction from everyone there. I started giggling, shaking my head as I thought: a tattered old shack, sitting on wobbly red vinyl stools split open from years of supporting fat bottoms, eating hot dogs with my dad on my wedding day...could it get any better?"

"We sat at a counter which faced out, running along the front windows."

"We should go dere sometime. Sounds like a place I'd like." Willie looked so sincere I just had to smile.

"Then we shall." I responded with a smile.

After a pause he nudged my shoulder.

'You think we really can?' His tone was one of regret, his face sad. But he seemed to snap out of it saying, 'Cain't wait to hear what yer dad had ta say ta you. I thinks he musta had a good reason ta get you alone."

"And you'd be right. My dad spoke as we settled ourselves, watching the noonday traffic.

'I know we haven't really talked much through the years,' He began. 'I sort of left most stuff up to your mom. But I want you to know that it's not because I haven't wanted to. It's always been hard for me, you know, to talk about how I feel.'

"I could see how very uncomfortable this confession had made him. As he stared out the window into the rain-drenched, crowded street, he continued.

'When your mother and I first got married, we decided to have children right away. I wanted a baby girl. Zeda.' "He was my grandfather." I explained. Willie just shook his head in understanding but kept quiet prompting me to continue. "My dad said, 'Zeda thought I was crazy to be carrying on about having a daughter. *Richard, he'd say pray for a boy. A son will carry on the family name.'*

"I have to stop here because at the time I thought this *carrying on the family name* was pretty silly since my grandfather had changed our real name to Gates when he arrived here from Russia, because it sounded less ethnic than our real name." Willie looked totally confused.

"A name change was pretty common at the time because immigration authorities couldn't understand them to get the name right or the immigrants themselves wanted a more American sounding name...you know they wanted to fit in."

Willie sat looking somewhat amazed. "Huh, I never knowd dat."

After a beat with Willie appearing deep in contemplation he said, "So, he wanted to talk to ya about your grandfather?"

"No, he was using my grandfather's advice to him to frame what he really wanted me to hear..." She stopped when total confusion spread over Willie's face.

"Look all of that's not important. I'm just telling what he said."

He sensed that she might be a little put out with him. "I jess whats to understand you. Please go on wiff the story." And, he smiled that smile. How could she not respond to that?

"So, my dad told me what my grandfather had said to him. I laughed at my father's flawless accent, as he not only took on my grandfather's voice but his posture as well. With one wave of the hand, I was silenced and awaited the rest of the story. Jeez, he was really serious. He continued.

'I wanted this child to be a girl. During the nine months all I talked about was my daughter. Then when your mom delivered and I saw your brother, my first born, I was filled with pride. A son. I liked the idea after all. So, the next one would be a girl.

And a couple of years later, your mother was pregnant again. All I kept telling everyone was that this one would be my little girl. I drove them all nuts! Your Aunt Dee finally refused to be with me unless I promised not to mention my soon to be born daughter, that's how crazy I was! Then another boy was born. When they let me see him for the first time and he was so blonde, just like your mom, and so very beautiful, chubby and round...almost nine pounds. He looked like he was two months old already! I had to just love him.'"

"I sat silently watching him. I could imagine the jet-black hair without the streaks of gray which now distinguished his temples and a bit less of the thick body sitting there beside me. The middle-aged, well-established father of three was not who was sitting with me now in that hot dog shack on Dempster Street. Instead, a young, handsome man, just starting a family in years past...in places I have no recollection of having been was beckoning me to join him. Oh, what a journey he offered. One I was very excited to make."

"I spoke not a word, barely breathed. I dared not. I loved him so much just then for sharing himself with me in a way he had never been able to before. He trusted me not to abuse the fact that he could be vulnerable. Oh, Willie, it was amazing. And he wasn't finished yet.

'Finally, your mom was pregnant again,' he continued.

'This time I said nothing. I kept my mouth shut. I was afraid that if this child wasn't a girl, we would never have one.

When she went into labor, I sat in the waiting room and prayed. You know that I have never been very religious, but I prayed this time the best I could.

The nurse walked in beaming. I couldn't control my tears when she told me that I had a daughter...tiny but healthy. You were the answer to my prayers. When I called your Aunt Dee to tell her, she said, *Richard, what a JOY! You finally got that little girl.* As soon as she said it I knew what your name would be...Joy. For you were my Joy then and you still are.'"

"Teach, yo name's Joy? Why'd ya tell us it's Lauren?"

"Well, my mom had something to say about it too, you know. She wasn't quite as sold on the name as my dad. So, they compromised. My name is Lauren Joy Gates."

"Whuda joy...I think he's right. Joy does suit ya."

"What about Teach? I thought that was the name you liked for me?"

"Maybe fer now, but someday I'd like ta know ya as Joy..."

As if the implication of a future was just too much, he let his sentence trail off without fully completing his thought. With a slight shake of his head, he looked me straight in the eyes. We shared a moment of anticipation as I became aware of what felt like jumping jacks being performed in my stomach.

"So, how'd da weddin' turn out?"

It took a moment for the question to register. I think I hide my disappointment. Then I did note a glimpse of confusion darken his gaze to be replaced almost instantly by sincere curiosity.

"Well, my father delivered me promptly at three, as promised. I found my mother anxiously awaiting the bride. Then he drove us ladened with tote bags and garment-bagged gowns to the temple."

"The structure was a multi-million-dollar house of worship set back an acre from the street. It was the same street Glen and I used to take our summer drives along while we were dating. Lake Michigan lapped up below its back terrace. There was a bride's dressing room in the lower level of the enormous sanctuary where we would prepare ourselves for the grand event.

The storm had miraculously cleared so the clean, white structured reflection glistened in the sun-sparkled lake. What a perfect setting for a fairy-tale wedding. The wealthy North Shore Jewish community had commissioned a Japanese architect to design this massive temple to blend into its aesthetically peaceful setting. The huge trees on either side of the driveway leading to the entrance naturally formed symbolic praying hands and the design theme for the building itself was taken from that classic form. A huge sanctuary, complete with skylights, stained glass and a sixty-foot cathedral ceiling formed the stylized hands in prayer." She sighed deeply at the remembrance.

"You OK Teach?" He asked concerned.

When she answered with a radiant smile, "I just haven't remembered all of this in along time." He was relieved.

"Will ya tell me more? It's getting interestin!" They just smiled at each other for a moment before she continued.

"We were greeted at the front doors by the very friendly custodian. 'So, this is the little lady getting married, huh? Ya know I got ta look 'em all over 'fore I let just anyone get married in my temple!' he teased."

"We laughed and, as he nodded his approval, we took the stairs down to the bride's room. The scent of roses struck me as soon as we opened the door. There were roses everywhere: on the walls in the brightly printed wallpaper, on fabric and on couch cushion pattern. Rose prints covered the makeup stools, which stood in front of a huge brightly lit mirror.

171

Astonishment struck as I stared at the mirror. Reflected in it, behind me, were vases and vases filled with real roses decorating the entire room. Hundreds of velvety pedals in every color imaginable created a cocoon of soft luxury into which we walked.

My mother spotted a note taped to the mirror first and retrieved it for me. I hesitated for a moment before opening it, almost too overwhelmed. *To my beautiful bride, this is just a sample of the flower-filled future we will share. All my love, G.* was written in Glen's distinctive handwriting.

I handed the note to my mother to read. I was unable to speak.

'Well, sweetheart, I'll say one thing for him, he is thoughtful...if a bit excessive!' She handed me back the note and began to empty the make-up case onto the counter without another word about it.

'We'd best get down to business or Glen might be a bit disappointed when they start playing *Here Comes the Bride* and you're not ready.'"

"I just couldn't get over what he had done. What a guy! Who does such things?" I sincerely asked of Willie.

"Yea, who does? Makes da rest a us look pretty shabby, all right. I guess whens ya gots da bread, it's easy ta be romantic."

"I guess. But it was really something to see. I just sat there for quite a while and then I became surprisingly calm. I was truly convinced that marrying Glen was absolutely the right thing to do. If I had had any doubts they were certainly now gone."

"My mother and I sat side-by-side sharing the huge mirror. I found myself examining her reflection. She was so lovely. Her slender arm directed a delicate hand stroking mascara onto her eyelashes." Her golden- flecked, hazel eyes reflected with such beautiful energy the floral setting surrounding us. Even with no makeup, she looked bright, her skin almost glowing as if lit from within by magic. I sighed deeply. She had always been the beauty of the family.

Then I took a good long look at myself, knowing that I would once again be disappointed with the dark, drab, ordinary me reflected there, especially in comparison to her. But instead I noticed, for the first time, that my eyes were considerably larger than hers. And their dark, rich brown color coupled with my deep olive skin tone actually held a mystery, an exotic allure that I had never noticed before. I hadn't realized that my complexion had completely cleared and my skin was now smooth, stretched over high cheekbones almost in shadows created by thick dark eyelashes.

"I stood, startled. I stared at myself in that mirror surrounded by the proof of Glen's love, clothed only in bra and panties and I was astounded by the attractive figure, long shining hair...all that reflected in front of me as if for the first time. I looked again at my mother's reflection. She was still so very lovely. It hadn't been easy growing up with a mother that was prettier than I. But, I hadn't realized until that very moment just how much it had affected me. Our appearance was so very different. Our coloring, bone structure, everything, I had always tried to compare my looks with hers. But now I could see so clearly that there was really no way to compare. Before I could take in the extent of this realization, a sharp knock interrupted my thoughts. The custodian's voice reached us through the closed door.

'Flowers for the sanctuary just arrived. Thought you ladies'd like to see what they look like.'

The flowers, I thought excitedly, it was all really happening. I turned to face my mother.

'Do we dare go up into the sanctuary in our robes?'

'Oh, come on. No one's here. Who's gonna know?' She said as she tugged gently at the sleeve of my robe that I had hurriedly slipped into.

The two of us scooted out the door and up the stairs. Our footsteps echoed loudly throughout the empty, massive interior.

'It's kinda spooky without any people here.'

I grabbed her arm. I felt so conspiratorial. We were two naughty little girls sneaking somewhere we weren't supposed to be!"

"The sanctuary was awesome in the enormity of the emptiness. The cavernous ceiling produced a chilling echo with each footstep we took. Yet even with the grand scale and minimalist simplicity of decor, there was an aura, an unmistakable presence I found both comforting and exciting. To another's eye it might look stark and hard. To mine it appeared solemn and magnificent. Oh, I had made the right decision. This was indeed the place that our wedding vows should be exchanged.

I had been to weddings in this sanctuary before. Dozens of bouquets overflowing from atop a canopy and filling the area surrounding the bema in an attempt to create a garden setting was the usual effect desired. In reality it was nothing more than a kind of one-up-man-ship played by the congregants in their seemingly never-ending contest to outdo each other.

Before us stood a simple white canopy supported by four chrome poles. Just to the right was the one large flower arrangement of magnificent orchards we had ordered. Here now, in this place, the simplicity was truly elegant. We both stood motionless for a moment.

'Oh, Mom, you were so right. I am so glad I listened to you. Simple is so much more effective!'"

"How did she know? Most thought that one could never have too many flowers at a wedding. But this sanctuary was so extreme in design, so elegant in structure, the abundance of flora at all of the other weddings was just simply gaudy. Would I ever know things like that?

'It is lovely isn't it?' She said quietly, reverently. 'It's going to be just perfect. Even the rain has stopped.'

I looked out at the glistening waves of green lawn spilling into the crystal blue of the lake and saw a clear bright sky reflected there. I knew it too. Everything was going to be perfect."

"So'd it end up perfect?"

I sensed that Willie was ready for something not so perfect to happen.

"Is anything ever really perfect?" I whispered with much more emotion than I had intended. I continued in a much more matter-of fact tone.

"I wanted desperately to savor every moment of the day, but somehow it all just got away from me. I don't remember when nor how we got back to the bride's room or opening the boxes containing my bouquet and those of my bridesmaids. I do remember stopping for a moment when seeing my bouquet for the first time to marvel at the great job the florist had done. We had presented her with quite a challenge. My Grandmother and my mother had carried the same prayer book at their weddings and we had had the florist use it as the base for my bouquet. She had done a great job with it. It had turned out to be truly fabulous and at that moment, seeing it for the first time, I thought that one-day Glen and I would have a daughter that would carry this prayer book at her wedding."

"Then all at once my makeup was finished and my hair was brushed and my headpiece was secured. Then the room was suddenly filled with my bridesmaids. Cynthia made an entrance and everyone kept fussing with my dress. In unison a scream went up when I was about to sit down for a minute.

'Don't sit! You'll wrinkle your dress. The back is what everyone stares at for the entire ceremony!'

Since my less-than-petite derriere had always been my biggest - and I do mean biggest - figure problem the prospect of two hundred plus people staring at it for the entire service was not a thought upon which I chose to dwell.

And finally my mother, with tears in her eyes, was kissing my cheek.

'Bye, sweetheart; it's time. You are beautiful. Your father will be waiting for you at the top of the stairs. Remember, I love you.'"

"And then she was gone. They were all gone. I heard the door close behind her and I was alone. I looked around. To hell with them all...I sat down on one of the stools and looked into the mirror.

Something was very different. Not chubby. Not pimply. Not even awkward. I had become a woman without even realizing it. And I wasn't too bad to look at either. As soon as the thought came to me I pushed it aside in my mind knowing that a lot of it had to do with the gorgeous gown, a real dream come true. And the lace and seed-pearl headpiece; I mean who wouldn't look good in that get-up? Yet I knew. I felt the long sought after dream finally becoming a reality. All of those years of waiting, searching my dressing table mirror in my room; my wait was finally over. Today was that special day.

I was ready. I walked through the door and on up the stairs. My father stood awaiting me at the top. He smiled approvingly, as if he understood what had just happened to me, sensing the revelation I had experienced in that rose-filled basement.

'Lauren, you are truly beautiful,' he whispered as he tucked my arm under his.

It was the very first time I had heard those words and believed them."

The Wedding

"As my father and I approached the sanctuary, I could see all of the heads of our guests craning to catch the first glimpse of the bride. He leaned very close and whispered in my ear as we started down the aisle.

'I love you.'

I could say nothing. I mechanically proceeded down the white silk runner unable to move my head. It was as if rusted in place. *Oil can...oil can* the barely audible, croaky voice of the Tin Woodsman echoed in my head. I smiled, transported for a moment to the wonderful hours upon hours of pure childhood delight I had experienced watching Dorothy heroically struggle to find her way home. Then I realized that my smile had become fixed as well, the muscles frozen in place. God, this was getting worse by the second. Where was an oil can when you needed it?

I began to feel quivering waves of tension flowing through my extremities. My fingers numbed. My toes tingled in my satin pumps.

As I passed each row of guests, some familiar faces nodded, some just smiled. I could do nothing except walk...and smile. I felt my father's hand cover mine, as if he sensed my need for reassurance. And you know Willie, that simple gesture did the trick. His hand was warm, strong, reassuring. You will not stumble; you will not fall; I am so proud of you; you are truly beautiful. It was as if he was speaking to me through his touch, saying just the right things to ease my tension.

And then there was Glen in front of me. He stood smiling, no, absolutely beaming at me while all I could think was how had this happened? I still couldn't fathom why, but this man, this handsome, wonderful man was actually going to make me his wife. Glen Jacobson was simply the answer to all of my prayers." I became absorbed in thought, silent in reflection. Why was I telling him all of this?

He seemed to sense my hesitancy to continue.

"Whoa. Wished I was dere ta see ya come down dat aisle," he whispered.

I smiled at the compliment but was unsure whether or not to

continue.

"Will ya finish da story?" As usual it was as if he had read the indecision in my thoughts,

I answered simply, "yes."

"The Rabbi stood before us enormous, looming over the proceedings. In black robes with his steel gray hair, Charlton Heston's Moses, he appeared to beckon the heavens to bless this union."

"I guess it's natural fer ya ta keep comparin' it ta da movies. Sounds like a real production." Willie interrupted.

I would have expected this observation to be voiced with humor or sarcasm but instead it was offered with complete sincerity. I didn't know how to respond to him. I had never thought about it quite like that before. But I guess he had a very good point.

He expected no reply. I gave none as I continued.

"Throughout the ceremony I saw Glen very clearly. I remember nothing of what was said. But I do remember him standing handsome, glowing with approval...in his perfectly tailored tux!"

For this comment I received an appreciative chuckle from Willie.

"I don't remember one other thing from the ceremony except the relief I felt when it was over. Glen and I escaped back up the aisle. An all-encompassing flood of contentment overtook me. I remained wrapped in the comfort of it as we entered the waiting limousine for the short drive up the lakeshore to the Jacobson's estate.

Glen had been talking to me for the entire drive. I had heard nothing."

'Lauren, are you O.K.?' His voice finally penetrated.
'I'm fine.' I heard my words but couldn't figure out from where they had come.

"I held his arm tightly, pushing, snuggling tightly against him, trying to physically reach that place in his heart that I knew was now only mine to occupy. I could now truly lay claim to his heart. It was finally mine to inhabit. I could breathe free, relax surrounded by the strength and security of my new home within Glen's soul."

There was silence. Willie was breathing deeply as if inhaling what I had said. He had such a curious look on his face.

"Are you O.K.?" I asked, hoping that I hadn't totally bored him with my rambling. Then I looked again at his expression and realized that it was not boredom I saw there but rather a kind of melancholy longing. A slight smile, an envious smile met my gaze.

"Do ya got any idea how lucky you is?" He asked gently.

"I know," I laughed. "It was really something; every girl's fantasy."

He shook his head. "I don't means da dress an da fuss." He seemed annoyed.

Now I was the one a bit confused. He must have sensed it or seen it.

"Do ya knows how many times ya jess said someone told ya dat dey loved ya? Do ya knows how much carin n tenderness was directed at cha as if it was da mose natural thin in da world? And ya sure is used ta bein treated dat way, loved dat way 'cause ya didn't act like it weren't nothin special t'all! Do ya have any idea how lucky ya is ta have parents like dat?"

I bristled at the question and its implications. Of course I knew I was lucky. Hadn't I thought it, said it hundreds of times over the years? Or did I just mechanically think that I was lucky and never really understood just how lucky I truly was? Why was I letting this man confuse me so? Why had I told him all of this? He was now making me very uncomfortable in my own life.

Did I take it all for granted? In my world parents loved each other and they loved their children and they strove to create a safe, nurturing environment for their family. Why was I, all at once, feeling guilty because that was the environment in which I was raised?

"I guess I've gotten a bit carried away with my story," I said rather curtly. "It's getting late. You must be bored as hell with..."

Willie's expression became warm and endearing completely halting my train of thought.

"Go on," his tone imploring. "I really wants ta hear da rest."

I was restless now fearing that I had truly gone too far. What was

I doing here with him, telling him all of this?

"Really, go on. I's interested...really." He coaxed.

"There's just the party..."

"Tell me 'bout da party. Common, tell me 'bout da party," his request seemed utterly sincere.

I had to smile both at the recollection and even more so at the boyish pleadings coming from this mountain of a man. I tried not to, but I just couldn't help it.

After a deep sigh, I resumed my tale.

"There were two hundred and fifty guests entering the garden through trellises entwined with orchards. Exotic flowers were everywhere: they trimmed the edges of the grounds and bordered the blue stone terrace. They floated in the pool and adorned the cake.

And the people, oh, they were all so beautiful. Women in their gowns and men so handsome in their tuxedos; I watched them glide, drinks in hand, through the garden, smiling, having a good time, all in celebration of my special night. It was everything I had dreamed it would be.

The first person I caught sight of was Jane Janus. She was the only one of Cynthia's friends with whom I had grown truly fond. I had naturally gravitated toward her warmth and wit during the seemingly endless progression of showers and parties Cynthia's circle of friends threw for Glen and me. I can now see that she was the only genuine person among the whole lot."

"Ta me I's surprised dere was even one," Willie smirked.

Trying to hide a smile and feigning indignation, I continued.

"I was so overwhelmed with all of the attention and of course the elaborate gifts, that I was totally blind to the affectation which seemed almost to be a requisite of Cynthia's friendships. For in reality it all had very little to do with their happiness for us but rather they were desperately trying to outdo each other: who could throw the more elaborate party, who would give us the most expensive gift. But Jane was different. She had come to know Cynthia through a mutual friend, an art dealer in New York. One thing I have to admit about Cynthia; if she wanted to know something about a subject with which she was not well versed, she sought out those who were expert in the field to tutor her.

With her new found fortune she decided that she should not only understand fine art but own it as well. One chance meeting at the Gallery, one conversation with Jane, convinced Cynthia that this was a woman she needed to get to know better. Through the years, and with Jane's wise counsel, Cynthia had acquired a wonderful art collection.

I had the opportunity to visit Jane's home once and was so impressed. A classic Tudor, built on a hill, her home exuded warmth and good taste. The style and intelligence of the woman was truly reflected in the decor. And here she was standing before me at my wedding reception, looking beautiful in a floor-length navy-blue gown. More than any of the other guests, she alone instantly confirmed my hope that the evening was indeed going to be spectacular."

'Lauren, you are exquisite!' She kissed my cheek with genuine affection.

'Jane, I'm so glad you're here...and what a great dress!'

She dramatically unwound the artistically coiled length of fabric expertly tied around her neck and shoulders. When loosened I could see that it was attached at the bodice of the dress so when untied, it cascaded down supplementing the skirt and revealing a fabulous strapless neckline. The appreciative surprise I felt, must have spread across my face.

'I just love all of the options this thing provides.' She laughed.

'That's GREAT.' I gave her a hug. 'I am so glad you're here.'

"And you know what Willie, I knew in that moment that all of it was really happening. My fantasy had indeed become my reality. I was married to Glen and this was my fairy-tale wedding."

"Sounds like...so, jess partyin leff or somthin' interestin happen?"

"Not sure interesting is the way I would describe it, but something did happen."

With a smile and leaning back in his chair, Willie twirled his hand in front of him in that *come on, come on get on with it motion*. So, I obliged.

"By mid-evening, Glen's pockets were stuffed with envelopes. He was so happy. We were so happy together. And then Cynthia approached. She somewhat drunkenly draped her arms around our shoulders as she positioned herself between us.

'Hey, kids, let's go inside and see what kind of a haul you made.'

'Sure, Mom,' Glen answered to my great surprise.

I said nothing while reluctantly following them into the huge house.

We settled into the large leather chairs in the library."

"Hah! I members. Dats Glen's favorite room."

"Wow, Willie. You really have been listening." I teased.

"Ta every word," he replied with such sincerity I found I couldn't look at him. I immediately squirmed in my seat gently smoothing an imaginary clump of fabric I was pretending had gathered in my lap.

"Shall I go on or have you had enough?"

"Please, I wants ta hear it all."

"Well, once we were settled, in Glen's favorite room," I smiled. "Glen opened one envelope after another."

'Look at that. Only a hundred from Joel and Linda.' Cynthia's venom began to spew.

My stomach began churning as Glen continued to open envelopes to Cynthia's running commentary assessing our guest's generosity. I didn't want to be there. We were having such a wonderful evening and then, this. I wanted desperately for Glen to whisk me back, but Cynthia was in control, as she always was. I sat back, a joyless smile cloaking clenched teeth, went totally unnoticed by my husband and his mother. *The fascination will wear off soon.* My mother's words came back to me. But why did it have to happen at my wedding?

Finally, Cynthia had had enough and announced that she would escort us back to the party. We had just reached the French doors leading to the garden when she grabbed Glen's arm urgently.

'Look, Harvey Patton is over there with the Stones and your father.'

I was immediately pleased causing my spontaneous smile to erupt at the thought of seeing the Stones again. Gary Stone was Arthur's investment advisor and a truly impressive man. Born and raised in the small city of Linwood, Indiana, he held us totally rapt one evening with his tales of his somewhat wild country youth which contrasted so very dramatically with his accomplishments as an adult. After serving in Viet Nam, he went on to acquire his CPA credentials and a law degree, graduating from both the University of Chicago and Northwestern University respectively.

His solid advice and true financial savvy soon had him steadily climbing the proverbial corporate ladder in Chicago. But what I loved the most about him was the fact that he had returned to his hometown of Linwood to marry his childhood sweetheart, Laura, and establish his home there. This shift in location diminished not one iota his ability to make his clients a ton of money -Arthur included- which of course made him one of Cynthia's favorite people. This *big fish* had definitely found his *little pond* by building a trust department at Fieldstar Bank, envied by the *big pond big fish* in Chicago.

I genuinely liked both he and Laura for their obvious but not overt affection for each other and their very apparent caring for their friends and community.

'Come on.' There was a bit of urgency in Cynthia's insistence.

'Gary feels that Harvey might be interested in investing in a new venture your Dad is putting together. Let's go help your father out.'

She clung to Glen's arm as we crossed the path to where they were conversing. Cynthia used Glen as a brace, supporting her somewhat off-balanced approach. She made sure that her entrance onto the scene could not have gone unnoticed. Patton proved to be willing prey.

'Ah, there's the lovely Cynthia.' He extended a hand in greeting.

'Why, Harvey, you make me blush...'

I actually thought that I was going to vomit. Cynthia's sugary tone, coupled by a false flutter of her eyelashes was just too much.

"Are men really that stupid?" I asked rhetorically.

"Yes," Willie stated flatly.

I was not expecting an answer from him and certainly not the definitive one I received. After a moment and a brief emotionless, reconfirming of his answer with a nod from Willie, I continued.

"All I could do was stand mute, having not been introduced to Harvey Patton, as Cynthia went on and on. She cutely covered her mouth several times as if trying coyly to hide the slight slur of her words. Patton was thoroughly taken in by her apparent embarrassment at being tipsy.

'Why, Harvey, you simply must excuse me for being so giddy, but it's not every day one's son gets married.'

It occurred to me that I had fallen victim to a similar scene myself. Look out Mr. Patton I thought. I kind of felt badly that he didn't have my mother to come to the rescue like I had had. But he just kept falling into her trap deeper and deeper. The poor man didn't have a clue.

'Now Cynthia, this can't be your son. You're much too young to have a grown boy.' He obviously thought his hackneyed compliment to be very clever.

'Well, Harvey, if you can keep a secret,' she leaned in very close pressing her ample bosom against his arm and whispered just loud enough for all of us to hear. "Glen is from Arthur's first wife. Shhhh...don't tell.'

Her timing was impeccable. As soon as confusion had entirely engulfed his expression she continued.

'Why, Harvey, what a silly goose you are. I AM Arthur's first wife!' She rebounded beautifully.

He was instantly back under her spell, laughing at himself and ogling her cleavage.

'You are a lucky man, Arthur.' He turned and patted Arthur's back firmly.

'That I am, Henry. I only wish for Glen and Lauren the same happiness that Cynthia and I have shared throughout the years.'

'That's right, children, take a lesson from us.' Cynthia kissed Arthur's cheek noisily, dramatically.

'Lauren, you be sure to pamper my boy the way I do his father. That's what keeps 'em happy. Be a man-pleaser and he will please you back.'

I glanced at the Stones' who had been silent during this entire exchange. Gary bent his head slightly. Laura lifted her chin responsively their gaze melding, almost visual liquid heat flowing between them. His outstretched finger gently wiped beneath her eye catching an eyelash from her cheekbone, and without a word being spoken he held the tip of his finger up before her lips as she blew gently. Her mouth then erupted in a beautiful smile. It was oh so obvious that he was wordlessly conveying the sentiment that he hoped all of her wishes would come true by the slight nod of his head. Nary a word had been spoken but volumes had been conveyed in just that brief moment of time.

With a gentle touch at the middle of her back, they turned in unison and over his shoulder, Gary excused them by saying that they were going to the dance floor.

I looked at Cynthia. Arthur had a powerful grip clamped around her shoulder. I looked back at the Stones. They were now effortlessly in each other's arms, their gaze holding them together more so than their embrace as they swayed to the music.

That was what I wanted for us. That was what I wanted some young couple first starting out to see when they looked at us after 20 years of marriage. I knew it was possible. I would make it happen.

Meanwhile Glen had assumed the same position with me that his parents had struck. I felt the pressure from his embrace enfolding my shoulders.

'You don't have to tell that to Lauren, Mom. She couldn't please me more.'

And at that moment that was all I wanted to do."

I paused reflecting just briefly on the memory.

"So, that was how I started my life as Mrs. Glen Jacobson." I sat back and crossed my arms.

"But, enough of Cynthia and her silly games."

Willie sat back also. I hadn't noticed that he had been listening perched on the edge of his seat. I smiled. After all, my story was certainly not exactly a thriller! He shook his head but remained silent.

"What? What are you thinking?"

"Jess 'bout yer life. How differnt from mines it is. I only seen what you described on T.V., in da movies. I never know'd no one really livin like dat. Had whad ya had. Did da kinda stuff you done.

Two real parents, lovin each other, lovin da kids, havin money ta spend. Mansions, fancy weddings, rose gardens...like da fuckin White House, fer Christ's sake...Oh sorry Teach!" He was all at once angry with himself for the profanity. But He continued.

"I means, man, I cain't even begin ta 'magine how it were like growin up like dat. You're whole world is jess so different from mines."

I had to bite back an urge to correct his grammar. Why all of a sudden had that mattered to me? Up until this moment, I hadn't even noticed his misuse of words, his faulty grammar, and improper tenses. What the hell was this all about?

I sat, confused not only by my thoughts but by what he had said. I didn't know how to respond. I had been so wrapped up in the events that I was reliving, I hadn't thought of the impact the environment of the story would have on him. Talk about stupid. If his world was such an overwhelming puzzle to me, why hadn't I thought that mine would be the same to him? He was so intrigued with it all, was so interested in all of the details of my everyday existence. That which I thought would surely bore him seemed to hold his attention like an engrossing film, set in unfamiliar locations, portraying lives of unfamiliar characters...or maybe it just held the voyeuristic appeal of a melodramatic soap opera.

"So'd Cynthia keep on callin' da shots or what? Dat why ya quit her boy?"

"Whoa, you do ask the tough ones, don't you?"

I paused to think for a moment.

"It wasn't only because of her. For sure, she had something to do with it. I think when any relationship breaks up it's for lots of reasons. It's never simple."

"Life's never simple, period. Why would dat be any differnt?"

"You have such a gift for summation. You should be a trial attorney."

He laughed much harder than I thought the comment warranted, but he began speaking again before I could find out why.

"So, how'd ya handle her after dat?"

"It took awhile, but I did finally get the ammo I needed to hold her at bay. I have often thought how unfortunate it was that the timing was so off. If I could have gained control over her before Glen and I started to have real problems, maybe we could have worked things out.

"When was dis?"

"I guess it was about two years after Glen and I were married."

"So wha'd happened?"

"It began with a phone call from my mom. I knew something was very wrong instantly. After much prodding she finally told me that one of her friends had overheard Cynthia discussing my sex-life in a conversation at the beauty shop. Apparently, Cynthia had gone into graphic detail about what Glen and I were doing in bed.

My mother was mortified. I don't know if you have a good picture of the kind of person my mother is. This is a woman of subtle style and grace. This is not someone wanting to hear that her daughter's sex life was the topic of a public conversation involving Cynthia and her cronies!"

"I thinks I got it." He spoke seriously as if he too had been offended by Cynthia's actions.

"If you could have heard my mother's tone of voice, the embarrassment, humiliation...and I felt it was all my fault for bringing this lunacy into our family. The last person in the world I would talk about sex with was Cynthia Jacobson. So, imagine my shock to find that our supposed blissful sex-life was being discussed and analyzed at the beauty shop. Who knows what Cynthia's vivid imagination came up with? If I weren't so irate it would have been truly funny considering that our sex-life was pretty pathetic. But I gotta tell you, at the time, I was genuinely appalled."

"After hanging up with my mom I could not get the conversation out of my head. I was angry and sickened and very confused about just how to handle the situation. Cynthia had really gone too far this time. I was not about to let her get her sick kicks at my expense. Glen and I had enough problems without having Cynthia compounding them. I thought long and hard as I waited for Glen to get home from work. I finally decided that the best course of action was to simply tell Glen the story and let him handle it. I knew that his wrath would surely put Cynthia in her place once and for all."

"Yo sex-life, huh? Sounds like she needed a good bangin' herself. Was she fer real?"

"I don't know. I mean what mother goes around talking about her kids like that? Is that sick or what? This was so far removed from any reality with which I had ever had to deal. I just couldn't handle it. As the afternoon passed, I was convinced that letting Glen deal with her was the right action to take. Actually, what I really wanted was for Glen to beat the shit out of the bitch!"

"TEACH!" Willie feigned shock.

"Well, I was really upset." I sheepishly stated. "We were at a point in our marriage where I knew that it would take a lot of work for us to get back on track...if we ever were on track to begin with. I had had enough to worry about just trying to figure out her son. I didn't need this nonsense thrown into the mix."

"Waiting for Glen, I began to pace around the house. As I walked past the bookcases in the library, I realized that Cynthia had worked with the architect to design them for us. Then into the dining room, I had changed my mind on the dining room chairs because Cynthia had thought that these chairs would be better for Glen's sometimes troublesome back. Then through the kitchen toward Glen's study, I spotted Cynthia's influences everywhere. The hallway mirror was a gift from her. The powder room chest: *It's just perfect for this space; I just couldn't resist buying it for you two.* The couch in the den: *You simply must have suede, it's so chic.* My God, she had infiltrated almost every room in my house without my even realizing it. But this was going too far. I was not going to allow her to occupy a place in my bedroom as well! My anger was building with each step I took.

Finally, Glen came home. I sat him down and calmly told him exactly what my mother had told me. I was very proud of myself for remaining so calm because I was sure that he was going to explode and I didn't want to unnecessarily add fuel to the fire. 'So what?' Was all I got in response from him.

'So? Is that all you can say?' I was almost too shocked to respond. Whether it was the incredulity of my tone or the sheer volume, whichever, he became aware of just how upset I was.

'Relax, baby. So, the old lady has an imagination. What's the big deal?'

'She lied. She said that I had told her all about how ecstatic you make me in bed. Details, she made up sick pornographic details...' I couldn't go on. The thought of a mother talking that way about her children literally nauseated me.

Glen came over and stood in front of me with a gloating smirk on his face.

'Is that so far from the truth? I do know how to push your buttons, Baby.' And he tweaked my breast.

I lost it. I didn't know at whom I was more angry, Glen or that whacko mother of his. I honestly don't even know what I said. I had never been so angry. I guess all of the months of unhappiness that I had experienced began to spew forward. The arrogance of his attitude, the audacity of his mother sent me into a rage. What a pair they were. And I was stuck in between them. I began to rant. Rage spit forth through profanity the likes of which I had never before used. I had enough of their collective craziness and games. I wanted him to do something about this lunacy. Do it fast and with no wiggle room for her to misinterpret his message.

He sat there for a moment dazed in total bewilderment. I had never erupted like this before. For a moment I thought that I had gotten through to him. For just a moment I thought that he had finally seen what I had been putting up with. I felt a slight spark of triumph at the prospect of it finally being over and the promise of a normal life finally emerging from all of this mayhem.

Then I saw the confusion on his face slowly turning into his own brand of rage. My joy at the prospect of attaining resolution to the nonsense that defined my married life was replaced with a moment of sheer terror thinking that his inevitable tirade would be directed at me. But I was quick to realize that his mother had all at once gone from being an imaginative old lady to the Vicious Villain."

"Oh, Teach, you was in wiff a real bunch a loonies!"

"Wait, it gets better."

"I don't knows if I can handle *better*" he joked.

But I was on a roll. I just kept talking; emotion driving every word.

"Then Glen gets the phone and calls her yelling and screaming, and all of it so obviously for my benefit.

'No I don't think she's exaggerating,' he shouted. 'Don't you call her an over-reacting child! She's my wife God Damn It and I won't stand by and let you upset her like this.' He countered her objections, never with his indignation only with mine."

"I was helpless to move as I listened to Glen's side of the conversation. Cynthia's responses were so loud I could also hear some of what she was saying. It was not pleasant!"

'I'm telling you to just leave us out of your conversations in the future.' He interrupted her before she could continue to defend herself. 'I DON'T CARE IF THE STORY GOT TWISTED OR NOT...'

I stood and left the room. I had to get out of there. I couldn't listen to anymore. What a huge mess. It wasn't turning out the way I had hoped at all. And all at once, I could hear from the hallway Glen's voice become deadly calm.

'Get your jollies at someone else's expense next time!' he hissed viciously and hung up on her.

I waited in the darkness for Glen to find me in his study. I knew he would come. He put his arm around my shoulder as he forced me to stand. Turning me toward him, he kissed me before I could speak. Wrapped in a tight hug, I felt his hardness and knew the reward that he would demand for defending me. And I knew I would give it. But I also knew that now I had a weapon I could use against Cynthia. From the bravado of the battle just fought, I was confident that I could stop Cynthia from interfering with our lives...I was the one controlling her son's affection. There was no doubt in my mind that if I were to give the ultimatum, Glen would choose me over her."

I felt Willie's arm around me., surprising me. I was shocked to realize that he had scooted his chair so close to me. I was equally surprised at the tears slowing making their way down my cheeks. He kept one arm about my shoulders as he gently wiped the tears away with his thumb. The action was so tender, so sincere, I paused to look at him. How could this massive man be so gentle and caring?

Shaking my head in an effort to clear my thoughts I said, "Sorry, I've never spoken of all of this to anyone. I didn't realize how it would affect me."

"It's OK. I's sorry fer makin ya so sad. Ya don't needs ta tell anymore."

"It's not that I'm sad. Please, stop looking as if any of this is your fault. I think I needed to talk about this to someone. It's cathartic." I shrugged.

He took his arm from my shoulder and leaned forward placing his arms on his thighs. He gazed intently into my eyes.

"Don't know why ya chose me ta hear yer story but seems like ya had to get it out and I's glad ya chose me ta tell it to. But, if dis is makin ya feel so bad, jess stop; we can talk bout somethin else." An anticipatory little smile grew on his face.

"God Willie, I wish I could explain this better. It's not making me sad. I think the tears are more of a cleansing that has been a long time coming."

He looked a bit confused, "So's dis is a good thin?"

"I think it is. I don't know why it's happening now, in this place, with you."

"Maybe don't try ta figure it out. Maybe if it's a good thin, jess let it happen."

Maybe if it's a good thing just let it happen.

I couldn't help but think he was talking about more than just my story telling. And yet the sincerity with which he spoke, the concern in his eyes; I realized that I was the one imagining the double entendre.

"Are you sure you want to hear all of this?"

"If you's ready ta keep talking, I's ready to keep listnin."

I nodded as I continued.

"The next morning I drove to the Jacobson's estate. Annette greeted me at the door.

'Miss Lauren, why are you here so early?' she asked concerned.

'I want to see Cynthia,' I stated simply. An alarmed expression crossed her face.

'I'm afraid she's not up yet. She hasn't rung for her breakfast. Why not come back later?'

I guess she was afraid of what Cynthia might do if she let me in uninvited. But I would not be put off.

'I'll wait,' I told her as I followed her back into the kitchen.

Almost an hour later we were both startled by the loud buzzer signaling Cynthia's awakening.

'There it is. She's up and wants her tray.' She immediately busied herself preparing Cynthia's breakfast.

'God, that buzzer is awful.' I had never heard it before.

'It's better than having her screaming...she's not so pleasant first thing in the morning. You sure you don't want to come back later?'

She was scared and I must admit that her words frightened me a bit, but I stayed determined. I would confront Cynthia. I would put an end to this, here, today. If my marriage was going to stand any kind of a chance at all, I had to be free from her interfering. The memory of Glen's expression, the humiliation and anger I felt the night before, my own mother's chagrin served to strengthen my resolve. I had to take charge of my life. It was time to trim the rose of its thorns.

'I'll take that to her.' I grabbed the tray from Annette's hands as she approached the stairs.

'But I haven't announced you. She's not expecting you.' There was real panic in her voice.

'Don't worry. I will take full responsibility,' I tried to calm her. 'Really, it'll be fine. Don't worry.' It was easy enough to say, but could I pull it off?

With each step climbed, my courage grew. I paused for one deep breath as I reached Cynthia's door. I knocked strongly.

'Come in, Annette. Set it up on the coffee table. I'll be out in a moment. That will be all then; you can leave.' Cynthia's voice sounded strong not like someone just awakening.

I pushed the door to her sitting room open. The room was empty. The door to the bedroom was closed, so I set the tray down on the table. As Cynthia burst into the room, shock covered her face when she saw me.

She stood naked. At seeing me she straightened up, standing tall, totally unself-conscious. I had to force myself to return her steady gaze. While I was filled with embarrassment, I could not let her see or sense that I had anything but pure strength buoying me up. God, if she only knew the truth, I would be dead in the water. But somehow I pulled it off. I don't know how, but I stood my ground and stared right back at her.

Her skin looked smooth and as silken as her expensive body lotion had advertised it would be. As I looked at her lovely, well-tended body, I realized she had no reason to be self-conscious. As if reading my thoughts, a slight smile came to her lips. Her eyes, however, remained piercing, cold. Her hand moved gently up her thigh and over her youthfully protruding pelvic bone. As her hand reached her belly, she paused at the only interruption in the perfection that was her body. A scar running from pubic hair to navel halted her hand's journey. This stitched up mar in the beauty had been her son's passageway to life. She brought my attention to it as if to emphasize her claim to his affection by right of sacrifice.

'What the hell are you doing here at this ungodly hour?' All pretense of civility was gone.

'After last night's fiasco, I felt we should talk.'

She was surprised by my tone. I was surprised by my tone. But I hoped it was a signal to her that she had underestimated me.

She threw open one of the closet doors without a word more and wrapped a white satin, feather-trimmed robe dramatically around her. She then began to strut around the room. Her red disheveled hair formed a comb-like tangle atop her head. And as she paced around the room with her hands clasped behind her back and her head bobbing up and down, she looked like a rooster eyeing an opponent at a cockfight. The analogy made me very uncomfortable."

"You was lucky ya din't get bloodied...or did ya?" Willie smiled as I replied with a hint of unguarded self-satisfaction.

"I wasn't the one that took the hits this time.

'What is it you want, Lauren?' She demanded angrily.

'I want to set some ground rules, Cynthia.'

She actually flinched at my tone as I cracked out her name. But she came back strong.

'Why you little bitch! How dare you come in here and use that tone of voice with me?'

I was ready. I had been up all night thinking about just what I would say.

'How dare I? I dare because I control the one thing that is going to keep you on good behavior from now on.'

She started to laugh.

'Oh, really?' She smirked. 'Little girl, you are out of your league.'

'I think not. All I have to do is say the word and you lose your precious boy.' Her laugh seemed a bit less confident this time.

'You're sorely mistaken if you think you have that kind of power,' she hissed attempting to convey total confidence. But, to the contrary, there was even less confidence in this response. I moved in for the kill.

'Need I remind you of what happened last night? Would you like to know what Glen said about you after he got off of the phone?' I didn't wait for her to respond. I was on a roll.

'He thinks I need protecting from you. He vowed to do whatever it takes to keep me happy. I'm to let him know if you ever upset me again.'

I paused as she, without changing facial expression, took in what I was saying.

'I could easily play into that scenario if I have to.' I lowered the volume of my words to almost a whisper. 'And you know how it would play out, don't you? I can make sure that there is room for only one of us in Glen's life. Whom do you think he'll choose?'

While her face remained expressionless, I knew nonetheless that I was scoring big time. Now was the time for the real venom, fangs to the throat.

'And don't doubt for one moment that I will make him choose if I have to.'

She actually grimaced and stared coldly at me for several seconds.

Finally, she spoke.
'What do you want?' She hissed."

"Hah! Ya had her!" Willie proudly stated.

"I had her. I did it. I didn't know how I had managed to pull it off...but I had. However, I also knew that I could still blow it if I wasn't careful. I had to keep my cool. I forced calm to reign.

'Just leave me alone,' I stated without anger or emotion. 'It's that simple. Don't talk about me. Don't order me around. Don't buy for me. Don't interfere in my relationship with Glen in any way. Just leave us alone and you can keep your son's affection.'

She sat and picked up her coffee cup with no expression on her face at all.

'That's it?' She asked staring into her coffee cup; taking a few sips.

'That's it,' I replied casually dropping into a chair.

She took a bite of toast as I watched. Without another word she lifted her orange juice, holding the glass in the air for just a second. She then offered it to me.

'I have no problem with that,' she smiled."

"I ignored the glass in her outstretched hand, and I rose to leave. This was going to be great. I had rehearsed a terrific exit in my mind on the drive over there. I spoke casually over my shoulder.

'Just remember one thing. I don't threaten idly. I will be cordial for Glen's sake. But interfere or cause any trouble and, as God is my witness, I will see that your son never speaks to you again.'

I then quietly closed the sitting room door behind me as I left. I immediately heard the crash of the juice glass hitting the other side. Whew! She was mad!

So that was it. She left us alone from then on...but the marriage still failed."

I sat silently with Willie just looking at me. I grew very uncomfortable.

"Why have I told you all of this? I've never told anyone these things," I was self-consciously aware that I was repeating myself but

I was still trying to wrap my head around what was going on here.

"Cause I could listen ta you talkin' forever."

It was such a sappy thing to say yet he was utterly sincere. He continued.

"Sometimes ya jess gotta talk ta get thins straight in yer own head. It's jess yer time ta talk dis whole thin' out 'n I happens ta be a good listener."

"But I'm not usually a talker, that's the thing. What is it about you? You're one of my student's, for God's sake. Why have I told you these really very private things?"

He looked so pensive, then so sincere.

"I's jess whats ya needs right now. Sometimes thin's jess happen dat way. I knew it right from da firs...I think, so did you. Yer at a place right now where's ya jess needs me, and here I is. Dat's dat."

He was actually making sense. Questions began flooding my thoughts.

"Who are you, Willie? How did you end up here? What was it that brought you into my life?"

I felt the tension, saw the discomfort and finally sensed the resolution. He had decided to tell me his story. At that moment it was all that mattered to me. Everything else had disappeared, vanished in that resolve to let me into his life. There was no more Mr. Jackson, no more Mellie Thomas, there was no more Glen or Cynthia; there was no one but Willie.

"I's here as part a my parole requirement," he stated.

"Parole! For what? What did you do?" I couldn't have masked my surprise even if I had tried.

"Murder," he paused briefly. "Two counts a murder."

He said it so effortlessly, almost comfortably. It took a few moments for the word to register. Murder. I kept replaying the word voiced so softly, the tone and tenor completely camouflaging the meaning.

"Murder? You?"

It had to be a joke, a really bad joke. I couldn't be so out of touch with human nature. He had to be teasing me.

"I kilt two guys. It was a long time ago. I was sixteen. Been out ten months now an part a da condition fer my release is I comes here ta school."

He watched with apprehension as I tried to sort through what I had just heard. But he said nothing further. No explanation. No pleading innocence. No insisting that it was all a mistake. No defense. He just waited for me to say something.

Oh, SHIT...not Willie too! I knew that he expected me to say something, but how could I respond? My instincts told me that I was in the presence of a warm, gentle, considerate man, while not well educated, a truly smart man. And now he tells me that he is a murderer? I had just started to make progress with my class and Mr. Jackson threatens me with bodily harm. All I wanted was to make a few copies of my lessons and Mellie spits in my face. I walk into my classroom on the first day expecting...I don't know what, but certainly not the insult that I received from Henry Baton, before I even told them my name. What the hell was going on? I expected to hear that creepy "Do Do Do Do," music and Rod Serling's voice announcing that I had entered *The Twilight Zone*, at any moment.

My life had always been so, I don't know, linear but since I came to Dawson there have been no straight lines at all, only roller coaster climbs and dramatic dips. My life up until now just went along. I just went along. I was simple; go with the flow Lauren Gates. The kinds of things happening in my life now just didn't happen to me. I didn't come in contact with murderers let alone get involved with them. Oh God, all that I had told him. What an idiot I was. What was this place?

As I looked at Willie's face. I began to shake my head. I wondered if as so often before, he knew exactly what I was thinking.
WHO WAS THIS MAN?

It's About Privileges

"You O.K., Teach?" The familiar concern coaxed me gently from my thoughts.

"I'm not sure, Willie."

"Kin I help?"

"I don't know if I can explain it to you, if I can make sense of it myself."

He looked so anxious to help, to please.

We sat two desks angled so our shoulders almost touched as we faced each other. He was close. I could smell the familiar sandalwood; feel his power. I looked down at those big hands, hands that I had associated with giving comfort and support. Could they have killed? I remembered the fast, violent reaction he had to Henry Baton that first day and his vicious comment about killing Mr. Jackson. Could he really kill? Without realizing it, I had begun to voice my thoughts.

"Do I know so very little about human nature? I come here thinking...O.K. so it's an all- black school. I'm a good teacher. It won't make a difference, but is that enough? Is being a good teacher enough? I guess not. All of my schooling, all those years taught me nothing about this world, your world. A place where a man like you, one of the most caring men I have ever met can be a self-proclaimed murderer. How did I get to be twenty-three years old and really know nothing about all of this?

All of the campus rhetoric, all of the protests, we credited ourselves with being such liberal thinkers. We marched for equality, so sure that we knew what was right. We knew what should be. We knew it all. When in reality; we knew nothing.

Why didn't I learn that there is a whole different culture, way of life right here under my very nose? I never got a first-hand look at your world. I've never had to sweat your concerns or have any kind of a sense of your life. The emotions are so heightened here: exposed more easily, explode more readily. Even if you're not a part of this world, you get caught up in it. It's that powerful. How could I not know this? Why wasn't I taught this?"

"Jess lucky I guess," he whispered, smiling, laughing an uncomfortable little laugh.

I shook my head and couldn't help but smile too.

"Just lucky," I agreed softly.

"Don't be so hard on yerself. I never knew of a life like yers till yer stories took me dere. Wasn't yer fault any more den it bes mines. You was jess born ta a place in da world dat had da privilege ta ignore my world. Never touched ya bafore. Jess like yer world done never touched me...still don't touch me. But difference is yer here. Right in da middle a my world now. You walks deese halls. Yer nose is filled wiff da smell a da tension we sniff as daily breathin air. You jess can't avoid havin' da might of da hands a our life lain on ya when you's here; leavin' its powerful fingerprints all over ya. Changin' ya from den on."

"But I have had contact with black people before. That's what's so confusing about all of this. I know, am friends with lots of black kids. We went to school together, lived together in the dorm..."

"Ya don't gets it. It ain't 'bout black en white. It's 'bout PRIVILEGE. Not jess color or even money but privilege. Somes got privileges fer whatever da reason that others jess don't got. And how many an da kinds a privileges ya got sets a kinda peckin' order in da world, where ya fits in, how ya fit in."

"Privilege, not race?"

"Well, yea race enters inta it. The very nature a bigotry is denyin' privileges but dere's lots more to it."

We both sat thinking about what he had said. It seemed like such a simple concept. Privileges.

"Do you think we can ever get to a time when we are all just people? I hate to sound like a simpleton, but wouldn't it be something if it wasn't race or color or religion or neighborhood or privilege or anything but just people? I'm embarrassed to admit it, but I thought that we could. Deep down inside, truly in my heart of hearts, I thought we really could. But here, now...I don't know anymore. I was so naïve, so totally unaware of places like this, cauldrons of such intense fire, emotions bubbling; constantly spurting reactions in all directions. Reactions so intense, spewing forth, scalding all in the way, all of the time. Oh I knew about ghettos and crime and poverty. But I thought we could just pull together and clean up the physical mess and establish programs for educating. I never had a clue about the culture of it all. Classes and a scrub brush won't bring equality. I didn't have a clue."

"The places in my life aren't like this. I'm lost here. At every turn I'm struck in the face with such passion...as I think about it, maybe you're right. Maybe it's not a black or white thing at all. Maybe it is a privilege thing instead. Maybe those with possessions and position use them to serve as shields, not so much from the discomforts of poverty but from the emotional realities it promotes. Without the distractions of privilege, every yearning, each pleasure, every moment of fear or dread, hatred and scorn is unencumbered, free to explode to the fullest degree of one's nature...in direct contrast to the propriety dictated reactions of my experience."

"God, am I just rambling or am I making some kind of sense here?"

"Dunno. What makes sense ta ya is a differnt thin all together from me. Ta me yer mother-in-law did't seem ta have propriety dictatin' her reactions." And he shot me a *uh ha you gets me smile*

I was taken aback. Cynthia surely didn't take a back seat to anyone when it came to letting her emotions run rampant. But somehow it wasn't the same. At least it didn't seem the same until I was forced to really look at it.

"I don't know. I can't get it all figured out."

He laughed the first genuinely hearty laugh of the day.

"If it bees easy, It'd all be takin' care of by now. All's I knows is we all gotta find da way ta get through en hopefully along dat way we can choose da paths dat might, jess might, lead us, each of us, ta a better place. We gots ta take advantage of it all...all dat comes ta us. If dere's one thin I know; we gotta make tings happen fer ourselves. Dere's ways ta do dat. I didn't always think so, but now I knows dere's ways."

"Sounds like you have given this a lot of thought."

"Had nothing much better ta do for all a dose years locked away. I was one a da lucky ones. I had me some help."

"What do you mean help? In prison?"

"Dere was dis program. Most guys went fer da cigarettes. But dere was dis lady...white woman, Mrs. Gardner. Somethin 'bout her, I knew from da firs she was gonna be important ta me. Kinda like when I firs seen you."

Hearing that last statement, his comparing how he felt about meeting me to how he felt when he had met another woman, a strange sensation passed through me. What was that? Jealousy? Was I feeling jealous? I looked at this man whom I had known...no not even truly known, just met such a short time ago and at the mere mention of a woman whom had been important to him, I'm reacting with jealousy?

What was the matter with me? This man just told me about his experience in jail...JAIL! He committed two MURDERS and of all the emotions that his incredible admission should evoke, the one I'm feeling is jealousy? What has happened to me in the brief time I have spent here?

"She was dere teachin' a readin' program" he was continuing.

"Came twice a week da whole time I was dere. Still goes, I bet. She cared. I was no one ta her. Gang member, murderer, everyone else but my ma didn't give a shit wah happened ta me. But she came twice a week. Drove from her soft little life ta help me. It did somethin' ta me, seein' dat small spit of a gal stare down dem brothers when dey got outta line. Kinda like how you done ta Barton, not sayin' a word...not needin' to."

Oh God, if he only knew the truth...

"She had more courage den anyone I ever knowd. So I studied. Learned. Truth is I really couldn't read too good at all, but she taught me. Stuck wiff me. We talked about anythin' dat came up. We talked politics, history, literature. An she helped me ta get out."

"Sounds like you were very lucky to have her."

"Jess one a da privileges dat come my way dat I took 'vantage of. Maybe some folks calls it luck. Howsever ya wants ta call it, I learned ya gotta take 'vantage, kick da shit outta any opportunity dat comes to ya. She taught me dat. Just like you gotta git back in dis here fight."

"What fight?"

"Jackson. Don't let him get away wiff keepin' ya from givin' some of dem privileges ta us. I knows what a difference ya can make."

"I don't know..."

"Where is dat strong determined gal who stood up to da likes a Cynthia? Don't tell me she's not still in dere somewheres."

He tapped my shoulder.

Good question! Where was that strong determined girl? Why did she keep disappearing on me when I really needed her? I knew that I had made progress since my insecurities led me into my marriage but it seemed every time I made some strives forward, I soon started falling into the same old habits. Look what I was doing with Willie. Wasn't he just another strong man that I thought I could rely on to take charge and handle things for me? Or was he?

To him it all seemed so simple. And he had helped make it simple for me too. He had taken me from utter confusion to such clarity. He was right. I could and I would get back into this fight. But how?

With Cynthia the solution just presented itself. The beauty shop incident was the impetus, but the resolution just evolved, painfully for sure, but I never really had to work at it. The solution to this problem was a whole different matter. Then, there was total clarity. Now, I only felt confusion. I truly did not know how to proceed.

As I looked at Willie, I could see the anticipation on his face. He expected so much of me. I didn't want to disappoint him. He was waiting for me to detail the course of action that he was sure I had devised...HAH! What course of action?

"So, let's say I'm going to take your advice and get back into this fight. You know more about this guy than I do. How would you handle him?"

"I'd kick his sorry ass up frough his throat 'n out his mouf...but you'd best take a differnt way; yer own way. What feels right ta you? If I wasn't here, wha'd ya do?"

I felt a moment of panic. He wasn't going to help me. Wait a minute. I had come too far from that frightened little girl needing someone to do her thinking for her to allow her to appear again. Wasn't I the person who had effectively neutralized the likes of Cynthia Jacobson?

And then it hit me.

Don't you love those moments when all of a sudden you begin to see things really clearly? I call them kaleidoscope moments when the jumbles of multi-colored, multi-shaped smatterings of half-formed ideas or concepts in utter confusion seemingly, miraculously morph into an unexpected, well-defined, intricate, previously undetectable pattern of absolute beauty making strikingly-clear sense.

I had to think for a minute. What should I do? My dad had always told me that focusing on the basics was always the best approach to solving any problem. Keep it simple. So, I began to go over, in my mind, the criticism Jackson had leveled at me.

"I'll concede the minor points and stand firm behind my teaching methods." The assurance with which I spoke surprised me.

"Aw right den. DO it! He should understand a little give 'n take. He couldn'ta gotten where he is wiffout it."

"O.K., that's it then; O.K., I'll see him tomorrow."

"Yea, jess git right up inta his face."

I looked at my watch. It had gotten very late.

"I've got to get home."

"Me too."

We both sat waiting for the other to make the first move to leave. It was apparent that neither of us wanted to go as we both broke into laughter.

"I do have to go," I insisted.

"Me too."

He finally rose.

The whole drive home, Willie's words were with me. Privileges. It was all about PRIVILEGES. I had never thought about it in that way before. But from my experience, it made perfect sense. The black people I had been so quick to point out to Willie that I knew were among a certain social economic group that he would consider privileged. Of course so were the whites by whom I was surrounded. With like-environments, issues of color certainly had less impact.

But just because I had no experience with other groups of people didn't mean I hated them. It didn't mean that they should hate me.

Would I feel differently if I were among the unprivileged group?

Motivational understanding didn't make dealing with the likes of Jackson any more pleasant to contemplate. I didn't want to understand him. I didn't even much care if he understood me. I simply wanted him to deal with me fairly. I'm sure if confronted (which I was not going to do) even he would admit that he hadn't come close to attempting that so far.

All evening I readied myself for my meeting with him. I'd logically lay out my position. We would probably exchange a few words and it would be over. I was willing to compromise. I was certain that he would be willing to do likewise.

How simple it now seemed. How lucky I was to have Willie on the sidelines. But what had he really done for me? Could it be that in reality I wasn't as needy as I thought? Was I simply not seeing my own strengths? Was I mistaking advice which I was free not to act upon and often didn't, with essential decision making without which I couldn't survive?

In actuality he had *not really done anything* for me except be a friend and help me work through my own thoughts. He wasn't making my decisions for me. He had merely led me back to realizing that I could do it for myself.

I had made progress. But, would the day ever come when I wouldn't need anyone else to get me refocused on my internal strength? Or does everyone need someone at times for that?

Finally, as the night ebbed I saw the sun rising, I had been unable to sleep with all of the possible scenarios of my conversation with Jackson playing and replaying in my head. I have always believed that there are people who, for whatever reason, are simply lucky in this lifetime. Then there are those who walk through life under a little black Winnie-the-Pooh rain cloud. I felt that I had always been blessed to be among the lucky. So now I would see if my luck would hold.

Somehow I knew that Willie had been put into my life to assist in my getting through this. He had made me see that it was within my own power to mend the appropriate fences and get on with teaching.

By the time I reached school, I had my whole speech prepared. So, by the end of the day, as I walked the halls to Jackson's office, I felt totally comfortable in what I was about to say.

I began as I sat down across the desk from him.

"I've been giving a lot of thought to our discussion yesterday. I feel that all of the problems that you mentioned can be worked out. I'd like to respond to your comments about the complaints that you've received about me."

I waited for some kind of sign that he agreed with my logic and wanted me to continue but I received none. I proceeded anyway.

"While personally I feel that my clothes are entirely my own business, I will make every effort to be more conscious of my appearance in the future. As far as your second complaint, I'd like to explain. I do not let any of my students smoke in my class. I have, however, *looked the other way* when Harlen Davis lights up in the hall because he is a fifty year old man, the same age as my father and it was just very uncomfortable for me to call him on it. But I will in the future, comfortable or not, make sure it never happens again.

Now, as far as the French..."

I leaned forward, my arms on the desk, looking him squarely in the eyes. He held my stare.

"I realize that teaching English Grammar through the usage of French is unconventional, but I am seeing real progress in the class, measurable progress with their English Language skills. I can't technically explain it but this incorporating some simple French word usage and grammar a couple of hours a week is really working. I know you'll agree that I need to teach using the most effective methods available to me. That's what I am paid to do. My students deserve no less. And this is working."

I sat back. Boy, that came out great...sounded even better than in front of my mirror. I was proud of myself. I waited to hear his agreement. How could he not agree with that logic? After all, we were on the same side in this. We both wanted what was best for the students at Dawson. He causally glanced up from some paperwork on his desk that had drawn his attention midway through my explanation.

"Wait right here," he barked as he stood abruptly and left the room obviously unimpressed with my monologue.

I sat stunned. What the hell was going on? All I wanted to do was the best job possible yet this man, this supposed administrator whose job it was to be of benefit to the students, to provide an environment in which they could grow and learn and thrive was throwing roadblocks in front of me at every turn. How was I to do my job if he was thwarting my every effort? I could feel my anger growing. I could sense my emotions blocking, blocking something...what? There was something I was missing. There had to be something going on here that I was definitely missing.

As I sat trying to calm myself, trying to figure out what it was; I scanned the room, distracting myself in the hope of gaining some insight. What was going on here? What did I know about this school, this program? Looking around my eyes happened upon the folder on his desk. He was holding it when I entered and didn't put it down until he left. Did I dare? What the hell? How much more trouble could I possibly get myself into? I rose and made my way behind the desk. The tab on the top file was marked "$ Received."

$ Received? What could that mean? I knew the center received its funding from the federal government but certainly documentation of the government funds received would need a larger folder than this measly little thing lying on the desk.

I looked around. Oh, what the hell! Without giving myself time to chicken out, I opened the folder to the first sheet of paper. The heading actually made me gasp.

DECEMBER DEPOSITS

Under that heading were weekly totals of the money per student received from the government. The next column was titled "Amount Reported." And the final column was "Difference Deposited."

It was so very simplistic, almost juvenile. Could it really be what it looked like? "Difference Deposited?" What difference? Why would there be a difference? Could there be some other explanation than the thoughts running through my mind? Deposited where? Could this blatant indictment of Jackson's malfeasance be for real? As I stared at the columns of numbers all I could think about was if he was smart enough to be syphoning money, stealing from the government, would he be stupid enough to be keeping such childish records? And could he be so clueless as to leave me in the room alone with them lying around on top of his desk? How could such a moron possibly be in charge of large sums of government educational funds? And, how in the world was he able to get away with it?

Monthly reports had to be filed on each student. The reports were the mechanisms by which Dawson received the appropriate funding to run the program. That was why taking attendance was so important. That was why my weekly progress reports on each of the students were meticulously filed. Without those reports, funds would be discontinued. So, what was his scam?

I scanned the names. There were several that I recognized belonging to students who I know had dropped out of the program and yet there were numbers under the amount received column. The amount deposited were the same. And then I noticed that other names belonging to students still attending had one number under amount received and another lesser number under amount deposited.

I slammed the folder shut. Holly shit, what had I stumbled onto here? This was fraud, major fraud. Oh my God. Unknowingly, I had become a part of it.

I went back to my chair. Thoughts were whirring through my head. I was part of a something here, something bad.

Did Jackson sense that I was some sort of threat? Is that why he seemed to be doing everything in his power to make it so uncomfortable for me? Was he hoping I would just quit? Had my assumption that the antagonism I felt from almost everyone wasn't about a white teacher in a black school or the clothes I wore or anything personal about me at all but rather the concern that I might find out what was really going on here and blow the whistle?

What should I do?

Before any feasible answer entered my thoughts, Jackson entered the office barking even before he took his seat.

"You're fired. Mellie's got your check. Clear your stuff out and leave immediately." He, very matter-of-factly, opened the top file and with head bent down peered at the paper without another word.

Fired? I sat stunned. Fired! He couldn't do that.

"You can't do that," I stated firmly as my back stiffened.

Without even looking up he replied, "I just did. Get out. I have no time to discuss this. There's important work that I have to attend to."

"But I have a contract."

"Not anymore. I was in meetings all morning about you. You can fight it...you'll lose. Now leave."

Fired. I had never even considered this possibility. At every turn I kept being slapped in the face with my naiveté. Well, no more. I was not going to let him run roughshod over me any more than I had let Cynthia. It might have taken me awhile, but I finally realized that once determined to act, no one was going to control me.

"You bet I'll fight this. Believe me, this is not over yet," I stated firmly resolving to leave little doubt about my determination.

"Bad attitude. Even worse decision. I thought you were smarter than that." He spoke quietly as he shook his head in feigned regret. I took his attitude as a direct insult.

"Oh, I'll just bet you did..."

He looked up at me with eyes blazing.

"I'm warning you. For your own sake, give it up now. This ain't suburbia...no sugar-sweet kids whose biggest problem is which Ivy League school to shoot for. These folks do a different kinda shooting." His voice took on a quietly threatening tone as he softly continued. "Go back to where you belong before you get hurt."

"I am a teacher, and a damned good one. I won't be scared off by idle threats."

"I hoped you wouldn't but I figured you'd say something like that. Too bad. Don't say I didn't warn ya." He once again buried his head in his paperwork.

I could see that it was pointless to try to continue this now. It would get me nowhere. I had to think this through. Figure out a strategy. Talk to a lawyer. I was sure that the law was on my side, but it would take time to get this straightened out, and my students were just starting to make progress. Merde. Merde. Merde!

I had to get control of my emotions. I wouldn't give him the satisfaction of knowing that he had upset me. In any confrontation, half the battle is the bluff.

As I rose and calmly walked out of his office, he grabbed a walky-talky from the corner of his desk. He watched me leave, impatiently waiting to make his call until I was out of earshot, obviously anxious to get back to business as usual. But it was anything but the usual business for me. I had to plan my next move carefully. I didn't want to make any mistakes by reacting in anger.

Mellie Thomas threw a check at me as I passed her desk. Amazingly, my reflexes were sharp, and I made a great one-handed catch, snatching it up before it floated to the ground.

"Nice toss, Mellie," I said sweetly over my shoulder as I left the outer office.

I was getting pretty good at effective exit lines.

I could almost feel the intense heat from her irate stare searing my back as I walked calmly away. But once out in the hall, out of her line of sight, I totally lost control of the anger that I had managed to contain while in Jackson's office.

I rushed through the hallways and slammed into my classroom. Who the hell did he think he was? Well, I would leave, but I would be back. This place had not seen the last of me yet. I would be back.

It took a moment of pacing around my empty room to realize that Willie was not there waiting for me as he had said he would be. No matter, I would gather my things and leave...for now. But I would be back, God damn it!

There really wasn't much to pack up: some papers, a few personal things. But I couldn't bring myself to walk out the door. Despite all of my bravado, deep inside, I had the feeling that once I left, I would never be coming back.

Where was Willie? I could use his clear thinking. I needed someone to tell me that I wasn't crazy.

I needed to say good-bye. God, how was I ever going to say good-bye?

And who was going to tell my class? What would they be told happened? I didn't want them to think that I was abandoning them. Oh, how I hated not having control over the way this would be handled.

I decided to leave a note on the blackboard. I had no idea if it would still be there when they came back to class, but it was my only chance to let them know the truth and I felt that I had to take it. As I wrote in a very unsteady hand, tears began to fill my eyes.

Due to a serious dispute with Mr. Jackson over my teaching methods, I have been fired. This does not diminish the significant progress that you all have made through your own hard work. It has been my great pleasure to know all of you and a privilege to be your teacher. If you keep working hard, I have every confidence that you will accomplish your goals...I believe in you. Adieu mes eleves. "Until we meet again my students" Lauren Gates.

I had hoped that writing the message would make it easier for me to leave. It had not. I just could not bring myself to walk out of the door.

Where was Willie? I realized that I was actually waiting for him to show up. The more time passed, the worse I felt. It was late. It had gotten dark. I had reached the point where I just wanted to get home. I couldn't wait for Willie any longer, I just couldn't. I had to get out of there.

Where was Willie?

Just You and Me, Baby

I was struck by the cold and by how instantly I had become so very tired as I left the building. I looked around enveloped by my now very familiar dark, barren, desolate surroundings. Why would anyone want to fight to stay in a place like this? Why did I? I shook my head at my own disturbing thoughts. I was just too tired to think about it now.

I walked to my car. It was the last one in the lot. I guess Mr. Jackson's pressing paperwork wasn't that important after all. All at once I was very aware of just how dark and deserted this lot truly was. There wasn't even an El train to break the eerie, cold calm of this night.

I opened my purse looking for my keys. God, it was so dark. For the first time I was suddenly aware of how totally secure I felt having Willie with me in this lot at night and how scary it was right now not to have him with me. I continued my search for the elusive keys as I realized that I had never really thought about my safety here when he was with me. I never had to.

No luck finding the keys yet. I looked around nervously. Not a soul to be seen. All I saw was my breath in the cold air...more and more of it as I continued my search in the abyss of my purse. Desperation mounted. I checked the zippered pouch for the millionth time. They weren't there. I bit the tip of my index finger, tugging off my glove with my teeth so I could really hunt in earnest.

One final, enormous, cloud producing sigh; I found the keys and was in my car with the doors locked, sweating in my bulky winter coat. I sat for a moment supporting my very heavy head on the steering wheel. What was I going to do now? Oh, I talked a good show, but now I actually had to figure out what to do. Was I kidding myself? I wasn't up to this. I put up a brave front to Jackson's threats, but if a dark parking lot could scare the hell out of me...?

I finally got around to starting the car...starting the car...trying to start the car. I kept turning the key. The engine wouldn't turn over. I looked around me as the reality of my situation sank in. True panic was next to sink in.

My anxiety level was building with every subsequent turn of the key. I kept trying and trying but the car would not start. The engine just simply kept grinding. I waited several minutes hoping that it was just flooded and would start after a rest. But I smelled no gasoline odor. I didn't think that it was flooded, but what did I really know about cars? The cold breath smoke billowed from my mouth as I inhaled and exhaled quickly. The windows began to fog over.

I had to calm down, think. Think logically. So, that is exactly what I did. One last deep breath and then I concentrated on my breathing and heartbeat. Slowly they both decreased to normal. O.K. Now I could begin to think sensibly. So, doing just that, I came to the very sensible realization that I was in deep shit!

The doors to Dawson locked upon closing after 4:00 P.M., another security measure. No way to get back in there. The only establishment with a phone within walking distance was the bar across the street...the same bar that Willie had warned me to absolutely stay away from. The conversation came flooding back into my memory.

"Maybe sometime we can have a drink or somethin' after class," he had shyly suggested.

"Maybe so. There's the bar across the street." I had replied.

He began to laugh. I remembered quite clearly my degree of anger growing proportionately to the intensity of his amusement. I didn't like being the brunt of a joke, especially one I didn't even understand. He finally realized that I did not share his amusement.

"Sorry. I's sorry. Ya gotta jess picture...I really couldn't bring ya dere."

"Well, maybe I'll just have to go there and see for myself just how funny it is." I was never one to be told I couldn't do something. I didn't like this at all.

Noticing the defiance spreading across my face, he became deadly serious.

"It's not funny. I's sorry. I don't wantcha ta never go in dere. It's no place for ya. Yous gots ta understand, dey's places 'round here dat ain't safe fer...no one ta go.

"You mean places that are not safe for a white woman to go." I smiled broadly, "like Dawson Skill Center." The tension was broken when I began to laugh and soon we were laughing together. And just as quickly Willie darkened.

"Jess don't never go dere." His command was ominous, and I nodded my assent.

Sitting in my car, in the dark, with the windows fogged up, shaking with...I don't know, was it just the cold making me shiver? I remembered the tone of his voice. And I remember very clearly the fear he instilled in me. That fear had returned now, big time.

What was I going to do? That bar seemed my only option. I certainly couldn't stay in the car all night.

Then I saw him. A man had opened the door of the school and was looking out into the lot. A moment later he was looking directly at me. Was it Willie, still in the building waiting for me?

Simple relief replaced the momentary joy of that prospect when I saw the man put a walky-talky to his mouth and I realized that it was a security guard. I was further calmed when I caught sight of the uniform as he opened the door wider and became fully lit from behind. It had never occurred to me that the Skill Center would have manned nightly security. I had seen none before, but then I wouldn't have. Once we decided it was time to leave, Willie always whisked me quickly out of the building each evening. I thought that the building was just locked up at night.

I was never so happy to be wrong in my life.

I got out of the car and approached the guard. When he saw me coming toward him, he nodded understanding, spoke a few more words that I could not make out, then, replaced his walky-talky in its holster type case, which hung from his belt. He opened the door further to let me in. Thank God my luck was holding. He was even wearing a gun to protect me. Relief flooded through me. I was safe.

"Car trouble?" He asked, taking one more look around the parking lot before slamming the door closed.

"It just wouldn't start, wouldn't even turn over. I can't understand it. Maybe the cold, but it has never done that before. I have to tell you; I was sure glad to see you. I don't know what I would have done..."

He interrupted my appreciative enthusiasm with a sentence-stopping sneer.

"I guess it's jess you 'n me, baby." He stroked his gun and then grabbed for my hair.

I ducked and ran. I don't know how I got away. I don't remember even having a conscious thought. My instincts and pure panic just took over. I was too scared to scream, not that it would have done any good: we were totally alone. I ran. I heard his heavy steps behind me. I was desperate. What could I do? I had to get to my room. I was about to turn and throw my purse at him, my only weapon, but suddenly realized that even if I could get to my room, I would need the key to open it and I kept the key in my purse. Then I remembered, shit, I didn't have the key. It wasn't my room any longer. I had left the key on my desk...my room was open! I hadn't locked it when I left. There was hope. I had somewhere to go. I'd worry about what to do when I got there...when I got there.

As I ran the building's hallways toward my room, I could hear his heavy breathing. He was a large man, a man of excess weight. The extra pounds were taking their toll. Though his steps were steady behind me, his breathing became more labored. Maybe I could outrun him, tire him out...who was I kidding? He had a gun!

The image of him standing in that doorway appeared in my mind's eye. The look on his face as he grabbed for my hair exploded into my thoughts. The terror of that first moment when I knew I was in trouble began flooding my memory. He had a gun. No matter how much distance I could put between us, even if I secured myself behind my locked classroom door, he had a gun. I could find nothing in this train of thought to reassure me. I was better off not thinking.

I reached my room ahead of him and slammed the door shut, locking it from the inside just as he reached it. I could feel him grabbing the knob on the other side. As I held it, the knob shook and jiggled, but the lock held firm.

What to do? What to do? Think, Lauren. My pulse throbbed in my neck. I heard every tha-dud, tha-dud echoing through my head.

There was quiet from the other side of the door. Every silly, slapstick, *I Love Lucy* episode where she rigged up some kind of booby trap to befall her pursuer came to mind in a rush. What could I do against a gun?

I tried to listen past the thud-dud, thud-dud of my heart beating. Not a sound. God, what was he doing? Where was he? Why was he waiting? If he was going to...why didn't he get it over with? Moments passed but there was still noth...CRACK,CRACK, CRACK. Three shots shattered the knob and surrounding wood. I was still holding onto the knob as something sliced across the back of my hand. I remember thinking that it must be a large shard of wood. I jumped back as he slammed into the room.

I could feel the wet warmth of blood seeping between my fingers. Oh God, the look in his eyes. A gleeful hatred beamed at me from those awful eyes.

I was powerless to move for a moment as I stared fixedly into that hate. I became aware of a fear growing within me the likes of which I had never known before Then, all at once I felt an overwhelming surge of repulsion which seconds later was replaced by fear. And then, blessedly, tremendous anger replaced the fear as I shoved one of the desks at him as hard as I could. It slid along the tiled floor and hit him mid-thigh. His hatred changed instantly to fury. He flung the desk aside effortlessly and started for me. I skirted around another desk and pushed it towards him. This time he anticipated it and with a sweep of his meaty hand, pushed it aside before it struck him.

I scooted down one isle making for the door but gauging my intention he shoved a desk in front of me to block my escape. A few more seconds of avoiding desks being shoved at me and I found myself backed into a corner. God damn it, I was trapped. The son of a bitch had me trapped.

He slowly walked the few steps to stand right in front of me.

"Wouldn't listen, huh? Think you'll be makin' a fuss now?"

I wanted to keep him talking. I had read somewhere that the best defense against an attack was to get the attacker talking and keep him talking.

"What do you mean? Listen to what?"

"You know."

"No, really. Tell me. I'll listen to you. Please, explain what you're talking about."

"They said you was smart. I heard 'em talkin'. Pretty, too...for a white girl. But you can't be too smart ta be here, huh?"

I couldn't think about what he was saying. All I knew was that I had to keep him talking. I had to figure a way out of this.

"What do you mean?"

"You, in this place, not too smart, are ya?"

"I'm a teacher. Why shouldn't I be in a school?"

He grunted a half laugh.

"This ain't no school..."

My attention was suddenly shifted from my safety to what he meant by that comment and to the file I had seen on Jackson's desk. Maybe I could get some information out of him.

"Then what is it if it isn't a school?"

He didn't answer. He just started toward me.

"What did you mean?" I tried desperately to engage him once more in conversation.

He didn't answer me. Our conversation was obviously over.

"So, what now? You've got me cornered. What do you intend to do with me?" I tried to sound calm, in control, but the words came out in a less than confident whisper.

I only caught a glimpse of a demonic grin and then the blur of his cocked arm before he struck my cheek with a powerful blow. I felt the bones of his knuckles crack with his slap into the side of my face sending a thunderous clap reverberating in my head. It was as if there was no flesh, no meat buffering the collision of the steel-like back of his hand and my cheekbone. While I guess it was technically only a slap, the blow, so intense, sent me stumbling back into the wall. I hit my head hard and then I saw only black.

I wasn't totally conscious but not totally out either. While not being able to see at first, I was aware of his considerable weight on me, all over me. There were no more slaps only the awful smell of him and the weight of him to be endured. He reeked of hatred. I was gagging. I think he had his arm across my throat, holding me down. I was kicking, thrashing, fighting, trying to get him off of me, but he was so heavy, crushing. I couldn't catch my breath. I saw only blackness, felt only his tremendous mass upon me.

Then all at once I felt no weight at all. I stopped kicking, stopped fighting. The weight had been lifted off of me as quickly as it had dropped onto me. Was I dead? No. I was gasping for breath, my windpipe suddenly free. I began to see something through the blackness. I saw the forms of two bodies, struggling, coming into focus. I recognized the uniform and suddenly I was able to make out the other...it was Willie.

There was no time. Swarming blurs of motion, cracks of sound. Had the gun fired again? I was there and then not. I saw Willie come for me. He took off his shirt and ripped a long strip of cloth and wrapped it oh so gently around my hand. Why did he do that? I was gone again.

I was outside. I was floating above the ground. No, that couldn't be right. And then, once again I was gone.

Suddenly I realized that it was very cold. And then the sensation left me. In what seemed like the next moment I was inside somewhere small, alone. I saw the car hood up in front of me. Heard it...no felt it slam shut. My head hurt. Then there was movement...driving somewhere.

I saw stars in a blue/black sky. I was gone again. And then, I heard...music...yes it was music. I was in my car. I don't know how I knew, but it was my car. And I was gone again. Who was driving? I turned my head. OH, GOD, MY HEAD HURT! I tried to focus. Who was driving?

It was Willie. What was Willie doing driving my car? What was I doing slumped in the passenger seat? I tried to straighten up, sit more upright but a searing pain halted my effort. What had happened?

"Where are we going?" I heard a little voice come from my throat.

"I's takin' ya to a hospital."

"Why? What happened?" I tried once again to straighten up in the seat.

It hurt. That sharp pain stabbed my head. It was a searing agony, but I did manage to get more upright. I opened the window just a bit. The cold air felt wonderful against my face. Trees whizzed by. Huge winter-barren, trunk-and-limb skeletons dotted the lakefront. The lights of Lake Shore Drive glittered upon the still water. No, not just lights. It had started to snow ever so lightly. While everything else was pretty much a blur, I could see the intricate detail of the flakes as they fell all about us, sticking to the car's window before melting. Why was that? How could I see the snow so clearly?

"You say somethin'?" Willie asked gently.

But I was unable to answer. Had I spoken?

I was aware of no other cars, and there were no people on the beach. God, what was I thinking? It was winter. No one would be on the beach this time of year...this time of night. I was so confused. Tiny flakes hit my face through the opened window with wonderful cold wetness.

"Ya O.K. over dere? Maybe ya should lay back down till we get dere."

"I don't need to go to a hospital." I was amazed that I was making sense. I continued. "Really. Please, just take me home." The events of the past few hours began to bombard my thoughts. "Really. I need to go home." Even to my ear, there was strong resolve in my voice. I closed the window. I was getting wet.

"Ya sure?"

"Positive. Willie, please."

I don't remember telling him where I lived or how to get there. He pulled over to the curb and quickly made his way to my side of the car. All at once his gentle strength was all around me as he gingerly lifted me from the seat. I draped my arms about his neck and inhaled deeply, relishing his smell. I relaxed immediately as he tightened his hold of me ever so gently. Looking down, I saw a dark splotch of color on my seat back where my head had rested. The reality that it was quite a bit of blood, my blood, struck me and I nuzzled into Willie's neck. So that's why my head hurt so damned much!

He had parked the car down the street from my apartment building. I could have told him that there was a garage to park in, but it was so comfortable, safe in his arms. I needed to feel that way, if only for a little while longer.

"Better give me yo key," he said.

"There's a doorman," I replied.

Willie looked a bit nervous. So did the doorman as he opened the front door for us.

"Miss Gates, what happened? Are you alright?"

"Yes, Jack, I'm fine. Just a bit of an accident." I felt Willie tense at Jack's glare.

"Jack, this is my good friend, Mr. Taylor. I don't know what I would have done if he hadn't come to my rescue."

"Pleased ta meet cha." Jack mumbled, appeased but not happy.

We entered the elevator.

"I think you can put me down now." I really didn't want him to ever put me down.

"Ya sure you's O.K.?"

"Only one way to find out..."

He placed me ever so gently, feet on the ground.

"There, see? A bit wobbly, but O.K."

The door to my floor opened. I stepped out but Willie didn't follow. I looked back at him standing there...looking at me.

"Please, come in, Willie. I'm still a bit shaky." I continued in a whisper. "I'm afraid to be alone just now."

He didn't smile. Didn't speak. He just walked off of the elevator. He took my purse from me and instantly found my house key.

In that moment I realized that I still had my purse flung over my shoulder. After all that had happened, my purse strap had remained on its perch. The thought made me laugh. Ooooh that made my head hurt even more. But with everything that had happened, I was, perhaps inappropriately, amused that I still had my purse over my shoulder. Another squeaky, small laugh escaping my lips caused excruciating pain to sear through my head. My hand reflexively touched the back of my head. Warm wetness covered the now throbbing area. I found that if I synchronized my gait, as I somewhat wobbly made my way down the hall towards my apartment, with the throbs; it lessened the pain.

When I stopped at my door, he opened it. He then stepped aside so I could enter first.

I turned on the lights and went to unbutton my coat. The buttons weren't there. Where were the buttons to my coat? At first this was a total shock. What had happened to my buttons? Then realization struck. That man had ripped opened my coat. I hadn't even been aware of it. Oh God, the thought of what had happened...what could have happened; I bolted back into Willie's arms crying, no, wailing uncontrollably.

We just stood there, Willie gently stroking my back saying nothing, just holding me until I had quieted a bit. Then he helped me to the couch. My breath came in huge gasps as he sat cradling me. Then, I was merely sobbing and finally the tears stopped, and my breathing became more regular.

"Who was that man? Why would he...?"

"Dunno," was his simple reply.

I knew they were useless questions being asked of the wrong person, yet I was unable to control my asking. I sat silent for a moment and then one more question came to mind, one that Willie could answer and one that I was determined he would answer.

"Where were you? I needed you. I..." My anger flared.

All of my fear and pain was all at once directed at him. But my totally unfair, condemnation was silenced by one look into his guilty, so very sorry face. What was I doing? He had saved me. None of this was his fault. I was only making myself feel even worse by lashing out at this dear man. And look what I was doing to him. I raised a hand and tenderly stroked his face.

"It's not your fault." How lame it sounded.

"Mellie found me waitin' fer ya in da classroom 'n toll me dat she got a call. Said my Ma was in a accident. I din't think...just left. God, I's sorry. I's so sorry." His whisper was barely audible from his hung head. "I rushed right back soon as I knew."

"You mean this was planned? I was set up?"

"Looks like."

The walky-talkies...Jackson!

Now I was angry, very angry, so angry my head began to throb with such force I had to close my eyes for fear that they would explode from my skull. And then the anger turned to fear, intense, debilitating fear. What had I gotten into?

"Why would Jackson do this to me? Why would anyone do this to me? It makes no sense."

I was having trouble breathing and talking at the same time, my breath coming in huge gasps again.

"It's my fault. I know'd what kinda place Dawson is. I thought I could protect ya. I din't wantcha ta go. I shoulda thought more 'bout you and less 'bout what I wanted. It's all my fault."

"That's ridiculous. Don't even think that way. This was not your fault. I would never have let you talk me into leaving even if you had tried. To the contrary, without you...I don't even want to think what would have happened."

The tears began to flow again. The last thing I wanted was for Willie to feel guilty but I was helpless in controlling the flood of emotion.

He just sat there with me, not saying a word for what must have been hours. He just let me do whatever it was I had to do to get through the night. At times it was all out crying, other times whimpering sighs. Very few moments passed in utter silence. There seemed to always be some sort of noise coming from me. Still, no matter what God-awful sounds I made, he held me fast and let me get it all out, until finally he spoke.

"Best do somethin' 'bout dat cut head."

He turned me so he could look at the back of my head. I felt him gently lift my hair.

"Not too bad," he diagnosed. "Be right back."

He eased me out of his embrace and made his way to the kitchen. He returned with two wet towels; one was soapy. He began to gently wash the cut. While certainly not comfortable; it didn't hurt as much as I had expected it would.

"Now, let's see what I's can do here." As he spoke, I felt the slight tug of him knotting several strands of hair on either side of the gash.

"Dere dat'll hold it t'gether till it heals. Rest a yer hair'll cover it up so's no one'll see it. As soon as da knots grows out, ya jess cuts 'em off n no one'll ever know. God's own stitches, we calls it."

"Where'd you learn that?"

"Dere's times ya jess can't go ta no doc. You needs ta improvise." A broad smile crossed his face as he emphasized *IMPROVISE.*

I leaned against him, making myself comfortable in the security of his presence, smiling to myself at his wonderful way.

After what seemed hours of settling in, he sighed deeply.

"Ya up ta talkin'? I'd really like ta know what finally happened 'tween you 'n Glen. Why'd ya finally quit him?"

I knew exactly what he was doing and why. I was so grateful to get my mind off of my terror. I gladly cleared the thoughts of all that had just happened from my mind, buried all of the questions, the answers to which I wasn't even sure I wanted to know.

"Well." I forced myself to focus on my past with Glen.

"I guess I was just finally forced to admit that he was never going to be the man I was hoping he would grow into. No, that's not exactly right. I realized he had never been the man that I had thought he was and then expected him to grow into. Fairly or unfairly, I had expectations that he couldn't live up to and that I couldn't compromise on. And by the same token, I was certainly not, nor would I ever be the wife he wanted and needed."

"How long was ya married?"

"Three years, just long enough to become truly miserable."

"Any 'mount a time is too long ta be unhappy."

"In all fairness, I wasn't unhappy the whole time. We had our moments. Given the right type of woman, I guess he would make a good husband…. I just wasn't her. But I do feel good about the fact that I really did give it every chance to work. I really did try. Even near the end when I knew in my heart, I would have to leave him, I still wanted to make one last effort."

"So was dere a 'somethin' dat ended it or was it jess time ta call it quits?"

"Oh, there was a definite a something."

Glen Revealed

I stared out the window for a moment. The snow had stopped as I sat warmed in the comfort of Willie's massive embrace. How strange that it felt so right to have him here with me, to be telling him about my life, my feelings; feelings I had so ardently avoided dealing with in the past.

It seemed to be late, very late, but I had no way of knowing what time it was or even what day it was. I was not at the right angle to see the face of the Waterford clock that was on my desk at the far side of the room. It had been a wedding present from one of my parent's friends. *May the joys of your life together be as multifaceted as this gift.* They were the words I have so often written on the card of the many wedding gifts Glen and I gave to friends and family. The cut crystal of Waterford, so delicate, fragile, yet, it always seemed substantial, sturdy, unlike some other crystal designers. Waterford looked to last.

After receiving the clock as a gift, it became my favorite offering to a bride and groom representing unlimited possibilities for a future filled with beauty and substance, a promise of all the good times they would share in their lifetime together. It was one of the few precious things that we had received for our wedding that I had taken with me after the divorce. I hadn't wanted to fight over things. I hadn't wanted to fight anymore. I just wanted out.

I remembered back, back to sitting on my den couch looking at that clock, watching the minutes tick away, feeling my life tick away with them. I finally realized that day, I really only had three options as I sat there in my beautiful home, surrounded by such opulence: I could kill myself, but that seemed so melodramatic. I couldn't really consider that a viable option; I could stay married to Glen and be taken care of and pampered in such elegance and style and truly go insane. Oh, I could probably pull it off. No one would ever know that I had gone nuts, but I would know and that has to be the worst kind of insanity...when no one else knows about it; or I could simply leave. As soon as I had given thought to it, it was easily decided. I had to leave him.

"Hey, Teach. Where'd ya go?" Willie tightened his embrace.

I was pleased to be brought back to this place with this man.
"I'm right here." I dug in even closer.
"So, ya wanna finish da story or do I gotta tune in next week?"
"I need to figure out just where to begin to tell you the end."
"Take yo time. I ain't goin' no wheres."
And I was so glad of that. I sensed that he knew it too.

"We had been married two and a half years and even Glen had to
finally admit that something was wrong between us. So, he decided
that we needed to get away on a little mini vacation, just the two of
us. He arranged to surprise me with a long weekend in Vegas. He
had convinced himself that getting away would cure everything that
was wrong with me. I knew it was useless to continue to point out
that there was nothing wrong with me, that it was the "us" that
needed fixing. But he was trying the only way he knew how to make
me happy and I was determined to try also.
So, we boarded the plane, taking our seats in first class."
"Firs class!" Willie whistled. "I ain't never been on no airplane,
'specially firs class!"
"When I remarked about the extravagance to him, Glen said, 'if
you don't think you're first class and are willing to spend the money
to prove it, why should anyone else treat you like you're first class?'"
"I guess he kinda had a point." Willie acknowledged.
"Maybe so, but then he said, 'Besides, we're RICH!' He said it just
loud enough for the other passengers to hear him.
I was so embarrassed as everyone turned to look at us. I was
ready to call the whole trip off, but the wheels started rolling.

I have always loved to fly. To hear the powerful rumbling, feel the
powerful bumping produced by the tons of the pure, energy-filled
mechanical giant racing down the runway. Like a well-disciplined
long-distance runner controlling the urge for an all-out sprint, it
waits, steadily building, building momentum until the final release of
reserved energy that, once tapped, explodes into the thrust skyward.
As many times as I have experienced it, I still find that I have to
stifle a gasp as I am magically lifted towards the heavens.
And this lift off was even more special. I allowed myself to feel
hopeful as we embarked on five days of luxury. Maybe getting away

was what we needed, neutral territory in which to make a new start at being happy."

"During the trip, Glen attended to my every whim. I mean he really went all out to please me. Anything that money could buy."

"Sounds like da man was tryin'."

"Oh, he was. He always tried. That was never the problem. The problem was that he always tried the wrong things. What I so desperately needed couldn't be bought. All of the gifts, the cars, the house, could not create a loving, caring, sharing environment in which our life together could grow and prosper. Yet, he was convinced that all of these material things could do that. He had only to buy the right things, find the proper combination and he would make me happy. He was determined to buy my happiness. It never occurred to him that that might not be enough. It was compassion, a true sense of sharing our lives and a sense of contentment that I so desperately sought."

I could see from his expression; I had lost him.

"Does this make any sense at all?"

Willie looked rather bewildered. To tell the truth I wasn't so sure of my explanation either.

"Well, all of that doesn't really matter. The point is he was trying and I was determined to have a good time upon which I was hoping to begin to build a better future with him. I had to believe that I would be able to get through to him.

And we were having a good time, at first. Las Vegas is such a crazy, fabulous place. Have you ever been?"

"Me? Ta Vegas? Naw, never got dere. Never got most anywheres."

I was instantly sorry I asked. How stupid could I be? I searched his eyes but gratefully saw no hurt or discomfort in them. I felt selfish and inconsiderate. I would have to really try harder to think a little bit before I spoke. I didn't want to hurt this man who had saved my life.

"Well, it is a complete escape from reality. But it is not a place to stay for any length of time. A long weekend is more than enough time."

"Hows come?"

"It's just such a crazy place..."

"Ya already said dat. What's so crazy?"

"It's hard to describe. Everything is upside-down. You're up all night between gambling or seeing great shows and so you sleep most of the day unless you're into pool sitting. Some people play golf. Most people are there for only one thing...gambling. And you can pay for everything with the casino chips. It's like a whole different country with its own monetary system and currency. Glen was throwing chips at all of the hotel staff for their tips. You can lose all track of the fact that these little multicolored discs are actually money. It's so easy to forget that.

And Glen was so happy. I was determined to try.

I'm not much of a gambler but when I do play, my game is blackjack. I knew I could always find Glen at the craps table. When I would take a break, I would stand watching him from across the casino. He loved shooting craps. The way he stood, the look of pleasure, winning or losing, on his face; he just enjoyed it.

There he stood, tall, good-looking with such striking green eyes. They literally shone with excitement all the way across the room. They sparkled so, they put the deep green of the felt covered tables, reflecting in the crystal chandeliers above, to shame. He was handsome. His looks still caused a reaction within me. Oh, nothing earth shattering like in the porno books, but just a subtle pulse which seemed to vanish as soon as I consciously acknowledged its existence."

"Sounds ta me likes ya still had somethin' fer him."

"At that point I guess I did. But I didn't know what it was. Was it just physical attraction? If so, why couldn't I build that into at least physical satisfaction? I yearned so for contentment."

"Bad sex'll bust a marriage every time," he stated flatly.

"And are you speaking from experience, my friend?" I teased.

"HELL NO! Oh, Teach, sorry."

It continued to embarrass him when he swore in front of me.

I couldn't help but smile at him. After everything I had told him, how could he still have this idealized view of who and what I was?

"I weren't never married. I gotta get my own self in order firs. I got my Ma 'n sister ta take care of."

"Were you born sensible?" Amusement spread across his face as he realized that I had repeated the words he had spoken to me during our very first talk.

"So, I guess da trip turned out ta be a bust, huh?"

"It was just the beginning of an incredible sequence of events that changed my life forever."

"Now ya gots ta tell me. Dis sounds good."

"Well, the five days came and went and although I was tanned and rested, nothing between us had really changed. I had hoped that Glen was right and that a change of environment would produce a positive effect on our relationship. But sadly, it didn't.

Glen, remaining true to his nature; felt that he had done his part. He had determined what it would take to solve *my problem* and then made sure he provided the appropriate solution. Now he assumed that everything was fine. But in reality nothing had changed at all.

That last morning in the hotel, he left me to my breakfast in the coffee shop to go check out. I watched him walk away, his powerful swagger that heralded supreme confidence brought an ironic smile to my lips. That which had attracted me from his first kiss was at the very root of our problems. What was I to do? When, how could I tell him?

Our waiter interrupted my thoughts when he arrived, with phone in hand, at my table.

'Phone call for Mr. Jacobson, you want to take it?'

'Yes, I'll take it, thank you.' He plugged the phone into a jack at tableside.

Glen's father was on the line.

'Oh, Lauren it's you. Is Glen there?'

I knew at once that something was very wrong."

"How'd ya know?" Willie stopped my tale.

I looked at him. I could see that he wanted to understand more about me.

"Well, his voice sounded strained. He hadn't even bothered with the obligatory niceties. No *how are you or how's the trip going?* No pleasantries at all. This was not like the ever-considerate Arthur I had grown to love. I could sense the tension; feel the tightness.

Anyway, I looked up and saw Glen approaching.

'Yes, he's right here.' I answered and handed Glen the phone. 'It's your dad.'

Glen looked as surprised as I felt. He waited a second and then took the phone.

'Hi Dad. What's up?'

As soon as Glen heard his father's voice his expression changed. He must have sensed the same distress that I had. With phone cradled in the crook of his neck he dug into his pocket and handed me several hundred-dollar bills. He didn't even count them.

'Here, baby, go pick something out in the gift shop. I'll meet you there.'

From the look on his face I knew not to question what was happening. I took the money and left.

It took about ten minutes for him to join me there. His anger was so intense; I felt it even before I saw it on his face.

'Glen, my God, what is it?'

I couldn't imagine what Arthur could have possibly said to get him so upset.

'He's so fucked up, even I can't help him now,' was all he would say."

"I knew something really bad had happened as soon as I heard Arthur's voice. And it wasn't just his voice. Why would he be calling when he knew we would be home in just a few hours and he could talk to us then? But I didn't expect whatever it was to have such an effect on Glen. Oh, Willie, you should have seen him. He was a maniac. He began throwing money at the hotel employees, shouting out their instructions. The desk clerk, the doorman, the bellboy all took their turn at receiving his verbal abuse. It was a real scene."

"After what Cynthia pulled in dat clothes store, seems like he comes by it natural."

"Natural or not I was embarrassed and worried and scared.

'Glen, what's happened?' I asked trying to get his attention but it was as if I wasn't even there. He was so wrapped up in his tirade. I had seen him explode on many occasions, but never like this. Something was really wrong and I had no way of finding out what it was.

In his haste to usher me into the limo that was to take us to the airport, he brushed against the doorframe of the car. With a fluid, powerful stroke he smashed his fist into the door yelling, 'God damned door! 'and literally threw me into the backseat.

I didn't know what to do. I thought for sure that he had broken bones. I went to gently take his bruised fist into my hand but he snatched it back and stared silently out of the window. I made no further attempts to comfort him. All I could do was grow more and more worried. Not knowing the cause of such an emotionally charged outburst was scaring me to death."

" We drove to the airport in complete silence. Once there, the scene at the ticket counter mirrored the horror of the one he had created in the hotel lobby. After Glen had totally humiliated several of the airline personnel we were finally on the plane. When he seemed to have settled down a bit, I thought it safe to once again try to get some answers. I took his arm, hoping to get some kind of response. He said nothing, did nothing but he let me hold onto him.

'Glen, you're scaring me.' Was all I could manage to say, and that came out in such a low whisper, I doubted that he even heard me.

It took a few moments but he finally turned to look at me. To my utter shock, his expression was totally relaxed.

'I'm so sorry, baby. I didn't mean to frighten you,' was all he said as he put his arm around me.

He might have thought that that made everything O.K., but I was not about to let it drop. I wanted some answers. I deserved some answers.

'What's going on? What did he say to get you so upset?'

'Dad resigned from Leasco,' he stated flatly. I mean there was no emotion in his voice at all...nothing. It was really spooky. And that's all he would say."

"Wa's Leasco?" Willie asked.

"Leasco was Arthur's company. He had started it when he was Glen's age and from absolutely nothing he had built a multi-million dollar conglomerate. For him to resign meant that he was in big-time trouble. The business was like one of his children. He loved it, nurtured it. He'd never just resign. I realized that the nature of Glen's reaction was certainly not called for, but the degree of his concern was.

For the entire plane ride, I kept thinking about all of the comments that Glen had been making about Arthur's abilities and management style since we had returned from Des Moines. I couldn't help wondering now if Glen had been right in his criticism. Maybe Leasco had gotten too big for Arthur to handle.

'They are meeting us at the airport.' Was the only other thing Glen said as our plane approached the runway for landing. I sensed that I shouldn't ask any more questions and Glen didn't volunteer any more answers.

Cynthia's red hair was the first thing I saw upon exiting the plane. You should have seen her, Willie, as always, she looked stunning in a green wool walking suit with a red and green paisley silk shirt. I remember the outfit so well because I couldn't help but be amazed at how she could take the time to put herself together down to the smallest detail when her whole life could, quite possibly, be falling apart."

"Might jess be da way she copes, ya know? Some people needs ta sweat da details as a distraction from da reality." He shrugged. "Jess a thought."

I looked at him with renewed respect.

"I never thought about her in that way. God, I'd hate to think that she is really human after all!"

He shrugged again.

"So, why'd he quit?"

"At that point I still didn't know. And judging by Cynthia's greeting, you wouldn't think anything was wrong at all. She was waving and smiling like nothing had happened. For a brief moment I thought that perhaps Glen had misunderstood or was simply over-reacting. Then I spotted Arthur. Slumped in a corner of the waiting area sat a skeleton of a man. I'm not exaggerating. His usually tanned face was gray as ash and his clothes seemed to hang limply as he slouched in the chair."

"Whad happened ta him?"

"I wasn't sure but in five short days he had gone from hale and hearty to shriveled and sickly. I couldn't believe it. I left Glen talking to Cynthia about our trip as I approached Arthur.

'My God, Dad, what's this all about?' I couldn't speak louder than a whisper. His appearance had literally taken my breath away.

He had always seemed the sanest of the bunch but looking at him then, in that truly pathetic state, I wasn't so sure anymore. I needed answers. I was hoping to get some from him. But I was disappointed. He simply ignored the question and asked if we would join them for dinner. He obviously was in no hurry to talk about his trouble."

"Den why'd day meetcha guys at da airport?"

"Well, I think he realized that whether he wanted to talk about it or not, he knew he had to. I guess he wanted to get it over with; it just took some time to build up to the explanation. God, Willie, you should have seen him. I mean he had been the most elegant man I had ever met and now his hands shook, and a constant tic kept closing his left eye."

"As we rode the escalators to the restaurant, the suspense was killing me. What could have made such a drastic change in him in just five days?

And then there was Cynthia. You should have seen her swishing through the room making sure that she was noticed by each and every table we passed. Emphasized by the cream colored booth in which we were seated, the brilliance of her hair and the outfit she wore created quite a vision, much to her satisfaction, being enjoyed by a number of other diners.

I understood completely how they could be taken in by her appearance. I certainly had been. If you didn't know her, you couldn't help but be impressed. I, however, had achieved a degree of satisfaction in the knowledge that I had truly grown with regard to our relationship. I had started out in awe of her. Then I felt nothing but contempt. Then I had gotten to the point where I only found her to be terribly amusing. And finally, now, I felt only pity for someone requiring such attention. I think I made real progress!"

"An in only three years!" he teased.

"Some of us are just a little slow on the uptake. I'm sure you would have had her number right from the start." I said it

sarcastically, but in truth I believed it.
"Ya got dat right!"
We laughed.
"So? What was wiff ol' Arthur?"
"Very long story."
"I gots time...'n so do you."

I didn't want to think about the present. I just couldn't yet. Willie
knew that and was making it so easy for me not to. He was aiding in
my avoidance. He instinctively knew that I was just not ready to
deal with what had happened to me. I didn't know if he was really
interested in all of this or not. All I knew was that he made me feel
like he genuinely wanted to hear every detail and that was good
enough. While my past was painful to examine, it was nothing
compared to the harsh reality of my present. I was more than
willing to escape back to those former problems. So, I began again.
    "Remember I told you about the day Glen came home so upset
because Arthur had expanded the board of directors without putting
him on it?"
    "Yea."
    "Well, Glen's prophecy, at the time, about it coming back to bite
him in the ass came true. Arthur had taken the advice of his
attorney about expanding the board and who should be placed on it.
Then, this same attorney, and the new members put together a kind
of coalition. Once they had a majority of the board members united,
basically, they threw Arthur out of his own business."
    "Say What! How'd he let dat happen? Ya gotta stay on top a yer
boys when you's da boss or they'll walk all over ya." He shook his
head. "He shoulda knowd dat."
    "Glen's point exactly."
    "I hate ta be agreein' wiff dat man, but I's right there wiff him on
dis one. Da ol' man shoulda know'd."
    "By this point it was too late for shouldas. The scene was truly
painful. Arthur's voice actually cracked several times as he was
telling us the story. I mean here was a man who had been so totally
dominated- no castrated -by his wife at home and now it had
happened in his business life as well. To go from being successful
and powerful one day to being totally broken the next was just a

pity. My heart was breaking for him."

"Wait a minute. Did dey get all his cash too?"

"No. He had his money. But he had lost so much more..."

"Still, havin' a few mill here an dere, I gots a hard time feelin' too sorry fer da man."

"I suppose if you look at it that way, but there was so much more to all of this than merely the money. Maybe you had to be there. You know, this might be one of those situations that loses something in the retelling. But as I sat across the table from this now pitiable man, I remembered one night, in particular, at the Jacobson's house. It was the night I truly got to know Arthur and love him. The memory of our conversation that night is still so very vivid."

"Glen and I had just recently returned from our honeymoon. Arthur and I found ourselves alone in the dining room after dinner. It seemed so silly, just the two of us sitting miles apart at the huge table. I figured he probably dreaded having to entertain me while Glen and Cynthia attended to something in the library. I knew I had to put him at ease, so I rose and walked the length of the table and kissed his forehead."

"'I'll get the pot,' I teased.

He was taken aback momentarily.

'The coffee pot, silly, what did you think?' I giggled and he laughed and the ice was broken.

It was the first time I ever really had a chance to talk with him alone. Actually, now that I think about it, it was the only time.

'So, tell me about yourself,' I prompted after pouring us both a cup of coffee and sitting down next to him.

'Why in the world would you be interested in me?'

'Because,' I leaned forward making my expression of sincerity unavoidable, 'you know all about me and I know very little about you.'"

Willie smiled. "I kin jess see ya doin' dat." I looked deeply into his soft brown, oh so very brown eyes as he continued. "N I betcha he talked too." He broadened his smile.

"Yep. He began to talk about how Leasco had first become a reality. I had asked him about himself and it was his company that he talked about. You see, Arthur felt he was his company."

"'It was really the beginning of everything for me,' he began.
I remember the smile. Just the mention of his accomplishment
brought genuine joy to his face.
'Cynthia and I had saved two thousand dollars. That was
everything we had. It was quite a bit for a young couple just
starting out back then. We were scared as hell, but Cynthia had
such fire and passion and she believed in me. I had what I thought
was a good idea. She made me know, unequivocally, that I would
succeed. Together we would succeed.'
He paused and took a beautiful gold cigarette lighter from his
pocket. He lit a cigarette and inhaled deeply.
'This lighter cost more than two grand, can you imagine that? But,
at the time, that was everything we had; all that we had worked for,
all that we had saved for.'"

"Real American Dream stuff, huh?" Willie nodded his head in
understanding as he asked the rhetorical question.
"Heavy-duty American Dream stuff. I don't know if you can
imagine it. I sure had a hard time, but he said that he and Cynthia
worked together back then. As he continued his tale, I was
absolutely transfixed in the telling."

"'Cynthia brought the baby with her to the office every day. Glen
would be in a playpen we set up for him while Cynthia did the clerical
work. We both worked very hard. And our timing was perfect. No
one was leasing heavy equipment at that time. I had been working
in the truck leasing industry and decided that it was an idea whose
time had come, so we started a heavy equipment leasing business.'"

"Timin's everythin.'" Willie interjected.
"Yes it is and the Jacobson's seemed to have it timed just
perfectly.   But I gotta tell you, I still have a hard time visualizing
Cynthia typing in an office." I had to laugh.
Willie was silent. When he spoke it was with great sadness,
regret.
"Sometimes our pasts is like differnt lives altogether," was all he
said.

He looked so troubled, pensive. I decided not to press him. I was sure that he would talk when he was ready. For now I would just continue the story.

"'Well, the business boomed,' Arthur continued.
'Within a year we were expanding and hiring. No more clerical work for Cynthia. She was now the wife of the president.'"
"There was such pride in his voice. You should have heard him talking. In only a few short years he had taken the company public."
"Wha's takin' a company public means? Dat da stock market?"
"Exactly. Basically, it means that the public is allowed to buy shares in the company. If not technically, the Jacobson's were in essence the ones selling the shares. So, they made a ton of money. Then in the future, when the company makes more money, the stockholders share in the profit. That's when everyone involved, including the Jacobson's, make even more money.

Now, what's important to our story here is that the stockholders also have a voice in how the company is run. Most of the time they just support whatever management does or wants to do. Arthur, being management, never had a problem until he expanded that Board of Directors. He was unaware that the new members of the board, whom he had appointed, would turn against him and vote him out of the presidency. So, now they were management and he, had no say at all in how the business was to be run day to day."
"Whoa, dat's some story. I still don't see how Arthur coulda let dis all happen right under his nose?"
"That was Glen's question too. He was appalled that his dad could have been that stupid. He confronted Arthur right there in the restaurant."

"'How could you have just blindly trusted Joel?' Glen's voice, while not raised, was unquestionably angry.
'He was my lawyer. He recommended that we expand the board, so I did,' Arthur answered defensively.
'But you didn't have to appoint the people HE picked to sit on it. You should have gotten your own people! My God, Dad, how did you ever get as far...'
Cynthia interrupted with clenched teeth rage. 'It wasn't your

father's fault...those bastards were supposed to be our people! We made them all what they are today. We made every one of those greedy sons of bitches!' She screamed.'"

Willie had an ironic smile on his face. "Least she's loyal ta her man. But wha'd she mean? How'd dey make 'em what dey was?"

"All of the new board members were CEO's of Leasco's subsidiaries. They all basically worked for Arthur. According to Arthur and Cynthia, and it did appear to be the case, they all got greedy. Even though they each had become rich in their respective positions, they were not satisfied with Arthur getting so much of the pie, so, they turned against him."

"Money'll do strange thin's ta people. When it comes ta money, ya jess ain't got no friends."

"That was certainly the case here, but my focus at the time was on what we could do about it. Arthur explained that we had two choices. We could let them have the management of the company; after all, between us we had a substantial amount of stock which generated sizable income, or we could wage a proxy fight."

"O.K, I'll bite. Wha's a proxy fight?"

"Any stockholder who has a beef with management can call for a vote of all of the stock holders to determine the questions raised."

Willie looked totally confused for which I take full credit. I wasn't doing a very good job explaining the business details. I'd have to try harder.

"Look, Arthur had the right, as a stockholder, to challenge the new management team. All he had to do was convince a majority of the other stockholders to side with him and he could then be reinstated as president."

"Like when one of da gangs is goin frew a internal power play?"

"My guess is that it is very similar. Whomever has the most votes gets to call the shots. That's why they wanted to meet us at the airport. A decision, whether or not to wage a proxy fight, had to be made as soon as possible. The annual meeting, where the voting would take place, was scheduled in two months."

"So, Arthur and Cynthia wanted Glen ta make da decision? Sounds like Glen was wrong 'bout his daddy not givin' him sponsibility."

"Not exactly. I'm not sure why they needed us, because before

Arthur had finished going through the options with us, Cynthia began, once again, to scream."

"'We will fight those sons of bitches!'
The decision was apparently already made. I looked over at Arthur expecting to see him energized. I certainly was by the challenge ahead of us, but he just sat there staring into space. He was a changed man, a broken man. When he finally did speak it was through utter confusion, as if to himself."

"'Why did they do this? I know that some of the board members wanted to sell the equipment leasing division. But that was how we started the company. I couldn't let them do that.'
He turned to Glen.
'You know I just couldn't do that!' He was pleading for Glen's agreement.
'I can't believe you,' was Glen's seething reply. 'You mean to tell me that you can sit here and actually not know why they did this? You haven't figured it out? Use your head, old man; it's your own fucking fault!' He spit through his teeth. 'Ever since we acquired Manny Cannon's auto leasing company, he's had his eye on taking over Leasco. Everyone knew it...I told you a year ago to watch out for him. Do you remember me telling you that? But did you listen? You were too involved with making plans for that cruise that you and Mother were going on. And when Joel convinced you to expand the board and I told you to put me on it, that you needed another sure vote on your side. Did you listen? You took Joel's advice and put Manny on the board instead of me.' He paused a moment to regain some semblance of composure. 'This is no one's fault except your own' he stated calmly. Then he turned to me.
'Didn't I tell you he fucked up? Didn't I say something terrible was going to happen because of his mismanagement?'"

"I sat stunned. How could he be so cruel? I looked at Arthur. I didn't think it possible, but Glen's tirade had caused him to shrink even smaller. What kind of family were they? How could Glen turn on his dad and strike when he needed comfort and support? They were all nuts!"
"I dunno. Sounds ta me like Glen made a good point."

"O.K. So, he had warned Arthur. So, Arthur had screwed up...royally...I'll grant you that. But it's at times like that when a family has to stick together. The strength, the beauty of being part of a family is knowing that they will be with you, on your side, during the bad times."

"Yea, Teach, sounds great, but it ain't always dat way. Ya gotta way of only seein' good, spectin' good. Da world ain't always da way it's s'pposed ta be an people don't always act da way dey's s'pposed ta act. Dat's why you's always so set back when da bad comes out. Jess like da folks at Dawson. Not everyone has yer sense of *should be*. Ya gotta learn it once an fer all or you'll jess keep getting' tripped up by it.

Dere's no perfect nothin' in dis world, an dat's O.K. so long as ya knows it. Ya obviously din't learn it from dem folks, but maybe now you'll learn it from dese here at Dawson."

I sat motionless, stunned, catching my breath, needing to actually think about breathing. Was he right? It seemed so simple. Was I really that naive, that stupid?

I didn't want to hear that, not now. I just couldn't deal with that now. This was just too much reality for me to handle. I simply didn't have the strength, not right now. And yet his words had rung so very true.

Escape. I had to escape. I needed to retreat back into my story. I was entitled to a bit of avoidance wasn't I? I chose to ignore his observation, what almost sounded like a challenge to how I had lived my life. I would exercise the strength and self-preserving self-confidence he was challenging me to embrace. In the spirit of what I had just learned about myself, I *chose* to simply continue my story!

"Ironically, all of the trouble with Leasco kinda helped Glen and my relationship for awhile. I mean Cynthia had an enemy, so she was in her glory, and Glen and I had a diversion from our problems. We were all working together, making phone calls, sending out pamphlets to stockholders; we were trying to effectively get the true story out. We detailed the conspiracy and the duplicity hoping to garner support from the average guy by appealing to his sense of fair play.

The other side was emphasizing the elaborate entertaining, expensive trips and of course the Rolls Royce. They were detailing the decadent lifestyle to which the Jacobson's had grown accustomed at the company's expense."

"Sense a fair play was yo only ammo 'gainst Rolls Royces, huh? I thinks I knows where dis is goin!"

"Surprisingly, as the date for the meeting grew closer the vote seemed to be a toss-up, but we weren't totally naïve to the reality. Afterall, if you had your life savings invested in a company and then heard that the president had and did all of those things instead of paying you a larger dividend, would you side with him when he cried that he had been cheated out of that cushy position?

It didn't look great but since we, collectively as a family, controlled a huge block of stock ourselves; we thought we had a chance. I had to believe that we had a chance.

But then Glen's behavior changed dramatically. As the day of the stockholder's meeting approached, Glen started acting really weird. He was very secretive. There were unexplained meetings and whispered telephone conversations well into the night. But most alarming was the fact that he seemed totally unconcerned about the proxy fight. Our entire financial future was at stake and he didn't seem to even care. I managed to push the concern out of my mind rationalizing that it was just his way of coping with the pressure. Afterall, he'd be inhuman if he weren't worried about his future, our future."

Willie sat watching me with a faint smile on his face. I didn't quite know how to interpret his expression. Was he making fun of me? Then, all at once, that totally sincere gaze of his resurfaced and I was reassured that he was really interested in all of this. God only knew why.

I had no idea of how long I had just sat there watching him watch me.

"So, ya gonna go on or what?" He broke into my thoughts.

I took one more moment in silence, just gazing at him, memorizing his every feature, before continuing. I wasn't sure why it was so important to me to get every line, every facial contour stored into memory, it just was. Once I was sure that I would forever be able to bring up the image of the way he was looking at me at that very moment, I sighed and continued.

"By the time the alarm went off the morning of the meeting, I was exhausted. I flipped the lever on the clock radio and flopped back down hoping to recapture the blissful peace from which I had been so abruptly awakened. The harder I tried, the more the anticipated unpleasantness of the day ahead kept creeping into my calm solitude.

Finally, I accepted the fact that it was no use. I was up and nothing could prevent the fear from reigning supreme. Proxy Fight. The words kept echoing in my head. Proxy Fight. Up until a couple of months before, I had never even spoken those words. Oh, of course I had heard them, was familiar with their meaning, but I had no personal experience with what they truly meant, how they could affect, the impact they could have on a person, on a family. Just knowing how to define a word does not guaranty that you really know what it means.

I guess, now that I think about it, that's always the case in life. We think that we are truly sympathetic when we hear of others' troubles, but in reality, we don't have a clue until we face the trouble ourselves. Language is such a deceptive tool. We must rely on words. We think that by using the correct ones we are communicating effectively. We think that we understand what something really means if we are familiar with its definition, yet in reality we haven't a clue."

"I don't git it. If you knows whad a word means, ya knows whad a word means."

"Not necessarily." When I saw the look of confusion on his face I continued.

"I'll try to explain. Some years ago, my mother shattered her hip. Until that moment and the months of recuperating afterwards I thought that when I heard someone talking about a relative who had broken a hip that I genuinely understood the horror of that disability. I was sure I knew what a broken hip meant. I genuinely felt sympathy. But, I hadn't a clue. I couldn't have understood totally not having seen or experienced it firsthand. In that one moment when she fell she went from independent, strong and confident to frail and almost totally dependent. That's all it took, one second to create an entirely different reality for her...and for me. It was one of the hardest things I had ever had to face. This was a proud, independent woman. She was one of the most competent people I had ever met. And in that split second, she needed help with most everything. While using crutches, she couldn't even carry a cup of coffee for herself. Thankfully, it was only temporary, until she healed."

"The point I'm trying to make is that there are words; so many words whose meaning, their truly based-in-reality meaning, can never fully be understood until one is faced with their impact directly."

"I see what yer sayin.' It's da 'ya gotta walk in my shoes thin.' Ya knows, focusin' on word meanin's."
"Exactly!"

He continued to amaze me with his spot on analogies between my world and his. How could he shift so seemingly effortlessly between the two of them when I was having such a hard time with the transition in reverse?

"And so it was with the words, Proxy Fight. These words now forced their way into every conversation I had, smashing all other topics. Everyone I spoke with, everywhere I went, someone asked about the impending fight. *How's it going? Are you going to win? How's Glen holding up?* These questions had been asked of me so many times; win or lose, At least after that day it would all be over. I walked around to the other side of the bed to awaken Glen.

As I stood above him, I traced his contour beneath the covers. He lay deathly still, on his back with hands folded on top of his chest. I always envied his ability to totally relax and sleep a deep, calm sleep the entire night through...every night.

His strong, angular face was completely relaxed in a serene handsomeness which hadn't been visible during his waking moments in months; perhaps it had been years.

As I stood there watching his rhythmic breathing, I was struck by how much he had changed since the overthrow of Leaseco. I simply couldn't get a handle on it. On the one hand, he appeared detached and almost devoid of feeling when it came to the fight. Then, he'd become almost violent in expressing his desires for the future."

"Dis don't sound good, Teach, Ya shouldda packed a bag right dere and den and left 'fore he woke."

"Maybe you're right. Yet, looking at him while he slept. So calm, so at peace; I pushed away the thoughts of what had happened, what problems we had in our marriage. I knelt by the bed spreading my arms wide to hold him. His warmth felt so good, comforting against my body. I needed to be comforted. I was so very needy. Just to escape the insecurity of my life, my failing marriage, our questionable financial future; I just needed a little contentment. Just a few moments of contentment. I yearned for a bit of peace."

"As I laid my head on his chest, I took the first really contented deep breath I could remember. I felt warm and protected. We could build from this moment. We could start afresh. We could! I could feel him beginning to stir from his deep sleep. Instinctively, he wrapped his arms around me. Oh, God yes. A few moments of simple peace, I rose to my knees and gently eased myself atop him, not wanting the quietude of the moment to be disturbed.

I allowed my mind to wander, grasping at the hope that perhaps things could stay like that, calm, quiet, so very warm and wonderful.

Then, all at once I felt Glen's awareness of the situation heighten."

"Oh, Teach..." Willie whispered almost mournfully, fully anticipating what was to come.

"I know," I answered before I continued, my own voice now filled with sorrow for my loss, all that I had lost."

"Before I could plead for just a few more moments; he forcefully rolled us over, trapping me beneath him. An instant later, he was violently ripping my gown from my body. Then, through my confusion, I felt bruising kisses and painful squeezes of my breasts."

"I tried to shake the confusion from my mind. We were so good together for those few moments. Oh, God I can't believe I was still thinking that. No, we weren't good together. I was, even then, as he once again, painfully squeezed one of my breasts, still defending a relationship long since destroyed. What was wrong with me? Those past few minutes of calm and peace had nothing to do with *us*. Glen had been sound asleep for God's sake!

I was the one who was finally waking up. We hadn't ever been good together. My confusion turned to revulsion. I was disgusted with myself as much as with him. What was I? How had I deluded myself into thinking that what we had was any kind of a marriage at all? Just because our union was legal, did that make me any better than a two-bit whore trading her dignity for money?"

Willie gently but firmly grabbed me by the shoulders. "Ya gotta stop bein' so hard on yoself. Ya was young, dat's all. Don't go puttin' blame where dere ain't none. Yer not da bad guy here."

I knew that he was trying to help, but I couldn't respond. I just kept talking.

"As he entered me, he growled, 'now this is the way to start a day off right. Especially this all-important day. You always know exactly what I need, baby.'"

"And like that, it was over. I lay there kind of numb but silently vowing never to submit myself to that kind of hurt again. If he came to me, I would not deny him, but I would never again attempt to reach out to him. Never, never again would I allow that kind of hurt."

"That somnabitch! How could he dun dat to ya? I'd a kilt him. I'd a..."

"It's OK Willie. It's all over." I took his hands in mine. I saw true fury in his eyes. I didn't know what to say, what to do. All I could think of was to stop my story which was so upsetting him.

"Maybe I shouldn't go on."

It was as if he had been slapped. He sat straight up suddenly realizing that he had overstepped his boundaries, or at least the boundaries that he had put in place for himself.

"Maybe id jess better go." He sounded so contrite.

The thought of his leaving terrified me.

"No." My voice had the distinct sound of panic. I took a deep calming breath before continuing.

"Maybe I just shouldn't go on if it's upsetting you so. I know it is unfair of me, but I don't want to be alone just now. Will you stay?"

He wiped from my cheek the tears that had been streaming down my face. I hadn't even realized that I had been crying. His expression had changed from fury to concern. I was grateful for his touch. I marveled at how quickly I had given up all pretenses. I wasn't even self-conscious.

"I caint stand ta see ya so upset. Caint stand ta see ya cry like dis. I wants ta hear what else happened but not when I sees da way it hurts ya to tell it. I wants ya ta go on, 'less ya don't wants to."

"No, Willie no. You're misunderstanding my emotions. It actually feels cathartic to be telling the story. The tears are in a way cleansing." The confused look on his face made me instantly aware that I had lost him.

"I think it's good for me to be telling you. Hearing it after feeling it, living with it...oh I don't know how to describe it. I've never actually heard all of this before. I mean I've never told anyone, so, I've never heard, you know, the actual words." I sighed heavily trying to make him understand.

"It really puts the whole thing into perspective. I think this is good for me. I mean, for me to be doing this now, tonight. But I don't want you to be upset."

God, I was having trouble getting the words out. I didn't want him to go. The bottom line was I did not want him to leave. He smiled reassuringly as if reading my thoughts.

"I's not upset. I jess hate dat you's so hard on yoself. Dey was all hard 'nough on ya wiffout you joinin' in."

I was grateful for his assessment but very aware of just how unrealistic it was. I could not be held harmless for all that had happened. I was an active, willing participant. I could have stopped it at any time. In my defense, I just hadn't been aware that I had the strength. But having said that, I cannot get away from the fact that I should have been aware.

He looked at me with encouragement, so I took a deep breath and continued with my story.

"After Glen's wake-up greeting to me; we dressed in silence. I don't think Glen even noticed that I had not said a word. And we continued not speaking the entire trip to the bank where the meeting was to be held. Nor was the silence broken as we waited in the lobby for Arthur and Cynthia to arrive.

I had no idea what Glen was thinking. He was obviously concentrating on something important. One thing I had learned was his facial expression when he was deep in thought or figuring out a plan of some sort. As usual, he chose not to include me in on it. To be perfectly honest, not only couldn't I care less, I was actually grateful for the exclusion.

Cynthia had summoned Glen and me the night before to a family strategy session. She had decided that we, as a family, would make a spectacular *united entrance* after everyone else had gone in. We were instructed to meet in the lobby by 9:15 for the 9:30 meeting. It was now past 10:00. Patience has never been one of my virtues. And Glen's continually looking at his watch and swearing at his mother under his breath was adding to the discomfort of my nervousness.

I spotted Cynthia's flamboyantly colored, lightweight coat hem swishing about her legs within the revolving door as she energetically entered the bank. There was that flaming hair freshly coiffured, thanks to her extremely accommodating hairdresser and her elegant air gusting through the lobby.

Arthur followed. The revolving door seemed to be dragging him along as he clung to the chrome bar instead of pushing it. Cynthia was radiant with enthusiasm and confidence. Arthur was pale and troubled.

She began her reprimand of me halfway across the bank lobby. 'Lauren, for Christ's sake! Why so sullen?'

Bank tellers and depositors alike strained to catch a glimpse of the obviously sullen Lauren. As she approached me, every eye followed her progress. Upon reaching me, she linked her arm through mine and whirled me about, without missing a step, carrying me along at her pert pace.

'Morning, darling.' She shot a sweet smile at Glen. Then returned to my instructions.

'Now, let's have that million-dollar smile of yours, dear. We don't want the stockholders to think we're nervous. Would you vote for someone who lacked the self-confidence to win?'"

"As much as I hates ta say it, she had a point." Willie accurately observed.

"Oh, she wasn't without her...well, let's just say she did have her moments.

Anyway, the four of us proceeded down the escalators to the bank's large meeting room. There she held up the procession for a moment of last minute instructions. She slipped her coat off and casually draped it over her shoulders.

'Now then.' She straightened Arthur's tie and then Glen's. 'Are we ready'? She didn't wait for an answer. 'Look confident. Smile. And above all, be charming. You'd be surprised how many people will wait to commit their vote until they actually see for whom they are voting. First impressions are just that...what they see, what they sense first. You never get another chance to make a first impression.'"

"Oh, God Willie; I almost laughed in her face at her using such a hackneyed adage. But, my nerves quickly surfaced and I was once again just wanting all of it to be over."

"Who'd made her da expert anyway?" Willie quipped.

"Cynthia, as usual." I shook my head. We exchanged smiles as I continued.

"In one swift movement, her most confident expression securely fixed, she flung the double doors wide and triumphantly exploded into the room. We all followed right behind.

There were seven people congregated around a buffet table arrayed with coffee and sweet rolls. That was it. Seven people."

"Ouch! Dat don't sound so good."

"Not only were there no people, but there was very little food."

"You was worried 'bout da food?"

"No, but the lack of it meant that the new management team obviously knew that very few people would show up. As that realization took hold, I couldn't stop a quiet gasp from escaping my lips. Things did not look good. But Glen seemed totally unmoved by this latest development and Cynthia, while momentarily stunned, gallantly recouped her composure and wandered straight into the center of the group at the table. I couldn't help but marvel at her as she worked the *crowd*."

"Glen and I took our seats waiting for it all to begin. I fidgeted nervously. I had a very bad feeling about all of this. Glen sat perfectly composed. He put his arm around me and whispered into my ear. 'Stop worrying, baby. I'll take care of you. I've got it all covered. You have nothing to worry about...except what we should do for lunch when this is over. Where do you want to eat?'"

"You know how I was trying to explain about language being so lame at times? Well, there are no words to adequately describe how shocked I was at that moment. Was he kidding? How could he be thinking about lunch? I just looked at him unable to answer. My expression must have displayed the incredulity that I felt.
  'We have to eat, don't we?' He defended his question."

"And that's when that comic strip light bulb burst on in my mind. Not only was something very peculiar happening here, but by his almost smug expression; I knew I wasn't going to like it. I needed to find out just what had prompted his bazaar behavior.
  'I know we have to eat, but the meeting hasn't even begun yet. Who knows what will happen? If we win, I'm sure your folks will want to celebrate with us. We'll have a lot to talk about.'
  He leaned very close to me. I felt his breath, warm against my face, smelling of Listerine, as he whispered almost gleefully.
  'Baby, we are not going to win this one.'
  His words were like a slap in the face. I jerked to look at him.
  'What do you mean? How do you know?'
  I didn't even realize that I had shouted my questions; I was so surprised to hear with such certainty that our greatest fears would be realized. We had never even put the possibility of losing into words before.
  'Shhh,' he snapped sharply as he tightened his grip around my shoulder.

'Ease up, baby. It's the best thing that could possibly happen to us.'

I looked at him with what I'm sure was sheer horror. At least that is the way I was feeling. What was he saying?"

"'Don't you see? At Leasco, I would always just be his son. No matter what I accomplished. No matter how much better I was than any of the others, just HIS son. But now that we've lost the proxy fight, I can sell our stock without the folks having a fit and I can start my own company with the money.' I sat dazed.'"

"'See? This takeover was the best thing that could have happened, a real blessing in disguise.'

'But how can you be so sure we will lose?' I managed to whisper.

'We have lost. Just think a minute. How many hundreds of proxy notices do we receive in the mail from our investments?'

'I don't know. I don't pay much attention.'

'Precisely. We just ignore them and by not responding, our shares automatically vote with management. That's how it works. I did my homework. On average, ninety percent of stockholders don't actively vote their shares in a proxy fight. Ninety percent of the people who own Leasco stock will do just what we do, ignore the proxy notice. So, in effect, they are voting with Joel and Manny. They are management now.'"

"I was once again squirming uncomfortably as Glen got that look on his face and continued to explain, this time in his most condescending tone.

'Baby, this fight means a lot to us, but it doesn't mean shit to most everyone else who owns stock. Look around at how few bothered to show up this morning. All the others, more than likely, just threw their proxies away and by doing so voted with management.' He was smiling as he continued. 'Awe, common Baby, don't look so defeated. This is exactly what I wanted to happen. Don't you see? You and I will win by losing this fight.' Explanation made to his satisfaction, he turned to the podium as the meeting was called to order."

"I thought about all that he had said, trying to sort out the logic. How could he be so sure? Wasn't there still a chance? We still had a chance to win. After all, Glen and I alone held tens of thousands of shares. And if you added that to all that Cynthia and Arthur controlled...then it hit me. Oh my God, I could see it in his face. Glen had made sure we would lose the proxy fight. He had not added our votes to those of his parents. He had not voted our shares for his father."

"Everything now started to make sense, his moods, all the secrecy. What had he done? How stupid of me."

I took a deep breath through whispered sobs. Willie responded with a gentle hug then I continued.
"I knew exactly what he had done. He had double-crossed his own father."
"Whoa! How was ya married ta a man like dat?"
I shrugged, not knowing what to say. After a moment to recoup my composure, I decided simply not to reply and continue my story. Afterall, how could I provide an answer to a question to which I had no good answer. So, I just continued.

"I sat in silence. What could I possibly say to him that would have done any good...any good, Hell, I wouldn't have even been able to come up with something that would have made any sense. I just sat and stared with fascination as Glen watched his father walk stiffly to the front of the room to present his case. Before the votes of those present were cast, he had requested and was granted the opportunity to speak."

"Arthur looked like a walking dead man as he approached the podium. His skin so colorless, face so gaunt; his once confident stride had been replaced by a teetering shuffle. I feared he would be unable to garner the strength to stand for any length of time. But he stood steady before the pathetic little assemblage. He waited a moment before speaking. I prayed he hadn't lost the ability to communicate effectively. When he finally spoke, his voice was weak. More than making a simple plea, he was pleading for his life.
'Many of you don't know me. Many of you know very little about Leasco Corporation except that you own shares and you receive a very nice return on that investment every quarter.' He began. 'I

would like to tell you a little something about myself, and Leasco, before you make your decision as to how you will vote on the important question of who should run this company.'"

"As he spoke, his voice grew even weaker, quivering with emotion. Then, he began to ramble
on and on, detailing how he had started this company from nothing and built it through the years into a multi-million-dollar conglomerate. His left eye kept twitching from the nervous tic he had developed. He kept shifting from one foot to the other like a four-year-old needing to pee. His voice, now almost hushed at times, had a whining quality as he was reduced to begging for understanding.

Then, he totally lost control, screaming accusations at the new management team. They had conspired against him. They had plotted this devious take-over and had to be stopped. He was pointing a shaking finger accusatorily at them, shouting across the room. The cadre of conspirators sat silent, smirking, every one of them. There they sat, assured that any witness to Arthur's almost incoherent tirade would have to agree that they had done what was in the best interest of the company by removing this lunatic from power. He was obviously incapable of running a lemonade stand let alone a huge corporate conglomerate.

Arthur's last-ditch effort had deteriorated into a horrible spectacle to watch.

I had to bury my face in Glen's arm. I couldn't stand to watch Arthur; gentle, stately, elegant Arthur; make such a fool of himself. It was a pity to watch. Oh, Willie it was such a pity to see.

But then I was aware of a whispering from the audience. I looked up to see, Cynthia, head high, expression defiant, approaching the podium. I didn't know what to expect from her. She reached Arthur and took his arm tenderly, quietly guiding him away from the podium, down the aisle and silently out of the room.

In spite of everything, my heart broke for them. When I looked up into Glen's face expecting his expression to mirror my emotions, he was smugly gloating. He actually sat there reveling in his father's misery."

I had to wait a moment before I could continue. The emotion of the recollection was so overwhelming. Willie sat silently, patiently until I could finally finish.

"You had asked me a while back if there was a *something* that ended the marriage. Well, that was it. As of that moment, that expression on Glen's face; my marriage was over. There was no way I could live with a man who was capable of doing that to his own father. How could I have rationalized what he had done?"

"From then on there was just the hassle of getting the divorce."

"Wow, some story, Teach. So, how'd Glen end up?"

"On his feet, of course. Within a week his business was up and running. He owns Unilease International."

"I hearda dat company! Yer ex-ol' man owns dat company? Teach, ya sure ya couldn't put up wiff him? Dat's a lotta bread ta give up!"

At first I couldn't tell if he was teasing me or not. His comment was spoken so seriously. Then his huge smile responded to my confused, almost angry reaction.

"I's kiddin', jess kiddin," he insisted with hands raised in mock surrender. "Don't shoot!"

As soon as he said the words his smile vanished. He quickly lowered his hands. Both of us were instantly back to the reality of what had happened to me earlier in the evening. I didn't know what to say. He didn't know what to say. So, we sat. We sat just looking at each other.

"You seem to bring out things in me that I thought were buried deep a long time ago." I found my voice.

"Ya musta had ta sort 'em frew agin, or no one coulda gotten at 'em. It's not so much me as it must jess be da time fer ya ta finally learn from 'em an den frow 'em away an get on wiff it.

Maybe dis was yo way of findin' da strength ta deal wiff what happened at Dawson. Yer way of remindin' yoself jess how strong ya can be. Ya gotta trust in yer strength. Use da power dat knowin' it's a part a ya gives ta you. You's come a good long way from dat awe-struck little girl. Ya jess gotta realize how much ya gots ta offer...ya always had da strength. Ya always had a lot ta offer."

My tears started flowing again as if his words freed them up to wash away the past. He continued quietly but forcefully.

"Ya din't need no one ta tell ya dat. Ya jess needed da time ta find it fer yoself."

I smiled as I thought to myself that I didn't even have any ruby slippers! I could almost hear Glinda saying to Dorothy, *You have the power. It was there all along...* but it was Willie continuing.

"Glen, Cynthia, even me, we jess pushed ya tord seein' it fer yoself. Da Cynthia's n Jackson's n Mellie's a dis world, none of 'em can touch you when ya know who ya are, what you's made of."

He made me believe it. He made me feel it was true.

All at once I thought of Jackson....

"Willie, I saw something, something I wasn't meant to see and I don't know what to do about it."

"Whud ya see?"

"A file on Jackson's desk."

"What was it?"

"I'm pretty sure it was proof that he is defrauding the government, scamming money meant for the center."

Willie shrugged. "Yea an?"

"And? And? What am I supposed to do with this information? I can't just go on as usual as if I didn't know.

"Why not?"

"Because it's illegal. He's keeping funds meant for the program. He has a file with it all documented by date, student and amounts. Amounts he received and the amounts he deposited in his own account."

Willie had that strange smile on his face as if he was musing at my naiveté.

"Oh, Teach, do you got a lot ta learn!"

I ignored his playful sarcasm. "I need to get back into that office."

I was startled at my own resolve. I sat pondering the reality of my decision. What was I thinking? I couldn't get back in there. Shit!

Willie sat mute just watching my resolve melt.

"I guess that's a pretty silly idea, huh?" Even to my own ears there was self-deprecation in my voice.

He eyed me quizzically.

"What?" I demanded. "Why the look? The idea that I could get back into the office?"

"How's come?"

"How come what?"

"How's come it's a silly idea?"

I laughed. "Look, I'm just a kid straight out of school. I happened into this job by pure luck and I now find myself in a situation that is so far over my head I am having trouble believing it myself. I am not even sure what it was I actually saw. I know what I thought it was but maybe I misinterpreted it. Maybe it wasn't what I thought it was at ... but I think it was. I think it's really bad..."

"Are ya done havin' dat conversation wiff yoself tryin' ta talk yoself outta what ya seen?" He was laughing at me. "For a teacher ya ain't too smart!"

I swallowed my anger at being mocked and asked, "O.K. big shot, what am I missing here?"

"Everybody scams da system. Dat's jess how it is. Da students come ta get more money in they's checks. Da staff do as little as possible ta get they's pay. An ol Jackson skims off da top. It's da system. It's how thins work. It's da 'merican way."

"But, it's not right. The money is supposed to be helping people."

"It is! Helping students get they's drugs an keeping da bookies off a they's backs. Helping da staff get they's pay checks fer minimal work. An helping ol' Jackson keep up dat shiny new Mercedes he drives 'round in."

"I don't know why I'm surprised," I whispered into the air.

Willie's look hardened. "Ya really wants ta get back inta dat office?"

"Yeah, like that's possible."

"Oh it's possible."

"How?"

"Center's closed on weekends. No guards 'cause dere's nothin' ta steal."

"What about the cameras?"

"They's jess fer show, ain't never really worked."

"But the doors are locked."

He gave me a *who are you kidding* look.

"O.K., say we can break in, but I don't know…"

"Whoa…not us, Teach … me. You ain't gonna be dere."

"I can't let you do this. You could end up in jail again and it would be all my fault."

"No jail, no fault, not if ya jess lets me get in an get out on my own."

"No. No, absolutely not!"

He just sat there smiling at me.

"I mean it, NO!"

All at once enormous drowsiness overtook me. I really hadn't been aware of just how exhausted I had become. And as if he knew he moved to lay me down on the couch and covered me with a throw he retrieved from the back of one of the chairs in the room.

"Ya needs some rest." And he gave me one of those Willie Taylor smiles.

What could I do? And within moments, I was asleep.

Willie Gets the Goods

The day had been bleak. A light snow fell throughout the afternoon hours. Steel grey clouds obliterated any hint of winter sun. As evening approached what little light might have been star-generated chose to hide behind those ominous clouds still hanging over the entire city. Streets were deserted. Not a soul was around to hear the thunderous roar of the El trains as they rumbled on their infrequent weekend schedule. The train cars looked to be every bit as empty as the surrounding neighborhoods they screeched through. Any Chicagoan worth their salt knows that on a Sunday late afternoon in December the vast majority of Chicago residents sat munching on snacks and watching the Bears setting their fans up for yet another disappointing season.

Had there been someone on the street they might have caught a glimpse of something; some shadowy mass whisping toward the main door of the Dawson Skill Center...but no. It was just an illusion, there one moment and in the next, gone. But then again, for a flicker of second, a huge, dark mountainous man stood at the door and the next second was gone. Had there really been something there?

Willie walked the halls in total silence. For such a large man his step was light and soundless. The lock on the outer door to the administrative offices was as easy to pick as the main entrance had been for a man with Willie's streetwise experience. Willie found the lock on Jackson's door to be an even bigger joke. He looked around the office and smiled...piece a cake he mused to himself.

There were no files on the desk. *Sonnabitch cleaned up fer da weekend,* he thought. The only thing he saw there was an antique inkwell which shared space with an ornate quill, both perched on a small silver tray occupying the center back half of the desktop surface and a crystal candy dish off to one side. He helped himself to one of the colorful hard candies and made his way to the file cabinets at the back of the office.

They weren't even locked. Da idiot musta thought dose pussy-assed door locks would keep anyone out! Dat or was jess so cocky he coudn't imagine anyone would have da nerve ta mess wiff his stuff. Willie just shook his head in disrespect.

The first file drawer he opened had student files alphabetically sorted. He could not resist the urge to pull his own file and take a brief look at its contents. He shrugged as he read about his past... *yep dey jess 'bout had it all right dere on paper.* Then he smiled broadly when he found the form assigning him to Lauren Gate's class. Lauren. *Dat little spit of a girl wiff dose eyes a hers and dat heart...yea her heart... what was dat expression he'd heard his ma say once 'bout a person wearing dey's heart on dey's sleeve. Yea dat was it. Lauren wore her heart on her sleeve fer anyone takin' da time ta look see what a really good, really "real" person she be. How had he gotten so lucky? Who'd a thought he would meet someone like her, get to know someone like her, come to care 'bout someone like her?*

Dere was somethin' about her, a hidden strength she din't even know she had, an a pull, a power ta make him want ta be better den he knowd he was.

The next drawer contained teacher and staff files. He resisted the urge to pull Lauren's file. He already knew all that he needed to know about her and he didn't want to waste any more time.

Finally, he found the right drawer. YES! There they were. As he read the first few sheet in three of the files, he knew he had hit pay dirt. He saw the one sheet that Lauren had described to him and he found oh so much more. He even found Jackson's bank statements. Hah! He had all that he needed.

In the outer office he picked up a large manila envelope off of Mellie's desk and placed the files into it. He gave the room a once over and closed the door behind him. Leaving the building without a trace was even easier than entering it had been. With the files-filled envelope tucked under his large black coat, he once again became that fleeting dark specter stealing unnoticed through the night.

When I woke Willie was sitting in a chair across the room just watching me and yet I felt not a bit self-conscious.

"What time is it?" I asked, not really awake yet.

"It's 7:30 or so."

I guess he could see the questioning in my face for he continued before I could formulate what to ask.

"It's 7:30 Sunday. Ya needed dat rest after alls you was put through on Friday. Ya slept a whole day an a half away."

All that I was put through on Friday? The pieces of memory surfaced in my groggy mind but nothing really made too much sense.

"Something bad really happened then?" Why was I so confused? What had happened?

He nodded solemnly, walking over to sit next to me. With his big arm around my shoulder he pulled me to him in a firm embrace. That's when I realized that he still had on his big, heavy, black coat. I smiled.

"You've been wearing that coat the whole time?"

"Yes'um," he answered with a grin.

"Fine hostess I am and this being your first time in my home. Please Willie, take your coat off."

He stood without a word. He took the coat off to reveal his naked torso. The blurry recollection of him taking off his shirt and ripping it came flooding back to me. Why had he ripped his shirt? A throbbing in my right hand began when I remembered the gash. I had been cut by the flying wood...or was it one of the bullets? Had I been shot?

"I could have been shot!" I spoke my thoughts aloud in a desperately frightened tone.

"I knows," he whispered and I saw tears filling his eyes.

"Oh, Willie, don't. I'm fine. Really, I'm fine. Look..."

And he looked at me with such tenderness I had to move, change the subject for fear of what I might say, might do.

"Well, since you sacrificed a perfectly good shirt, let's see what this hand looks like." I said as I unwrapped the blood-stained, makeshift bandage.

"I think I better get this washed off."

With that I was relieved to leave the room. As I walked through my bedroom to the bathroom, I examined the cut more closely. It looked pretty good. A clean, straight line angled down from index finger to wrist. The bleeding had stopped. It burned like hell as I washed it but the bleeding had definitely stopped. It would not require stitches.

I leaned on the vanity to look closely into the mirror. I was having trouble focusing. I felt hot, so very hot. I splashed some cold water on my face and tried looking into the mirror again.

A pretty decent-sized swelling had purpled on my cheek. Moving my jaw side-to-side produced no sharp increase in pain, and since I was able to talk without fainting, I concluded that there were no bones broken. In reality, the truly painful pounding in my head and the stinging of my hand, the tightness of my jaw and even its discoloration, as I looked in the mirror; all in all, my injuries seemed rather minor. And God, my hair looked a mess! I ran a comb very carefully through it. It kept catching on the dried blood. Then I saw that my sweater was stained with a deep crimson slash from my shoulder down then lessening to a spattering across the front. My face was smudged with dried blood as well. Upon further focused inspection I was all at once struck with the fact that blood, my blood was smeared all over me. How had I not noticed right away?

Oh my God, I had to get clean. I had to wash away every trace of what had happened. And I had to do it right away! I felt a sudden gush of heat from within. And then instead of the internal inferno, I felt as if I were being scalded by the blood stains from without. I could almost smell the stench, sizzling, charring wisps of smoke as the blood left its mark upon me, branding me forever.

I ran the cold water and held my wrists under the tap. I couldn't remember how I knew to do this but somehow, somewhere in my memory I had learned that applying cold to the underside of your wrists, the pulse point, not only cools the body but helps relieve anxiety. I had braced myself for the shock of the cold water but felt only relief. It was as if my very blood was being cooled down as it coursed from my wrists spreading calm throughout my body. AAAH. I was able to lose myself for just one moment, change the heat, the searing heat engulfing me into soothing coolness...if only for that moment; if only for one moment.

Then I caught sight of my obscenely blood smeared clothes and the heat began to rise once again.

I tore off my clothes. I had to get in the shower immediately.

I scrubbed and scrubbed everywhere that man had touched me. I scrubbed my hair, my arms, my neck until my skin glowed red from the irritation. My hand burned. The gash on my head was on fire. I didn't care. I scrubbed some more. I had to get it all off of me. I had to get him off of me.

Then my tears erupted as I sank to the shower floor. I could see myself sitting there huddled in the corner of my shower, almost as if I were detached, looking down at myself. I was watching a scene from a predictable movie where a woman got raped or beaten and she sat on the shower floor crying. But it wasn't a movie. I wasn't some actress emoting. My ribs hurt from the depth of my sobbing. My hand throbbed. My head was threatening to explode. No, this was no movie. This was real. This was really my life happening here.

Thoughts were bombarding my brain. Dawson, Willie, Glen, that horrible man; what did it all mean? Was I supposed to understand something, get something out of my past being merged into the present?

Then I could think of nothing. Feel nothing. Only the deep, mournful sobbing was all that was left. What was I mourning?

Finally, the sobbing stopped. I hadn't forced it. It had simply run its course. I dried myself. I re-bandaged my hand, which, not surprisingly, had begun to bleed again. As I wrapped a robe around me, I caught my reflection in the mirror. I basically looked the same as I had Friday morning when I got out of the shower readying myself for work. Same body, same face...but so very much had changed. I knew I would never truly be the same again.

So, It Begins

He was leaning against the bedroom doorframe with the light from the living room aglow behind him. He had been watching me. I don't know for how long.

I heard a faint sound of a siren twelve floors below heralding the misfortune of some soul being rushed to a nearby hospital. Then, there was silence.

We both stood perfectly still, in that silence so palpable, it created a noise of its own. Neither of the lamps on the bedside tables nor the overhead fixture were on, yet I saw it all, saw everything so clearly. How beautiful he was, as if glowing from the back lighting, he stood there just watching me, his skin as if polished, his eyes adoring.

I was drawn to him, without a word, neither of us needing any words. I couldn't have stopped myself even if I had wanted to. I didn't want to.

I moved across the room without effort, barely aware of the steps taken. I stopped close enough to feel his warmth, his heat. We stood.

His body had very little hair, just smooth, soft skin, seemingly oiled to a slight glisten. Tightly stretched over solid muscle, it was cool to the touch as I hesitantly stroked his chest. How could so much heat be emanating from within such a cool exterior? Everything about this man was a paradox.

His eyes held mine as he spoke softly.

"Soon as I walked inta yer class dat very firs day an saw ya, wiff dat long sleek hair hangin' down almost ta dose legs...girl ya gots some great legs dere. And den da way ya stared down ol Henry Baton...wiffout sayin' a word, ya jess took charge wiff dat look, not flinchin', not speakin', jess dat look. I says ta myself, *Willie, dis woman might jess be too much fo' ya, but ya jess gots ta try.*"

He brushed my wet hair back from my face with both hands and pulled me to him. I felt one strong hand at the base of my back the other wove into my hair at the nape of my neck. His lips were warm as he kissed my forehead, my eyes. Then, he everso gently kissed the bruise on my cheek.

"Dis hurt?" He whispered gently.

"Not bad." My answering whisper prompted a subtle smile. His kisses then turned hot as he engulfed me, totally, in a hug, kissing me heavily on the lips.

I closed my eyes, aware of nothing else except his full soft lips on mine. No sounds, no conscious thought, only the sensations of his mouth against mine. He turned me gently to face the wall, my back to his front. He raised my arms and held my hands up with his. It was so gentle, so very gentle, that when he removed his hands, I never thought of not leaving mine above me against the wall.

He raised my hair to kiss the nape of my neck then trailed kisses down the rest of the exposed side of my neck and on down my back. Even though my front was pushed up against the wall, I felt cushioned, enfolded in secure softness. He held me there, pinned me there, kissing me, just kissing me. As his other hand drew around me lightly pushing on my stomach, urging me to back into his hard body. Seemingly having a mind of its own, my body complied, and I felt a surge of pleasure as his body heat merged with mine. He kissed my shoulders, as his hands caressed my breasts, then down to my thighs then up again. I think I moaned. I'm not sure. I'm not sure of anything other than his touch, his kisses, his tenderness.

Then he turned us both around, his back now to the wall, my back to him.

He surrounded me from behind, moving my hair, gently sucking my earlobe and then kissing below my ear and down my neck. As he kissed, occasionally gently sucking, his hands rubbed my shoulders and across the top of my chest. I arched my back, straining for at least a slight touch of my breast, but he continued kneading my shoulders, kissing my neck, my cheek when I turned my head to nuzzle against him. I felt his tremendous strength through such tender caresses.

My robe fell to the ground at my feet. How it untied and came off, I didn't know. Had he done it? I wasn't sure. I couldn't make any sense of it. Why did I always have to have things make sense? I kicked the robe and my thoughts aside.

No thoughts, just feeling. Feeling his breath on my neck, feeling his body pressed so tightly against my back, feeling his hand moving oh so gently, achingly gently across my shoulders and down my sides. He still held me from behind, hands on either side of my waist, as he began to sway, lovingly guiding my movements. A sensual rhythm began to build as he nudged my hips side to side...side to side. I felt his rhythm, got caught up in his dance. Such primal sensations, the smell of him, the feel of his bare chest against my back, the weight of his hands conducting the rhythmic swaying, the swaying keeping pace with my steadily increasing heartbeat. Or was it his heart beating that I was feeling? I couldn't distinguish between them for it was as if we had already melded into one, even though we had shared nothing more than those kisses. It was as if we were already eternally joined.

I lost my train of thought as I felt myself being lifted. He held me cradled in his arms. Higher, such a heady high infused my being, until somehow we reached the bed. Down deep into inviting soft, his weight seemed to push mine, yet it felt like no weight on me at all. I was totally unencumbered. I was free.

I opened my eyes to see him so very clearly. He leaned on his elbow, his face just above me, looking at me, warming every part of me with the fire in his eyes.

"You is so beautiful," he whispered softly. So softly, I wasn't really sure if he had actually spoken the words or not. Then with a wonderful smile, he put his hands under the pillow upon which my head rested. Gently, he drew the pillow up toward his face and kissed me, kissed me, kissed me again.

I don't think I spoke and yet he seemed to be reacting to me. Did I speak? What could I have possibly said? Every time I started to think, become aware of actual thoughts, I would all at once lose it. It was as if he could somehow banish rationality; he would not allow me anything except feelings...and I liked it.

I kept losing myself. I don't know how else to describe it. The room was so very hot. The orange glow of dawn shown through the drawn curtains.

His tongue, sort of rough, almost feline was on my body. God, how it felt. I heard the contented moan of an irritating itch, finally, finally being scratched, come out of me. Yes, yes, scratch it!

The smell of him, that sumptuous smell of sandalwood, and I wanted more of it. I inhaled deeply again and again, filling myself up with him. And the taste of him, once again such a paradox. He skin tasted smoothly sweet, yet hinted of spice. I had never known that skin could have such flavor. There was so much that I had never known. That he was teaching me. Now I the willing student. And, I wanted more. I wanted everything. I wanted the heat and the friction and the rough and the gentle.

Tangled and rolling I found what I had needed, needed for so long. Willie was a great teacher.

We both lay breathless. I wasn't aware that I was crying until he gently kissed my tears.

"I din't mean ta hurt'cha. I's so sorry..." he achingly said with tears of his own threatening to spill.

I pulled him to me, stopping his apology with a kiss.

"Don't be sorry." I kissed him again. "That's not why I'm crying. I don't know why I'm crying. I feel wonderful...God, I feel so stupid for crying." I started to laugh at myself and at his confused expression.

"Oh, Willie, don't look like that. You didn't hurt me, silly, couldn't you tell? You gave me nothing but pleasure."

His relief gave way to passion. This time, slowly, easily, I was aware of every touch, every breath. This time there was no confusion, only the pure joy of him. We lay for hours, forever, stroking each other, nuzzling, speaking not one word.

I didn't want to think. Why should I have to think about anything except how easy it was to forget what had happened to me when in his arms?

Lying there with him, I could lose myself in marveling at how well we fit. He so massive in stature, me, well, I was considered petite, small-boned. Yet we fit so comfortably. I had never before been with a man built like Willie. I was fascinated with the outline of his muscles. I traced their borders with my finger. His forearm had a long sleek muscle while his upper arm seemed filled with a tennis ball.

He flexed as I stroked his arm. I laughed. Why do muscular men always flex when you touch their arms? He certainly didn't have to impress me. Not after all that he had done for me.

What exactly had he done for me?

What had happened? God, what had really happened?

So many realities all at once crashed through my newfound euphoria. Oh, God, I tried but could not banish them back to dormancy. I wanted the euphoria back. I didn't want reality to reign supreme. Wasn't I entitled to just a few more moments? Didn't I deserve more time of peace?

As if we were of the same mind, I felt his body tense, his jaw tighten. I don't know if he knew what I was going to ask or not. I had a feeling he did. I think he knew I was powerless. I had no choice but to ask.

"Did you kill him?" I whispered hesitantly, not knowing if I wanted to hear the answer.

He kissed my forehead so tenderly. Then he lifted my cut hand and brushed it with a feather of a kiss as well.

"No," was all he said.

I hadn't realized that I was holding my breath until my relief released it.

We fell back into silence. Oh, how I wanted to stop my mind from thinking. Just a little longer, please let me stay in this wonderful blissful state of ignorance. I don't want to know anymore. I don't care what happened and I especially didn't want to think about why. But I couldn't stop the question. What had happened?

My mind retraced what I remembered. I had been fired. I had been threatened. I had been shot at. I was attacked. I was rescued and I was truly made love to. My mind was racing once again. What was happening to me? I felt the now all-too-familiar fear building again. No, not yet. I'm not strong enough to face all of this yet. I need to hide just a little while longer...

He was there, seeing straight through me, all around me, inside me, protecting me, comforting me; helping me through.

His hands on my back as he rolled me on top of him were warm as they rubbed and patted comforting, soothing my sobs. His chest was a firm pillow for my mildly aching head. I never wanted to move. I wanted to stay in this embrace forever. The tears stopped as suddenly as they had started.

"Are you hungry?" The question startled me as much as him, but I was all at once aware that I was starving.

"You? I'll getcha somethin' if ya want. Ya probly shoun't be up...ya needs ta rest," he offered.

"Don't be silly. I'll make a little something for us both."

I scooted off of him and out of bed. All at once, I realized that I was standing there naked. I turned, embarrassed.

"You's beautiful," he whispered.

And it was all right.

I bent to pick up my robe. A sharp pain attacked my head. I brought my hand up to the gash hoping to stop my brain goo from oozing out. The wound was dry. It was O.K. I felt woozy as I grabbed for the robe on the floor with the other hand.

"No, don't put it on." He was out of bed beside me.

He substituted his arms around me for my robe, then his kisses for his arms.

The hell with the food, it could wait!

Once again, he seemed to just know, to instantly provide everything I needed. Yet this time was different. There were questions, important questions, questions about him that now lodged in my thoughts, would not allow the total oblivion, the complete abandonment I had experienced before.

What was it that he was actually providing? Was a good lay all that I needed? Or was it a safe haven from all of the violence of which I had found myself a victim? Could he be that? Could any man? Did I need a man; did I really need anyone for that? And if I did need him for that, how could a murderer be any kind of safe haven?

I had so many questions. As hard as I tried to ignore them, to get back to that place of just feeling the moment; they kept seeping into my thoughts. Did I really want answers? I tried to make Willie, my Willie, here with me now. all that mattered. But in the warmth of his embrace, with him holding me against anything bad, I felt I had to ask him. I needed to know about his past.

We lay quiet. Our breathing had calmed. While I couldn't see his face as I lay with my head on his chest, I knew he was awake.

"How could you have murdered anyone?"

As soon as I asked it, I was struck with the irony. Hadn't I just witnessed, firsthand how it could have happened? Wasn't I just the cause of a possible similar scenario? He might have killed that man to save me.

Oh God, what a relief! Of course, that was how it must have happened. Willie, this man within whose warm embrace I found such comfort, such compassion, was no cold-blooded killer. He couldn't be. He must have perpetrated some act of heroism, come to someone's rescue and due to his color or some other horrible miscarriage of justice been mistakenly put into jail for it.

It all made perfect sense now. We were alike in this way. Like me, Willie had fallen victim to circumstances, surroundings. And how easy it was to do that, didn't I know? Willie's world was filled with places like Dawson. Places in and of themselves providing the backdrop of violence, a kind of daily horror I had only read about before, certainly never been exposed to. Read about and then easily forgot about. But he couldn't forget. This was the world in which he lived, a world not of his making, not of his choosing. A world that had turned on him in the cruelest way.

I was gratefully able to, in that moment of realization, convince myself that he had paid a horrible price for being better than his environment, more caring than that world of his allowed. He was the victim, not a murderer. I felt ever so much better.

Then he began his story.

Willie Revealed

"Guess second grade started it." A deep sigh released his words.

"Guys, big guys, flashin' bread, braggin' clothes, come ta me 'bout joinin, bein a brother. Dey was Blackstone Rangers, my neighborhood. Dey rocked! An dey come ta me. Dey come ta school lookin' fer ME! See, I was big fer my age even den. Always had a big mouth so's everyone know'd me. I jess never was a blendin in kinda guy." He smiled, almost embarrassed as he continued.

"Dey come one day lookin' special fer me. You shouda seed my friend's eyes. I musta been important fer dem ta come find me. Firs time in my's life, I was somebody."

"Second grade?" I mused.

"God, in second grade I was mad for Jimmy Thompson. I hated my teacher Mrs. Kramer but loved studying the American Indians. We built a tepee right there in class. We had to sign up to do quiet work in it. Jimmy and I always signed up together. We traded dog tags in the spring but his folks made us trade back for the summer. I remember Mrs. Kramer being so mean, but I loved second grade."

"Ya 'member yo teacher's name?" He sounded so shocked. I was shocked that he would be shocked.

"Of course, everyone. Hodges, kindergarten; Franklin, first grade; Kramer, second; Gault, third; Boyd, fourth; Stout, fifth; then in sixth we started having multiple teachers for different disciplines, that's when I started to take French as an elective. Want to hear all of their names?" I asked playfully.

"Ah, no..." His smiled faded as he became very serious. "I don't 'member any a deir names."

I was struck by what he had said, the way he said it.

"God, Willie, school was the very center of my life growing up. Everything I did revolved around it."

"Mines was differnt. School was jess another place. No better, no worse n any other ta hang out when ya had nothin' better ta do. My ma tried ta tell me, Lord knows she tried ta git me ta take vantage of learnin', but alls I could see was how important da brothers was, da bread dey had in rolls wound up in big rubber bands bulging out deir pockets.

Dey was IT in my neighborhood. Den, 'cause a dem, I was IT. Dere jess wasn't no reason in da world ta be nothin else."

"So, we made some trouble, got some scars; only made us more special. All da kids looked up ta us. Dey looked up ta ME. Grown-ups was even scared a us. Now it was me had da green rolled up in my pocket. I walked down da street an people noticed me, got outta da way fer me, respected me. Dere weren't nothin' better. Jess nothin' better. Seemed ta me it coud't get no better."

"So, when you's was splittin up subjects in sixth grade, I got 'nitiated inta da Rangers full force. Whud I need school fer? I got brothers, I got bread. I got girls...lotsa girls!" He blushed without blushing.

I sat intrigued, the full force of what he was relating not yet registering.

"Girls, huh? Well, in at least one way we were alike back then. In sixth grade I had a huge crush on Bobby Martin. I knew at first sight that I was destined to love him. He was kinda smallish but he had great blonde hair and an adorable little pug nose..."

"Jess like me!" Willie jumped up pointing to his definitely not pugged nose.

I flew at him and we rolled on the floor wrapped in each other's arms and our laughter.

"Yes, just like the first time I saw you." I kissed him, his lips, his ear lobes, around the back of his neck.

He batted me away playfully.

"Stop. Don't! Dat tickles!" He was all over me using just enough of his tremendous strength to roll me over without hurting me.

"Don't ya know ya never tickles someone's bigger n you?"

He held me hostage as he kissed me, poking his nose, tickling my ribs. He looked up startled when I didn't laugh. He tried again, this time tickling in earnest. Still I didn't laugh. I watched smugly as his expression changed from surprise to intense curiosity.

"I learned control very young." I explained seriously.

"I have two older brothers. I couldn't afford to be ticklish. I couldn't afford to show any weaknesses."

Now it was his turn to be totally serious, shaking his head in understanding and agreement.

"Den ya understands. I couldn't 'ford no weaknesses neither."

I shuddered at his intensity. We both knew exactly what he was talking about. I waited a moment then had to ask. "Will you tell me what happened?"

He rolled over on his back. He just lay there, staring at the ceiling, for what seemed a long time.

"Sometimes thin's jess happen. Thin's ya got no control of." He sighed deeply.

"It was summer. I was sittin' on our front porch one afternoon wiff my ma an sister. Jess sittin. It was hot. Ma had made some a her special iced tea, kinda a combination a tea an lemonade. Real sweet. Real good. We was jess sittin' dere, weren't even talkin. I was sixteen."

He stopped. I wasn't sure he was going to continue. I wanted so desperately to know it all, everything about this man, like I felt he now knew about me.

"What's she like?"

He looked confused by my question.

"Your mom, what's she like?"

"Ma?" A huge crater of a smile cracked his jaw.

"Ma's da best. Worked housekeepin' at Billing's Hospital since I kin 'member. Raised my sister Eleanor an me. She be named fer Mrs. Roosevelt but we calls her Ellie. Mine's really Wilson not Willie, named fer da president, Woodrow Wilson. Ma's real big on dis country.

Anyways, my Ma did it all alone. Worked, saved, sang choir at church, bought herself n us a house. I had it better 'n most a da other boys. I always know'd I was loved."

"Then why the gang? It must have been so hard for her to have you involved in all of that"

He just looked at me, amazed.

"She weren't stupid. Prayin' fer me, lecturin' ta me coud't overshadow money an cars an girls. Sure, she tried. Sure, I heard 'bout what she wanted fer me, all da time. But what our folks want or even what's bess fer us, dat don't make it come true. Ya said you was young an naïve, I say I was young an stubborn."

"Don't know, maybe we ain't so different, huh? Young gives good excuses fer an awful lot."

God, that was so true. I nodded my agreement.

"What about your dad? You said she raised you guys alone; did you know him at all?"

As soon as I asked, I was uneasy. I hoped I hadn't overstepped my bounds. It just came so naturally for me to inquire about someone's parents. I had to keep reminding myself that this was not someone like anyone else I had ever known.

Willie tensed. All signs of the smile were gone.

"When I was little I was always askin. *Who's he? Where's he?*
'You like Jesus. God's yo daddy' was all my momma'd say.
Dat was good 'nough fer me...upta a point. But no matter how hard I'd try, no matter how I begged fer somethin' 'bout him, she jess wouldn't, couldn't say nothin' more. But den my Grandma finally gave me a story. I was so young an hungry fer anythin bout my Dad, I believed it ta be true. Lookin' back now, I guess it was probly da story a some movie she seen, but at da time it meant da world ta me ta have somethin' a him. Jess hearin' it made me happy. Gave me a image a him. Even if it ended wiff him leavin' us; I still had somethin' a him ta 'member. Once my Ma heard what my Grandma toll me, she went along wiff every detail. Don't know fer sure, ta dis day, if it be's true or not, but back den it was enough."

He sighed as if signaling the end of his tale. He couldn't think that that was going to satisfy my curiosity. I looked at him with all of the incredulity I could muster.

"You don't think you're going to get away with just that do you?"

"What? What'd ya mean?" He gave me an, *I have no idea what you are talking about,* look.

"Come on. Let's hear the story. I've been spilling my guts out to you, providing every ridiculous detail of my entire life, the least you can do is give me one little glimpse of yours."

And so he began.

"He was a big, handsome man, older man, come n jess bowled little Evelyn Meade over. She never stood no chance. Know'd him jess a couple a months n he married her."

Looking at Willie now, having been taken in so thoroughly myself, I could see just how that could happened.

"Dey said he played da saxophone...travelin' man. He was away a lot. But he always come home bringin' giffs. Three years dis went on, two babies dat he missed da birffs of. He missed anniversaries. He missed Christmas. But when he'd start ta missin' her, he'd load up dat big ol yellow Buick a his wiff giffs an he'd drive back home."

"And she loved him. She was an still is a one man woman. Took him in like no time passed tall. Grandma said he'd play his music n fill da house wiff comfort."

"What happened to him?"

"Easy ta guess da endin'." He shrugged with resigned acceptance.

"What I do knows fer fact is some time in da fourth year, he leaves fer a gig in St. Louis...never pulls dat big ol Buick up ta da house again. I was four, Ellie almost three, last time he seen us. But I swears I remember dat car, shinny bright yellow wiff black seats dat got hot in da sun. I remember shoutin' in shock an pain when I got in ta da car one summer day wearin' shorts an nearly burned my butt off!" He became serious again.

"Took five solid years fer Ma ta admit he was gone...and I also know she still ain't over him yet. If he was ta pull dat ol Buick up today, she'd give him a smile an help him inta da house."

Sadness covered him. I wanted to replace it with the comfort of an embrace but he pulled away. I realized that if I made things too comfortable for him, he would never be able to tell me the rest.

He jerked his head to the side as if shaking off a glancing blow. The sadness had now turned into a cold resolve. His body tensed as his mood changed dramatically. With no emotion, and with what was certainly his street face, he continued.

"Anyways, dere we was, my Ma, Ellie n me sharin' a beautiful day on da porch. Alls a sudden two of *Da Nation* comes prancin' by as cool as can be. I mean dey was jess 'strollin, walkin all puffed out wiff attitude, right? Dey was walkin' right in front a my house, on MY STREET!"

He turned on his side, leaning on his elbow to face me. I saw indignation covering his features. I didn't understand the point he was trying to make and I certainly did not understand why having two guys walk by his house made him so indignant. When he caught the bewilderment obviously displayed on my face, he began explaining, trying to make me understand.

"Dey was on our turf...our turf! Two of *Da Nation* on *Ranger turf.* Dey know'd da rules. We all gots rules but dere dey was, right up in my face. I looked at my sister. I looked at my ma...took da time ta think a minute, took dat minute ta calm myself down. I had deese womens here ta think of."

"I decided ta do nothin, let 'em pass on by. I did't want ta upset my sister n ma. Figured da boys'd get da lesson dat was comin' to 'em a little further down da block if any a da other Ranger's was around."

He sighed and shook his head.

"But no, dey was out lookin' fer me. Dey had come specially fer me. It came out in da trial, dey was real life brothers, ya know blood kin an I had done somethin' ta deir other brother. Guess I messed him up pretty bad in a fight. Ta be honest, don't even member – ta dis day can't say I member a thin' bout him. But dat's why dey was dere. Dey was lookin' ta get some revenge. I guess dey thought da two of 'em could take me easy." He sort of smirked with pride at their obvious mistake.

"Dey shore was shocked when dey realized I was gonna let 'em pass. It weren't what dey 'spected, not what dey wanted at all. So dey started mouthin' off, sayin' stuff dey shoudn't in front a my ma an sister."

He stopped abruptly, irate at the mere retelling, yet actually too embarrassed to tell me what was said; he didn't want to offend me. I sighed in bewilderment. Who was this man? How could a murdering gang member still possess all of the dear, kind, even caring attributes he had shown to me. My God, he was concerned that the bad language would disturb my sensibilities. Could he really be a cold-blooded killer? No, of course not. What was I thinking? He wasn't a cold-blooded killer.

Suddenly, I didn't have to hear any more. I knew what must be coming. These men had attacked Willie's sister, maybe killed her or his mom. That's why he killed them. Why was I putting him through this? Oh God, the horror of what he must have gone through. And now here I was making him relive it all. I didn't need any more details. I could hardly bare the look on his face as he interrupted my thoughts.

"Dey couldn't get away wiff dat, not walkin' in fronta my house n sayin' what dey said ta my ma." He continued. "I had ta put dat right. No one insults my ma, 'specially in her own front yard." He paused for a moment. Another deep almost contented sigh.

"We fought. I won."

A man totally justified in his actions spoke the words. He shook his head emphasizing his agreement with the justification.

"We's all got rules we gotta live by. Dey broke da rules," he ended matter-of-factly.

I lay there. All I could do was just lay there. He had killed two men for that, over words spoken to his mother? No, no, no, that couldn't be right. That can't be what happened. There had been no attack on his mother or sister? No physical violence? He had killed two boys because they had broken some sort of street rules; said the wrong thing?

I was stunned, appalled. Before I could even think clearly I heard the words coming from my mouth.

"You say you punished them because they had broken the rules, but Willie, the ultimate rules are the law. You broke the law, they didn't. You broke the law, Willie, not some arbitrary street rules. You murdered those boys." I could not comprehend his attitude about this.

He looked shocked by my outburst. His face, momentarily contorted exposing his internal struggle, his inability to grasp my not understanding what in his mind had been totally justified. No, more than justified, required! His tone became pleading.

"Some rules are too important ta let da law stand in da way..."

This was too much. My thoughts were racing. My head began to ache again. My bandaged hand reflexively went to the gash skillfully tied closed at the back of my skull. The throbbing had returned in full force. Willie took the hand from my head and lightly kissed the bandages. Defensively, I snatched my hand from his gentle grasp. He flinched at the unintended insult.

"Who decides which rules are more important than the law?" I couldn't mask the anger I felt, even if I had wanted to.

He sat silently as I continued.

"This isn't some game we're talking about, with all this *rules* stuff. Who made these rules, some whacked out gang member? These groups of underachieving, uneducated thugs created this life absorbing game and everyone is expected to follow their rules? This is no game, Willie. This is murder. This is the law we're talking about. You just can't ignore the law and expect to have a functioning society."

"Who says?" He spat back, then calmed instantly. "We gotta live in da neighborhood. Dat's what ya gotta understand. We live in da neighborhood; gotta live by dose rules," he justified.

"But the law supersedes any other rules."

He just shook his head no.

"O.K. then what about jail?" I felt helpless, the right words just wouldn't come.

He grabbed my arm firmly as if the impact of his strength could force my understanding, my acceptance.

"Gotta live by da rules. Even if it means doin' time. We all knowd dat goin' in. Jess part a life on da streets."

He paused a moment then released my arm when he realized he hadn't gotten through. I could see him mentally trying to hit on an effective way to explain it so I would understand. Again, he took hold of my arm, more gently this time.

"Maybe firss ya gotta understand 'bout gangs: what dey is, what bein' a part of it means."

"O.K. help me understand."

"Dey is life." He began instructing.

"Da diffrence tween bein' beaten down day after day till dere's no pride left in ya an havin' respect an power. When you is young alls ya see is da dead-ends ahead of ya an den all's a sudden ya can be a part a something; somethin dat lifts ya up, a family dat takes ya in an treats ya like ya got value, shows ya some respect."

"Hearing 'bout yo life I can see dat dis muss be hard fer ya ta understand. You's always belonged. You's always had hope. You's always know'd ya could succeed. Only way I know'd I could succeed was ta be a part a what ruled our streets. Cause dat was where I would always be, on da streets. See, I had ta succeed too, an it was da gang dat paved da way fer me. Dey was my home an deir rules was my law."

He could see that I just wasn't getting it. He sat up. His instructor's tone had not worked to his satisfaction so he changed it to that of stern, fatherly lesson giver.

"I bet you's got one, maybe two people who loves ya nough ta die fer you, huh?"

I was stunned by the question.

"I've never really thought about it. I guess my folks would die for me. I don't really know. I have no way of knowing for sure." I had no idea where this was taking us.

"Well, bein' a Ranger, I gots a whole mess a brothers who'd KILL fer me! Dat's right, I said kill fer me. I don't got ta think 'bout it, wonder if, I knows dey would kill fer me. And dey knows I'd do da same fer dem. Dat's somethin' huh? Dere's no excuses, no bullshit. It's jess pure."

I sat up totally debilitated. What could I say to that? What could I possibly do?

We remained both sitting straight up, for a long silent moment. He was still holding my arm. A pained grimace grew on his face. I sat staring, bewildered, into his now cold eyes.

I knew. I knew at that moment, as did he that I would never, could never understand what he had done for the reason he had done it.

The one thing I did understand, all too clearly, was that he would unequivocally do it again. He would kill two boys, with his bare hands, because they had the audacity to walk across his lawn and insult his mother.

We all got rules we gotta live by, he had said. He wanted me to understand the justice of his actions. His eyes turned soft, pleading for understanding. Then they went cold again. There was just silence.

My heart broke for our differences. We both felt it at that moment and he shifted to hold me tightly. We struggled to return to where we had been before this conversation. In the silence that ensued we agreed never to speak of any of this again. There was no need.

I don't know just how long we lay there in silence, wrapped in each other's arms. I felt his deep breath, heard sad resolve in a heavy sigh.

"So, whatcha gonna do 'bout Dawson?" His voice had changed. Everything had changed.

"I don't know. I'd like not to have to think about it. Silly isn't it? I know I have to think about it, have to come up with some course of action." Even I heard the lack of resolve in my voice.

I held on tighter as I thought about all that I had experienced, all that I had learned from my time spent with him. Oh, what I had learned. It was another moment before I realized I was voicing those thoughts.

"I understand now that I have always believed that I really had very little control over my life. I often lamented the fact that I had led a pretty ordinary existence. And I actually felt kind of sorry for myself always being at the mercy of others, stronger, more confident, capable people, who seemed to take charge of my life, determining the directions it took.

When I entered the doors of Dawson, with everything that happened there, I was sure it had to be *that place.* When I was telling you all about Glen and my life, I was sure it was *the situation* or Glen and his family directing the action. And even listening to you just now, I had convinced myself that you too were some kind of victim, not really responsible for your actions. But you know what? That's a bunch of bullshit!"

"I think that most people consider their lives pretty dull. I sure did until I really examined it...until you made me really examine it. We all go along day to day and bitch about all that is or isn't happening to us. But if you sit down and really take a good look at your life, like I did over these past days...there is real drama, not just in mine, but in everyone's life.

Truly dramatic events occur all the time over which, in most cases, we do have some control...if we take it. It's true, real-life drama and we have the power to make the choices as to how we will play the leading role.

And I think most people are just like me, not even aware that we do have the ability to choose just how we will act or react on our own life's stage.

Oh, it's not easy, Hell no. Life keeps throwing stuff at us, for sure, but it is up to us, each of us ourselves to decide just how we handle any given situation, how we react and then it's up to us to move on."

"So, I guess that's exactly what I am going to do. In answer to your question, after that lengthy rationalization, I'm going to just move on."

There was finality to my statement that I hadn't intended but it pleased me nonetheless. Willie too looked pleased.

I rose in confidence and grabbed my robe on my way to the kitchen. When he followed me a few minutes later, he was showered and dressed though still bare-chested.

"Sorry 'bout your shirt...but I can't think of anything that I have that would do."

He smiled.

"Don't need no shirt wiff dat big ol coat. I'll be fine till I gets home. And you'll be fine too." He warmed me through with his smile.

I knew he was right. I smiled back. I actually felt a rush of excitement. I would be fine.

I found myself puttering around the kitchen trying to avoid looking at him. All at once it just wasn't comfortable having him sitting at the table watching me. I made bacon and eggs but found that I could eat very little. He finished all that I made. We sat in silence.

"I'd best be goin'."
I didn't argue.

As we stood at the door I had to reach up on tiptoes to help him on with his coat, returning the favor he had done for me so many times. As it covered his shoulders, I knew it would be the last time I would see the bronze of his back. I smoothed out the fabric across those huge shoulders. I could feel the strength even through the heavy black material. A few more moments were filled with silent sadness. I knew I would never return to Dawson. I couldn't. But I also knew that I would find some other way to get back into the fight.

As had happened so often since meeting, he spoke my thoughts.
"You can't go back ya know? Ya won't will ya?"
I couldn't answer for fear of crying.
"I don't want nothin' worse ta happen ta ya."
"I know, Willie." I whispered.
And he was holding me in that wonderful, comforting hug. Tears wetted his shoulder. Were they only mine? I couldn't tell.
As we embraced, over his shoulder, I saw something on the table. What was that envelope doing there? It hadn't been there last night.
"Willie, what is that?" I pointed toward the table.
Without even looking he said, "somethin' dat might be a use ta ya."
I let him go and walked over to the table. I opened it up and found all of the documentation anyone would need to blow the lid off of Jackson's crimes. As I stood gazing at the documents it came to me exactly what I would do with them. Without even a moment's

hesitation, I grabbed a marker from the drawer and addressed the envelope to Mike Royko at the Chicago Daily News. I knew that no explanations or identification need be included. Royko was the man that would know what to do with it.

"Give dat here. I'll mail it fer ya. Ya needs ta stay put an get some rest." He spoke quietly taking the envelope from my hands.

There was a somewhat awkward moment, but I finally nodded in agreement.

We stood. We looked at each other. We both smiled.

How is it that sometimes you know? You just know when it's right and God damn it; you know when it's not.

We both knew.

He kissed my mouth, gently, with the tenderness of good-bye.
"I doubt ya will, but if ya ever needs me, Teach..."
The door opened and closed and he had vanished.
I leaned against the doorframe. I did know if I ever needed him...I shook my head as a huge smile crossed my face.

WHO WAS THAT MAN?

Epilogue

The Entitlement Fraud Scandal in Chicago was one of the biggest news stories of 1974. The series of articles exposing the full extent of the misuse of government funds garnered a Pulitzer Prize for excellence in reporting that year.

As for me, to this day I'm caught in a breathless flood of emotion at the thought of him...of us together. He was tall and proud, so very strong and truly beautiful, totally strange and appealing, dangerous and gentle. What is it that attracts that which is different? Is it mystery, curiosity, or even just stupidity? In my case I don't think it was any of those things, or was it all of them?

I have tried to analyze, to understand what in the world I was doing. I had never before felt so completely emotion driven, leaving all logic, all of that common sense I thought I possessed, of which I was so proud, even defined by; ignored, purposely stashed away. I was needy of him, so hungry for what he was, all that I wasn't, didn't understand, never been exposed to.

Friends and family, what would they say if they knew? A secret. I have a wonderful, tragic secret that I will cherish forever. A memory of such uncharacteristic behavior, feelings, incredible life-altering realizations; and that face, a face I knew right from the start that I wanted never to forget...it's all mine...sensually, lovingly, forbiddingly mine.

Made in the USA
Middletown, DE
08 June 2021

40985594R00159